REGINALD DWAYNE BETTS · JILL BIALOSKY · MARK BIBBINS · FRANK BIDART
JOHN BIGUENET · TOM BISSELL · THÓRDÍS BJÖRNSDÓTTIR · SOPHIE
CABOT BLACK · GABRIEL BLACKWELL · BRIAN BLANCHFIELD · TABITHA
BLANKENBILLER · ANDREJ BLATNIK · EMILY BLIQUEZ · AMY BLOOM · RYAN
BLOOM · MARIA BLOSHTEYN · ROY BLOUNT JR. · DEBORAH BLUM · ROBERT
BLY · JUSTIN BOENING · LAURA BOGART · EAVAN BOLAND · ROBERTO BOLAÑO
ALICE BOLIN · KERA BOLONIK · EUGENIA BONE · YVES BONNEFOY · BRIAN
BOOKER · KYLE BOOTEN · CAMILLE BORDAS · ANNE BORN · ROBERT BOSWELL
PATRICIA BOSWORTH · ELEANOR MARY BOUDREAU · LOUISE BOURGEOIS
GAVIN BOWD · TIM BOWER · PAUL BOWLES · WILLIAM BOYD · ELIZABETH
BRADFIELD · ARTHUR BRADFORD · PER AAGE BRANDT · MICHAEL
BRAUNSCHWEIG · ADAM BRAVER · BREYTEN BREYTENBACH · SARAH BRIDGINS
TIFFANY BRIERE · SUSIE BRIGHT · JAMEL BRINKLEY · LUCIE BROCK-BROIDO
KEVIN BROCKMEIER · MELISSA BRODER · OLIVER BROUDY · JOEL BROUWER
CARRIE BROWN · JERICHO BROWN · MOLLY MCCULLY BROWN · TIFFANY
LEE BROWN · JENNY BROWNE · RUBY BRUNTON · KIMBERLY BRUSS · JULIA
BRYAN-WILSON · NINA BUCKLESS · GARTH BUCKNER · JUDY BUDNITZ · RITA
BULLWINKEL · ROSE BUNCH · FRANK BURES · ERIC BURG · WENDY BURK
MICHAEL BURKARD · THOMAS BURKE · JENNY BURMAN · DEBORAH BURNS
LAETITIA BURNS · LISABETH BURTON · BARBARA G. BURWELL · FREDERICK
BUSCH · MARIA BUSTILLOS · ROBERT OLEN BUTLER · WILL BUTLER
MICHAEL BYERS · SARAH SHUN-LIEN BYNUM · TOM BYRNES · SHANNON
CAIN · MARK CALDWELL · KENNETH CALHOUN · NICOLE CALLIHAN
GABRIELLE CALVOCORESSI · PATRICK CAMILLER · ERIK CAMPBELL · ALBERT
CAMUS · KEVIN CANTY · MARY CAPONEGRO · MEL CARLSON · RON CARLSON
STACY CARLSON · KAI CARLSON-WEE · BOGDANA CARPENTER · CHRIS
CARROLL · TOBIAS CARROLL · WILLA CARROLL · HAYDEN CARRUTH · JAMES
CARSE · ANNE CARSON · LISA CARTER · STEVEN CARTER · CODY CARVEL
ORLY CASTEL-BLOOM · BRITTANY CAVALLARO · CLARE CAVANAGH ·
NICK CAVE · MARY ANN CAWS · ABIGAIL CHABITNOY · MICHAEL CHABON
FRANCESCA CHABRIER · JESSAMINE CHAN · L[...]
SAMANTHA CHANG · RYAN CHANG · VICTORIA CHA[...]
CHATTI · ALEXANDER CHEE · ANTON CHEKHOV · C[...]
CHENG · EMILY CHENOWETH · KATHRYN CHETKOV[...]

DIANA M. CHIEN · RITA CHIN · CHRISTINA CHIU · JAE CHOI · SUSAN CHOI · CHIN-HO CHONG · KATY CHRISLER · INGER CHRISTENSEN · KATE CHRISTENSEN · HEATHER CHRISTLE · NICHOLAS CHRISTOPHER · CHUANG-TZU · SONYA CHUNG · LISA CICCARELLO · DREW CICCOLO · GEORGE MAKANA CLARK · JONATHAN RUSSELL CLARK · MARY HIGGINS CLARK · ADAM CLAY · CASSANDRA CLEGHORN · BRIDGET CHIAO CLERKIN · EMMA CLINE RACHEL CLINE · MICHAEL W. CLUNE · CHRISTIE B. COCHRELL · ANDREA COHEN · JOSHUA COHEN · PAUL COHEN · ROBERT COHEN · TEJU COLE BILLY COLLINS · JIM COLLINS · PAUL COLLINS · KATIE CONDON · LYDIA CONKLIN · JAMES CONRAD · BRENDAN CONSTANTINE · DIANE COOK · JULIA COOKE · LUCY CORIN · LEELA CORMAN · MARGARET JULL COSTA · BRANDON COURTNEY · ALEX COX · EMILY COX · KATIE COYLE · PETER CRABTREE · JIM CRACE · TONAYA CRAFT · ALLEN "LORD WHIMSY" CRAWFORD · MEEHAN CRIST · JENNIFER CROFT · KATIE CROUCH · JOHN CROWLEY · M. ALLEN CUNNINGHAM · AMY CUTLER · CHARLES D'AMBROSIO · STACEY D'ERASMO TONY D'SOUZA · TADEUSZ DĄBROWSKI · MICHAEL DAHLIE · SUSAN DAITCH JOHN M. DANIEL MARK Z. DANIELEWSKI · KATE DANIELS · BEI DAO KYLE DARGAN · ALICE ELLIOTT DARK · MAHMOUD DARWISH · KAVITA DAS JENNIFER S. DAVIS · LYDIA DAVIS · OLENA KALYTIAK DAVIS · TERI ELLEN CROSS DAVIS · OLIVER DE LA PAZ · MÓNICA DE LA TORRE · ALEŠ DEBELJAK KENDRA DECOLO · JONATHAN DEE · BRIAN DELEEUW · DIANA MARIE DELGADO · AMANDA DEMARCO · RICK DEMARINIS · DARCIE DENNIGAN ROB DENNIS · AMBER DERMONT · TOI DERRICOTTE · ANITA DESAI · MARCIA DESANCTIS · HEATHER DESURVIRE · A.N. DEVERS · CHRISTOPHER DEWEESE DAN DEWEESE · ANNIE DEWITT · PATRICK DEWITT · JANINE DI GIOVANNI JUNOT DÍAZ · NATALIE DIAZ · MATTHEW DICKMAN · MICHAEL DICKMAN ALEX DIMITROV · LIDIJA DIMKOVSKA · JOHN DIVOLA · ARIEL DJANIKIAN CORY DOCTOROW · ELIZABETH DODD · ANTHONY DOERR · SARAH DOHRMANN SHARON DOLIN · NATHANIEL DOLTON-THORNTON · CHRISTA DONNER ARIEL DORFMAN · MARK DOTY · BRIAN DOYLE · JOEL DRUCKER · AMY DRYANSKY · ALLISON DUBINSKY · ANDRE DUBUS III · RIKKI DUCORNET CAROL ANN DUFFY · DANIEL DUFORD · DONALD DUNBAR · CAMILLE T. DUNGY IRIS JAMAHL DUNKLE · STEPHEN DUNN · JONATHAN DURBIN · P. GENESIUS DURICA · LEE DURKEE · STUART DYBEK · CORNELIUS EADY · TONY EARLEY

RICHARD EDSON · RONALD "STOZO" EDWARDS · JENNIFER EGAN · WILLIAM EGGLESTON · NATALIE EILBERT · DEBORAH EISENBERG · EMMA COPLEY EISENBERG · CARL ELLIOTT · JULIA ELLIOTT · STEPHEN ELLIOTT · THOMAS SAYERS ELLIS · LAURA EVE ENGEL · NATHAN ENGLANDER · SEAN ENNIS ELAINE EQUI · LOUISE ERDRICH · PAMELA ERENS · ERIN ERGENBRIGHT BLAKE ESKIN · VERONICA SCOTT ESPOSITO · JOHN ESTES · JEFFREY EUGENIDES · CJ EVANS · DANIELLE EVANS · BRIAN EVENSON · EVE EWING KATHY FAGAN · ELLEN FAGG · FAIZ AHMAD FAIZ · SONIA FALEIRO · NURUDDIN FARAH · JOSEPH FASANO · FARNOOSH FATHI · GIBSON FAY-LEBLANC MELISSA FEBOS · DAVID FEINSTEIN · PAUL FELDMAN · ADAM FELL · AUDREY FERENCE · MEGAN FERNANDES · JENNI FERRARI-ADLER · MONICA FERRELL JOSHUA FERRIS · DAVID FERRY · CHELSEA LEMON FETZER · MADELINE FFITCH · THALIA FIELD · ABBIE FIELDS · MICHELE FILGATE · ZACK FINCH JOHN FISCHER · JAMIE FISHER · JESSICA FISHER · JANET FITCH · ADAM FITZGERALD · F. SCOTT FITZGERALD · GUSTAVE FLAUBERT · COLIN FLEMING EMILY FLOUTON · NICK FLYNN · MARK FORD · RICHARD FORD · STEPHANIE FORD · T'AI FREEDOM FORD · AIDAN FORSTER · JORDAN FOSTER · JOSHUA FOSTER · CARRIE FOUNTAIN · DIANA FOX · THOMAS FRANK · JOSEPH FRANKEL TOM FRANKLIN · DAN FRAZIER · LYNN FREED · HELEN RUTH FREEMAN JOHN FREEMAN · MEG FREITAG · GABRIEL FRIED · MARK FRIED · PHILIP FRIED · SETH FRIED · TYLER FRIEND · ANDREW FRISARDI · ALBERTO FUGUET ALICE FULTON · MARY JANE FUMARE · TIFFANY NOELLE FUNG · RITA GABIS PETER GADOL · GINGER GAFFNEY · MARY GAITSKILL · ANN GELDER · EDUARDO GALEANO · AMY GALL · JAMES GALVIN · SARAH GAMBITO · SERGEY GANDLEVSKY · LUCIA GANIEVA · BENJAMIN GANTCHER · GABRIELLE GANTZ ANGELICA GARNETT · PHILIPPE GARNIER · SAM GARRETT · WILLIAM GASS BILL GASTON · DAVID GATES · NATHAN GAUER · MICIAH BAY GAULT · EDWARD GAUVIN · ROSS GAY · ROXANE GAY · WILLIAM GAY · TIM GEARY · CHARLIE GEER · JAMES GENDRON · BEN GEORGE · DINARA GEORGEOLIANI · DAVID GEORGI · GREG GERKE · AMANDA GERSH · DAVID GESSNER · HAFIZAH GETER PANIO GIANOPOULOS · D.W. GIBSON · CELIA GILBERT · AARON GILBREATH JENNIFER GILMORE · SARAH GIRAGOSIAN · WILLIAM GIRALDI · PETER GIZZI ANN GLAVIANO · TEOW LIM GOH · ELIZABETH GOLD · GLEN DAVID GOLD ALBERT GOLDBARTH · JIM GOLDBERG · REBECCA NEWBERGER GOLDSTEIN

MANUEL GONZALES · REGAN GOOD · JOANNA GOODMAN · FRAN GORDON
NEIL GORDON · AMELIA GRAY · ROBERT GRAY · ROBERT DUNCAN GRAY
LEAH NAOMI GREEN · ARIELLE GREENBERG · GARY GREENBERG · ANDREA
GREGOVICH · KIMBERLY GREY · LISA GRGAS · PAUL CHARLES GRIFFIN · TIM
GRIFFITH · RACHEL ELIZA GRIFFITHS · ALISON GRILLO · TOM GRIMES
PAUL GRINER · CARRIE GRINSTEAD · J. P. GRITTON · LAUREN GROFF
MICHAEL JOSEPH GROSS · ANNE CHOTZINOFF GROSSMAN · LISA GROSSMAN
NIKOLAI GROZNI · DAVID GRUBBS · PAUL GUEST · JAMES GUIDA · SUZANNE
GUILLETTE · SHUSHA GUPPY · NICHOLAS GUREWITCH · ALLAN GURGANUS
CAMILLE GUTHRIE · DEBRA GWARTNEY · RACHEL HADAS · EVA HAGBERG
FISHER · RAWI HAGE · MERLE HAGGARD · KIMIKO HAHN · MICHAEL HAINEY
LAUREN HALDEMAN · DANIEL HALL · DONALD HALL · JUDITH HALL · J.C.
HALLMAN · MARK HALPERIN · DANIEL HALPERN · AARON HAMBURGER
MOHSIN HAMID · ANDRÁS HÁMORI · EMIL HANDKE · DANIEL HANDLER
JESSICA HANDLER · BRUCE HANDY · BARRY HANNAH · RON HANSEN · JARED
HARÉL · BAIRD HARPER · MICHAEL HARRIS · KATHRYN HARRISON · HEATHER
HARTLEY · RYAN HARTY · MATTHEA HARVEY · JOHN HASKELL · CJ HAUSER
EHUD HAVAZELET · CHRISTIAN HAWKEY · AMANDA HAWKINS · JEREMY
ALLAN HAWKINS · ALIX HAWLEY · TERRANCE HAYES · TODD HAYNES · K.A.
HAYS · RYAN HEALEY · THOMAS HEALY · SEAMUS HEANEY · STEVEN
HEIGHTON · KATHERINE HEINY · HELLE HELLE · MICHAEL HELM · ERNEST
HEMINGWAY · ALEKSANDAR HEMON · AMY HEMPEL · LAUREN MILNE
HENDERSON · SMITH HENDERSON · KEVIN HENKES · EDWARD J. HILL
KATHERINE HILL · SEAN HILL · BRENDA HILLMAN · EDWARD HIRSCH · JANE
HIRSHFIELD · TONY HOAGLAND · JAMES HOCH · ANN HODGMAN · MISHA
HOEKSTRA · ADINA HOFFMAN · CARY HOLLADAY · SANTI ELIJAH HOLLEY
C. HOLLOW · T.E. HOLT · ETHAN J. HON · ANN HOOD · HORACE · CAITLIN
HORROCKS · MICHEL HOUELLEBECQ · CHRISTOPHER R. HOWARD · GERRY
HOWARD · MARIE HOWE · GREG HRBEK · THOMAS HRYCYK · DANE
HUCKELBRIDGE · KAREN HUDES · RHODA HUFFEY · CAOILINN HUGHES
EVAN HUGHES · SOPHIE HUGHES · ANDREW HULTKRANS · DONNA HUNT
HOWARD HUNT · SAMANTHA HUNT · FRANCES HWANG · LEWIS HYDE · KARL
IAGNEMMA · COLETTE INEZ · ANNETTE INSDORF · VICTOR INZUNZA · SIR
MUHAMMAD IQBAL · MARK IRWIN · KRISTEN ISKANDRIAN · TARA ISON

HENRY ISRAELI · GARY JACKSON · GREG JACKSON · MAJOR JACKSON · MARCUS JACKSON · MITCHELL S. JACKSON · NAOMI JACKSON · SHELLEY JACKSON · SHIRLEY JACKSON · MIRA JACOB · KATE RUTLEDGE JAFFE · TANIA JAMES · THOMAS JAMES · LESLIE JAMISON · DUNJA JANKOVIC · TOVE JANSSON · LUIS JARAMILLO · TAMARA JENKINS · MALIA JENSEN · MORGAN JERKINS · YANG JIAN · HA JIN · KRISTINA JIPSON · ADAM JOHNSON · DANIEL JOHNSON · DENIS JOHNSON · JESSICA JOHNSON · JULIA JOHNSON · LACY M. JOHNSON · TAYLOR JOHNSON · BRET ANTHONY JOHNSTON · TROY JOLLIMORE · HOLLY GODDARD JONES · LISA JONES · PATRICIA SPEARS JONES · SAEED JONES · TAYARI JONES · THOM JONES · LAWRENCE JOSEPH FADY JOUDAH · ANNA JOURNEY · MIRANDA JULY · JOHN KACHUBA · ISMAIL KADARE · RACHEL KADISH · TONY KAHN · KEN KALFUS · GEORGE KALOGERAKIS · YORAM KANIUK · CYNTHIA KAPLAN · KAREN KARBO · KAPKA KASSABOVA · RAFIQ KATHWARI · STEVEN KATZ · YASUNARI KAWABATA CAROL KEELEY · DEBORAH KEENAN · ANNA KEESEY · DONIKA KELLY · JAMES KELMAN · JOSH KENDALL · JANE KENYON · BETH KEPHART · MAZEN KERBAJ ETGAR KERET · KARL KESEL · KEN KESEY · RACHEL KESSLER · RACHEL KHONG · TRACY KIDDER · LYNN KILPATRICK · ALICE SOLA KIM · HA POONG KIM · SUJI KWOCK KIM · JULIE KING · RICH KING · STEPHEN KING · JOHN KINSELLA · PAUL KIRCHNER · KARL KIRCHWEY · WALTER KIRN · MATT KISH PHIL KLAY · ALEXANDRA KLEEMAN · AMELIA KLEIN · MARK KLEIN MICHAEL KLEIN · MARK KLETT · MARSHALL N. KLIMASEWISKI · PETER KLINE · JOANNA KLINK · NATE KLUG · ALEXIS KNAPP · CHESTON KNAPP KARL OVE KNAUSGÅRD · ALYSSA KNICKERBOCKER · BILL KNOTT · CAROLINE KNOX · MICHAEL KOBRE · NOELLE KOCOT · JEFF KOEHLER · LEAH KOENIG JILL KOENIGSDORF · WAYNE KOESTENBAUM · JOHN KOETHE · EMMA KOMLOS-HROBSKY · YUSEF KOMUNYAKAA · ERIC KONIGSBERG · SCOTT KORB ANNA KORIATH · NINA KOSSMAN · CHRISTINA E. KRAMER · MATTHEW KRAMER · CHRIS KRAUS · PAUL D. KRETKOWSKI · ANDREW KRIVAK · ROBERT KRULWICH · SIGIZMUND KRZHIZHANOVSKY · KEETJE KUIPERS · MILAN KUNDERA · STANLEY KUNITZ · RACHEL KUSHNER · PETER LABERGE CATHERINE LACEY · AMY LAM · DANUSHA LAMÉRIS · DEBORAH LANDAU KRISTA LANDERS · DYLAN LANDIS · HEATHER LARIMER · REIF LARSEN PETER LASALLE · DOROTHEA LASKY · BEN LASMAN · BRETT FLETCHER LAUER

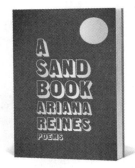

MAGAZINE

Tin House

Volume 20, Number 4

But the time ain't tall

Yet on time you depend and no word
    is possessed

By no special friend

And though the line is cut

It ain't quite the end

I'll just bid farewell till we meet again

—BOB DYLAN

Tin House

MAGAZINE

EDITOR IN CHIEF / PUBLISHER
Win McCormack

EDITOR	Rob Spillman
DEPUTY PUBLISHER	Holly MacArthur
ART DIRECTOR	Diane Chonette
MANAGING EDITOR	Cheston Knapp
EXECUTIVE EDITOR	Michelle Wildgen
SENIOR EDITOR	Emma Komlos-Hrobsky
EDITOR-AT-LARGE	Elissa Schappell
ASSOCIATE EDITOR	Thomas Ross
POETRY EDITOR	Camille T. Dungy
SENIOR DESIGNER	Jakob Vala
PARIS EDITOR	Heather Hartley
COPY EDITORS	Meg Storey & Jess Kibler

CONTRIBUTING EDITORS: Dorothy Allison, Steve Almond, Aimee Bender, Charles D'Ambrosio, Natalie Diaz, Anthony Doerr, Nick Flynn, Matthea Harvey, Jeanne McCulloch, Rick Moody, Maggie Nelson, Whitney Otto, D. A. Powell, Jon Raymond, Helen Schulman, Jim Shepard, Karen Shepard

INTERNS: Jeremy Cruz, Elena Ender, Nike Laskaris, Morgan O'Sullivan

READERS: Leslie Marie Aguilar, William Clifford, April Darcy, Selin Gökçesu, Todd Gray, Lisa Grgas, Carol Keeley, Louise Wareham Leonard, Su-Yee Lin, Maria Lioutaia, Alyssa Persons, Sean Quinn, Lauren Roberts, Gordon Smith, Jennifer Taylor, J. R. Toriseva, Charlotte Wyatt

"It is a fact that when I was a young editor and thought I'd stumbled across a new writer, I'd discover that @Tin_House had already published them. The magazine was editorially catholic and adventurous--exactly what you want from a lit mag."

—NICOLE RUDICK (@nicolerudick)

"Wow, I'm really sad to hear this. But also @Tin_House has had one of the greatest runs ever. So much stellar fiction and careers have come out of this magazine. One of those lit magazines that helped define the last 20 years of American lit. Thank you!"

—LINCOLN MICHEL (@TheLincoln)

"A sad day for fans of Tin House magazine. You had a great twenty-year run. Thank you for promoting new voices and lifting up overlooked ones. And thank you for always being supportive of your writers. You've left an indelible mark on the literary landscape."

—RENEE ZUCKERBROT (@RZAgent)

As far back as when I was an earnest young man in the MFA program at the University of Oregon in the early 1970s, I nurtured the idea of one day starting a literary journal. But over the years, every time my mind returned to the thought, I rejected it out of hand. A literary quarterly, I would conclude, made no sense: a harrowing expenditure of money would garner you a modest circulation at best; you could have no real impact on the world, even the purely literary world, with such a publication. Meanwhile, I had entered the magazine publishing business for real, founding a general interest magazine about my adopted state called *Oregon Magazine*. After a fifteen-year run I sold that enterprise to a conglomerate back East, which put both myself and my art director, Richard Jester, out of work. One day he said to me, "I know you've had this fantasy about a lit pub forever—why don't we just start fooling around with some possible designs and see what happens?" What happened was, once the project took on a concrete aspect, I was hooked. I hired Holly MacArthur to help me and Richard put together a sample issue, and after the product we produced persuaded me to undertake the project for real, I hired Rob Spillman and Elissa Schappell, who had come recommended by almost everyone I talked to in New York, as editors. It took us one year to produce the first issue, which we then brought to the annual convention of the Association of American Publishers. A friend of mine who was also attending the conference met the staff and said to me, "McCormack, you have an exceptional talent for finding really good people." Let that statement stand as an explanation for why the Tin House project has been as successful as Nicole Rudick, Lincoln Michel, and Renee Zuckerbrot, along with many others, say it has.

Win McCormack

EDITOR'S NOTE

There is not space or time enough to thank everyone who has been a part of the building, renovation, and maintenance of *Tin House*. But I am going to try. First, thank you to our writers, all 1,582 of you, each of whom is named at the opening and close of this issue. It has been an honor to publish your work and to champion it in the world.

Tin House would not exist without the generous commitment that publisher Win McCormack made to the quixotic venture. My co-founding editor and partner, Elissa Schappell, has been the magazine's heart and conscience. From day one deputy publisher Holly MacArthur has somehow managed to keep the place afloat. Michelle Wildgen has been our most thoughtful and insightful reader, at every turn a voice of reason and compassion. Cheston Knapp has likewise been invaluable; his deeply considered and nuanced editing has earned the admiration and loyalty of scores of writers. Emma Komlos-Hbrosky, with her editorial acumen, dark humor, and daring, has been my rock in Brooklyn. Thomas Ross consistently surprised and challenged us by bringing in pathbreaking work. Week after week I was astonished by the depth and breadth of the poetry Camille Dungy shared with us. Copy editor Meg Storey is that rare grammar genius who is also an elegant and sensitive editor. The art team of Diane Chonette and Jakob Vala managed, issue after issue, to delight us and readers with their imagination and innovation.

Thank you also to Jon Baird, our first art director, who drew up the blueprint of the initial design, as well as past poetry editors Amy Bartlett, Brenda Shaughnessy, and Matthew Dickman, art directors Bill Stanton, Laura Shaw, and Janet Parker, and editors Desiree Andrews, Christina Chiu, Lance Cleland, Serena Crawford, Brian DeLeeuw, C. J. Evans, Diana Fox, Ben George, Randy Gragg, Heather Hartley, Tucker Malarkey, Jeanne McCulloch, Lee Montgomery, Jason Nickerson, Jon Raymond, Tonaya Craft, Greg Villepique, and Anne Yoder.

Twenty years ago I believed that stories, poems, and essays could build bridges and save lives. I still believe this. Thank you for sharing the dream with us. I can't wait to read what you write next.

CONTENTS

ISSUE #80 / THE FINAL ISSUE

||||||||||||||||||||||||||||||||||||||||||||||| **Fiction** |||||||||||||||||||||||||||||||||||||||||||||||

Poetry

Nonfiction

1999

Lost & Found

Readable Feast

Blithe Spirit

Last Word

FICTION

The
Gondoliers

Karen Russell

I. THE CHORUS

Dr. Glim was supposed to be my last fare of the evening, but when I am a quarter hour from home I hear a man coughing on South Jetty. Against my better judgment, I am drawn down the foamy water of a side canal toward the rattling sound. Through the keyhole spaces in the mangroves, I glimpse a tall figure in a long green slicker pacing on the jetty. He cries out when he sees me, flagging me down with his whole body.

The sky is two-toned, fiery pink above the green horizon line. It's too late for a passenger, even a regular, someone trusted and familiar. A happy story ends here; a responsible gondolier poles homeward. I can hear my sisters doing just that. They are singing in a wide canal, three boats pulling into a line. Echoes fly into the birdcage of my sternum. Even miles apart, we are always audible to one another.

When I am twenty feet from the jetty, I raise the pole and wave it slowly at him. Power gathers in my cracked heels and pulses upward. Will I take him to his destination? We are equals in our suspense.

"What luck," cries the man. "Are you going north?"

"Push your hood up. I want to see who's asking."

Sunset is less than an hour away, and he won't find another boat if I refuse him. His fear reaches out to stroke my cheek. It makes me feel tenderly toward the white-faced old man; also, powerful. On the poling platform, I am almost eye level with him. Old, I guess that's always relative. Older than me, I should say. Thirty? Forty? But perhaps I look old to him.

"Thank God you spotted me. Please, I'm in a real jam."

He keeps a finger trained on me, as if at any moment I might disappear.

"The boat I hired never showed."

From *Orange World and Other Stories*, published by Knopf.

His voice catches. Now that I am closer, I can hear how deeply this rattle has lodged itself inside his body. Even at dusk, it's still eighty degrees, but this stranger is shivering. His desperation perfumes the air, a soaking underarm smell. Under the jutting limestone, as if in secret mimicry of him, a thousand tiny, sharp wavelets jump and fall. He is nervous. I am making him nervous. Power whips through me again, and I almost laugh, it feels so good to be alive on the poling platform. Song gathers under my navel and I make no effort to contain it.

"OoOoOoOo—"

I watch him jump.

"Miss, won't you help me?"

"Miss," I smile. "That's a first."

I have two names: Janelle Picarro and Blister. My mother gave me the first name, my sisters, the latter. My regular passengers rarely address me at all.

"Can you take me to the seawall in Bahía Rosa?"

A visitor to New Florida usually wants to see the jungle, the ruins. Locals hire us to pole them to the fishing nets, the floating markets. We take children to their school in the morning, weaving around the leviathan shadows of the wrecked cruise liners, helping them up the gangplanks to their classrooms. Nobody asks to go to the seawall. My sisters won't pole within a mile of the black buoys.

"We don't go there."

"We?" The man opens an antique red wallet. "But I'm asking *you*."

Two miles away, behind the tangled red mangroves, home calls to me. My sisters and I live inside the ruins of a seaplane hangar built out of metal and glass a hundred years ago. By now my sisters will be rinsing the salt water from their gondolas. Only my boat slip will be empty. I can hear the twangy echo of my absence in the hangar, a hollow note that gives me a queer twist of pleasure in my gut.

"Money can make sense out of almost anything, can't it?" I watch his black thumbnail riffle the paper. "It's magic that way. But no amount of money can turn a trip to the seawall into a sane journey."

The seawall was erected by the Army Corps as a last-ditch attempt to protect the city from getting swallowed. It failed, of course, and thousands

> A happy story ends here; a responsible gondolier poles homeward.

drowned. Now it rises out of the middle of the sea, the fossil of an old boundary line. We call the silent bay that surrounds it Bahía Rosa—a pretty name for a rippling nowhere. Once, the green lights used by fishing boats draped the ocean in a miasmic fog, so bright it was visible from outer space. Now reddish blooms of a fish-killing algae cover the entire bay. Bahía Rosa gets blamed for everything from cancer to bad dreams. A desire to go there suggests a highly contaminated assessment of risk, reward. Smugglers supposedly meet at the seawall, a rumor I did not much credit until this moment.

"Please, miss. I am already behind schedule."

He offers me a stupendous sum of money. More than I make in a month as a gondolier on Bahía del Oro.

"Double that," I tell him.

As we pole away from the jetty, I hear a faint, awful rumbling, but I can't decide if this is the true echo of some future disaster or only my guilt. This man is sick, and he has no supplies, no food. But if my last fare wants me to leave him in the middle of the sea, that's his business; my business is transportation. He didn't hire me to ask questions.

> **Only a lunatic or a criminal goes to the seawall.**

Only a lunatic or a criminal goes to the seawall—that's what Viola would say. Viola is my oldest sister, the most responsible of us and in some ways the most guileless; she wouldn't understand the humming in my body that begins when I hear the words "Bahía Rosa." The truth is that I badly want to go there, and I'm grateful to have this stranger's money as my alibi. Once I deliver him to the seawall, I'll have hours to myself in the unmappable dark. A part of me is already flying into the future, where I am rid of this person, free and alone, and swimming under the blind moon of Bahía Rosa.

His coughing jolts me back into the boat, and I feel sick myself for a miserable moment, wondering if I should turn back. It's a relief to pull clear of the mangroves and join up with the fast-moving current. Now the tide is carrying us toward the sea, and the echoes make my decisions for me.

Two birds, one stone. The old, brutal saying returns to me out of the blue. I can't remember where I first heard it; I house thousands of these fragments. Echoes of unknown origin. Words that went skipping across minds for centuries, apparently, before sinking into mine.

. . .

The current races us through the ruins of Old City, where a teenaged boatman drowned just last week. My sisters and I have a monopoly on this territory. Even locals lose their way here, where the debris rearranges itself in a slowly turning kaleidoscope, the garbage mountains always changing shape. The glare of the sun is intense at six o'clock, splintering around the concrete grottos. We enter the shade of a domed ceiling, poling around the brass and silver letters: MI I PL ET RI UM. Former home of the phony night sky, where hundreds of translucent fish now sway, nibbling at the algae on the auditorium walls. Rows of spongy seats glide just below us, a reef of huge brown scallops. Staircases that move like our singing does, lunging in two directions at once.

"OOOoooOOOooo—"

Middle C to E minor. Orange to pink to blue. The song sweeps in front of the bow. I crutch around the drowned beams that fill the planetarium's lobby, singing at the top of my register. Echoes shower into me. My spine feels ignited by them.

New Florida is composed of grassy water, the bleached reefs of submerged and abandoned cities, and dozens of floating villages. It's illegal to live here, although thousands of us do. Holdouts and the spawn of holdouts. Old Florida is a glassy figment in the minds of the soon to be deceased. If you think our song is monotonous, you should hear our neighbors reminiscing: *Oh, the highways, the indoor malls! Soil as far as a man could travel. Funerals, remember those? The coffins we planted like seeds in the ground.* That Florida, if it ever existed, has no reality for me.

We go mazing between the toppled condominiums, which loom like dark whelks lying on their sides. Golden awnings bloom on the former city's northern border; the tenanted ruins rise in the west. Generator lights glow in several of the third- and fourth-story windows. My passenger turns on the bow seat and shouts over my singing, "Miss, didn't we just come from that tunnel? Are we going in circles?"

"Yes," I call down, enjoying my height. "It's the only way out."

Satellites have been down for decades. Even those who navigate with salvaged equipment fail to detect the dangers hidden under the water. Perhaps these vintage technologies work on sleepier seas; I have only ever lived here. My sisters and I navigate these margins with breath and bones. We sing, and we absorb the echoes into our skeletons. A map draws itself inside us, revises us.

Three hard strokes, brake. Pivot and pole around a forest of streetlights. Launching my voice against a wall, I can hear the sunken pylons that mean to kill me and I swerve, changing the future. This happens hundreds of times a day in New Florida.

"Lean back," I tell my passenger, and he folds himself into the gondola as if it's a casket, crossing his arms against the crinkling slicker. It ripples across him, and it's easy to pretend that I am transporting the sea itself, the wind made flesh. We enter the archway to a vanished city park, now a deep green pool. Smells change as we travel: rotting wood, salt-eaten aluminum. The song boomerangs around a flooded parking garage, once large enough to stable hundreds of cars. I close my eyes as we spin into a stone nautilus. Hiding just ahead of us is the decaying, waterlogged hulk of a poinciana tree blocking the exit. Echoes push its branching shape into my skull, and into the skulls of my sisters in the distant, adjacent hangar. Always, we are this close and this remote. Vibrations unite us. We can hear the golden algae that gloves the underwater city and the long bald stretches of sunlit wall. Spongy sounds and waffled ones. But tonight the map is my own creation, the product of a single looping input. C stroke. J stroke. I brace the pole against my chest. The song hunts for an opening, and water spits us into unbroken sky.

When I open my eyes, the man is staring up at me.

"Ah. I've heard about you." He smiles uncertainly. "You're one of those bat girls. The echolocators."

"What luck," I smile back at him. "I am."

· · ·

We call ourselves the gondoliers. Four singing sisters, poling the canals of New Florida. There are other boats on the water, but only my sisters and I take passengers through Old City. According to Vi, when our mother was alive, people would count four girls seated behind her on the long skiff and reliably say, "Trying for the boy?" "As a matter of fact," she'd snap, "God has blessed me with daughters. If I could, I'd make a hundred more."

My sisters tell this story all the goddamn time. So often that it feels like *my* memory. She drowned when I was three years old, before the cameras in my mind turned on.

Our regulars suspect there's more to our nasally singing than we let on. For sure they know it's not Italian. "Lady, can I please pay you to shut up?" tourists have begged me. I used to think that we were very special, the best boatwomen in the world, but Viola says no, we are only vessels ourselves: something wants to be born. Perhaps there are many others like us around the bays of New Florida and elsewhere. Women who know enough to be silent about what is developing inside their bodies.

This sensitivity grew in us softly, softly. I can only compare it to seeing in the dark. We sing, and shapes tighten out of an interior darkness. Edges and densities. Objects sing back at us: Turn hard left to avoid the fallen tree. Pole southwest to miss one of the many gluey hills of floating garbage that block the canals. Pillars thin as lampposts push fuzzily into our minds; a heartbeat later they rear out of the bay, fatally real.

Our mother could not echolocate, according to my sisters. When I was a child, I found this frightening and sad. Imagine seeing a thousand colors streaking the sky and realizing that your mother saw only one unbroken gray. But Viola says our mother could hear us crying from impressive distances, and I wonder now if she had some precursor of this ability.

Our gift is not a true clairvoyance, or what I imagine that to be. There's no time for anything like that. It's more like a muscular intuition of what the water is going to do next. And with our poles flying, rattling the oarlocks, we move to accommodate the future of the river.

We call ourselves the gondoliers. Four singing sisters, poling the canals of New Florida.

. . .

In this neighborhood of Bahía del Oro, pollution tints everything with phosphor. Mosses drop in shimmering clumps around the stern. I pole from starboard, my bare feet planted against the cypress boards. Orange plants with soft drunken voices slide around the hull, drawling a beautiful lace behind my eyelids.

"I like your boat. Very pretty."

The man's deep voice startles me and causes the shy plants to fall silent. He raps a fist against the hull. I can hear the solidity of my gondola behind the hollowness of his compliment. "Such an unusual design . . ."

Suck my dick.

You can't say that to a paying customer, chides Viola in my mind.

"Suck my cock," I hear myself say.

He slams a laugh into my chest.

"I haven't heard that one in decades."

I read it on the wall of the flooded school, which is covered in adolescent hieroglyphs: Suck my dick. Ride my dick. Lick my juicy pussy. Names that are still legible at low tide: *Paola was here. Gabriel was here. Say my name. Hurt like I do. Kiss me, Someone.* Writing that survives the bodies that produced it is always haunted, I guess. But the underwater graffiti of the lost world feels especially so.

"I don't like false praise," I tell him. "And I see that you have eyes."

I have a bad thought, staring at his bony face—that I can answer him without fear.

My gondola is decorated with crude stars that I knifed into the wood. The end result was less like artwork than an attack my boat survived. My boat looks nothing like my sisters' perfectly lovely gondolas, and that is how I wanted it.

After that, there is a long silence. The sun seems to tarry behind the trees, extending our opportunity to beg it to stay. Bright water ripples around either side of us and the black mangroves slant off into the distance.

"Do you live on Bahía del Oro, sir? I've never seen you out here."

"No, you haven't. That is certainly by design."

"What a feat. A recluse among recluses."

"You don't like false praise. I don't like false people. I choose my company carefully."

Undeterred, the man taps at the steel ornament fixed to the bow, my birthday bird, welded for me by Luna as a counterbalance to my weight in the stern.

"Your work?"

"My sister Luna made it for me. She's the family artist."

The heron is painted a somber madonna blue, my only criticism of it. Turquoise would have been my choice, I tell him. "Turquoise is what that blue would look like if she divorced the night and went on a fabulous vacation."

He laughs again, a laugh that I bounce back to him at the same low frequency. Warmth stirs in my belly.

"Do you boatwomen ever take a vacation?"

"Oh, never. I feel like I'm always working, even when I'm sleeping. Our beds are practically floating. Our home sits half in water."

"Home." It sounds like a foreign word, the way he intones it. "Where is home?"

It's taboo to ask this question of a stranger in New Florida, but perhaps he does not know our etiquette. I have a bad thought, staring at his bony face—that I can answer him without fear, because he is very close to the end of his life.

"We live in an old seaplane hangar."

"Almost like a cave. Perfect for a bat girl."

"Water laps inside it. You should see the four of us, poling home at night. Like horses swimming into a barn stall."

He smiles at me strangely, his eyes crossing a little.

"Horses. Have you ever seen a horse?"

I shake my head, embarrassed. Only in books with waterlogged pictures. Stories fly out of the mouths of my oldest neighbors. But I have never seen a swimming horse myself, it's true. "Tell me, when were you born?"

I whisper the year to him, and something like awe crosses his face.

"How lucky! So you remember nothing, then—none of the evacuations, none of the flooding. None of the floating bodies . . ."

His face puckers and relaxes, a quick civil war.

"You don't remember any of that."

"I know what my older sisters tell me," I say. "It's almost like a memory."

"And what do they tell you?"

"Very little."

We skirt the cathedral, half hidden in a tangle of mangroves. A brass steeple soars over the trees, a canted X on which several anhinga dry their wings. Framed by the sun, their glossy feathers look emerald. Hundreds more roost around the ruins. Snakebirds, the ocean's swans. Egret, pelican, heron. Someone lives here now, I think. Rope ladders tumble down the walls. As we glide under the cathedral window, a dog begins to bark.

We are only allowed to stay here, says Viola, because officially, we don't exist. Most mainlanders have forgotten us. New Florida has been declared a "wasteland," which is a hilariously inaccurate term for our living, liquid world, where the southern marshes teem with thousands of fishes and birds. "A resurrection," say the old-timers. But for me, it's the world as it always has been.

"We're almost there," I keep promising the man. I don't like the way the eastern clouds are rumbling. "Twenty minutes," I say. The standard lie. Like a cracker you can hand people, to put off their appetite. Every twenty minutes, you repeat this. But his impatience seems to burn off him as soon as we pull away from Old City. He begins to hum along with my singing, a beautiful surprise, like someone walking beside me, taking my hand.

"Look," he says dreamily, and points to where the moon is rising, bright and enormous as the door to another galaxy, on the opposite side of the bay.

· · ·

OoOoOoOo.
OoOoOoOo.
A whiskery sun flashes between the sunken rooftops, but dark clouds have rolled in from the southeast, a bad surprise. I imagine my sisters pointing up at them, shaking their heads.

"Do you feel that?" His frowning face retreats inside the cowl. "Rain."

Glimmering threads begin to fall. A hissing starts in the back of my brain. Rain is no good. Rain scatters the echoes. I can feel the massing thunderheads like gloved hands at my back, pushing me to go faster and faster. The current is moving us steadily seaward, at a speed of perhaps fifteen knots.

The clouds racing toward us give me a tingling déjà vu, and I realize it's a sky I've seen in dreams, lowering itself into my home. The great floods occurred in a distant world: before Bahía Rosa was Bahía Rosa, back when everything had a different name. I wasn't born when the ocean rode across the peninsula. Still, I hear the waves rearing back, slamming forward, causing the walls to buckle. The cries of the families on the rooftops, the ambulance boats with their droning sirens. My older sisters become quite agitated when I describe these dreams. "You have no idea what it was like then," Vi told me. "You never lived a day on land. Quit stealing our stories."

Perhaps the memories filtered into me through our mother's blood? I once suggested to my sisters. Viola, in her most condescending voice, then told me to "leave the grieving to the grown-ups." She still thinks of me as her three-year-old ward. It will shock her, some day, to look up and discover that I am an adult now, with secrets of my own.

"The algae." I stir some around my pole. "You see? It's changing color." Brownish-gold to reddish-pink. Which means we are drawing very near to the seawall. The worst pollution seems to be concentrated here, under the algal blooms.

"Do you ever see mutants out this way?" the man asks me, turtled in his hood. He keeps his voice nonchalant, but I watch him peering into the darkening water.

You hear tales of goliath grouper with multicolored eyes, two-headed manatee calves.

"Never once. Does that disappoint you?"

In fact, when I first entered Bahía Rosa, I found something even stranger. A silence that almost erased me. But I don't tell the man this; why burden him with a new fear, when we are finally sitting level on the water?

II. THE BRIDGE

One slow afternoon last May, I found myself in the middle of Bahía Rosa. For two hours I'd been tailing a dolphin through the polluted zone, reasoning that if she could breathe here, so could I. When I reached the outermost limits of our territory, where the black buoys warn boaters

"Do you feel that?" His frowning face retreats inside the cowl. "Rain."

to turn back, I continued onward. By this point, the dolphin had disappeared, but I'd already traveled so far from home that it seemed obligatory to continue exploring. My sisters could feel the growing distance between us, but they were singing in Old City, hours behind me.

Long before I saw the seawall, I heard it lifting out of the ocean. At last it appeared, a thick hallucination striping the ruddy bay. I knew the stories but I'd never seen the remnants of the great wall for myself. There it was, rising out of the ocean, a monument to its own failure. This mile-long stretch of the seawall was largely intact, with bright moving gaps where the maroon water had eaten through the crumbling stone. First I heard, and then saw, what must have been the seawall's former landside edge. It curled toward me, as if uninformed that the land had pulled away, and it was easy to imagine the whole peninsula slipping out of this relaxed embrace and sinking.

What must have once been solid, unbroken coastline, in our mother's youth, is now a pointillist landscape of small tree islands. Many are less than one acre wide, knuckles of limestone covered in flowering vegetation. I had been hugging their muddy shorelines for the past hour. Now I let the springy echoes from the seawall choreograph my passage into deeper water, poling toward the northern edge of the wall. As smoothly as a happy thought turns black, I found myself in the middle of Bahía Rosa, where the algae waves in every direction. The absence of birdsong made the sky feel empty and tall. A stinging odor lifted off the water. Almost immediately, I developed a terrible headache.

I poled up to the huge, broken molars of the seawall. Three hundred yards behind me, the bald mangroves lifted onto their tiptoes, as if they too were surprised to find the barrier still breaking the waves. I could hear its secret skeleton, the weep holes and the reinforcement rods. I could hear, also, the gargling cracks where it had failed at the waterline. I was poling through a pocket of dense red algae that had collected around the wall's barnacled edge when something astonishing happened to me. The echoes ceased entirely. My sisters' singing fell away, and I was alone. The suddenness of this silence

> All I could hear was a single, flattened cry.

shocked me more than any detonation. The deep sonority of our chorus vanished, and all I could hear was a single, flattened cry. This, I realized, was my voice—separated from the others. Fear spun me around: What had happened to my sisters? Somehow, it seemed, I had poled out of range; I was floating in a kind of *deadspot*.

I watched the waves gonging into the limestone wall for miles and miles, a birdless sky stretching above me. Nothing sang back to me. The present seemed to spill eternally around me, and no echoes reached my ears. I removed my clothes and slid into the toxic water. I don't know what possessed me to do this, but it was no accident: I pushed my head below the surface, through the slippery blooms, kicking down.

I'd never felt this far removed from my sisters. Under the water, I stopped hearing even the whoosh of my blood. What happened next, I'll never know, because I sank out of earshot of my thoughts.

I surfaced to a grogginess that exceeded anything I'd ever felt in my waking life. A ruff of pearly blue seascum encircled me. The plants seemed to emit their own red glow. A light independent of any moon. The raw throats of cypress trunks scraped the sky. I didn't know who I was, what I was. The face floating on the water was not mine, not yet. It wrinkled and smoothed with a foreign serenity. Nothing remembered me.

The seawater I spit out tasted poisonous. Creature-like, I watched my limbs moving through it. I could name the colors of the bay before I knew what sort of animal I was. An acrid smell lifted off the water, impossible to ignore at low tide, bringing with it visions of putrefying flesh. A smell that should have been incompatible with my bliss, but somehow was not. *How interesting*, I thought from a great distance, rolling my arms through the rosy water, turning onto my back.

"Sensation returned" conveys none of the extraordinary pain I felt coming to consciousness. Like a numb foot tingling awake. My joints began to pulse. A bad sunburn crackled across the mask of my face. When I heard the waves slapping against my gondola, memories swept through me: I was Janelle Picarro again, one of four gondoliers, afloat in the forbidden waters of Bahía Rosa.

My sisters. Queasily I swam for my gondola. The seawall loomed on the horizon, and once I poled out of Bahía Rosa I could hear them again. Viola. Mila. Luna. Seeping back into my skull, a wailing harmony. Only then did I take the measure of what I had done.

Just this once, I thought. *Once, and never again.* This magic phrase inoculated me against my guilt. I pulled the red weeds from my hair and climbed into the boat. I didn't know that I was setting a precedent. It felt like coming back from the dead that night, poling into the seaplane hangar under a full moon. My sisters were very angry with me. They wanted to know where I'd been. Their heavy tones fell into me like lead weights after the freedom of the afternoon.

The lie was spontaneous.

Ordinarily it is very difficult to lie to my sisters. But the deadspot had inspired me. Without thinking, I screamed back at them. Swinging my pole, striking at bedrock. Using tone alone, I changed the night's direction.

"Where were *you*?" I counter-accused. "Why didn't anybody answer me?"

I began to sob. I let them witness the release of so much blackness from my body, recalling the silence that had flooded me while I floated under the wavy ceiling of algae. "I was calling and calling for you. I have never felt so all alone on the water."

The best lies have a fleck of truth folded inside them. All good performers know this. Real gold to bite down on. The ringing truth overrides the hollowness of the lie. I could see from my sisters' horrified expressions that they believed me. The transfer of my guilt into their bodies was a success. I even began to believe myself.

My sisters apologized to me. They blamed the weather, interference from the scattered raindrops. We embraced. My relief could not have been more sincere.

That night, I lay awake for hours in an itchy reverie, curling my toes on the bed railing. We sleep in cots stanchioned to the walls. Luna's body was a lump in the cot above mine; Mila was snoring down below. Waves lapped at the metal hangar, the salt water breathing with us in the dark. *Never again*, I promised my sleeping sisters. I could always return to the deadspot in my memory—it was enough to know that kind of quiet existed. I went to sleep feeling warm and lucky. Grateful for the strange experience, and snug in my conviction that I would never repeat it.

Seven hours later, I was poling back toward the deadspot.

III. THE DEADSPOT

We vowel down the channels. Darkness reaches around the eastern sky-scrapers, and then those stalagmites are behind us. A pink line stitches day to night. A few early stars have appeared, but that light tells me nothing about our position. Unless I am singing, I really can't tell south from north after dark. Barking seagulls scatter the echoes, and I get caught in a swirl-ing cul-de-sac of water on the outskirts of Old City.

Once the seagulls fly on, I hear my sisters' voices crackling into my body, combing the darkening bay like searchlights:

"AAAaaaaaAAA—"

"UuuUuuuUuu—"

Disappearing can make you feel like your own biographer. You hear the absence of your voice, the notes you fail to hit. You unlid the spaces ordi-narily hidden by your body: a new song comes fluting through them. When-ever I hear my sisters singing without me, I get a flash of my own silhouette.

I bounce back a B-flat at the top of my register. The note quivers there, reassuring them: I am alive, in Old City. The songlines connecting us pull tight, relax. I hear a pulsing silence: my sisters listening as I move away from them. When I return, I will pile money on the table. I will give my sisters hundreds of reasons to forgive me. What will Viola say, I wonder, when I tell her I've made more in a night than she makes in a summer month on Bahía del Oro?

My passenger cranes around to stare at me, wearing the oddest look. The slicker lays heavily on top of him, alien as frogskin. It seems to breathe all on its own.

"Old MacDonald had a farm. E-I-E-I-O—"

I stare down at him, stirring the gold from the bay.

"You sound like you are calling pigs to the trough," he says, but he is smiling.

I like this man. He fixes me with a lolling curiosity, despite his urgency to reach the seawall. He does not offer to help me to steer the gondola, as some of the nervous men do. He does not snap at me when I pause to rest my voice. His eyes are mild. He is turning his palms, catching the fat droplets of rain.

"Were you born with the ability?" he asks. "Or is it something you taught yourself out here?"

I feel the song idling in my belly, changing slyly inside me.

"Both, I think."

People talk about heredity as if it's linear and vertical. Dead people passing things "down" to the young. But my sisters and I are evolving together, I tell the man. All day, we swap notes around. We blur our voices into one song. Something grows in the fast-moving channels between us and it's changing all the time. It moves with us, this thing we are inheriting.

> Disappearing can make you feel like your own biographer.

To our left, ivory columns stand guard over a submerged pavilion.

"That was a bank once," I tell him. "Did you see the vault in the middle of the floor?" Ferns are twining around it now. "Can you believe that? People kept their money at a great distance from their body."

"I believe it," he says. "But I'm quite a bit older than you."

"My oldest sister, Viola, says—"

"You youngsters only know the stories."

His tone is wistful, but I hear the scolding note. My sisters and I are no strangers to this attitude. Older passengers often seem dismayed that they have to cede the earth to creatures like us. They are aghast that we know so little about their world, and bewildered by our happiness in this one. *We know more than you can imagine*, I want to tell him. But not as badly as I want my tip.

"I wish that I remembered the land, for what it's worth," I tell the man, watching his pale eyes swim over my face. "I would have loved to know what my mother's yard looked like."

"*Yaaard.*" He looks up at me thoughtfully. "What an odd word. I never noticed that before. Don't mind me, miss. You should forget even the stories. Look how lightly you sit on the water, remembering only water . . ."

I picture the healthy eelgrass waving in the limpid shallows of Bahía de las Nubes. "The grass is always greener, I guess."

He laughs at that. "Where did you hear *that* one? I'm surprised that it survived the floods. You know all our corny sayings. You're like a jukebox, miss."

His face reminds me of the wild dogs we see on the tree islands, panting with silent laughter. He speaks in a monotone, so I don't know if I should be complimented or insulted. Perhaps I'm being invited to laugh with him.

"A *jokebox*—"

"A jukebox. It was a machine that played the same stale songs over and over."

Blood rushes into my face. Does he think that's what I'm doing? Repeating myself? Can't he hear my singing changing on the air?

> "Down here, the world has already ended. It's very peaceful, in its way."

We blink up at the washed violet sky behind the rotting ceiling. The bank shrinks into the distance. When the stranger turns, his face is as composed as a poem, its symmetries perfectly mysterious. My fantasies don't run in his direction. But fear prickles my neck, and it feels almost like lust.

"Hey. What's your name?" I ask him. "Who are you going to meet in Bahía Rosa, where nobody lives?"

He cranes up at me, his Adam's apple jumping. I feel the oddest déjà vu.

"Make up a name for me. Any name you'd like. Give me a nickname while you're at it. I am always in the market for a new name."

"Let me think on it," I tell him. "Maybe we can borrow a name from the posters."

I say this to make a joke and wind up frightening myself. The MISSING PERSON posters flap against the walls of Old City, most bleached beyond recognition. Men and women and children who disappeared in the floods. There is no way to read them as anything but obituaries today.

"Ah, the posters. Yes. I've seen those. A missing person. How perceptive you are. That's me to a T."

He turns back to the light rain misting on the water, his hairy knuckles wrapped around the heron's throat. I've retreated into my own thoughts when he calls back, "All of those faces are my face, why not? All of those names can be me. We are fungible sponges, we missing people."

I can't get my bearings in this conversation—is he joking? Is he really a MISSING PERSON?

"Were you here for the floods?"

He turns and stares at me for a long moment before answering.

"I'm part of a dying breed, bat girl. An *Old Floridian*. I grew up on a street called Coral Way. In a house with a foundation."

"But you stayed."

"No, miss. I fled. I was in the first wave of evacuations. But I wanted to come home before I died. To see my home again." His laugh becomes the phlegmy cough. "I'd need a scuba suit to find it, I guess. I've been here for three weeks and I can't find a trace of that life."

It does not surprise me that I have a neighbor whose face I've never seen. Millions of people once lived in the coastal cities; thousands of us remain. "Squatters rights, bro," someone spray-painted on the tallest standing condominium in Old City. But property disputes are rare on moving, glowing water. You have to live here to discover that the pollution isn't strong enough to kill you.

"Where are you moored?"

"I've been camping at the university. On the roof of the library, I believe. It's a good retirement home. The twilight zone, for my twilight years."

"Come on. You're not *that* old."

We laugh together, a sound I often draw like tarpaulin over what I do not understand.

"Down here, the world has already ended. It's very peaceful, in its way."

It always surprises me when visitors treat New Florida as if it's a graveyard. Our home is no afterlife, no wasteland. Not an hour earlier, we poled through a rookery that shook with the hungry sobs of fledgling birds. Wood stork chicks and starry white ibis and young stilt-legged green heron wading through the rooftop sloughs. But if my passenger failed to hear them, I doubt my voice can convince him that our world is newborn.

"Do you have a family, sir? Up north?"

"I did. A wife, two sons. Terrestrials, all."

"They must be worried about you. Do they know where you are?"

"They drowned."

"Oh. I'm so sorry."

"I killed them," he elaborates. "I was one of the engineers who designed the seawall."

"I don't blame you," I blurt out.

"You should. People my age are criminals. We ruined the world."

Reminiscing about his guilt seems, perversely, to cheer my passenger. His voice brightens as he describes the scale of the failure. "We built the wall to withstand winds of 150 miles per hour. Does that sound naïve to you?"

I wonder if he can hear the note of pride inside of what he seems to mean as an apology to me. He's chosen a funny moment to have this conversation, I think, with the wind picking up all around us and rain slanting between our faces.

"You failed," I say, echoing him—it's the line he's written for me to say.

"Our imaginations failed us. Our models failed us."

A smile is still playing at the corners of his mouth. I wonder if he knows he's smiling. There is a profoundly unchaperoned quality to his gaze, now that his mind has traveled back in time. I try to listen to the details of his story, but it's his slack, abandoned face that fascinates me. His eyes roll up to the gray clouds, as if something is dragging him skyward by the roots of his hair.

"We all knew the end was coming. Don't let anybody tell you otherwise."

It would be cruel, I decide, to remind him that life is flourishing in New Florida; that it is our world now, not his any longer; that actually, he is the one who is dying.

"This used to be paradise. I'm sorry, little bat. We ate up the whole horizon. We left you a ghost town. Not even a town. A toxic slough—"

"This is our home," I tell him. "And we are not ghosts."

I stop poling and stare down at him. Water rolls down his slicker, capturing the light. As if the green skin is sweating for him. In his voice I hear a longing for release so close to my own that it is almost unbearable.

"There is a place I like to go," I hear myself say. "To fall silent."

As I describe the deadspot to him, he listens in perfect stillness. Even his blinking slows. Several times, I hear him swallowing his coughs. It feels like a betrayal to entrust this secret to him when I've told none of my sisters. But almost anything I say to them provokes a terrible reverb. Whereas a stranger is an open field—no buried stalagmites, no love lost between us, no history and no expectation of a future. These turn out to be the perfect acoustics for confessing a secret on which I do not actually wish to reflect.

"And you don't think the pollution is damaging you?" he asks at last. *Deranging you*, I hear.

"No." The skin under my breasts begins to burn. "Not really."

An odd rash has spread silently over my belly, unnoticed by anyone. Even I forget it's there during the daylight hours. My hands remember it at night.

"You choose to swim here," he says. "In the world's most toxic waters."

"It hasn't affected us."

"Hasn't it, little bat? It's affecting all of us."

He drums his knuckles on his temple, his smile softening like something boiling at the bottom of a pot. His voice curls inward, so that it seems he is talking mostly to himself.

"The gondoliers. The birds of Chernobyl."

"What's that mean?"

"Nothing. A bad joke."

Algae drags behind us like an old-fashioned wedding train. You have to sweep the lantern over it to arouse the red glow;

"This is our home," I tell him. "And we are not ghosts."

the unlit bay is entirely black now. Soon I will deposit this person on the seawall, I think with relief. Then I will go night swimming. I imagine the water closing over my head, swallowing me into it. The feeling that this water is gestating me, my secret life. So secret, that for whole minutes I know nothing about it.

We drift for a while while I rest my voice. Very gingerly, the man lowers his left arm into the water. Then he drops his soaking hand into his lap, where it looks like a netted white fish. I watch him frowning down at the hand, as if waiting for it to change before his eyes.

"Tell me something," he asks. "Why do you keep returning to this *deadspot*?"

For some reason, I feel myself blushing. "I'm the youngest in our family. My sister Vi was like a mother to me. At the hour of my death, I'll still be the baby sister to them. It doesn't seem like I can age out of the role . . ."

This is certainly part of why I feel entitled to my lonely hours in the deadspot, I explain to the man. Their entire life before my birth is a secret from me. Whereas everything I've ever done has been visible to them.

"Out here, I float into my own element. It's a relief to fall silent. When I am silent, when I am alone, I feel free. I don't have to sing along with anybody. Even my thoughts stop."

Under the water. Far from my sisters. Outside the chaos of our breaths. Only then, when I am nothing to anyone, do I feel the great peace.

It's as if I've released something living into the narrow gondola. I picture the secret floating between our faces, a jellyfish emitting its soft violet light, blowing open and shut. I wait for the man to turn it into a joke, or to shame me for coming here alone.

"Yes," he says quietly. "That's it exactly. What a discovery."

The man lifts his eyes to mine with naked surprise, and I feel equally astonished. The longer we stare at each other, the louder a pure tone grows inside the gondola. Audible, I think, to both of us. He pushes back the green hood, smoothing the wet leaves of his hair. Gray or brown, there's no telling in this lighting. His wide smile sends all his wrinkles into hiding.

> "Who doesn't dream of it? The silence that blots up thought."

"Who doesn't dream of it? The silence that blots up thought. The silence that frees one from the burden of being oneself."

His smile opens a portal back to the stranger's infancy. Every prior grin I've seen tonight, I realize, was a counterfeit of this one. Understanding someone can make you feel understood in turn, and I smile back at him, to let him know that we have this thirst in common. Poling forward, it occurs to me that I should thank this white-faced man, the engineer, along with everyone from the last century who heard the water coming and failed to stop it. The deadspot is their creation.

• • •

We gondoliers operate by the Golden Rule. You do not take any risk you wouldn't want your sister to take. You don't pole into bad weather, or shoot the tunnels at low tide. You refuse any passenger who might overpower you. I would kill my sisters, for example, if they risked their lives to take a fare to Bahía Rosa.

My sisters and I all pretend to live by this code. To prize safety over profit. But I have always felt quietly certain that perfect adherence to the Golden Rule would sink our business. We'd never leave the hangar. When I started breaking this rule routinely, it was easy to rationalize. I needed a darkness that would have killed the others, and they needed me to keep that a secret from them. This did not feel treacherous, not at first. It felt like a loving choice.

People will tell you that Bahía Rosa is a fatal place, but for months it was my paradise. The black-walled horizons. The silence that lets me ripple out of my body, until at last I feel entirely at peace, whole and unfractured. One with the wildest turnings of the universe.

But at the same time I had begun to wonder, poling home from the deadspot, *How true can this sensation of unity really be if you need to leave everyone you care about to get it?*

. . .

We float over a school of pompano, dozens of frozen grey faces skipping in front of the bow light. Something has frightened them; perhaps its long body is saucering beneath the transom. The man beckons me down from my platform. When he asks his question, his words quiver like the fishes.

"Do you and your sisters ever hear the voices of the drowned in this bay?"

"No, sir. That's not . . . we don't have that kind of range."

"I see," he nods, but I don't think he believes me.

The man helps me by bailing water, leaning carefully forward. His green slicker bunches around the stringy muscles of his shoulders. The humming grows inside me until there is no room for worry. What will it feel like, I wonder, to enter the deadspot with another person? To fall silent with him? He thinks my home is a cemetery, and I want him to hear how wrong he is before we part company. The end of his life is not the end of all life. Something wants to be born.

. . .

We pass the line of black buoys. They strain after us on their long tethers; just as quickly, they are lost to sight. They push against the back of my mind as I sing, nodding on the surface of the night.

OoOoOoO . . .

OoOoOoOo . . .

For a long time we see nothing at all, only water and more water. But I reassure the man that I can hear the seawall drawing nearer with each booming wave. And then we both see it, the bleached wall, looming like a motionless wave on the horizon.

I touch my tongue to the inside of my cheek. For hours I've been waiting for this moment, but now that the end is in sight, I don't see how I'm going to manage the pivot. It's impossible to imagine leaving this sick man alone on the seawall with no supplies, no fresh water. Tantamount to pushing him off a roof on a night like this. The nausea I felt when I picked him up on the jetty returns with a force that nearly doubles me over.

We shadow the soft shoulders of the tree islands, matted with laughing-yellow, snarling-green vegetation. In twenty minutes, I tell the man, we will reach the northern edge of his wall.

But when we are perhaps three hundred yards to the northwest of the seawall's rocky edge, the rain begins to fall in earnest. It pounds into my skull, drawing a caul around the gondola. More water splits the sky; in an instant, the map inside me dissolves. If I were home right now, I'd be listening to the rain falling on our home's domed roof. Luna would be snoring above me, Mila below me. I'd be drifting off myself under my blanket, at the beginning of a dream. Can my sisters still hear me? I hear nothing but rain. I swing my light across the chop and feel the stirrings of real panic. By sight alone, in such a punishing crosswind, there is no way I can make this passage.

"Violaaaa?"

"Milaaaaa?"

"Lunaaaaaa?"

My voice flies off and does not return. Nothing answers me. Nothing steers me here. I place the pole in the oarlock and climb down from the platform. Perhaps my poker face is not on straight, because the man gives me a wild look and grabs my wrist.

"Why aren't you singing?"

"Forgive me, sir," I say, avoiding his eyes. "I made a mistake. I thought we could beat this storm. But we'll have to ride this out. I'm losing my voice. I can't map the channel. If I miscalculate this passage, we'll capsize."

On a slack tide, I explain to him, I'd shortcut across the bay, but the water is alive with eddies, and I don't want to get smashed against the wall or sucked out to the Gulf.

"Girl," he says slowly. "Take me to the goddamn wall."

His voice shakes with a rage I could not have predicted even a heartbeat earlier.

"I can *see* it. We could *swim* there, practically—"

"No. We can't risk it." His face is almost unrecognizable to me, winched tight with anger. "I won't risk it," I clarify, as it becomes clear to me that he is making very different calculations.

"You won't *risk it*. You'll bathe in poison, but this is too dangerous?"

The man tugs me toward him, shouting over the wind.

"Tonight is the anniversary of the storm surge. Do they teach that date in your floating school?"

I had forgotten the date; it isn't one we celebrate. Our mother was alive to hear it: the night the pumping systems failed. The night the seawall was breached by the towering water. The wailing night that did not kill our mother, who would live for another seven years so that I could be born.

He tightens his grip on my wrist, gazing at the gray beam from the bow light, where the angled rain is steadily visible. Horror seeps into me, his or my own, I am no longer certain. Large chunks of darkness lift and fall around my gondola.

"I traveled a thousand miles to die here. I chose this spot, this date. I wanted to walk across the seawall on my last night on earth. That was my wish. To die at home, on the anniversary of my children's deaths."

> More water splits the sky; in an instant, the map inside me dissolves.

Beneath the sagging hood, he peers up at my face. Here is a man who has written the last scene of his life, I realize, who is furious that his stage directions are getting eaten by the wind. His voice lowers, and inside of the anger I can hear a grinding disappointment.

"Don't hold out on me, miss. It's cruel to stop here, within sight of our destination. I didn't come this close to the end to turn around."

Our destination. Rain pounds into the hull, water we should be bailing. His feet are bare, I notice—at some point, he must have removed his boots. The toes waggle at me, as if their good humor is still intact, even as the rest of him seems bent on destroying us.

"When the rain stops, I'm returning with you." I take a shaky breath. "I cannot, in good conscience, take you to your death."

"In *good conscience*." He laughs angrily, reaching a wet palm to my cheek. "Miss, you already have. Look around you. We've arrived." The scolding note reenters his voice. "Now, be honest. You knew where you were taking me. The *deadspot*, you called it." Raindrops go jumping off the green slicker, outlining him in fizzing silver. "Get your pole. Finish the job I hired you to do."

"No." I climb back onto the platform and begin to turn us toward the lee side of the nearest tree island, which I can just make out through the rain. When I look again, the man is rising to his feet. We ride up one swell and down into a deep trough, and I have time to feel amazed that we have not capsized just before he lunges at me. Perhaps he is a better echolocater than I am: when my arms lift, he shadows them, a rhyming motion. Quite easily, he wrestles the pole away from me. He gives me a terrible grin, gripping my pole to his chest. Sisters, I was wrong about my last fare. He is stronger than I am, and he is much sicker than I imagined.

"If you refuse to continue, I'm afraid I'll have to take command of this vessel . . ."

Warm liquid seeps through my trousers and I am crying now, I want to go home. OoOoOoOo, I scream. The man releases my arm. For a moment, his eyes shine with some trace of our earlier understanding.

"Poor little bat. You just wanted to disappear for a little while, didn't you? You don't actually want to die."

I don't. I don't, but I had to come a great distance to learn that, sisters.

> **My mind is like the sky between the stars, void of shapes names facts.**

"You should stop swimming out here, then." Again I hear the scolding note, but it's much fainter now. He is trying, clumsily, to push off the rocky bottom and turn the prow toward the seawall. I watch him struggling with the pole, its foot now choked with mud. "This whole bay is a stomachful of bile."

Then comes a rippling instant when the scene I am imagining becomes the action I am taking. I watch my hands reach out to grab the pole back, my fingers closing just above his knuckles; he doesn't let go, but twists around with a cry, jerking me with him. I lurch forward and bite his hand until he howls. He is still clutching my pole when a strong wave washes over the gunwales. I let go to brace myself and the man falls backward, with my pole, into the rainy water.

I scream with him as he falls, and I go on screaming after he splashes into the bay. But I don't jump into the churning water after him, terrified that he will drag me down. "Sir?" I croak, but my voice is almost gone and I'm sure he doesn't hear me. It occurs to me that I don't even have a name to call. It's so dark that I can't see where he surfaces, but I hear his arms crashing heavily through the algal mats. If I were to swivel the lantern, perhaps I would see him bobbing mere feet from the boat, his pale face staring up at me, wreathed in the glowing algae. Perhaps I could save him. *Save him*, I command myself. But I don't move from the floor of the boat.

Instead I curl into myself and cover my light. As the staccato thrashing sounds fade, I realize, with relief, that he is swimming away from me. He must be trying to make the wall.

Eventually, my wish is granted: the splashing ceases altogether. Either the man has drowned, or he's swum out of earshot. But the new silence he leaves in his wake is far worse. I lie flat on the wet boards, pushing my fists against my stomach. My pole, I imagine, must be riding these same waves into the Gulf, or sinking to some depth I cannot hear. And my passenger? He is a true MISSING PERSON now, I think. A special amphibian, dead and alive, swimming behind my eyelids. The last splash he made is a sound that will not leave me. This bay will swallow his face soon, if it hasn't already. *You killed him*, I try not to think. The moon shines into my eyes; very slowly it occurs to me that the rain has stopped. I have a peculiar, nerveless awareness of the water's trembling surface. Where am I? My mind is like the sky between the stars, void of shapes names facts. But I don't need to sing to guess.

IV. THE CHORUS

I stare up at a busy construction pit. Tiny white spades are tossing huge quantities of darkness around. Stars—these are the stars.

I'm not sure how long I drift like this, trying not to see the man's face as he fell, trying not to hear the terrible splashing. Without my pole, I'm in bad trouble, but I screamed for so long that I must have blasted all feeling from my body, and it hardly seems to matter that no boats will find me in this distant bay. My bow light plucks at the stringy algae. Perhaps I sailed right through a break in the seawall without realizing it. My song is a pitiful hissing, and it returns no depths or dimensions to me. When I hear a voice rising out of the darkness, I think it must be my imagination. My light swings in the direction of the singing.

A gondola is arrowing toward me, flat-bottomed and opal white in the powerful beam of my lantern. My good feeling immediately flips into horror. A gondolier stands on the poling platform, her hair blowing loose. The pitch of her singing rises. *God, please, no. God, please, keep us separate. No, no, no. I am not ready to meet her.* OoOoOoO, she sings at me. Can this be possible—am I about to run into my doppelgänger? Is she poling out of the past or the future? Perhaps the man will be seated in the bow, smiling out of his green slicker. Will he be dead, I wonder, or alive?

But it's not my double that draws into view; it's my sister.

Viola glides silently past me, wearing a blindfold with trailing ribbons, her thin face illuminated by the gray orb of her bow light. Her droning song floods into me. I hear the same sound that pours from my throat in the deadspot—an emptying hiss, like grain spilling from a sack.

Her gondola moves much faster than my mind does. Lethargic thoughts chase each other in slow, widening circles: She's come out here to find me. She's put herself in terrible danger, all to find me.

But soon I realize that Vi has no idea that I'm out here. The blindfold is a trick of last resort; tight pressure across the temples can sometimes help us to hear better in bad weather. It doesn't seem to be working. Her hair flies raggedly behind her. Her singing has the strange, flayed quality of all sounds in the deadspot, shadowless and flat. Now I hear, with excruciating clarity, how much trouble we're in. Vi didn't come out here to save me. She's lost herself.

"Vi!" I scream. Too hoarse, I'm sure, to be heard.

But Viola unties the red bandage around her eyes, using the blindfold to wipe at her face. Had all the drowned risen up to address me tonight, I could not have been more astonished. Shaking her hair out, she turns and looks right at me: "Blister!"

Fury wheels around our boats, shrieking at such an earsplitting volume that it's impossible to pinpoint the origin of the feeling.

She poles up to me, our pupils shrinking in the doubled glare of the bow lights. Two voices swing out like hooks, each catching at the other:

"What are you *doing* here?"

The answer floats between us, mocking us. Rain lashes the water between our boats. Vi has always seemed to be light-years ahead of me. Perhaps she is as surprised as I am to discover how we overlap.

"Did you come here to find me?" Vi asks me in a stricken voice.

Her face seems to float, unanchored, isolated by the light. I think about lying, then shake my head.

"No. I wanted to come out here to swim."

"So did I," says my sister, with the ghost of a smile.

Our calamity strikes me, suddenly, as terribly funny. No less astonishing a coincidence, in its way, than being born into the same family.

"How long have you been swimming here?"

"Oh," Vi says pensively, chewing on her thumb pad. "Years."

Years!

One of us asks: "Why didn't you tell me?"

One of us says to the other: "It is so selfish to come here."

One of us is burning with shame—is it hers or my own?

One of us shouts: "Who am I hurting?"

And we scream at each other: "Me!"

Silence rips apart down the middle. Silence reveals its tiny serrated fangs. Have we loved each other well? Could we love each other better? I realize that there is so much we have never told one another, and likely never will. Secrets multiply throughout our hangar. A hundred doors that we refuse to test with speech. A hundred others that we pretend are walls. If I were braver, I would fling my voice against them, at the exact pitch to pick the locks. If I were braver, and if I were a better singer.

In a whisper, I tell Viola about my last fare. How I listened, paralyzed, while the moment when I might have saved him flipped into the moment of his death.

To my great surprise, she does not pull away from me. I watch the story fall into her open pupils, and prepare myself for Vi's disgust, her anger. But it's love, uninjured, that floats to the surface.

> Silence rips apart down the middle. Silence reveals its tiny serrated fangs.

"It's a shame we weren't alive then," Vi murmurs. "We could have told them how to build the seawall. We could have listened for the weak spots."

Over her shoulder, I see a rolling darkness. I have the nauseating thought that the man's green slicker might come floating our way, carrying the glowing algae.

"Can you hear anything out there, Vi?"

"Just you, talking. But let's keep trying."

I crawl into Vi's gondola and hitch my boat to her stern. We try and fail to find a signal. The rain begins again, lashing the black water between our boats. Soon she, too, loses her voice. This rain stings wherever it touches our skin. Vi gives up on poling and sits in the stern behind me; I feel the weight of her chin on my left shoulder. She runs the flats of her palms down my curved spine, pressing at the bony knobs. She used to do this for me when I was very small and still frightened of open water. She told me that this was how sisters tuned one another.

I wonder if we will ever reach the end of the deadspot. It seems to keep spinning us back into it, a hungry red mouth.

"Blister," Vi says, in her flattened voice. "Do you remember the mice?"

We had a single children's book when I was growing up, with a superficially cheerful, apocalyptic plotline. One mouse after another tumbles into a muddy hole, each trying to rescue the others. A family of mice doomed by their clumsiness and by their love, perhaps by a secret wish to save themselves. And saved they must have been, by some tractor pull of grace, because no children's book ends with the death of every protagonist.

But my mind cannot conceive of a way out of our predicament; in fact, my mind has become the hole.

"Are we going to die now?" Vi asks me.

I shake my head, touched that she's sought out my opinion. Another milestone.

"We should never have come here." Vi shudders. "I am sure they are out looking for us."

Mila and Luna. Perhaps we'll hear their voices soon, behind the curtain of rain. I imagine the storybook mice, steering a teacup on the high seas. In a family of sisters, everybody gets to play all the parts, the brave ones and the cowards, the doomed ones and the saviors.

We toss our raw voices into the wind. We are drifting sightlessly, possibly in circles, when the keening begins. When the first echo reaches me, I mistake it for a symptom of exhaustion. Another echo returns to me, although my lips are sealed.

"Listen," Vi says, tugging at my elbow.

"I hear it, too. You're not crazy. Or we're both crazy."

Behind me I feel Viola tense. The ocean is breaking into pieces. New pairs of eyes shine up at us below the gunwales: fluorescent enormous discs, orange and purple and white, inlaid in the angular faces of some schooling species I have never seen before. I know the old stories about dolphins saving humans, but these are not dolphins, and they seem wholly oblivious of us, even as their keening penetrates our bones. A humming enters my chest and begins to grow—a deep, marine roar. Vi wraps her arms around me, and I feel grateful for her heartbeat; I'd go mad in a second if I was hearing this alone. This new song is wrenching my mind wider than it wants to open, faster than I am ready to go. "I'm not ready!" I scream hoarsely, because I can feel myself getting spun into something vaster than I am, vibrating at a frequency that is not human. Echoes leap into us from dimensions that seem impossibly remote—shivering treetops and submerged walls, the tiny bones of unborn animals. We hear the hollows, the where-to-gos. Spaces in the ruins that cry out to us with the tides: *This is not the end of the world. This is not the end of the world.*

Without turning, I can feel Vi's lips parting, preparing to sing along. *Vi, Vi,* I want to beg like a child, *please, wait for me.* I had wanted to dissolve on my own terms, and only temporarily; if we go through this door, what will we become? Other singers push into my mind, the gibbering moon and the silver mangroves and the buried coral. I am afraid of the voices lifting out of the dark. I am afraid to join them. But perhaps we will have to, if we want to survive. 🔒

ROSEANNE BARR

Is there anyone worse
than Roseanne Barr?

she is the spear tip
of white resentment

her fake working class
caustic humor

can be irresistible
as an opiate

you take to rebel
and become an accomplice

which makes laughing
a kind of fascism

when the time comes
someone should bury her

in the forest
like a mushroom

and put up a big sign
that says don't eat

this poisonous mother

POEM FOR HARM

Walt Whitman
you cannot know

how a live oak feels
much less a woman

or anyone sold
does it help

to think that way
to wander

into everyone's experience
with love you told yourself

and therefore believed
was innocent

to break off a twig
and bring it back to your room

then write
by its harmless light

to listen to you
has helped me

in dark times
and when you said

you were like the grass
a uniform hieroglyphic

growing with equal
distant affection

"among black folks
as among white"

I believed you
your whole life you made

one book some people
now take out into the forest

to ritually burn
because elsewhere you wrote

when you were more than
old enough to know

what you truly thought
of the intellect

of black folks who
were not inside your song

Walt Whitman
should your words

here be said
in pain and shame

or left for only dead wind
to hear

if we keep it
like a secret does its dark

force grow
for my whole life

I thought words
could not harm

I too looked down
but then I had a son

about whom people say
what even I once said

Walt Whitman you are still
my favorite poet sometimes

but what poison
can you drink and live

is the question I ask
in the few moments I have

before my son
lying in bed singing

about feeling like a volcano
slams open the door

and demands
of everyone to be loved

Note: In an essay opposing the extension of suffrage, Whitman wrote, "'As if we had not strained the voting and digestive calibre of American Democracy to the utmost for the last fifty years with the millions of ignorant foreigners, we have now infused a powerful percentage of blacks, with about as much intellect and calibre (in the mass) as so many baboons." (*Prose Works*, p. 762) The phrase "keep it/ like a secret" comes from the title of a record by Built to Spill.

Sharon Olds

ANIMAL CRACKERS

I liked to bite the hindquarters off the hippopotamuses,
and the humps off the camels. I loved tails,
and ears, like those of the hollow chocolate
rabbit who appeared in my house when Jesus rose.
The indented spots on the leopard sent me,
the deep engravings in the zebra's side . . .
Sometimes I liked to save the head, then
pop it in and attend, to feel
that brain of dumb sugar and flour
added to mine. And now that I am half
old, I want some poet crackers,
some Smarts, some Whitmans, little busts or
cameos of everyone,
to eat. I ate Christ, and the bunny,
I want a Levine matzoh, I want
Dickinson by her own recipe,
and Keats, bright oatmeal brooch. I need to
read, lip-read, tooth-read, Ruth
Stone, Miss Gwendolyn Brooks, oh sweet
salty Rukeyser cracker! And I would like
to be one, to be in those little boxes
with woven handles like shed snakeskins—
edible Kinnells, Cliftons, and Oldses!
I wish, when I am dead, I could be
among the English and American animal crackers.

THE FIRST TIME

It was after the birth of a child, it was in that
small, dark, back room,
deep in the building as a kingfisher's summer
tunnel in the bank of a pond leading in
to its nest of eggs, it was in that slight
feeling of sadness after coming, and then it
came up from inside the earth of my body,
it wasn't sadness, it was more desire—
and that desire, from within the satisfied
desire, broke
with the force of both
desires, and then, after brief rest rose
higher, deeper, and broke harder, longer,
and then another, and it went on
awhile like that, until the changes
had been wrung from the whole cloth of a life
up to that hour. And of course I thought it
was love, and it was. And when we unswooned,
the world was not the world I had known,
and I wanted to go stand inside
a blossoming blossom tree, a cherry,
and look up
into it,

and see the bright ganglia
of blue sky, and the many gathered
skirts of the multiple blooms—I came to,
there, where I would spend my life,
decades more with him, then decades without him.

I THINK MY MOTHER

I think my mother had never met
anyone like me. Not her mother,
Victorian of corrosive suffering,
dead when my mother was seventeen.
Not her father, blue-eyed Quaker
in his Stutz Bearcat, dead when she
was five. Not her sister, or her brother—
they all had those blue eyes,
as if they had fucked for hundreds of years
to develop that glaze, its pinnacle
the refractions of my mother's raking
lighthouse mirrors of diamond and sapphire
combined. "Shary does not have what one
would call conventional beauty," she wrote
in my Baby Book, "but when she smiles
her whole face lights up." I think she hadn't
met anyone who felt things
as intensely as she, and showed it. And she
had never been adored by someone so much
smaller than she, nor someone who tried so
hard to explicate to my mother my
mother's adorability, to
express in words and looks the ardent

preference the small heart
had for the big troubled one.
Nor had she known
anyone who was
such a mixture of her and my father,
as if he had brought by force majeure
the rude glory of shapely buttocks
and long legs and curly hair
to bear on her family escutcheon. Nor was there
another person she had beaten. And there was
something not breakable in this girl,
something not quenchable in this odd,
funny, flirtatious child, her little
familiar whom my mother had pushed,
right after a bowel movement,
out of her body, as she wrote in my Baby Book.
She was so ashamed. Today I'd say
the birth-room smelled like a fertilized garden,
like pungent nourishment, and haste,
and eagerness, and hard work, and waste.

LANDING IN SAN FRANCISCO ON THE WAY TO THE COMMUNITY OF WRITERS (WITH A LINE FROM TOM WAITS)

When I emerged through the oval hole in the side of the fuselage,
there was the old smell of home: sweet
diesel, and the faintly rotten bay.
When you reach into a cardboard box of human ashes,
you drive soft shards of ground bone up under your fingernails.
We dropped fistfuls of my mother through the rising and falling surfaces
    of the swells.
Across the continent, the towers were intact,
as if the footage of a few months later had been run backward,
ashes to flesh, ashes to floors and ceilings.
Thousands of families in the dream of the ordinary,
of having a body which would remain whole during death.

First light the next morning, a figure of smoke
is walking out a long pier over San Francisco Bay,
followed by a dog of smoke.
No, it is a coat of ashes
and a cat of ashes—
Hash browns, hash browns—
it is a man pulling a cart out to the fenced oval at the end of the dock.
He unpacks, and starts praying, and another man comes, they are singing,
no, they are fishing. Galway, I'm glad
you were buried whole—as little of you as was left,
it was all of you there was,
deep in the ground on the slope of the mountain hillside,
and you called all those who could come, to come to you,
the carrion and deathwatch beetles, and the worms you loved to honor,
the insects and bacteria and molds and spores, and,
close enough up, they could be heard at their work,
chhhrrrrrrrr, gsmck gsmck gsmck, j-j-j-j-j-j-j-j-j-j-j,
so your body could sing its way into the earth,
so your fellow creatures could dance you back into matter.

Fuck '90s Nostalgia

I moved to Seattle in 1992. At the time, music meant everything to me and I approached songwriting with an agony of earnestness. Freshly sober, I owed everyone I knew apologies or money or both. After years of being an unwanted houseguest, a bad renter, and homeless, I was trying to become a functioning American. I'd forced myself to learn how to drive and got a social security number. I took my GED and found a legal job. Having already squandered several musical opportunities, I decided to apply my newfound diligence there too. This time, I would put my head down and work. I would finish the things I started. I wouldn't complain. I wouldn't disappear when I was supposed to go on tour. And for nearly seven years, I did just that.

If you just look at the pictures today, the '90s seem like an orgy of freedom. But when I hear people speak of that time nostalgically, as carefree or pure, I want to eat glass. I know everyone has their truth now, but if you were trying to make music in Seattle then, you were objectively

Vanessa Veselka

miserable. The demands of the market fractured the music community. While money was the reality, the rules were still punk rock: Every band should be a democracy. Don't ever look like you care. Don't ever look like you're trying. All the while people were climbing over each other to put their signatures on a contract. Word was, if you'd been a band for over six months and weren't signed, you should break up and start over because it wasn't going to happen.

We all existed in this hierarchy we didn't make. Some bands were above your band, others below. You could smell the fear when you opened the paper to the music column. You were rated every time you walked into a room. As a woman, this experience wasn't new, but it was particularly painful. There are all kinds of beauty, but there's only one kind of cool. It wasn't so much that I wanted to be famous, more that I wanted to be part of something and celebrity was the price. Of course the truth of hierarchies is that nobody is looking down on you; you're all looking up. But I didn't know that then. By 1999 all I knew was that I was done.

On New Year's Eve of that year, I stood on an overpass in Capitol Hill with a crowd of people and watched the fireworks and waited for Y2K to wipe everything out. I knew one thing with my whole body: my artistic life was over. I was exhausted from keeping my chin up, badly in debt from touring all the time, and ashamed of everything I'd ever made. I decided to leave the band on a Friday. We played a show that night and I told everybody the next day. They took it pretty well, said we should play a final show. I said we already had.

There are many things bigger than a band. Probably everything. There had to be a place for someone who had failed so profoundly at art. In the center of the WTO demonstrations, watching Niketown get demolished, I saw a path out. I would organize unions. I would work and never sleep. I would put the whole music thing out of my mind.

A few years back I got a call from an old friend in the Seattle music scene. She was collecting oral histories from the women in bands then and turning them into a play. She asked if she could interview me and use some of my music and I said yes. On opening night I sank in my chair as they played a track off my first record while people were seated. The lights went down and it got worse. I'd expected the material from my interview to be buried among forty others' but it was featured heavily, my rants and my discomfort spilled verbatim from the mouths of four different characters. One woman wrote one of my songs on stage. A band broke up over another song of mine. It was a Jungian nightmare. I fled as soon as it was done.

Unfortunately I'd agreed to play a show the following week in support of the play. Bands were flying in from everywhere. A local radio blitz drew young people wanting to live for a night in the fun times of the '90s. I went up at midnight to a packed house in the best spot you could have with energy high from the band before and everyone just drunk enough to be totally on your side. With all eyes on me in this festival of joy, I played a ballad of despair about waiting for your life to start. It wasn't what they'd paid for. Which was only fitting, because it never was.

Grief is like a channel. Once you know where it is on the dial, no matter what else you're listening to you always know it's playing just a few clicks down. Or maybe it's like a frequency. Once your ears adjust, you can always hear it bleeding through. Tune it out. Train yourself. Change the station. The grief channel, broadcasting alongside everything else.

My sixteen-year-old daughter is in a band now. Sometimes I am privileged to hang out while they rehearse. I adjust a mic or tilt an amp so the guitarist can hear himself. Other than that, I stay out of it. Lately they've discovered '90s rock and it comes up through the floorboards. They hear ecstatic distortion. I hear choppers. She's done internet searches but there's no proof of the band I spent seven years in. I know she's told her friends that I opened for the Ramones and the White Stripes, which is true, but we weren't all that glorious. Afraid she'd find the CDs someday and be disappointed, I decided to give them to her as inoculation.

I hadn't heard them in twenty years. Playing them in order, I tried to stomach the shame. I was testimonial. There were lyrical high crimes. We had pop band production but were never a convincing pop band. Deeply influenced by classic rock, I tended toward the anthemic. Later I gave up exposing myself and the songs turned tough and guarded. I played them as fast as I could, as if racing through them would get me out of where I was in life. Listening to the records years later, I just hear my twenties.

We were sitting in the car when I gave her the CDs. I wanted to warn her that my band hadn't been all that great, to tell her we were better live, say it didn't matter—but this was my daughter, a young drummer with her own band, and there's a special hell for mothers who lie to their daughters. So I took her hand and looked her in the eye and said the only honest thing I could: I want you to know that I meant every word. 🛡️

The Master's Castle

Anthony Doerr

Basil Bebbington from Bakersfield isn't good at basketball, wood-shop, or talking to girls, but he's fair at physics, and guts his way through technical college, and lands a job grinding lenses for Bakersfield Optometry, and his parents move to Tampa, and Hurricane Andrew floods their basement, and by age twenty-two Basil begins to worry that he's missing out on things—women, joy, et cetera—so on a whim he applies for a job as an optics technician at an observatory on the summit of Mauna Kea on the island of Hawaii.

The interviews take place at sea level, with a rotating slew of astronomers in flip-flops who warn him that the job involves heavy-duty solitude, weeklong shifts alone atop the volcano, "like being a lighthouse keeper on Mars," one says, but Basil is eager to adjust the trajectory of his life, so he signs the papers, completes the training, leases a Jeep, and on the day of his first shift, drives from sea level to fourteen thousand feet in two hours. By the time he gets out of the truck, the wind is throwing snow across the summit, and his skull feels as if a hatchet has been dropped through it.

A tiny flame-haired woman opens the observatory door, seizes him by the collar, and hauls him inside.

"Ow, what wa . . ." Basil stops midsentence.

"Get in here, Mr. Basil Bebbington from Bakersfield." She force-feeds him four aspirin and twelve ounces of Fresca, and shows him the composting toilet and the telescope—which is not the big Copernicus-type cylinder-with-eyepiece you might expect, but a three-hundred-ton compound mirror thirty-three feet across that adjusts its position twice per second—and she apologizes for the absence of the microwave, which, she explains, made spooky noises at night, so she dragged it to the edge of the road and pitched it off. Her name is Muriel MacDonald, and she's his age, and looks like a woodland elf but moves like a caffeinated jaguar. Before she leaves, she pours him a bowl of Raisin Bran, hands him a Stevie Wonder CD, and says, "When you get lonesome, put 'Higher Ground' on repeat."

By the time Muriel drags her duffel to her Dodge, orange hair blowing everywhere, yelling, "See you in a week!" Basil is ninety-six percent in love.

All that first night he listens to the wind crash against the walls. Fourteen thousand feet below, waves explode onto reefs and tourists gobble deep-fried prawns, but up here it feels to Basil as though life is finally beginning.

He measures wind speeds, radios reports to the astronomers in Waimea, analyzes Muriel's handwriting in the log. At night he puts on "Higher Ground"—

People keep on learnin'
Soldiers keep on warrin'
World keep on turnin'

—and dances idiotically in the mirror barn beneath the burly arm of the Milky Way, and when Sunday finally arrives, and Muriel churns back up the summit road to relieve him, his heart kicks against his sternum like a frog. He makes her coffee, tells her he saw fifty-six meteorites; her green eyes turn like whirlpools; she tells him she believes most stars in the universe support solar systems. "What if," she says, "*every* star has planets circling around it? What if there are hundreds of billions of Earths? Earths where you can high-jump eighty feet! Earths where little turtle-people build little turtle-people cities!"

All week in Hilo, flush with oxygen, Basil dreams of her, brushing her copper hair, flinging appliances off the summit. Cumulonimbi gather along the flanks of the volcano like battleships, and Basil watches them flicker with lightning: blue ignitions, as if Muriel were a god, incinerating things up there.

One hour each Sunday: that's all the time he ever sees her, sixty minutes on the boundaries of their respective shifts. Yet on the calendar of his life, what hours have shone more brightly? Muriel never touches him, or asks about his week, or notices his haircuts, but neither does she mention a boyfriend, and she always meets him at the door looking woozy and grateful, and ensures the cot in the control room has clean sheets, and one wondrous Sunday, after they have traded shifts for five months, she pokes

> Muriel never touches him, or asks about his week, or notices his haircuts, but neither does she mention a boyfriend.

him on the shoulder and says, "I always say, Basil, if you want something, you need to just go for it."

How many times during the next week, alone on the volcano, does Basil parse the possible implications of that sentence? Did she mean "you" as in the impersonal *you*, or did she mean "you" as in Basil, and "something" as in *her*? And could she have meant "it" as in *doodle-bopping*, as in *jingle-jangling*, as in *sexual relations*, and has she been waiting all these weeks for him to "just go for it"?

The next Sunday, after seven straight nights at fourteen thousand feet, Basil cuts fifty paper hearts from the pages of a protocol manual, writes a different simile on each—*I love you like a fish loves water; I love you like we're eggs and bacon*—and stashes the hearts all over the observatory: behind doors, rolled up inside the toilet paper, taped to the back of her Raisin Bran. Muriel comes up and Basil heads down, and all that week he imagines her discovering his valentines. She'll be euphoric, flattered, at least amused, but the following weekend, as he is packing for his next shift, the supervisor calls from Waimea to say that Basil has been reported for making inappropriate advances, that a lawyer is involved, that they are going to have to let him go.

> **Around this time Otis starts wearing an off-brand black superhero cape day and night.**

. . .

He finds a job at an ophthalmologist's in Eugene, then a LensCrafters in Pocatello, the ninth happiest city in Idaho, hoping that an increase in distance will correspond with a decrease in heartbreak, but every few nights he dreams of volcanoes and flame-haired goddesses and humiliation. *I love you like the sky loves blue. I love you like putting up the Christmas tree.* What happens to all the one-sided desire in the world? Does it dissipate into the air, or does it flit around from soul to soul, anxious, haunted, looking for a place to land?

The '90s turn into the 2000s. One Thursday at a foosball tournament, eleven years after leaving Hawaii, Basil is handcuffed by a drunken English department secretary named Mags Futrell who makes fun of his name for half an hour, then kisses him right on the mouth.

Mags drives a Ford Ranger, has eyes like holes burnt into a blanket, prefers Def Leppard to silence, and wears a T-shirt to sleep that says, *Lips that touch liquor touch other lips quicker*. She and Basil have a backyard wedding, and mortgage a two-bedroom rancher on Clark Street across from Al's Comix Warehouse, and Mags stays mostly sober through a pregnancy, and produces a bug-eyed infant named Otis, and during Otis's first year on Earth, Basil pushes his stroller up every hill in Pocatello, shedding pounds like he's shedding insecurities, and on his best nights he stops brooding over what life could have been and starts appreciating it for what it is.

But when Otis turns five, Basil catches Mags mixing Jack Daniel's into her morning Pepsi, and discovers a fifth in her glove compartment and a pint in her snow boots, and when he confronts her, she says, "Sure, Basil, I'll cut down on my drinking, how about I only drink on days that end with Y." Then she books a room at the Ramada and does not come home for four nights.

Around this time Otis starts wearing an off-brand black superhero cape day and night, every hour of every day—to kindergarten, to dinner, to sleep. Dr. O'Keefe says the boy is responding to "an atmosphere of stress" in his home environment, that he'll outgrow it, but soon Otis is six, then eight, and Mags is regularly heading to the guest room at bedtime with a Solo cup full of enough Wild Turkey to tranquilize a zebra, and Otis won't take off his cape even to shower, and for Basil, driving home from Lens-Crafters every evening has started to feel like a prison sentence.

In October Al's Comix Warehouse goes out of business, and a portly, white-bearded contractor named Nicholas starts putting crews to work on the building, erecting drum towers on the facade, and hanging a portcullis above the entrance, and in March a sign goes up that says, THE MASTER'S CASTLE COMING SOON, flanked by two aluminum skulls on posts with spotlights shooting out of their heads.

Nicholas assures Basil that it's all family-friendly, zoned for "entertainment"—"just keeping it secret to generate interest," he says, and winks over his bifocals, and tries to high-five Otis, who wants nothing to do with high-fives from strangers—and although Nicholas has a kind face and even resembles a sawdust-covered, dentally challenged Saint Nick, it's hard not to worry that the Master's Castle is going to be some kind of S&M dungeon, that soon Clark Street will be clogged with perverts in hot pants, that Basil's already battered home value will sink to zero, that his wife needs the kind of help he can't give, that his son might be damaged in some fundamental way, and that his life has descended to a nadir only a few, very particularly sorry lives reach.

Today though, the first of April, Mags wakes before Basil and scrambles a dozen eggs, and announces she's going to clamber back on top of the heap, vacuum the truck, get an oil change, and promises Basil she'll drive Otis to his appointment with Dr. O'Keefe after school, and Basil leaves LensCrafters at 4:00 PM feeling buoyant, and he empties the house of alcohol—pouring out the cooking sherry, the mouthwash, even the vanilla extract—and prepares a mushroom casserole, and preheats the broiler, and watches an internet video of a cat doing yoga, and another about a dolphin who turns pink when he's sad, then clicks a link to a story about a new best-selling book called *Memoirs of a Planet Hunter* and Basil's heart catapults into his mouth because the face that blooms across his iPad belongs to Muriel MacDonald.

Same green eyes, same narrow nose, slim, dignified, posed against a pillar in a lab coat, an orange-haired Joan Didion for the telescope set. Even now, after twenty years, to see the pale knobs of her collarbone floods Basil with a longing that threatens to capsize the kitchen.

The article describes how Muriel leads a NASA astronomical team that has discovered 540 extrasolar planets, including a sister Earth sixty light-years away, a rocky world only slightly smaller than ours, with life-friendly temperatures, and now she is slated to win a National Academy of Sciences medal, appear on *The Today Show*, and eat lamb shanks with Queen Elizabeth.

He downloads *Memoirs of a Planet Hunter*. Chapter one opens with seven-year-old Muriel building cardboard rockets. Chapter two covers high school. By page forty she's in Hawaii, interviewing with the observatory.

"Okay," Basil says to the empty kitchen. "Okay, okay, okay."

Out the window Nicholas exits the Master's Castle carrying plywood. The sky is purple. Somehow it has become 6:15 PM, and shouldn't Mags have had Otis home by 5:00? Basil slides his casserole onto the center rack, and sits at the table beneath a waterfall of memory.

The way the observatory loomed in the dusk, its dome pale against the sky. The way he'd have to rest his hands on his knees when he'd get out of the Jeep just to catch his breath, heart thudding, dust blowing across the summit. He brought Muriel his grandmother's macaroni and cheese; he bought her a Michael Bolton CD because the guy at the record shop in Hilo said Bolton was the white Stevie Wonder.

I love you like Saturday mornings when you wake up and realize you don't have school. I love you like the wind loves kites.

Maybe he came on a little strong, maybe he was a little naive, but at least what he offered was pure, wasn't it?

On page forty-eight, he reads:

Every seven days the other optics technician, a man—they were always men—would roll back up, blinking and slow from the altitude, and I'd be blinking and slow from seven days of thin air and sleep deprivation.

I was learning things in the cold nights, in the silence, in the spray of stars that would show when the big door rolled back and they poured their ancient light onto the mirror. I was learning how to see.

When the other optics tech came up, I didn't ever want to go.

Then it's chapter three, and Muriel is off to Caltech, the Kepler program, a photoshoot with Annie Leibovitz, et cetera, and is it possible that in the 460-page story of Muriel's life, Basil didn't warrant a single sentence?

He scrolls ahead, scans for his name, uses the search tool—*no results found*. The clock reads 7:15 PM, Clark Street is dark, everything smells like a forest fire—the kitchen, his life—and the smoke detector screeches, and Basil opens the oven

"Okay," Basil says to the empty kitchen. "Okay, okay, okay."

door to a rolling wave of smoke and hurries his smoldering casserole out the door and flings the pan into the front yard. At 7:20 he's standing on a kitchen chair, yanking the smoke detector off the ceiling, when Mags's Ford Ranger rolls over the curb and skids past the casserole and comes to a stop with its front bumper inside the hedges.

Otis sprints through the front door sobbing, making for his bedroom—no cape flying behind him—and Mags leaves the truck lights on and the driver's door open and comes seesawing through the door with her giant handbag.

"Reeks like fuck-all in here."

"What happened to Otis?"

Mags paws through cabinets.

"Where were you? Where is Otis's cape?"

A half-dozen bottles roll across the floor. "I took it."

"Dr. O'Keefe said to confiscate his cape?"

"Not Dr. O'-Flipping-Keefe, me, me, me. I took him to O'Keefe's and then we stopped at the Ramada and everyone agreed that third grade is too old to wear a cape, that all the kids who don't think he's a freak already will think so soon, so I took it."

"You brought our son to a bar?"

"I took him to see people. *Sane* people!" and she slides to the floor, and Basil drops the smoke detector in the sink and puts a frozen pizza in the oven and goes out the front door and backs the still-running, still un-vacuumed Ranger off the lawn and parks in the driveway and sits a moment behind the wheel wondering about distance and the other world Muriel found sixty light-years away.

When he goes back inside, Mags is slumped against the dishwasher. "April," she says, "the month to throw yourself off things." Basil can just see the hem of Otis's cape sticking out of her handbag, so he balls it up in his back pocket and slides the half-cooked pizza from the oven and hacks it into slices and carries two plates and a glass of milk into Otis's room and shuts the door and the two of them sit on the carpet, and Otis sips his milk, and Basil ties the cape around his son's neck, over his parka the way he likes it, and Otis brings its hem to his face and wipes his eyes. They eat their

Across the street, the twin spotlights of the Master's Castle rise into the sky.

pizza, and the house is quiet, and after a while Otis runs Lego cars over the carpet. Basil imagines driving Otis straight to the Pocatello airport and flying all night and queuing up outside *The Today Show* just as Muriel begins her appearance. She'll see him pressed against the studio window and cock her head in amazement; she'll tell Al Roker—right in the middle of *Today's Take*—that she is realizing only now that she made a mistake, that you never lose by loving, you only lose by holding back, and at her insistence security will escort Basil and Otis onto the set, and Al Roker's producer will whisper into Al's flesh-colored earpiece, *Twitter is going bananas, keep this rolling*, and Muriel will throw her arms wide and say, "Get in here, Mr. Basil Bebbington from Bakersfield," and Basil will look thin on TV, and Al Roker will don a cape in honor of Otis, and by nightfall half of America will be wearing capes, everyone superhero-ing everything, and Al will invite them to spend the weekend in his brownstone, and Basil will cook his mushroom casserole, and Basil and Otis will monitor storms on Al's rooftop X-band Doppler radar, and Al will poke his head through the hatch onto his roof deck and say, "Basil, that was the best goddamn casserole I've tasted in my life," and Basil will say, "Thank you, Al, but please don't swear in front of my son."

Lego men colonize Basil's ankles. He retrieves the carbonized casserole from the yard and scrapes the remains into the garbage can in the garage. Across the street, the twin spotlights of the Master's Castle rise into the sky. He says, "We could go to Florida. Stay with my parents."

Back inside, Mags snores against the dishwasher. He places a pillow under her head, and hand-washes the dishes, and the boiler in the basement exhales its ancient, burnt-hair smell, and when Basil next looks out the window, he sees Nicholas the contractor set something on the front step. The old man gives a wave, and his truck drives off, and Basil is still a moment, then opens the door and there on the front step are two head lamps and an envelope that says, *Seems like you and the kid could use a night out.*

Inside: a skull key chain bearing a single key.

Basil looks at the iPad still on the table, the shape of Mags on the floor, the key in his hand. Then he walks into Otis's room and stretches the band of a head lamp around his son's head.

He leads Otis out the back door so he doesn't see his mother, and they switch on their head lamps and cross Clark Street and stand in front of the Master's Castle. In the strange, purple light it looks large and frightening, a temple risen from some Mephisophelean underworld.

"We're going *in* there?" asks Otis. Basil turns the key, imagining ball gags and pommel horses, middle-aged men in latex trussed up in clotheslines, but in the beam of his head lamp, maybe twenty feet away, he sees what looks like a ten-foot-tall toy castle complete with battlements and turrets and pennants. Spiraling around it are pastures and villages, populated with waist-high windmills and stables, and what appears to be an actual flowing river, and everywhere five-foot-tall miniature oaks hold up thousands of real-looking leaves, and three-inch woodcutters stand beside wagons, the whole thing meticulous and miraculous in the strange light, and Basil blinks on the threshold, confused, overwhelmed, until Otis says, "Dad, it's Putt-Putt!"

To their left, down a cobbled path, stands a sign saying, *Hole #1*, with two putters and two golf balls and a little scorecard waiting on an apron of real-looking grass. Otis, in his big blue coat with his cape trailing off the back and the little cyclopic light of the head lamp glowing in the center of his head, looks up at his father and says, "Ready?"

They pick up the putters, one long-handled, one short, and set their balls in the little dots, and begin.

They play over ramps, through tunnels, under staircases, little wooden ponies drowsing in little wooden stables, mini blacksmiths frozen beside mini anvils, tiny swallows nesting under the eaves of the tiny cottages, everything detailed down to the tongs in the blacksmiths' hands. With each hole they wind closer to the great castle at the center, and Otis keeps score, and they roll their balls over moats, and Basil watches his sweet, mysterious son bend over each stroke, concentrating hard. And so what if he's not a shadow in Muriel's memory? She dreamed her dream after all, found her other Earth, just like Nicholas found his, and sometimes people just love who they love and what can you do about that? There are advantages in not getting what you want. Basil starts computing the realities of moving to Florida—plane tickets, separation from Mags, custody, schools, the size of his parents' condo in Tampa—but rather than feel overwhelmed, he feels light, even dizzy, as if he has rapidly ascended from sea level to fourteen thousand feet and can see the vast glimmering platter of the Pacific stretched out below.

They reach the eighteenth hole, Otis up by twenty, and the castle walls loom in the beams of their head lamps, little wooden guards in guardhouses peering down at them and little archers in archer loops and little golden chains holding up the drawbridge. Otis places his ball on the tee and looks at his father and says, "I'm not ready to give up my cape."

"I know, kid."

"I just need it a little longer."

"You take your time."

Otis sets his feet and whacks his ball straight up a ramp, and it flies right into a hole in the center of the drawbridge, a one-in-a-thousand shot, and some kind of machinery inside the castle comes to life. The three-inch guards lower their four-inch halberds, and the archers on the battlements lower their bows, and lights glow in the windows of the keep and in the towers and in the miniature oaks, and what looks like real smoke rises from chimneys, and the drawbridge comes down like the maw of a terrible beast, and a royal guard of bannermen marches out from the castle and stands to each side, and between them a harpist slides out, moving on some kind of indiscernible track, and begins to pluck her tiny instrument, and though it might be his imagination, Basil hears the tune of Stevie Wonder's "Higher Ground" . . .

> No one's gonna bring me down
> Oh no
> Till I reach my highest ground

. . . and the harpist plays and the castle glows, and when the song ends she turns, and slides back into the castle, and the royal guard retreats, and the drawbridge rises, and the lights in the windows wink out one by one, and the warehouse goes dark again.

Otis waves the scorecard and says, "I wrecked you, Dad." They lock the door behind them and stop on the edge of Clark Street and switch off their head lamps. Above them a few stars burn above clouds. A jet glides past, flashing its wing lights.

FOREHEAD, AFRAID, OVERHEARING ITSELF

The heart's mud-colored fears sleek out like the many limbs
Of the octopus, floating in his pool of ink and highly

Calibrated intellect, his arms the rolling *rs* of a beautiful dead language
Ululating in the water salt, ready to grasp onto any free-floating

Terror, dexterous as a mind as it comes undone.
Did you really just say "ululate"?

Who is it, Miss Bliss, that you think you are.
A slut of queasy lays on the easy white laid page.

The sweetesse of the ingénue who lay down in dampened leaves
Blazing scarlet still in the sepia of early photographs—you,

Here, in the Victorian nightgown bought on Portobello Road, lay back
On the great snarled trunk of sycamore, knowing even more

Than you knew you knew, still
With all the earthly powers of this world. The September cattails

Open, billowing out their minks and power to procreate, you,
Fertile just like that, comely, untouchable,

As more than a handful of gentlemen had told you: a hummingbird
Just out of reach. You do go on.

If you are out of sight of him, i.e., if he is in the next room,
The next world, he is dead; you're sure of it.

In the kitchen, the mother's handheld meat grinder mincing tongue
Like earthworms squiggling pinkly

Into a speckled bowl. It will reappear
In a toasted sandwich which will never touch your lips.

In Tikrit, one man holds on to his egg that lays hens.
The surrealist is festooned in the orange jumpsuit of Guantanamo.

It is likely we will be punished soon, for having known of bliss, Miss Bliss.
Who would want to fuck you now.

I am afraid that in the one white room just one white room from here,
He will be dying before I can get back home.

I would not live with that. I was alive
When Obama was our president, witnessing

His lanky hand laid across Mr. Lincoln's Bible, bound
In burgundy, gilded heavily, transfixable, austere though in its decadence.

A brief history of a little hope. We have squandered such a grace.
The poppa in his attic darkroom, working only by red light, coaxing

The invisible out from its page. For me, of fear—
The problem is that Possibility is not distinguishable

From the Actual. And here it is—the photograph
Of the sisters all in snowscape, all in wool and early fox-fur hats.

One of them, cheeky, peeking through the black-slatted fence, smiling.
All memory is loss.

CJ Evans

WHAT THE SEAS WOULD MAKE US

I don't know how to tell you about
the rain. It falls as if all these woods

weren't owned. It bends the arcs
of meteorites and flies. It invites

uninhibited fucking on blankets of fir
needles. That night in Harlem we didn't

kiss: This lifetime of lovely almost-but-
never pain is the rain's. I want it

at my small end as a rioter in the flowers
that'll roof my grave. If we give up on

buildings, on all the laptops
and catalogs, all the automatics

and wantings and wires, rain will
grow us a world new, naked and wild.

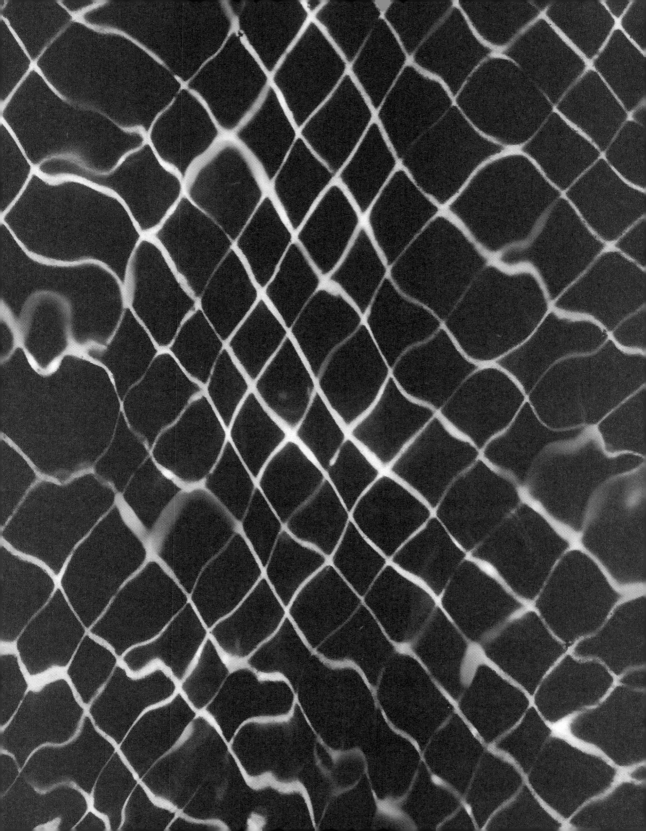

The Girl Who Did Not Know Fear

Kelly Link

A few years ago, I was on my way home to Massachusetts when bad weather stranded me in the Detroit airport for four days. I'd been at a conference in Iowa City—I travel rarely, but this was a point in my career when professional advancement required that I go. I was to receive a signal honor, one that conferred much benefit upon not only myself but also upon the university where I had tenure and no teaching responsibilities. My university had made it clear that it would be ungracious of me not to go. And so I went. I attended panels and listened to my colleagues discuss my research. Former students, now middle-aged and embarked upon their own careers, greeted me with more affection and warmth than I felt I merited; I bought them drinks in the bar, and listened to reports of their various successes. Some of them knew my wife. Others were Facebook friends, and remarked on recent photos of our daughter, Dido. How much she had grown. There was, of course, talk of politics and of the recent winter, how mild it had been. How wet this spring was turning out to be. I have never cared much for change, but of course change is inevitable. And not all change is catastrophic—or rather, even in the middle of catastrophic change, small good things may go on. Dido had recently learned to write her name. The children of my colleagues, too, were marvels, prodigies, creatures remarkable in their nature and abilities.

On the last day, I packed up my suitcase and drove my rental car back to the airport in Cedar Rapids. When I called my wife, she seemed distracted but then neither of us has ever been good at phone calls. And then, there was an appointment on my calendar that could not be postponed, and we were both thinking of it.

In Detroit, my connecting flight was delayed once and then again. Even someone who travels as infrequently as I do knows that travel in this age is an uncertain enterprise, full of delays and inconveniences, but eventually it became clear even to me that something out of the ordinary was happening here. There was a storm system in Atlanta so severe that flights operated by Delta had fallen off the grid all across the country. In consequence there would be no more planes going to Hartford tonight.

I called my wife so she would know not to stay up any longer. "How late is it there?" she said, "One hour back, isn't it? No, you're back in Eastern Standard now? So, not quite midnight. You go find a hotel quick before they all fill up. I'll call Delta and get you on a flight tomorrow morning. You'll be home in plenty of time. Dido wants you to pick her up after school tomorrow, but we'll see."

My wife is twelve years younger than I. This is her second marriage, my first. We look enough alike to be sisters, and she says sometimes, jokingly, that the first time she looked at me, she felt as if she were seeing her future. The longer we have been married, the more, I believe, we have come to resemble each other. We have a similar build; we sometimes wear each other's clothing, and we go to the same hairdresser. Each of us has a birthmark on a thigh, though hers is larger, three fingers wide. Her breasts are larger and her nipples are the color of dried blood. After she had our daughter, her shoes no longer fit and so she donated them all to a women's shelter. Now we wear the same size.

When we decided to start a family, there was no question that she would be the one to carry the pregnancy. Carry the pregnancy, she said. As if the doctors were talking about a bag of groceries. But she asked if I would supply the egg. And so I did and perhaps I should not have. I would have loved a child just as much, I think, if she had not been my child biologically. But then, Dido would not be Dido, would she? If she were less like me or even if she were more like me, would I love her more or would I love her less? Would my wife have fallen in love with me quite so quickly, if our resemblance to each other had not been so remarkable?

Dido is Dido and may she always be Dido in exactly the way she chooses to be. That is what I would choose for her. When Dido is older, will she look at me and see her future?

I do not like to think too much about the future. I don't care for change.

> When we decided to start a family, there was no question that she would be the one to carry the pregnancy.

· · ·

I was back at the airport at 7:00 AM for a 10:00 AM flight. In an excess of optimism, I went so far as to check my carry-on bag. And then, when that flight was canceled and then the flight after as well, I was told my carry-on was now in transit though I was not. It could not be retrieved. That night, I took a Lyft to Target and purchased a toothbrush, underwear, and a cheap bathing suit.

Just past the throat of the lobby of the airport Sheraton, where I was paying too much for the privilege of a cramped room with a too-large bed, there was an indoor courtyard with a concrete-rimmed swimming pool. There was a cabana bar, too, in the courtyard, shrouded in plastic sheets; unpersuasive palm trees in planters; deck chairs and little tables where no one ever sat.

> In all the years that I have lived with this condition of mine, I have learned it is wise to mitigate stress.

The water in the pool was a cloudy jade. No one else ever went into the pool, and the cabana bar was never open. The lighting indicated a perpetual twilight. Except for that first night when every seat on the shuttle to the Sheraton was occupied by a stranded traveler, all of us attended at check-in by a single teenaged desk clerk, I never saw any other guests in the public areas of the hotel.

In every way I am a poor traveler. I do not like to be confined in small spaces; I am a picky eater and easily overstimulated; in adolescence I was diagnosed with hyperosmia. I do not sleep well when I am away from home, but I have discovered that if I swim to the point of exhaustion, some amount of sleep is possible. The acridity of chlorine masks almost all other smells.

I wish I could make you see what the courtyard in that Sheraton was like. It had something of the feel of a subterranean grotto, or maybe a Roman amphitheater. As a child, I'd pored over a book called *Motel of the Mysteries*, in which archaeologists in the year 4022 discover a motel and attempt to deduce how the artifacts they dig up were used and by whom; when I floated on my back in the courtyard pool, one hundred feet above me a popcorn ceiling in place of sky, I was as liberated in time and place and purpose as I had ever been. On one side of me was my professional obligation, now fulfilled. On the other was my home and my family and an appointment that I knew I could not delay, and yet here I was. Four nights

I stayed in that hotel. I swam in the pool and tried to keep my head free of useless worries. In all the years that I have lived with this condition of mine, I have learned it is wise to mitigate stress. Stress is a trigger.

Four floors of breezeways rose up on all sides of the courtyard. No one came in or out of the hotel rooms that looked down on the pool, and neither did I ever hear anyone in the rooms on either side of the one where I slept. I swam silently so that I would not break the vast still spell of the place, staying in the pool for so long that when I went to sleep, my skin and hair gave off such a satisfactory stink of chlorine that the other smells in the room were little more than ghosts—the burnt-toast smell of the laundered sheets, lingering traces of perfumes and deodorants, stale remnants of repulsive foodstuffs, musk of sex and sweat, mildew-laced recycled air.

Each night I swam, and each day for four days I went to the airport, which was in every way the opposite of my tranquil courtyard. I woke up at 6:30 each morning and rode the shuttle as if I were going to my workplace. I waited in lines and passed through security and went to my assigned gate to see if my flight this time would depart. As the day wore on, and each successive possible flight was delayed and then canceled, I moved from one gate to the next, where, it was hoped, a plane might at last take off. I was one of several thousand people, all of whom were out of place, paused in transit. And here, this was the swimming pool, too, after all, it began to seem to me. A kind of suspended and purposeless motion.

The reason for the canceled flights might have been a storm system, but in Detroit the weather was mild and cloudy, like the water in the swimming pool. The bad storms had only truly affected Atlanta, but Atlanta was Delta's central hub and for many days, Delta planes continued not to be where they should have been and where there were planes, there were not enough flight crews.

I sat near outlets when I could, and charged my phone and texted friends, called home each time I was bumped to a new flight, and debated renting a car. If Dido was home, sometimes she would speak to me. She could not understand why I would not come home. My wife said that in my absence Dido was having nightmares again. Nightmares about what? "Toilets," my wife said. "An overflowing toilet. Yeah, it sounds comical but she wakes up screaming. And she wet her pants today because she didn't want to use the toilet at school."

I said, "I could rent a car. If I drove, I would be home in about twelve hours."

"No," my wife said. "That's ridiculous. You hate driving. You're a terrible driver."

Which was true. And every time a flight was canceled, there was a new gate where I could go and wait, suspended in the cloudy green day. I read the new Kate Atkinson. I drank iced coffee from Dunkin' Donuts. Passengers swapped gossip and stories. There was a family, I was told two or three times, who had flown over from London to take their three young daughters to Disney World. Now they had been stuck in Detroit for three days. They had not gotten to Orlando, and now they could not get home, either. Eventually, I, too, began telling this story, though I was not sure that I believed it.

Every now and then, a ragged cheer would go up at a gate. By this, we would know that a flight crew had arrived, and these passengers were escaping Detroit Metropolitan Airport. By the third day, I no longer waited only for flights that might take me to Bradley International Airport in Connecticut. I allowed myself to be booked for flights that might go to Logan or LaGuardia or even Philadelphia. But these, too, were delayed and then canceled. Each night I left the terminal between 10:00 pm and midnight and rode the shuttle back to the Sheraton. In my room, I washed a pair of underwear and socks with shampoo, rolled them in a dry towel, and put on my bathing suit. I swam until I felt as if I had washed time off of my skin again, and then left wet footprints across the courtyard that would be gone by the time I was asleep. In the morning, I woke up and traveled back to the airport. My wife was growing tired of her role as a single parent, but in the end we agreed there was no need yet for me to rent a car. My wife felt sure that I would be home soon. I told her the story of the English family. Still, she felt I would be home soon. I would be home soon and the appointment on my calendar could be safely marked off once again. Life would go serenely on.

In the middle of the night I woke from a terrible dream. Dreams, too, are markers of my condition, or so I have come to believe. It is possible that Dido has inherited my condition just as I inherited my mother's face, although it is possible her bad dreams are just bad dreams.

In my dream there was a pool in a courtyard, only it was full of moonlight instead of water, so bright I could not bear to look directly at it. But oh, there was a smell that was so delicious and enticing that I went into the pool, my eyes open so I could see what smelled so very good. The moonlight buoyed me up just as water would do, and I immersed myself in that wonderful smell, and my eyes watered and my mouth was so full of saliva that I had to swallow over and over again. I rubbed my eyes and then I saw that standing all around the pool were all of the people I have ever hurt or injured without meaning to. Some of them I didn't even know or maybe I didn't remember them, but I knew the reason they were standing there. There, too, were all the people that I would inevitably go on hurting even though I do not wish to—there was my mother, and my wife. There was Dido. Their eyes were so full of pain—I realized that they felt pain for me, because I was in the pool and I could not get out. I was in the pool because of my condition, and because they cared for me, they could not leave me here alone. I was hurting them in this way too, and when I realized this I was so full of anger that I burst into a thousand pieces and bits of my skin flew everywhere and that was how I woke up, soaked in sweat as if I had been running.

> I saw that standing all around the pool were all of the people I have ever hurt or injured.

I got out of my bed and put on my wet bathing suit and went to the courtyard pool. I wanted to make sure that everything was the way that it should be. I needed to see that my dream was only a dream and not something true. And, too, I could still smell that delicious smell. I needed to know if it was something real.

It was the middle of the night, but in the courtyard where nothing ever changed, it was only twilight. The delicious smell dissipated. I swam lap after lap and no one came to tell me that I should get out even though the hours were clearly marked on a sign tacked to the side of the cabana. No one came and so I swam until my head was clear again and my dream was gone.

. . .

All of my life, I have been a person in whom strangers have confided. There is something in my face that says, "I am interested in you" to some, and "I will keep your secret" to others. I have my mother's face, and it is true that my mother was sincerely interested in everyone she met, and that she was a faithful keeper of other people's secrets. I am not my mother. Sometimes, I think, I am not even myself. But whether a trick of physiognomy, or a habit of expression learned as her child in the way that all children mimic the behaviors and mannerisms of their parents, just as Dido sits at my wife's desk and makes a face at my wife's laptop and polishes the glasses that she does not wear, my face has said, all of my life, "I will listen to your story."

Pity the introvert with the face of a therapist or a classroom aide in a kindergarten room. Like the werewolf, we are uneasy in human spaces and human company, though we wear a human skin. The airport itself was bad enough, but even worse was the shuttle I rode back and forth between the airport and the Sheraton. The driver was a woman in her seventies, an ex-servicewoman, the mother of three grown children. One was an addict, and one had had a breast cancer scare. The other was estranged from her mother, though she lived only twenty miles away. The shuttle driver prayed every night to be reconciled with this daughter—who, it was determined, was my age almost to the month. With each ride, her presumption of our acquaintance grew deeper and by the third morning, she embraced me when we arrived at the airport in case she did not see me again. But although her daughter would not return to her, I did. I had no choice.

> Pity the werewolf. Wash off a stranger's sadness in a green pool.

Pity the werewolf. Wash off a stranger's sadness in a green pool. What should a stranger's story mean? Wash it away. Fall asleep in the clean reek of chlorine and inhabit the fragmentary and uneasy dreams of departed guests whose strands of hair, dander, lardy fingerprints, odd bits of trash, and inconclusive stains inhabit these transitory and poorly lit spaces. If you listen, a hotel room speaks too. It says: I will keep your secret.

• • •

I tallied my receipts on the fourth day. I checked in with my research assistant, who keeps the lab running on days when I'm looking after Dido, or when I have a flare-up and am confined to my home office. My university had covered my flight, the conference, and my hotel in Iowa City, but now there was the cost of airport food: coffee from Dunkin' Donuts, breakfast sandwiches, packets of unshelled pistachios and Snickers bars, bananas and burgers and power bars. There was my trip to Target; the room at the Sheraton at $119.00 plus taxes every night, checked out of so hopefully each morning; the five dollars I left on the bureau as tip; and the two dollars I gave each time to the shuttle driver. There was the cost of the babysitter my wife was paying to look after Dido while she was at work. My work schedule is flexible, coordinated with my wife's so that one of us can be at home most days with Dido when her school lets out, but still there was a great deal of business, now, to take care of at the lab once I was home and could go in. That would be more money for the babysitter.

My wife and I had decided that if there were no flights to Hartford or Boston or New York today, then tomorrow I would have to rent a car. This would give me two days to get home before my appointment. Even I could manage six hours in a car one day, and six hours again the next. I could even, my wife suggested, look around at my fellow would-be passengers. Maybe one of them might be willing to share the cost of a car. "Maybe," I said. "You think the English family has made it home yet?" she said. "Maybe," I said. "Next month we'll go camping," she said. "I ran into Molly at the co-op and she was telling me about this place in New Hampshire. Right on a lake. A little playground for kids, and lots of trails. She's going to send me a link to the campsite. That sounds amazing, right?" "Maybe," I said. It was a little hard to think past the next few days, getting home, and my appointment, and then catching up with work. I had my phone plugged into an outlet, and right then I was scheduled to leave on a 2:15 flight, and we talked until my flight was canceled and I had to hang up and unplug my phone and again go to book a new flight. Dido was asking about a dog again, because she'd snuck down the basement stairs to hunt for treasure. We have the usual sort of New England basement, which is to say that it is damp and cold, with a floor of tamped-down dirt. I have never liked spending time down there, but Dido is fascinated by it. The previous owner died in her nineties, and her children didn't bother clearing out the basement before they sold the house to us. There are old chests of drawers, some of them hiding photo albums or Depression-glass saucers, celluloid hairbrushes decaying around the horsehair bristles, the tangles of human hair coiled around the animal hair. There is the rocking chair, the hat rack and the hatboxes full of mouse droppings and shreds of silk, the washing board and the bundles of faded letters and the dog crate that is big enough Dido can stretch out inside it on her back and look at the gouges on the interior ceiling. Dido wants a dog so badly that my wife said she could almost taste it. Could almost hear clicks on the wood floor upstairs while she was downstairs, as if Dido were conjuring a pet into existence by force of her extraordinary will. And Dido was still having nightmares. She was making my wife go with her into the bathroom each time to hold her hand while she peed. My wife had tried to get Dido to explain what was so terrifying about a clogged toilet, but Dido could not articulate this to her. She could only dream it over and over again.

In the same way, my last day in Detroit followed the established pattern. I moved from gate to gate until there was only one flight left to wait for. This last possible flight into Hartford was scheduled for 10:30 PM, and then its departure was postponed and postponed again until eventually it was almost midnight and the agent at the gate got on the speaker to tell us that it was looking likely to be canceled. The airport was shutting down for the night.

On my phone was a series of texts from Dido. Dido loves texting, because she knows that it is something that adults do. Earlier in the evening she had somehow gotten the phone from my wife and used it to text me her name, over and over. Dido. Dido dido dido dido dido. And so on. There was a long string of emojis too, mostly made up of toilets, ominously, and then strings of words made up from predictive text. Then more toilets. By the time Dido is a proficient speller, perhaps it will no longer be necessary to spell at all.

I began to text my wife as people around me disconsolately collected their belongings. But the agent at our gate came over the speaker again to tell us new information had been supplied to her. It now seemed possible that a flight crew from Cleveland would be arriving in twenty minutes and might yet be assigned to our flight. So we were to wait.

We waited without much hope. We had all heard similar announcements over the past few days. But in the end, there was the crew, and here was the plane, and we all got on and the plane took off. It was a full flight, of course, and I had a middle seat. There was a woman a decade or two younger than me in the window seat, whose clothing was more youthful still. Dickies jeans, plum-colored hair, shitkicker boots, and a cropped T-shirt with DTF in a Gothic font. In the aisle seat was a woman just a little older, heavyset and tired looking, wearing the kind of clothing and minimal makeup that signals camouflage worn by lesbians in administrative offices. And when they looked at me, I knew what the two women saw. I was wearing the same slouchy black cardigan over the same black jersey dress I had worn for the past four days. It was my wife's cardigan, and days ago it had smelled like her, but it no longer did. I had on a wedding ring and a smoky eye, thanks to the MAC boutique in the Detroit airport, where a bored aesthetician told me about the Roller Derby match that her girlfriend had dragged her to the previous weekend and how she'd realized, watching the very first jam, that her girlfriend was cheating on her with the worst skater in the league. The smoky eye did not suit me. I'd been wondering, though, if it would stay on in a swimming pool. I'd been thinking all day about the swimming pool. Even here, on the plane and on my way home, I held that swimming pool, that cool and empty space, inside my skull as if by holding it there I might contain everything else that must be contained. I do not do well in small spaces. I do not feel safe when I am far from home. I am not safe when I am far from home.

I texted my wife again. On a plane! Getting in around 3, so don't wait up. I'll take a Lyft. Love you. Then I turned off my phone. You could feel every passenger on the plane holding their breath as we waited to see if we would, in fact, take off. And then the exhalation when we did. I clasped my hands tightly in my lap as the plane taxied and then rose up, the ground visible only as stacks and necklaces of lights that shrank to sequins, then bright pinpricks, shrank until everything was a velvety black.

I do not do well in small spaces. I do not feel safe when I am far from home. I am not safe when I am far from home.

There was no reason for it, but I thought of the shuttle driver's daughter. Though the daughter was my age, a middle-aged woman estranged from a woman who was near my mother's own age, her face was the face of my Dido.

"Well," the woman in the window seat said. "I guess we're going to get home after all."

On my iPad I had the first three episodes of a television show that my wife did not care to watch. But the woman in the window seat waited as I took out my headphones and just when I was putting them on she said, "I don't know you, do I?"

I lifted my headphones. I said, "I don't think so. No."

"No, I do," she said. "Don't I? Martine?"

"No," I said. "I'm sorry. I'm Abby."

"Oh," she said, disappointed. "Did you ever live up in Vermont? Burlington?"

"No," I said. "I've been there a couple of times, though. It's pretty."

"Yeah," she said. "It is. I lived there for a while. Oh, God. A while ago now. I moved up there because my girlfriend was opening a gallery, and I'd just gotten my degree. But then she dumped me a month later, and I should have just left but I didn't. It just seemed so embarrassing, packing up after just a month. So I slept on her couch for a couple of weeks until I found another place to live. And then I stayed there for eight years! Until another breakup, like one of those burn everything down to the ground breakups. But fuck, it's pretty up there. Just, you know, the dating scene is a little incestuous."

"Small towns," I said.

> There was something she was looking for, and I guess she just had to keep looking for it until she found it.

"Tell me about it," the woman in the window seat said. "I was trying to explain it to a friend in New York once. I ended up drawing her a diagram with everybody's name on it, and then these different colored lines. You know, who's dating, who used to date but now they're just friends, who broke up with who and now they won't talk to each other, who's in a poly relationship, who hooked up but thinks that no one knows, and then all the asterisks."

I said, "Being married makes everything a lot less complicated. Sometimes."

The woman in the aisle seat, on the other side of me, shifted. Her thigh rubbed against mine. She was pretending to read the in-flight magazine but I could tell she was listening.

"For Christmas, my friend took the diagram I'd drawn her and embroidered it all. Got it framed. I was like, what am I supposed to do with it? Hang it on a wall? But it was pretty. She used different stitches for the different kinds of relationship lines. What do they call that? A sampler, right? Anyway Martine was part of that whole scene. You look so much like her. I wish I had a picture. She and Leila. They were married when I met them, but then it turned out that Leila had this whole other life. She'd had a girlfriend in Quebec the whole time she and Martine were together, which you would think would not be easy to pull off, but Leila was a sales rep for a company in Quebec, this printing company, and so she was up there for a couple of days out of every month. Sometimes a lot more. But then Martine found out and threw Leila out and Leila moved up to Quebec, although she kept coming back to Burlington and telling Martine that she really thought they could work it out if Martine could just figure out how to get past it. She wanted to try therapy, and when Martine wouldn't go for it, Leila used her keys to let herself in while Martine was at work. She texted Martine and said not to worry, she was just there to pick up a pair of jeans she'd left behind, but when Martine got home, it turned out that Leila had actually been there to pick up her favorite strap on. Like, seriously? They don't have sex shops in Quebec? After that, Martine went through this whole phase. She was wild. She fucked any girl who looked at her twice. She would have fucked a cat if the cat had seemed into it. And she tried everything else too. People do that sometimes, you know? When they're going through something? Like my best friend growing up. She used to say she was putting the 'ho' in Hoboken. But you know, it turned out she was having all these other problems at home. It was how she felt in control."

"Did you?" I said. "Sleep with her? Martine?"

"No," the woman in the window seat said. "I mean, I hooked up once with Martine at a party. But we were both pretty out of it. There was some good shit at that party. This one girl, Viddy, she got this idea that she could juggle anything. She took a bunch of knives out of a kitchen drawer and threw them up in the air. Cut her hands all to pieces, and then everybody was just dealing with that. It was bad. I was an ambulance driver for a while, so I was doing first aid, and I had Viddy's blood all over me, and I really wanted to get cleaned up and this girl, Martine, it was like she didn't even notice the blood. But it kind of ruined the mood for me, and Martine went home with somebody else. There was something she was looking for, and I guess she just had to keep looking for it until she found it. I don't know what happened to her, but I hope she found it."

"Maybe she did," I said. And I did hope she had.

"Who knows?" the woman in the window seat said. "Maybe."

The flight attendant came down the aisle with drinks. I will be honest. I badly wanted a real drink. But I had a Coke instead. The woman in the window seat had a gin and tonic and the woman in the aisle seat asked for a tomato juice. She said, "I used to know a girl like that. In New York. A long time ago."

We both looked at her, me and the woman in the window seat.

"She worked in advertising," the woman in the aisle seat said. She drank her tomato juice and then wiped the red off her lips with the back of her hand even though there was a cocktail napkin right there on her tray. "She'd come to poker nights with a friend of mine. Tuesday nights. Penny something. My friend said Penny had the nicest apartment you'd ever seen. This enormous prewar apartment up near Columbia that no one could have afforded, but Penny was subletting it for hardly anything at all because it was haunted. No one else could live there. Apparently you couldn't even spend the night without seeing things or hearing things, really awful things, but Penny slept there like a baby."

"Some people just don't see ghosts," the woman in the window seat said. "They're not sensitive or whatever."

"No," the woman in the aisle seat said. "Penny could see the ghosts just fine. She could see them, she could hear them, for all I know she played poker with them on every night of the week except Tuesdays. She just didn't care. She wasn't afraid of them. She wasn't afraid of anything."

"I'm not really afraid of ghosts either," the woman in the window seat said. "All that kind of stuff is kind of stupid. No offense if that's not what you think."

The woman in the aisle seat said, "No, you don't understand. I mean this Penny literally wasn't afraid of anything. She wasn't afraid of snakes or the dark or thunderstorms or serial killers or being mugged or dogs or heights. She told my friend that she didn't really understand what fear even was. Her mother used to hide behind doors and then jump out at her, to try to scare her when she was a kid. Took her on roller coasters and to therapists. She was mugged at gunpoint twice in one week in New York and my friend said she just laughed about it. But she was curious about what it was like, to be afraid. So she and my friend would go to horror movies and afterward she would ask my friend why they were scary. What it felt like."

"That would be nice," the woman in the window seat said. "Not to be afraid of anything. I'm not afraid of ghosts, but I'm afraid of everything else. I don't even know what that would be like, not to be afraid of everything." She turned to me. "I mean, you're afraid of something, right?"

"Flying," I said. "Myself."

"Right?" the woman in the window seat said. "Right! I mean, imagine not being afraid of anything."

"Straight and curly hair," the other woman said. "People with straight hair wish they had curly hair and people with curly hair wish they had straight hair. You wish you weren't afraid of anything, and my friend said Penny wished she could be afraid of anything, even though she had this gorgeous apartment because she wasn't. She had a lot of girlfriends, but the relationships never lasted very long because none of the girlfriends would sleep over at her place. The ghost or whatever was there frightened them away the first time they slept in her bed. Nothing Penny could do could make them stay, and Penny didn't want to give up her apartment. But eventually she fell in love with this girl Min Jie, and she gave up the apartment for her and they moved in together and got married. My friend went to the wedding. Min Jie was a cheesemonger. She knew everything about cheese. Did you know that for a while you could buy a cheese made from women's breast milk? Min Jie said it was a soft cheese. A little like a goat cheese. She worked in this shop in Midtown that had every kind of cheese, imported chocolate, pâtés, tongue, marrons glacé. Lobsters, Golden Osetra caviar, tupelo and lavender honey, Sacher tortes, so the spread at the wedding was amazing, my friend said. The wine was some of the best wine she'd ever tasted, and there was plenty of it. Fountains of it. Tables of smoked fish and shrimp and mussels in carved ice bowls. Penny got up and toasted her bride and said that perhaps she would never know fear, but now she knew love."

> "Right! I mean, imagine not being afraid of anything."

"Very romantic," the woman in the window seat said. "Nobody's ever said anything like that to me."

The woman in the aisle seat said, "That night they went home and they made love and afterwards Penny lay in their bed in their new bedroom, which was so much smaller and dingier than the bedroom in her old apartment had been, and she was happy. And Min Jie came out of the bathroom with a bucket of live eels she'd procured at work, and she dumped the eels over the bed and all over Penny. And my friend said Penny sat straight up in the bed and started screaming because she finally understood what fear was."

"Seriously?" the woman in the window seat said.

"That's what my friend said," the other woman said.

"That's fucked up," the woman in the window seat said.

I said, "Excuse me" to the woman in the aisle. In the last few minutes I'd become aware that I was getting my period, days before I should have had it. Everything was wrong, everything was happening that shouldn't have been happening. But I was almost home. Surely we would be home soon.

I went in darkness down the aisle of the plane, passing women sleeping, women playing games on their phones or their iPads, women talking. That delicious smell from my dream was in my nostrils. Blood that shouldn't have been there was between my thighs. But we have no control over our own bodies. The things we feel. The things that happen to us, over and over again. The things we crave.

At the back of the cabin, there was an Out of Order sign on one toilet. The other was occupied. So I waited as patiently as I could. I tried to picture Dido, who would be asleep in her bed. Or perhaps she had had another nightmare and Martine was letting her sleep in our bed.

What my wife shared with former lovers does not diminish what we have together. It isn't as if, before, she killed a lot of people. She just fucked them. And perhaps we would not be together now, if Martine had not been who she was then. She was one person then, and is another person now. I never met that other person. That other Martine. And yet sometimes when I think of those years when I did not know her, I am filled with such a frenzy of jealousy that I imagine, as if compelled, finding those lovers in whatever homes or lives they occupy now. I imagine tearing at them with my nails, rending their flesh with my teeth. Making blood run in thick streams, enough to fill ten thousand swimming pools. So much blood it obliterates everything that came before she and I—

I pictured my swimming pool, cool and green and empty. Why would anyone be afraid of eels? Why be afraid of a creature, harmless, caught in a bucket? They only want to get out. In a plane, too, you are suspended. You cannot do anything. You cannot get out. You cannot always be the person you thought you were, no matter how badly you want to be her. Change is inevitable.

The toilet door opened and a woman came out. She said, "The toilet's clogged. I wouldn't go in there."

In the galley just behind us, one of the flight attendants turned and said, "Oh, that's not good. That's not good at all."

"Excuse me," the woman who had come out of the toilet said. I let her go past.

I began to go into the toilet and the flight attendant put her hand on my arm. She said, "No. I'm sorry. You can't go in there. We'll be landing soon. Can't you wait?"

The floor of the toilet was wet. The stench was intolerable. Swollen plugs of wet toilet paper sloshing in the metal basin. Writhing. I turned and looked at the flight attendant, and she recoiled. She took her hand off my arm and stepped back. She said something in such a small voice that I could hardly hear her over the sound of blood in my ears. Mice have louder voices. She said, again, "Are you okay?"

I could not answer her. I could not speak at all. What she saw in my face was not the thing that is usually there. It was the other thing, the thing that lives inside my skin. I turned and went back up the aisle to my middle seat. The moon in the window in every row went with me like a cold white lozenge that I could have slipped under my tongue.

It went with me like a thing on a leash, all the way back to my seat.

They would be announcing our arrival soon. I might get a little blood on the seat, but what's a little blood? Women bleed. Everyone bleeds.

The women on either side of me had been talking to each other. The woman in the window seat had a car in long-term parking, and she was asking the other, who didn't have a car, if she would like a ride into Northampton. She said to me, "Do you have a car, Abby, or is someone picking you up? Do you need a ride? Where do you live?"

I had a feeling as if I could have run the whole way home, all thirty miles or so. But I wanted to be home with my wife and my child. My appointment was waiting for me, though I thought perhaps I might be a little early for it this time.

"Sure," I said. "I would really appreciate that." 🛡

I WILL DESTROY YOU

Like laying a palm on the door of
a furnace to test

if it's still alive, I invite you up
to my hotel room. Let's

think of you as someone
I'd meet in a dream,

a representation of my own vast
recklessness. You're

the age my mother was
when she set our house on fire

—I'm asleep upstairs—I cannot
call it *accidental*. This vast

recklessness. My therapist points out

that fifteen minutes
of movie violence releases as many

opiates into the body as if

being prepped for major
surgery. For people like us it is somehow

calming. Tonight it's *Terminator 2*
again—let's go back to the scene

where the liquid metal assassin
assumes the form of a security

guard. We're in the mental hospital
where mom is locked up. As the real

guard gets a coffee from a vending
machine, the liquid

metal guy, disguised now
as the linoleum floor, rises up

behind him & slowly
takes on his features, even

the uniform
& when the guard turns & faces himself

he raises a finger to his own face
as if to point out that they are the same

but the finger turns into a blade
& he pushes it right into & through

his own eye
& then he goes looking for mom.

BACKSTAGE WITH KAREN BLACK

for David Trinidad

she swept in, slept in, the curlers
she slept in swept under a tablecloth
of a scarf of lavender and lime
a fed-ex package arrived, just bills
she laughed, no checks. the hotel bill
was paid, at least. this was the vertigo
hotel it's known as now, though then
it was the york, renamed vertigo later on
in honor of the movie that was filmed
there. she worked with hitch and loved
the association. she said her favorite
role was psycho, a film she hadn't even
been in

AT THE DELUXE

There's no use saying a dime. I'm
in my no use prettiness most of
the time, no outside food. No outside.
I go out to see live jizz and
blood on the corner. I used to be so
street, my fare was always fair
and my looks were fair when they
could have been injudicious, which
they also were it's funny how that works.

There's a mural on the wall where
I'm drinking you that starts in the
city and ends with a rural smoke stack.

In between, the laborers bent over
haybales and some cattle and a
distant locomotive. None of this is
real. Tipsy little clouds wander
around the bar of my affections. I
wandered lonely as a mural. I
stood at this same corner years ago
weeping out bad news as we used to
call it over what we called a
payphone it was that long ago. In my
head there is still a dial tone. My
band's name is Roe v. Wade, someone
says as if to shock me. So many
times I could shock back and don't.
The world is dirty enough to make
a dog sick. Come here and lick me boy.

WIND AND FOG GARDEN

the cypress bends
the city's always cold
that which holds
is what we cannot hold

from ABC

Matthew Dickman

The Alphabet Soup of a Troubled Soul

A is for *apple* and this particular apple being a green one. Being not a Granny Smith but a Golden Delicious. Not yet yellowing, still firm, and smelling exactly like cold rain. I remember in the third grade there was anxiety every day. The kids in class did not like me and teased me. The nun who was our teacher called all the kids by their first names but with me she became ruthlessly formal and called me by my last name, taking time to pause between the two syllables, the two parts of my name, *Dick* and *Man*. She would never say *Dickmin*, the way it's pronounced, turning the hard *I* into a soft *I*. No, instead she would say the word *Dick* and then take a long pause that felt like the distance that lies between two faraway countries before finishing with the word *Man*. She would say, "Come to the chalkboard and spell out the following

vocabulary, Mr. Dick——-Man" and all the kids would laugh because a dick was a penis and I was not a man. One day when it was time to learn about the ocean we were asked to take out our science books. I didn't have my science book. My science book was at home in my room. I hoped she wouldn't notice but she did notice, of course she noticed. Once all the other kids had their books set neatly on top of their desks and their hands clasped neatly on top of the books she asked me, "So, Mr. Dick——-Man, where is your book?" "Maybe it's in my backpack?" I said. "Then why don't you go to the coatroom and get it?" I stood up from my desk and began to walk to the back of the room, where all of us would hang our coats and backpacks when we arrived in the morning. As I passed the other desks I could hear, softly at first, the other kids

begin to snicker. Then I heard the teacher (I don't know what made her do this, what part of her or what you would even call that part) clear her throat like they do in movies and with something like music in her voice say, "And while you're back there, Mr. Dick——-Man, why don't you look for your brain too?" And that was it. The class erupted in laughter and I stood in the coatroom on fire. When I got home that day I stood in our yellow kitchen and picked up the apple and smelled it. I loved that apple because it seemed kind to me, it was something good, and it didn't want to kill me.

C is for *church*. I was born an Episcopalian. That is to say, my mother was an Episcopalian and raised us, her three children, in the Episcopal Church. We said our prayers before dinner yet I don't ever recall saying any prayers before bed. I remember feeling more than weirded out when I was ten or so years old and my twin brother and I were staying at a friend's house. His father was big into God and for good reason. He was Catholic. He had been a mean alcoholic, had lost his wife in a divorce, and had almost lost the privilege to see his kids. So when he got sober he also got a renewed friendship with Jesus though a rather strict one in his case. It's what he apparently needed to heal himself. Before going to sleep he gathered his three children, two boys and one girl, along with my

brother and me, and placed us at different corners of his own bed, where we got onto our knees, our arms resting on the coverlet, hands pressed flat together, heads lowered, and made us say the Our Father. Don't you think it's strange that he watched but didn't join us? Just stood there and watched this semicircle of children around his bed whisper prayers to a distant dad? And to do it where he slept and dreamt and masturbated and napped and tossed and turned and drooled onto the pillows and sweated into the sheets and suffered insomnia and farted and snored and talked on the phone to his ex-wife and woke up each morning. Isn't it odd he would make this kind of garland of children pray against his mattress, pray into and over his mattress? No matter where my family and I went to church I fell in love with all the priests. I wanted a father so much. I also fell in love with the ceremony of the Episcopal liturgy. Eventually my brother Michael and I became acolytes, which is the Episcopal way of saying altar boy. For a long time I thought the word *altar* was spelled *alter* and that being a part of the Mass altered a boy. I think it does. For a long time I wanted to be a priest. Nothing horrible changed my mind. I just ended up wanting to skateboard more than I wanted to go to church. Still, I miss feeling important in that way, wearing something that felt like a gown,

No matter where my family and I went to church I fell in love with all the priests.

helping a man that I got to call father break the bread and pour the wine.

D is for *dog*. And *dog* is for *god*. I can't think about dog without flip-flopping it. If you do turn *dog* inside out and make *god* then it is not a god of soft fur and panting, not of the eyes of the animal looking up at you from the bottom of a flight of stairs. If *god* is the inside out of *dog* then it is a god of organs and blood, the vascular palace, the bones and water, the muscle and tissue. God is inside each of us said the mom said the dad said the religion teacher said the priest.

Most of the people in a jury can't imagine killing anyone.

All of us dogs. Better to be a dog than a god. The first dog my siblings and I had was called Poppy. Our half-sibling's step-dad was also called Poppy when he wasn't being called Jim. Poppy had a coat of long black fur and usually smelled like an animal because we didn't give Poppy many baths. When I would spend the whole day being teased at school I would come home and curl up with Poppy. I would bury my head in one of Poppy's armpits. The two front legs dogs have, let's just admit it, they are really arms. I would bury my head and inhale all of Poppy, her sweat and musk, her dog smell, her warmth, and that was a way, through inhaling, to exhale all that had happened that day. I loved her. I would lie down next to her and watch her body go up and down as she breathed. I wasn't good at taking her on walks or taking her into the backyard to play, to throw a ball for her. That's not what I needed her for in the third and fourth and fifth grade. What I needed was a body to transfer all my sadness and anxiety into. I needed a god to take it all away, to move a hand in the air and part the seas of my school day, to turn one fish into many fish, turn the being pushed and hit and laughed at and pointed at and tripped from water into wine. I needed a dog and I had one. When Poppy got sick she slowed down. She would sit on my lap for longer periods of time. She would sleep and sleep. The last time I really held her I told her that I didn't want to be me. She licked the top of my hand and then I didn't want to be anybody but me. I was so understood in that moment. Then my mom took her to the vet because she was in too much pain to be a dog or a god and the vet gave her an injection and my mom held Poppy and cried and then Poppy the dog was put inside an oven or a bag or something.

J is for *jury*, this jury being the one selected for the murder trial of Andrew Whitaker, who was a year below me in high school, who left school one day, killed a twelve-year-old girl, and then drove to my house, sat on the couch, and talked about killing her, he rocked back and forth, his skin clammy, talked and talked and petted my dog. The jury was full of men and women with their own lives. One had a grandson that reminded her of Andrew. In television and in movies, juries meet in seclusion, they meet in a little room with coffee that they drink out of small paper or Styrofoam cups and they order lunch and talk about dead bodies, they talk about the people who took a living body and made it dead. They talk about what would make a person do that and some of them wonder about themselves. They wonder, *Am I capable of that? Do I have it in me to do that to another living person?* If the answer is yes it is most often a yes with caveats, it's a yes formed by a mouth in extreme circumstances. Yes, I could kill someone if they were trying to kill me. Or yes, I could kill someone if they were trying to harm my children. If they had harmed my children. When I tell my mother I don't agree with the death penalty she says fine but if someone came to your house and tied you up and made you watch while they first raped then tortured and then finally killed your wife and children you would be happy they got the death penalty. I remember thinking if anyone did that then death was the least of threats for them. Most of the people in a jury can't imagine killing anyone. They can only imagine being the one killed. They can more easily imagine being the one walking home who never reaches home, the one who answers the door, who opens the door to death, but they can't imagine being death. I think part of the reason this jury gave Andrew such a light sentence was because they couldn't dream themselves into the person of death, into the body of the killer, and because they couldn't have that dream they couldn't fully believe this high school kid was death. But the truth is this: we are both the ones being killed and the ones doing the killing, all at once. We are both. It's just that we sit in little rooms, drink coffee, and come to the agreement that we are not.

P is for *pause*. I had to take a pause writing this *ABC* project because a few minutes after the last section, O is for *Owen*, my son, I had a stroke. It feels so strange to write, like I'm not even writing it. Still, on Tuesday May 29, 2018, around 3:15 in the afternoon I suffered a cryptogenic ischemic stroke caused by blood clots in the carotid artery and the M1 branch of the right middle cerebral artery; cardioembolic or embolic in origin. Basically a stroke in the right side of my brain. I was having coffee with a young poet when I began to experience slurred speech, then collapsed out of my chair, sort of slid out of my chair, and did not have control of the left part of my body. My face was slipping down the left side and I couldn't lift or move my left arm or leg. I couldn't get up off the floor or talk very well. It felt like my tongue was asleep. I was lucky the barista at the café was so quick to call 911. I was taken by ambulance to the ER, where Julia met me. It was like a movie. We were both crying and I was feeling like I could maybe die. Anyway it feels like I'm always dying. While in the ER and my stay over four days in ICU I underwent the following procedures: *tPA, also known as IV rtPA, CT scans before/after (test), angiogram (test) thrombectomy, femoral artery descending aorta brachiocephalic carotid internal carotid left* MCA *stent retriever guide retriever with sheath, removed clot from right brain,* TEE *(transesophageal echocardiogram) (test), blood draws for testing (test).* I'm really afraid of doctors and needles and hospitals but it felt so normal there. Now I don't feel normal at all. I feel sad a lot and not like me. Physically I'm fine (I'm fine I'm fine I'm fine I'm fine I'm fine) and have been going to the gym. But inside I feel like I fell apart and can't come back together. All I really want to do is sleep and watch movies. I feel angry. I feel fat and I miss smoking cigarettes. I don't know who I am. But if I were going to die it would have been nice to die having a stroke. The part of my brain that wasn't dying was saying, *Oh it's okay you're just tired.* That's what my older brother said death was like before he killed himself. He said, Matthew, there's nothing to be afraid of: you like sleeping right? It's just like that; you just lie down and go to sleep.

X is for Xmas tree. When I was very young my mother would take all three of her children to the parking lot of a church where Boy Scouts or a Little League team would be out in the cold selling Douglas and noble firs, all kinds of spruces. There would be rows of trees leaning against each other. There would be a trailer where the boys could go get warm. It was like an office and they always had hot coffee and hot chocolate for the parents and their kids. We would walk around and be drawn to one tree or another, some feeling inside us, the wonder of the tree before it's taken home and decorated, before presents start to assemble like wishes beneath the lowest branches. We would pick one out and stuff as much of the tree as we could into the trunk of the car and then tie down the trunk so the tree wouldn't fall out onto the street on the way home. When we got it home we would cut the very end of the trunk off with a small, old, rusted saw, then place it in a stand with water. The tree stood right in front of the big picture window in the living room and almost immediately the house, which smelled of kids and dogs and cats, of cat piss and dirty clothes and lemon-scented cleaning supplies, of candles and dinner and wet fur, turned away from these smells and instead it was like walking into a forest. The whole house smelled like pine needles. When we were very young my brother and sister and I could only reach the middle of the tree and so when we went to bed our mother would take half the ornaments, the candy canes and glass balls, the ribbons, and rehang them in the top half of the tree. For weeks our house smelled like a forest, the tree covered with its green and sap all the messiness of our childhood, it promised hope and gifts and joy, it stayed lit, the red and green and blue and yellow lights hung over it all night in the dark living room so if you woke up from a nightmare, sweaty and afraid, all you had to do was walk out into the living room and stand in the light of the Xmas tree and it would X-out all your fears, all your doubts. Sometimes I would go out and sleep beneath it, curled up like one of our dogs, and breathe in the pine and sleep like a dog sleeps: without worry, without concern or fretfulness, just sleeping, just dreaming about cans of dog food.

Z is for *Zig-Zag* rolling papers. I loved smoking cigarettes. Some of my favorites were the light blue packs of American Spirit, the light green, elegant boxes of Shepard's Hotel, which you would open and inside the box were folded white ends connected by a sticker you would unfold to find the cigarettes neatly in a line, a kind of gift box, and the great, short Export "A"s from Canada. But my absolute favorite was a bag of loose tobacco, Drum or something else, and a pack of Zig-Zag rolling papers. Smoking was the best. It was a best friend. It was always there for me and no matter what was going on I could always walk away, find a quiet place to be alone, and smoke. I can't tell you how many times I tried to quit but failed. Right now I'm thinking about the times when I was in my late teens and early twenties, sitting on the front porch of the house I grew up in, rolling a cigarette, placing the tobacco inside the paper, moving the small taco of tobacco and paper between my fingers, back and forth, until the tobacco settled down, and

then bringing it up to my lips and licking one end of the paper, finally rolling it up so the two ends of the paper met and formed a seal. In this memory it is always lightly raining. I'm drinking coffee. On the Zig-Zag packet there's the face of a man who looks bohemian, looks like a pirate. For a little while I had a machine you could cup in your palm and you could put the paper and tobacco inside it and it would roll the cigarette for you but I preferred to do it myself. I feel so lonely all the time. Why did I just say that? Probably because I am? I love my family, I love being alive, but I feel so scared. Scared of living. Scared of dying. Afraid I won't be a good father, a good man. When I would stand beneath a big pine tree and smoke while it rained I could put all of that out of my mind, my body. I could put it on hold for the seven minutes I was smoking. I could forget about what was happening and make promises to myself about what tomorrow would be, about what I would be. I miss the sensation of brushing my hand across my jean pockets and feeling a lighter, a packet of rolling papers. I want to say I miss being born. That's what I want to say. So say it! I miss being born. I miss being something that wasn't anything at all. 🛡

THERE IS NO LAKE

there are no dogs
the right hand did not choke out the left
the brink wasn't inside you this whole time
there's no significance to the recurrence
of 9 on Wednesdays
the mole is benign
the platelet count is low but stable
the rock you skip across the lake
is not your self-worth
there is no lake
the candle is unscented
the slats on the roof are not shaped like frowns
the stew that tastes like poison
was poorly spiced
the knife at the shore of the lake
is not bloody
there is no lake
you are not swimming
in a murdered girl's remains
there is no lake
every woman in the café
has not been raped
the text message from your coworker

isn't that inappropriate
the ass grab at the concert
is an accident
the silence at the center of the book
is purely stylistic
there is no lake
stop looking for the lake

THE LONELINESS IS COMING FROM INSIDE MY BODY

what if I outsourced all my lonely shit into a poem
like in horror movies where the police say
    the call is coming from inside the house
what if I refused to be a receptacle
for this drop of blood in a dirty sink
this webcam and flared nostrils
and the highway reek
of the Purina dog food factory
this knowing that I only want
someone because he looks good in vests
crying in plant nursery bathrooms
the sad beating of broom on ceiling
the difference between those who play piano
and those who can break
a woman's arm in three steps
the signature cruelty of children
every poem I've started to write
called White Underwear
the stomach of the vacuum
the myths I tell myself about the tight borders
of bodies
turducken

the poems I've written to not have to write other poems
the nightness of lakes
the lakeness of night
imagining all my serotonin
marching in single-file lines
watching a plane bisect a cloud
wondering if someone on the plane
is watching me

Blame

Aimee Bender

It washed out at ten at night, after a day of cramping and lying on the sofa. An embryo, small and gray as promised, wobbling in a bed of blood on her supersize maxi pad. She had been warned it might be visible, and the doctor had said most women liked to flush and flush, to not look, to look away; "It can be distressing," he had said, pushing his glasses back onto his nose. "It is not your fault," he had said. She had listened while unhooking her feet from the metal stirrups, and nodded politely, and had thought she was interested in looking. She was different from those other women, she thought, imagining them all in a row, wearing the pleated pastel skirts of another era. She felt herself tougher, and better, which was pleasant to think about while in her blue paper medical gown with her hair in a claw.

But as soon as she saw it, she screamed. Yelled for her husband.

He'd been so busy, her husband—all day long he'd been on, on-on-on, watching her closely after she took the special miscarriage pills and turbo pain relievers, bringing her a heating pad, making her soup, calling to her through the bathroom door, and he was finally taking a break to relax into the science fiction movie about the werewolves and the car manufacturers. "You okay?" he asked, rushing in, wiping ice cream off his lips. She pointed at the pad, and he put his arms around her, and together they looked at it, and examined it, and she grasped his hands tightly and told him she thought it might have moved.

"Just a little bit?" she said, eyes big. "Like a shiver?"

He stroked her dampened hair.

"No," he said. He kissed her forehead. "I'm so sorry, love."

He kissed her again, but his eyes were still caught in the full moon of the other room, and who could blame him, really—the underwear around her ankles, the globs of body coming out of her own, all the crying all week after the shit trip to the doctor. Plus, he felt hopeful about their next round, their next try. He made a soft gesture about tipping it into the toilet.

"Do you want me to stay?" he asked, and she told him no.

After he left, she spent a little more time looking at it. The embryo, at eleven weeks old. It almost had tangible arms and legs, had maybe the slightest hint of a marine-like spine, and had, she felt while studying it, a firm and hostile personality. It was so small, barely the size of the top of her pinkie finger, and as she looked, a tiny slit seemed to split open inside the gray blur of what would've become a head.

She craned forward, to see better.

You, the slit mouthed, opening and closing. The word drifted up at her in the faintest of whispers.

You, it said again, the line wrinkling open. *Ma'am.*

She almost laughed, let out a cough. What? she said, leaning in.

You blew it, said the line. *I would've had a wonderful time. You had wine, right? What is your fucking problem? I was going to look like your grandfather. I already have a nice skull shape. I was beginning to grow my musical interests that would have led me to a piano. My spatial abilities are off the charts. My verbal—*

> "It can be distressing," he had said, pushing his glasses back onto his nose. "It is not your fault."

She was right up against it. Her nose almost touching. The words were like forms entering her, both heard and unheard. Her whole body twitched, and the way a bare foot will shiver and fling off a slug she tore the pad from her underwear and shook it behind her into the toilet. Flushed. Flushed again.

In the distant background, she could hear the sound of a werewolf howling and some gunshots.

She stood and changed her pad. It had not opened a little mouth, she told herself, walking briskly to the sink to wash her hands. Of course not, she thought, running the warm water tap, shaking out her arms and hands. It did not even have a mouth. It did not have language. It did not have access to family lineage, and comprehension about its fate. She scrubbed the soap over her palms. And what was it talking about, anyway? She whipped up a lather, let it froth past her wrists. What had she blown? She had taken all her vitamins. The wine was for a stew! French people drank wine all the time! The water grew hotter, pouring over her hands. And,

Ma'am? she said, aloud, rinsing her hands clean. She stared at her drawn face in the mirror. Seriously? Guitars surged in the other room, indicating the rolling of credits. Her husband called after her, and she turned off the tap and said she was fine, fine, in the same bright voice she had practiced as a child when looking at the cleansers under the sink.

I cut it off, she thought, vaguely. How long might it've talked?

Later, when she crawled into bed, he had settled on his side, clutching a pillow as if it were a woman. She placed herself carefully on a pile of towels, with a new dry maxi pad lodged into place, and he turned to spoon her back.

"Turns out it was a pain in the ass," she whispered. "We dodged a bullet."

"Honey," he said, in his dreams. "I'm so sorry."

"You don't understand," she said. "It's good news."

Though when she woke up, her pillow was drenched with tears, and her hands, as she made herself a cup of coffee, were trembling.

> She was a pretty girl; you could tell by the shape of her face and the elegant curve of her forehead.

She had, at one point, inserted within her underwear a paper cutting of a child that she had made out of expensive watercolor paper, thick, bumpy, beautiful, the cutout shaped by very careful scissor work, when she was nine years old. She was the best with scissors in her class and her teacher admired her for it and her friends often passed their work over for her to cut. She did not know why she was so skilled; she had a surgeon's eye for the movement of blade over paper. She made snowflakes like nobody's business, in their desert school where no one had ever seen snow, where in the distance the mountains were the color of sand, or sometimes the orange of sunset glazed onto rock.

Her teacher had recently announced to the class that she was pregnant, and on this day she had explained that she would be leaving class in March, and that the student teacher, whom nobody liked, would be taking over for the last few months. The class had audibly groaned, and the student teacher in her magenta headband had looked at them with a forced smile on her face and said, Aw, you guys! The main teacher, who now had a visible bump, once the kids looked—no one really had noticed before, she just seemed to be a better lap to sit on, a softer belly, more of her instead of her usual slightly brittle skinny self—shushed the class and said, in her warm tones: Kids, please. *Manners*. It was also clear she was glad to be the favorite. That afternoon, the girl, breaking from her friends, had felt taken by the desire to go home alone. She had a key, and her own mother was working, her father too, and she had been newly trusted with the means to get in, and her older sister was taking an extensive after-school piano lesson at the house next door, so it was hers, if she wanted it: the house. And she wanted it. Her friends called after her—Are you coming over? Are you coming? And she said no. She skipped a little, in her step. She had something to do. Talk to you later! she called, turning down her street.

The sharpest scissors were not hidden from her; even her family relied upon her careful cutting. They were admirers too. Not one member of her family could even tie their shoelaces properly; they were ham-handed as a lot and she was the one with the delicacy of fine motor. Like her great-grandmother, apparently, who had made lace and embroidered dresses that had sold for a good price long ago in Lithuania, land of bonnets and dill and tough men on roan horses. Inside the house, which was silent, empty, loaded with lit dust motes and silent insects crawling up walls, she found the best pair of scissors, a step up from orange handles into all silver, a pair her mother had actually mail-ordered as a way to encourage her daughter's capacity, and she went and got the nicest, thickest paper out from the drawer that held the art supplies and she set herself in her room, using a large picture book as a backing.

She drew a rough sketch of a girl doll on the paper, but pencil was not her forte, and it was with the scissors that she realized the details. First: the profile, the girl's proud lifted nose, the thick eyelashes, the curl to the hair. She was a pretty girl; you could tell by the shape of her face and the elegant curve of her forehead. Then, she did the body—the careful fingers, the moon-shaped fingernails, the nubby elbows, the crisp bows on the shoes. The girl had not really explored that part of her body, not extensively, and she did not even know what drove her to do it, but once the doll was done, the girl took her into the bathroom, rolled the doll into a tube, and inserted her into her underwear. She pushed the doll into herself, to whatever softness she could find, and the cuttings had edges and the paper pricked and scraped her. It all felt strange. Incorrect. She had not been touched there by anyone but herself, but it was not quite right, what she was doing, she could feel the not-quite-rightness of it, and how she was moving close to something in the neighborhood of harming herself, to finding something out about herself that she could not possibly understand. She knew babies came from there. She did not get how it worked. She had not enjoyed the conversation with her mother with the hardback book on their laps, the book her mother had taken off the shelf when the teacher had made her announcement. The girl perched there in the bathroom with the doll poking inside her, pricking, scratching, and then she reached in and pulled it out. Hello! she said, waving it in the air. Welcome! The doll, crumpled now, head tweaked to the left, hands torn from the rolling. The girl started to cry. What had she imagined? That contact with her body and her privacy would paint it with watercolors, imbue it with life, and she would come to school with a live doll herself, and she and the teacher could raise their children together? Yes, she had thought exactly that. She liked that idea very much. She pulled up her underwear more tightly, and put the doll in the toilet as she had done with that fish from the school pet drive, and flushed it down, which took two tries, and then she went into the other room and took the piece of paper where the doll had been, the negative space surrounding the shape, and for some reason she felt friendly toward that stencil and she found some tape and stuck it up on her wall.

She couldn't help thinking about it now, pulling herself out of bed, tugging on her slippers, turning up the heat. She remembered her mother seeing the stencil on the wall and praising it extensively, which had been annoying. Had her mother known the fate of the shape itself, she might've been concerned. Now, as the woman sipped her coffee at the table, taking two Tylenol and eating a small plain yogurt, she considered the flushed embryo, the flushed doll, the flushed fish, and all the other things flushed that were not usually meant for the toilet. The city our receiver, she thought.

Her husband kissed her goodbye and went off to work.

This had been their closest attempt at pregnancy yet—a pregnancy, yes, just not a workable one. They had been trying, through various means, for almost two years, and the embryo had died because of some chromosomal issue. She had now miscarried and would wait a month or so and then return to the doctor to do all the various preparation needed for another round. They had not been able to conceive naturally, and so the pathway to making a person had become overt, every hidden mystical step turned inside out so it could be looked at and replicated medically. The natural production of hormones in the body became shots they bought at the pharmacy for hundreds of dollars, which her husband prepped at the living room table, snapping at the syringe to get out the air bubbles. The natural process of conception becoming a series of visits to the surgical center—first, her under anesthesia while the doctor sucked eggs from her ovaries with a technological straw, her husband off in a red-painted porn-filled room with a plastic cup, and days later, her husband peering into a large wheeled incubator, hunched over a microscope to see the silvery cluster of cells, while she lay across the room stuck in the stirrups. The hope of implantation now being the doctor joking with them both as he crouched between her legs with a giant hollow needle packed with air bubble markers and blastocysts that he inserted into her cervix. It is all so inside out! she told her husband, as she leaned over the bathroom sink and he plunged a needle full of progesterone into her ass. It is all on the surface! He recapped the needle and called her the Pompidou. Pipes on the outside, right? he said. My little Pompy. That had been a good moment, a kiss then with his right hand needle-full, her right hand with a cotton ball pressing on her skin to stop any bleeding, the kiss good and funny and warm and rich. Then they went to watch TV. But once the embryos were inside her, mystery returned, and the body did what it would do, or not do, and the embryos did what they would do, or not do, and one absorbed fast into the bloodstream and the other lived briefly and then tanked. It is no one's fault, she said to herself, though those were only words because beneath she thought: it is my fault; sometimes she thought it was her husband's fault, and sometimes the embryo's fault. God's fault. The fault of the pharmacy that gave them the shots. The fault of January.

> This had been their closest attempt at pregnancy yet—a pregnancy, yes, just not a workable one.

On the way to work, she stopped at a donut shop. She did not usually buy donuts because she did not especially like donuts but today, paired with her aching stomach and uterus, they were the pinnacle of desire, and she had practically woken up with the word on her tongue: *donut*, the short spelling, the nickname. The store was called Yum-Yum Donuts and who could resist that? I sure can't, she said, pushing through the swinging doors. Inside, it was empty, and sun-splashed, as the early morning rush had already come and gone, as she was on a schedule these days of going to work late and staying late so she could incorporate doctor visits into the mornings as needed. The pink donuts with smooth frosting. The crusty old-fashioneds. The sprinkles and the jimmies. The jellies and the glazed.

She found most of them unappealing, but ordered a chocolate old-fashioned and a coffee, and the lady behind the counter picked the donut out with a hand masked by a square see-through sheet of paper, and the coffee had the pleasingly flat taste of certain things cooked with vegetable oil.

A dollar eighty, said the lady behind the counter.

The woman paid. She dropped twenty cents in the tip jar, only to see it was the give a penny/take a penny jar.

Oh, sorry, she said.

The lady looked at her funny. The woman dipped her donut in the coffee, and took a bite. That's good, she said, chewing. Wow. Mmm. It's been too long.

The donut lady began arranging fresh donuts into the rows on the shelves. Bad for you, she said.

The woman laughed. What is?

You'll die too, she said to the lady, dumping the half-full cup of coffee into the trash.

The donut, she said.

Not yum-yum? said the woman, pointing to the store logo on the napkin.

No, said the lady. Not really.

The woman waved her hand. It's okay, she said, lightly. I'm just trying to comfort myself.

The lady sniffed. She had sharp cheekbones, admirably sharp. Bad way to comfort, she said.

The woman sat herself down in one of the curved pink plastic chairs lining the walls of the store and ate the whole donut. She ordered another. She had had only that yogurt, she explained. She was hungry.

The lady nodded, and grabbed another see-through square sheet. The woman leaned back in her chair. She found it nice that the store was empty. The position of the sun made splotches of lightness on the orange tile.

To tell you the truth, she said, running her hands through her hair, I just miscarried yesterday. Eleven-week-old embryo. So I think I can have a fucking donut.

The lady, unflinching, placed the second donut on the counter, on its paper.

Miscarried, whatever, she said. Eighty cents.

What do you mean, whatever? Have you?

Oh, sure, she said. Three times. Four?

The woman crossed her legs. Well, she said. I'm very sorry to hear it. Three times?

Then I had three children, said the lady, sighing. Now I have to deal with children.

The woman got up and took her second donut. She asked for a refill on the coffee, and they both watched during the pour as the steam rose from the cup and filled the room with the smell of artificial roasting. She paid again. Her bracelet, a thick-cut chunk of ivory with a golden clasp, clanked on the counter.

That's a fancy bracelet, said the lady behind the counter. Look at that. Fancy, fancy. Poor elephant, but pretty lady.

The woman did not answer. She took the food and returned to her seat.

You're a rich lady, said the lady behind the counter.

According to whom?

To me, said the lady. In my estimations.

The woman dabbed her mouth with the napkin. It was true that she did make a good living. And so did her husband. And so had their parents.

You will have a rich child, said the lady, wiping down the counter with a cloth. Who will want rich things.

You think I'll have a child? said the woman, sitting up.

You will use up all your rich things, said the lady. You will want more rich things. And then you will die, said the lady, and she started to laugh. A cackle-laugh, high up into the rafters of the store.

The second donut was nowhere near as good as the first. It lacked the initial novelty and maybe this one was from an earlier batch because it was chewy in a wrong way and the woman stood and threw half of it into the trash. The coffee, too, had developed a chemical aftertaste.

You'll die too, she said to the lady, dumping the half-full cup of coffee into the trash, where it would drip out to the edges of the bag. And you're really not the nicest of people, she said.

We go to heaven, said the lady, folding the cleaning cloth into a square.

We? Who's we?

Store workers, said the lady.

And me?

You go to the rich person place, she said. Which is not heaven.

Oh, come on.

It's true, said the lady. You cannot go through the needle, so you will go somewhere else.

The woman brushed the crumbs off her lap. Outside, engines thrummed at the red light. You know, she said, stepping back to the counter. Personally, I don't like to be talked to about religion and doomsday while eating my donuts. I don't like unsolicited advice on my health. I bought this bracelet used. I don't want to compete over miscarriages.

You stayed, said the lady. She smiled, agreeably.

The woman pressed her hands on the clean counter. Listen, she said. She glanced around, even though the store was clearly empty, and dropped her voice. Just tell me one thing.

No, said the lady.

In any of your miscarriages, did you see the embryo?

No, said the lady. I did not look. Okay, one time, I looked.

The woman leaned closer. And? she said. Did it move? Was it dead? Did it do anything?

Mine was dancing, said the lady. She laughed a little.

Don't joke, said the woman.

Not joking, said the lady.

Dancing?

A little dancing, said the lady. She held up her arms in waltz-fashion.

Stop it, the woman said.

The lady wrinkled her nose, as if she was itching it from the inside.

No moving, she said. They were dead. One was older. Had eyes.

God, said the woman.

He waved at me.

No, really?

A little, said the lady. He waved bye.

She ducked under her words.

Are you still teasing me? said the woman. Because I am trying to get a grip here.

Not teasing, said the lady. Her eyes were dark. She was impossible to read. She was, the woman thought, the hardest-to-read person she had ever met in her life.

And you?

I waved bye back, said the lady. She shrugged. She didn't laugh.

Flush flush, the lady said.

The woman pulled her hair out from under her purse strap. Her back and stomach were still aching. She felt a latent sadness stirring deep in her legs, ready to journey all the way up her torso and to her face, where it would exit, if she let it, as streams of salt water.

Of course sometimes the body would construct a dam somewhere along that route that would block the path. Sometimes it would take a very long time to deconstruct that fucking dam to get to those streams of salt water.

Okay, she said, clearing her throat. That is helpful. Thank you.

Buy more, said the lady. Rich lady. Come back to Yum-Yum. Eat yum-yum. Clog your arteries. Enjoy life.

The woman bought a dozen donuts, all kinds. She left a generous tip. She went to the nearby bus stop and put the pink box, full of fresh donuts, some still warm from the deep fryer, on the bench. She pulled a pen from her purse and wrote FREE DONUTS on the outside so that people would know. Then she stood back and waited on the sidewalk to see if anyone would take them. She hovered close by for fifteen minutes before she had to head off to work, but no one took a donut. It was like a bomb there on the bench, a pink bakery bomb box, all the kindness and generosity she was trying to muster looking to everyone else like poison. 🏮

Louise Mathias

IN THE POEM NO ONE KNOWS IS ABOUT ME, I'M PRETTY MUCH PREY

Nightjars depend on their cryptic coloration.
Almost, he said, like a blonde peeing
in a field of goldenrod.

What's a leg when you're caught in a trap?
Moonflowers shriek from the side of the road.
Lord, let me die

in a godforsaken town,
not even the air

to notice.

THE ROAD IS THE SICKNESS AND THE CURE

In the truck it was both of us crying—
admiring each other's method in the dark.

Once, I ate needles for love.
Pried the poison from the flower and how

your moonlit kindness saved me.

In the long abandoned brothel,
we stood near the heart shaped hole

where the hot tub had been.
Red, I'll presume.

Implausible and finite as a rose.

Vive la Vie

It was to France that you returned in the century's final spring, as you did across most of those years. Alone in the middle of life, at the height of your career, the annual trips had become a sort of homecoming, an act of repatriation. You had developed a fantasy of living, sure, but also of dying in Paris, ideally in a richly upholstered penthouse at the George V Hotel.

At twenty-six, four years married, you first saw the city, together with your young husband, in the usual way: Eiffel Tower; Notre-Dame; Pernod at a sidewalk café. There was time, there was time; you slept late each morning, walked the shops each afternoon. The visit was brief, pleasant, part of a longer tour. No blinding flash, no transformational gong. Still, a mouthful of soft-boiled egg, during an otherwise unmemorable meal, sent a shock to some quiet, curled-up part of you. If only in that hidden place, life began anew.

Thirteen years later, back in Paris, something burst forth. Time was shorter, but life still seemed long. You had two children, a stalled

Michelle Orange

marriage, a new degree. Your style differed from that of your travel-mate, an old high school friend: you loved to dawdle; she kept it moving. You wished to be touring the Grand Palais and tasting steak tartare while in love, and by the end of the trip you were—with yourself, in France. You were sure then just how fine life could be. You left us soon after; not fully, but mostly.

Your diarist's impulse was bound exclusively to travel. You emerge on the page only in distant places, doing and seeing distant things. Your entries are overwhelmingly plain, a descriptive record, notes for a future self: stay on a higher floor; take a different autoroute; don't order the salmon. Advice for next time, and the next. Sometimes the second self to whom the pages are addressed appears, in lighter or darker ink, to converse with her former self, adjust a notation, confirm a prediction, congratulate a plan or wish fulfilled.

Back in France, that final spring, you traveled with your sister. You called your mom on Mother's Day. She was a French Canadian, born in Montreal. You never wondered, though, if some thread connected your passion for France and the essential distance between you two. If your habitual returns to Paris, your tours of the Basque Country, Brittany, and Provence somehow brought you closer to the homebound woman who raised you than you felt while breathing her same air.

While you explored the Lot Valley that spring, I too touched down in Europe. I filled my own travel diary with anguished, centripetal musings. There was time—endless time. That first trip, and again and again, I went to Italy—the seat of my father's paternal line. The connection was obvious because I had made it so: here is my allegiance, my history, my heart, my flag. I had and sought no husband. I lived with you, in fact, though soon after my return I took an apartment not far away, near the cemetery whose perimeter I came to trot each morning.

Today, the thought of my Florentine notebook beside your French one conjures the image of one figure charging forward, the other churning in her wake. It is the bodily quality that attracts me now to all of your travel journals: the sense of an avatar in motion, who might yet remain in motion; each day waking at a certain hour, eating a specific thing, leaving one place and arriving somewhere else. You too sought beauty, the sublime, and had learned that only the most ordinary persistence would reveal it. Your reverence was expressed not by language but accretion, careful line after line citing artworks and architecture, the local flowers of note. The pages themselves bear a living rhythm, marked by endless dashes, slashes, parentheses, strong underlines.

Virginia Woolf once observed that paging through the dull, voluminous diaries of an eighteenth-century English parson named James Woodforde "is not reading, it is ruminating." It is finding in his meticulous record of seasons turning, weather changing, of meals consumed—the endless pastries and jellies that "crumble and squash beneath their spoons in mountains, in pyramids, in pagodas"—a sense of repletion, the astonishing comfort of a steady heartbeat. If the kings and queens and indeed the reader are doomed to change and perish, Woolf writes, "we have a notion that Parson Woodforde does not die. Parson Woodforde goes on."

When it was declared, nearly two decades after our parallel fin de siècle journeys, that you were dying, one thought persisted among the many: *I must go to France*. Between hospital visits, I booked a flight for six months hence, late spring. At your bedside, I asked for help planning an itinerary, a survey of your favorites: Nice, Èze, Saint-Paul-de-Vence. You bequeathed me the remains of your airline points; it appeared your travels had ended.

But a new journey began. You did not die. You went on. You clung to family, fleet pleasures, your adored partner. For weeks and then months, in a dismal corner of a small ward, others died on the hour while you lived— one long, extraordinary day. There was time; you lay in repose. It is we who scurried back and forth, up and down a long hallway, bearing flowers, alive and then dead; dishes, full and then empty. Before you appeared vast quantities: towers of sliced *burrata*, avocado, heirloom tomatoes; marching hordes of squared dark chocolate, caramel, Turkish delight; haystack upon haystack of hot buttered toast, de-crusted and cut into thin strips.

Amid the meals and changing seasons, my trip arrived. You insisted I go: to Nice, to Arles, to Les Baux-de-Provence, where I ate a seven-course meal at your bidding, sending photos of each dish as it arrived. I did no writing in France, except to you. On returning, I had no more ardent wish than to reappear at the threshold of that cramped, dull, flower-lined room, to continue perfecting your four-minute egg, presenting it in a painted cup plucked from a French mountain perch. To watch your face, again, as you exclaimed over the cup's bright design, the exquisite texture, the comforts of a well-cooked egg. To remain still, at last, bound by a single mouthful, by the discovery that life might yet begin anew. 🗝

ODE TO ANTHONY BOURDAIN

As you move through this life and this world you change things slightly, you leave marks behind, however small. And in return, life—and travel—leaves marks on you. Most of the time, those marks—on your body or on your heart—are beautiful. Often, though, they hurt.
—ANTHONY BOURDAIN

I'm sitting on my couch watching a man on TV
get a tattoo of a symbol that means *epoché*,

a Pyrrhronic skeptic's term meaning *to suspend judgment*,
or as Montaigne translated, *to hold back*. The man

on the TV mentions Plato's dogmatic assertion—*All I know
is that I know nothing*. It does not strike me that either Plato

or this man on the TV knows nothing, at all. Maybe
just because they know more than me. The man on the TV

tells me that he doesn't really know who he is—no longer
a chef, not really a journalist, maybe (he says) he fancies

himself an essayist. Good. Essayists don't actually have to
know anything; *to essai*—in French it means to try, as in,

to attempt, but also, to test, to taste, perhaps for the first time,
a gleaming heap of tofu cubes doused in a red and shiny

ground-pork gravy, strewn with sliced-fine scallions. *Mapo dofu*,
says the man, *is everything you want in your mouth, in one perfect bite.*

The goal of Pyrrhonic skepticism is to arrive at ataraxia,
a kind of Western Nirvana—the man on the TV says

it means *to be unperturbed, happy in your life, not
tormented.* But who among us is not, somehow, tormented?

Plato, who said he knew nothing, also said: *Be kind
for everyone you meet is fighting a hard battle.* I know less

than nothing, but I know that to be true. The man on TV
laughs and raises a glass of beer to his companion, who

is relating a story of his infancy in Ethiopia, the tuberculosis
epidemic, how his sick mother walked her two sick kids

seventy-five miles to the Swedish hospital, how she died
and he and his sister ended up in Sweden—and then

the food comes, a vast expanse of spongy injera bread
islanded with *kitfo* (beef tartare blessed with hot chili)

and collard greens, *doro wat* (chicken stewed with eggs),
yellow lentils, carrots, and little bright vermillion mounds

of berbere spice. It's a painter's palate of delights, eaten
with the hands, as intimate and visceral as it gets, and

as they tuck injera-pinched lamb tibs into their mouths,
they close their eyes in a gesture that in every language

means, *This pleases me so much.* But pleasure is not
happiness. If anything, it's closer to—what? Oblivion,

I think. (Though thinking is not knowing.) Escape.
To please the body is to distract the mind from all

its striving after knowing, all its wheeling dread. Wine,
wonder, sex, song. And food—the slow-motion ooze

of baked Camembert from its broken crust, the gratifying
crackle of a fork through the edge of well-crisped *tahdeeg,*

the exquisite tang of a hand-whipped aioli barely flecked
with fresh dill, noodles slurped out of a steaming broth

afloat with bright green herbs, the way pit-barbecued pig
just unfetters itself in the pit-master's great gloved hand.

The man on TV is saying, about a nation to which he
is newly arrived, *You might not know this place is so lush,*

so often have we seen its name thrown up across a dusty
famine scene. What we think we know. How we think

we come to know it. How easy it is, to misunderstand
a man, or a woman, or a people. The man on TV, because

he is on TV, feels like a friend to me. He eats the same
trippa alla Romana I couldn't quite bring myself to swallow

when I was in that same terra-cotta city. He alludes
to his misspent youth, and I feel a surge of recognition

that washes some of my own regrets out to a further shore.
Perhaps I, too, will one day make it to Jerusalem. Maybe

I will get to recount, over a smooth black table lit
from above by a single bulb, how once in Hungary I ate

the perfect dinner—velvety pale green cream of celery
soup pebbled with bleu cheese and graced with flakes

of crunchy bacon, then roast goose leg on a white plate
daubed with demiglace, then sour cherries dark, round

like a word in another tongue you love the sound of
but cannot quite pronounce, cupped in fluted pastry, all

while sipping a silky wine called Bull's Blood, grown
and stomped just paces from where we were eating.

My sister took one bite and sighed, *Dear. People. Of Earth*—
because when we do find love, we cannot seem to help

but want to tell it. I love this man on the TV, in a TV way
and that's a paradox. The more visible one becomes,

the more lonely, too. Hidden in plain sight, in front of people
who don't all ask what they don't know, who don't all

suspend judgment, hold back. Who don't all try. Who
don't all understand why one might seek the oblivion

of pleasure, or of watching others live their lives in public,
or even of death. There is another word the ancient Greek

skeptics sometimes used—acatalepsy. It means, the in-
comprehensibility of things. Now the man on TV says, *I want*

to explore an African nation that was never colonized. And now,
after I napped and missed some stuff, the man on TV says

he doesn't think another tattoo will make him hipper, or
more relevant or interesting. The man is tall, snowy, has

some lank to him. And he's dead now. And now, he says,
forever and ever, *It's been an adventure.* He says, *We took*

some casualties over the years. Things got broken. Things
got lost. But I wouldn't have missed it for the world.

AMERICAN COWBOY

When the politician takes
his gun out on stage,

we're meant to feel wonder
he hasn't shot us,

grateful to leave with our lives.

It nears the feeling, maybe,
in Plath's "Daddy,"

the boot in the face . . .

when the white man walks on stage
in cowboy boots and hat,

a shorthand.

But I don't wish his body
near my own—*hear it*—

don't mistake terror for adoration.

There's no plot in the old Western,
only masculine delirium,

and the promise,
part childish, part challenge,

of frontier.

Gold humming in the nearest river.

Vigil of buffalo grazing through the night.

And the tumbleweed,
a complicated thing,

gaining momentum
around an emptiness.

Truly, inside is nothing,
and it protects that nothingness

that built it—

this, its language, its politic.

What will it take
to start over again

with a myth we might perhaps outlive?

It's the cowboy who the cowboy saves.

Colson Whitehead

THREE HAIKU

38.
Professor seeks grace
Making cars from coconuts
Sabotage escape

96.
Jumping roof to roof
Interrogating snitches:
Is that real leather?

131.
Pioneer hubris
Always the children suffer
Next—scarlet fever

from *The Little Book of Television Haiku, Chapter 3: The Devil Dreams of Syndication*

FICTION

Ladder

Etgar Keret

translated by Sondra Silverston

DIVINE INSIGHT

A few weeks before Rosh Hashana, Raphael called him in for a talk.

"So what's happening, Zvi, is everything okay?"

"Yes, more or less."

"Glad to hear it, because the truth is that lately, I've started worrying."

"Why? Did I do something wrong?"

"Heaven forbid, it's just that lately . . ."

"Yesterday morning I didn't rake with everyone, but I had permission."

"I know, I know. There are no complaints about your work."

"So what are the complaints about? Someone in the flock spoke to you? Amatzia?"

"No one spoke to me. No one has to speak, they just have to look."

"Look at what? Raphael, if you have something to say, just say it."

"How's your Yiddish, Zvi? You understand *farpishter punim*? It's the face a person makes when he's not happy."

"So my face is the problem?"

"Not your face, Zvi, but what's behind it. All of us here are, how can I put it, content. Not just because we have it good here—you do agree with me, Zvi, that we have it good here?"

"So?"

". . . but also because of the alternative. Any way you look at it, everyone who comes here feels lucky. More than lucky. Blessed, that's the word. Simply blessed. To be here with us and not with all the losers in . . . you know where."

"I know," Zvi said. "Did you ever hear me complain?"

"No," Raphael said, taking a deep breath, "never. But I've never heard you laugh either. I've never seen you smile even once since you got here."

"Okay," Zvi said, forcing a smile now. "You want me to smile more?"

Raphael became serious. "No, I don't want you to smile. I want you to be happy, all the time, truly happy. God knows that you have a lot to be happy about—"

"God is dead," Zvi interrupted him.

"I know," Raphael said and bit his lower lip. "Not a day goes by when I don't think about Him. But we're still here, and heaven keeps functioning just the way it did before. And you, as someone who once worked as . . . What exactly did you work at, Zvi?"

"I was a casualty assistance officer."

"That's in the army?"

"Yes."

"Something medical, right? You treated the wounded?"

"No. My job was to inform families that someone was dead. You know, a husband, a son, a brother."

"Terrible. I had no idea there was a job like that."

> Any way you look at it, everyone who comes here feels lucky. More than lucky.

"How could you, Raphael. Were you ever in the army?"

"Right. So you used to go to see the families and tell them that their loved ones were dead, and then you went to stand in line at the bank to pay your mortgage, afraid that you would die too. I'm guessing you were afraid of death, weren't you?"

"Afraid? I was terrified."

"And now you're here. An angel with no debts, no lines to wait in, nothing to be afraid of. You should be grateful."

"I'm grateful."

"You should be relieved."

"I'm relieved. Not right now, but in principle."

"You should be happy."

"I'm trying, Raphael, I'm really trying."

"So it's like, when you get up in the morning, you don't feel happy?"

Zvi cleared his throat. "I do, I do . . . But it's a limp kind of happiness. Like the elastic on underpants that have been washed too many times."

"I have to say, Zvi, that I've been here quite a long time and I've never come across the expression 'limp happiness.' The way I see it, happiness can't be limp."

"It can, believe me. Limp and faded and worn out. You know that feeling of wanting something so much that your whole body aches and you know that your chances of getting it are really, really small, and you stand in your living room in your boxers, covered in sweat, and try to imagine that moment when your lips meet the lips of the girl you've always wanted, or your son saying, 'You're the best dad in the world,' or the hospital calling to tell you the biopsy was negative? Did you ever want something that badly, Raphael?"

"No."

"Well I did. And I miss the feeling. You have no idea how much I miss it."

> Time moves in a completely different way here. Angels don't age, and neither do clouds.

"We don't force anyone to stay here, Zvi. If you're not happy, we can easily transfer you."

"I don't want to go to hell, Raphael. You know that."

"To the best of my knowledge, those are the only two options, and if you really want to be an angel here, you have to be happy. An angel has to be at peace with himself. Serene, that's the word I'm looking for. Because even if it's not written down anywhere, it's part of the job description. Not that being an angel is a job, it's more like an essence, and . . ."

"And about that business of raking clouds . . ."

"What about it?"

"Are there angels who do something else?"

"No, but if you're not interested in raking, that's something we can definitely . . ."

"I'm asking because Gabriel once told us that before our matriarch Sarah became pregnant, he went down to see her and . . ."

"It wasn't just him, there were two others with him."

"And I thought maybe . . . maybe there's a chance that instead of raking, I could do something like that? You know, visit people. Give them messages. I've already told you, I was a casualty assistance officer. I have a lot of experience with interpersonal relations in extreme situations and I'm sure that meeting people every once in a while would really help me. Not just me, the entire system. In all modesty, I'm really good at it."

"We don't do things like that anymore."

"But Gabriel said it wasn't only with Sarah . . ."

"True, but since God left us, we've stopped. It was always divine insight that influenced the decision to go down and establish contact with people. After all, even if that sort of encounter is efficient, it can cause damage, and none of us—neither I nor Gabriel nor Ariel—has the necessary insight to make that kind of decision."

"You don't have the insight? You're angels!"

"Ministering angels. Our job was to serve God, not to make decisions."

"But you're all . . ."

"Pure, not geniuses. But we're not stupid either. And if I may ask, why is all of this so important to you? Do you miss the world of the living?"

"Not the world," Zvi said with a sad smile, "people."

"I must say," Gabriel gave him a similar smile, "that is something I've never heard before. By the way, you know that it's quite possible they are no longer . . . no longer . . ."

"No longer what?"

"That they have been, you know, annihilated, or have annihilated themselves . . ."

"But I only just got here."

"Do you know how long ago you arrived here?"

"No."

"Neither do I. Time moves in a completely different way here. Angels don't age, and neither do clouds. I'm glad to hear that time has been passing so quickly for you. That's a good sign. But who knows how many human years it's been. One hundred? One thousand? One million? But however long it is, it's definitely long enough for such an unstable and vulnerable species to destroy itself."

"You sound like someone who knows something."

"I sound like someone who knows nothing and admits it. From the minute God died, people haven't been our concern."

"Okay. So if I understand right, the options are either raking clouds or hell," Zvi said.

"You understand right."

"So I'll go back to raking."

SWEAT

Angels never fail. It's almost impossible to fail when you're a pure soul with no desires or needs. But Zvi couldn't help feeling that he was exactly that: a failed angel. Floating on an ocean of serenity yet missing the pull of the whirlpools and waves. Something was wrong with him, something he couldn't share with any other soul. The problem was his alone, and if he didn't find a way to solve it, he'd end up in hell.

Hell was full of souls who had lived as if there was no tomorrow, and only after they died did they realize that they had to pay a price for their sins. He didn't want to be the first to arrive there as pure as the driven snow just because he couldn't manage to find himself some happiness in heaven. Zvi knew he had to find a way to stop missing things.

Angels never dream. The closest thing they have to dreaming is staring into space. And the first thing Zvi had to learn was how to stare into space, not to focus on concrete things and to avoid the frustrating place where he began to compare his now extinct material life to his present lofty existence. And he also had to smile more. Not fake smiles. Angels aren't capable of faking. He just had to find a smile inside himself.

A lot of time had passed since his conversation with Raphael. He couldn't say exactly how much, there are no clocks in heaven, but it was a lot. And even if his desire to return to the material world hadn't completely disappeared, at least it didn't nag at him. Zvi knew he'd never be a perfect angel, but he believed that if he kept working on himself, he'd manage to become a standard one, an angel that didn't worry or bother anyone. And despite all his angelic modesty, he knew that the change was visible. After all, of the dozens of angels, he was the one Raphael put in charge of garden tools. That was apparently Raphael's way of telling Zvi that he could see he was on the right path.

As the one in charge of garden tools, Zvi had to get to the shed before all the other angels, load the rakes onto the shiny wheelbarrow, and wheel it to the section of clouds scheduled to be raked that day. There were other garden tools in the shed: hammers, pruning shears, even a plowshare, but they only needed rakes. Zvi's favorite moment of the day was when work ended or, more accurately, the moment right after it. All the other angels relaxed, sinking into the sea of sublime serenity that Zvi never managed to experience completely, while he invested all his energy in collecting the rakes to keep himself from sinking into the familiar melancholy. And it helped, like real medicine. Every time Zvi spotted even a sliver of a thought about his former existence or a shadow of longing in his mind, he hurried to the shed and began to sort and organize the tools.

On one of his restless nights, Zvi discovered the ladder. It was a weird, incomprehensible ladder, a paradox with rungs: short enough to stand in the small shed and long enough to . . . honestly? There was no way to gauge its length in material measures, but if forced to do so, Zvi had to admit that its length was infinite. He asked Gabriel about that ladder, and with angelic patience and in great detail, Gabriel began to tell him the story of Jacob's dream, as if Zvi had never read the Bible. When Gabriel saw that Zvi was getting excited about the story, he introduced him to the angel who had fought with Jacob that night and even asked him to tell Zvi the story from an eyewitness's vantage point. And the angel did. He told Zvi that it had been the first and last time he went down to the material world and that the hardest thing about it for him had been the way people smelled. Jacob, the angel told Zvi, was very weak physically, at least compared to an angel, but he was supposed to hide that and pretend he was fighting a losing battle to defeat Jacob. Jacob, for his part, struggled and strained and sweat rivers. The smell of Jacob's sweat was so strong that it almost made the angel pass out, but he completed his mission, and finally, when he returned to heaven that night, the first thing he asked of God, who

Angels never dream. The closest thing they have to dreaming is staring into space.

was still alive then, was to never send him again on other missions that involved material creatures. When the angel finished his story, he raised both hands in the air as if to say, that's it, this story has no moral, and Gabriel, who was sitting with Zvi and listening, burst out laughing. "It's true," he told Zvi, "the smell is what always bothered me too."

THE SMELL OF FRESH LAUNDRY

That night, curled on a cloud, Zvi dreamed for the first time since arriving in heaven. When Zvi was still a newcomer, Raphael had explained to him that an angel's staring into space can sometimes turn into a dream, and that the dream never has a story, images, or time, only color. But the dream Zvi had that night was of a different kind. In it, he was raking clouds when his rake suddenly banged into something hard. Zvi dug in the cloud with his hands and found a metal box that had a picture of butter cookies on it. But when Zvi opened it, he found a small man, a mini-man, inside, and instead of speaking, the little man attacked Zvi in a fury. In the dream, the man was so small and unthreatening that Zvi couldn't understand where he'd found the courage to attack him. At first, Zvi tried to defend himself gently and get the little man off him by holding his shirt carefully with two fingers, but the little man wouldn't back down: he kicked and bit and spit and cursed, and Zvi realized in the dream that the little man wouldn't stop until he destroyed him, that this was a fight to the death. Zvi tried to squeeze the little man between his fingers, to crush him, to tear him to pieces—and couldn't. He didn't know what that tiny, hairy little man was made of, but it was a substance harder than diamond. When Zvi woke up and found a dewdrop on his forehead, he put it on the tip of his tongue. It was salty.

Zvi got up and went straight to the shed, picked up the ladder and dangled it from the edge of the cloud. The ladder had an endless number of rungs, and as he descended from one to the other, he tried to imagine the smells waiting for him below: the smell of sweat, of fresh laundry, of rotting wood, the sweet, scorched smell of cake left in the oven too long, the smell of something.

LONG AGO LOVES

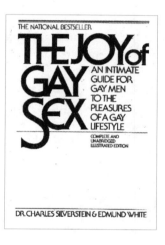

ON DR. CHARLES SILVERSTEIN'S

The Joy of Gay Sex

FRAN TIRADO

I was twenty at the time (but in gay years, scarcely eighteen months old), the artistic director of a local theater company in Indiana (corn-crunching, conservative, frat-run, middle-of-nowhere Indiana) putting on large-scale productions with small-scale budgets and a lot of found prop materials sourced from local dumpsters and Salvation Armies.

It was tech week, and we were in crunch time getting our set together—the show was some musical I can't even remember the name of, about a gay man and his romantic past life. Stacking old books and accoutrements onto a shelf in the set's living room, I pulled from a must-thick box a copy of *The Joy of Gay Sex* by Dr. Charles Silverstein.

1977. First edition. Co-written by Edmund White! The book found me. How bright and blinding this beacon of queerness was in the middle of Nowhere, Indiana; I felt like a video game protagonist pulling a 1000+ talisman with trumpet fanfare from a hidden treasure box. Its pages were aged to an old-lace white. They smelled like a stranger who would strike up an unprompted conversation on a park bench, one with strong opinions about why the Barbra Streisand *A Star Is Born* is the "definitive version."

I was out of the closet, sure—but there is a tender period between coming-out-of-the-closet and coming-into-your-ownness that leaves fertile soil for a lot of embarrassment. That period is like a second puberty, a pit in your stomach anytime anyone so much as mentions or alludes to the fact that you, or anyone in the vicinity, has a sexual or romantic life.

And here it was, that pit—the loudest, most pornographic reminder of the self I was still too scared to know, vintage, and with (very detailed) illustrations on every page.

My coming out had been unremarkable and anticlimactic, its thunder stolen by parents who, though they were conservative Evangelicals who fundamentally disagreed with the whole homosexuality thing, "loved me no matter what." Ugh! A writer's greatest nightmare realized. An experience traditionally inducing trauma (writing material) was met with uneasy warmth, tearful hugs, and contradictory statements that are difficult to give dramatic value. The chapter of my memoir that would have been filled with a scene of me getting kicked out of my home or bullied was replaced by a boring conversation on my front porch and the latent understanding that my parents would simply just always be a little sad that I'm gay.

But beyond their tentative approval, the easiest thing for all parties involved was to not talk about it, a well-intentioned but deeply Christian see-no-evil,

speak-no-evil policy. Our household kept this policy in regard to anything sinful, especially when it came to sex. Growing up (and still to this day) my parents would cover my eyes or fast-forward all the sex scenes. Kids in my school district received no teaching on the matter, and were instead shipped off by the busload with other seventh graders to Robert Crown, an education center forty-five minutes away that had the sole duty of giving students in the tri-state area "the talk" because our middle school health programs were not equipped, employing the help of silicone models of wombs and urethras, and corny CGI animations depicting the miracle of (straight) life, a product of the penis inserted into the vagina.

And this book, with the same confrontational quality as plastic fallopian tubes, put my embarrassment in full swell again. Not in my wildest dreams could I have imagined the gay version of my sexual education and the devastation that came with it. The internet was a thing by then, sure, but not the resource it is today. There was only so much information about anal sex beyond Wikipedia pages and porn, and I had neglected to dive deep as a consequence of the Jesus-Sees-You shame that ran through my blood.

"Oh, my God," said someone next to me, as I realized I had been holding the book and staring at it for an unknown length of time. "Who brought this?!"

No one knew the answer, or where it came from: a portent of sexual corruption. Someone grabbed the book and immediately started flipping through it, as a few more members of the cast and company gathered around. The book was opened to a chapter called "Fetish," underneath the title an illustration of a man with a large S shaved on the top of his head, his arms tied behind his back and his body chained to a pair of shining Doc Martens, which he was bending over in full child's pose to lick. The boots belonged to a muscled black man with high socks and a studded cock ring. The S man wasn't looking at the Doc Martens, but out, directly at the camera.

"Oh my God," came the refrain from the crowd now amassed around this book. Ironically, it was the furthest from God I had felt in some time.

With much giggling and pointing, the book was passed around and more illustrations were revealed. Eventually I got over my shell shock and joined in laughing, and we were proud to have come across such a find. We placed it on a shelf and deemed it an unofficial totem of our production. As a group, we decided it was ours, but deep down, I knew it would be mine.

Days went by. The book haunted every rehearsal and every performance. After the show closed, we broke down the set, and the minute I was alone, I stowed it in my backpack.

Learning to inhabit my queerness was less about pedagogy and more like Harry Potter discovering Parseltongue—surprised by his own fluency, lost to those who taught him his first language. Learning to inhabit my sexuality, however, was akin to

the experience of running through downtown Shanghai with a water-stained map, not knowing a word of Mandarin, and realizing someone has stolen both your wallet and iPhone. I felt lost, in perpetuity, or so I thought.

Back home, I read the entire book in one wild night, skimming through its alphabetical index of sex: "AIDS, Anus, Bars, Baths, Bisexuality . . ."; "Fisting, Foreskin, Frottage . . ."; "Phone Sex, Piercing . . ."; "Tricking, Types, Vanilla Sex, Water Sports, Wrestling." What I felt was not quite arousal or curiosity, but more like abject horror at the things I did not know.

The more I peeled through *The Joy of Gay Sex*, the further away I fell from the man I thought I had wanted to be. The book was a foreign, beautiful language. I paused over an illustration labeled "Fuck Buddies," an Adonis lying on the ground next to an empty condom wrapper, wearing nothing but a handkerchief tied around his neck. Lengths of rope wrap loosely around his body as he pinches the nipple of the man he has his legs around, a dark-mustached hombre donning a cowboy hat and boots. The cowboy beams down with the corniest smile as he grasps the blondie's penis with force, shooting semen a full two feet into the air. The look on the Adonis's face was seared into my memory, a look not of orgasmic pleasure, but bliss—a serenity I had never known.

As I finished the book, I felt isolated, ignorant. I shelved it on my nightstand and only ever picked it back up as a party trick to give guests a good laugh. I trekked through the year with that book on my nightstand. It was a retro, decorative wink, but also a shameful reminder.

It isn't until years later that I realize as I write: all this time, the book I thought had shamed me into demurity in actuality ushered me (okay, shoved me) into a clumsy sexual awakening. That year was the year I first "Bottomed," the year I first went to a "Bar," the year I first tried "Dirty Talk," "Doggy Style," "Fetish Play," and the year I had my first "Fuck Buddy." It was the year I first experimented with "Lubricants" and "Massages," with "Mirrors," "Phone Sex," "Role-Playing," and "Toys." It was the year I first "Sat" on someone's face and "Spanked" someone, and it was the year I nabbed my first "Trade."

I had never considered myself a sexual person, but as it turned out, consideration had little to do with it. My libido was a pulsing force inside me, dormant like the very book I found at the bottom of that props box. And though reading it was a slow unlearning of the things that held me back, and a relearning of the things my own body was able to do, the feeling of humiliation that had once run hot through me was replaced by a much different emotion—joy.

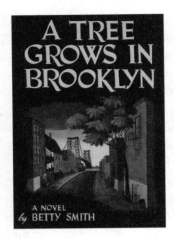

ON BETTY SMITH'S

A Tree Grows in Brooklyn

DANIELLE EVANS

The summer I was twenty, I moved to Iowa City to go to graduate school. I had applied months earlier with three short stories, two of which I'd written in the forty-eight hours before the postmark deadline, having just realized most of what I'd originally planned to send was no good. At midnight on New Year's Eve, my mother came downstairs with a glass of champagne and asked if I was sure this was a good idea.

I was not, but she proofread the new stories and told me I'd done it and drove me to the twenty-four-hour post office to mail my application, and a few months later there I was. I had a small paycheck and an apartment that was still being built when I arrived, meaning for a month I lived rent-free in a larger unit with other displaced tenants, including the reigning Miss Iowa. I had a great deal of confidence in my abilities and also a recurring nightmare in which I was summoned to the office and told gently that my admission was a mistake and I would have to go home.

I made friends mostly with black women who were attached to the university for other reasons. The first time I talked a friend into going to a workshop party, we drove through miles of cornfield to the farmhouse where a group of students lived, and were there only five minutes before she declared we needed to get back in the car and go home, because the occasion was a posthumous birthday party for Hunter S. Thompson and white people were shooting air rifles. I spent my twenty-first birthday at the Chili's at the mall in Iowa City's nearest suburb with a friend I saw as the intimidatingly glamorous older sister I'd always wanted. She had a wardrobe marked by dramatic draping, and gloriously picked-out hair, and drove a car with a *Wild Women Don't Get the Blues* bumper sticker, though she peeled it off the next year. "It turns out," she said, "that's not true."

• • •

My mother was my first audience. In high school I started reading books aloud to her. Before I got to college, this gave me my best preparation for what a workshop was—to read something, and then to step outside of your head and read it again, hearing it the way someone else would hear it. Betty Smith's *A Tree Grows in Brooklyn* was the first book I chose to share: I picked it when I got to the part where Francie's exiled Aunt Sissy puts an end to a teacher's humiliating bathroom break policy by inventing a cop husband and indirectly threatening her. Though not white, and not as long ago as the book's characters, my mother had grown up poor in New York City, too.

When my mother was five, a teacher sent her home from school for wearing pants. She waited hours in the rain because she wasn't allowed to cross the major Bronx street between the school and her apartment alone and the crossing guard was gone until school let out. A concerned elderly woman tried to walk her home, but she refused to leave with a stranger. The stranger managed to get her phone number and call my grandfather. He brought my mother home safely and had to be talked down from going to the school to "stomp that teacher," though my grandmother confessed later that she wished she'd let him go.

I loved in my mother telling that story what I loved in the book—the way a sentimental story doesn't have to be a cheap one, the way gentleness sometimes has to be fought for. I knew my mother loved the story of her rescue because the tenderness with which she was cared for then was not always present, the violence not always directed outward. In a life in which she'd so often been small with no one to stick up for her, it mattered the times someone had.

I thought my mother would love the book, and she did. Until she was actually dying and it turned out to be impossible to undo, she would quote it to reassure me when I asked what she was going to do about a problem that seemed insurmountable: "It takes a lot of doing to die."

. . .

Before I left for Iowa, my mother and I had a terrible fight. I can't remember what the fight was ostensibly about; I'm certain it was on some level actually about my leaving, and in some way a variation of the only fight we ever had: she thought I did not believe in things, or people, or her, enough, and I thought she had so much faith in things it bordered on reckless; we could see these things in each other only as a form of judgment and not as a love in which we overcompensated for each other's weaknesses. At some point in the shouting, someone walked out of the house and into the rain in her socks to end the argument. Sometimes I remember being the one who was so hurt she walked outside, and sometimes I remember waiting for my mother to come back, feeling annoyed and abandoned and worried. As much of my life as I spent angry at my mother for not acknowledging we were two different people, sometimes I also forget.

Where memory fails me, logic steps in. My mother never would have purposely dirtied a pair of socks. She would have relished the theatrics of putting on her sneakers before walking out the door, would have yelled something like, "Do you see how you are making me leave my own home?" The one who, once she was done, was out the door without a minute longer to think about it, who wouldn't even pause to put her shoes on: of course that was me.

. . .

My college and grad school years had been among the rockiest of my mother's life, a life that we all thought would eventually be back on the upswing, but as it turned out mostly put her through hell until she died of cancer just over a decade later. She wasn't sick then, but she was in the barely insured precarity that let her get to stage 4 with a liter of fluid in her lungs before knowing something was wrong. I had grown up with a great deal of cultural class privilege, but often little money; like a lot of first-generation middle-class people's, my mother's finances were without a safety net. I did not understand until I went to college what "paycheck to paycheck" meant, because I did not know that people outside of the obscenely rich had extra money just sitting in bank accounts. Increasingly, my mother viewed my every separation as a deliberate provocation, proof I was ashamed of her. I was not, but I was wrestling with the reality that at the first time in my emotional life that it occurred to me it was not my job to keep my mother alive, the conditions of her actual life seemed to suggest that someone was going to have to.

"I can still drive you to Iowa, but I guess you don't even want me there," she said, but of course I did, and of course she drove.

...

I came back to *A Tree Grows in Brooklyn* the year I moved to Iowa, without any of the baggage I would bring to it later. I would eventually feel more romantic about graduate school, but I believed then I was in the state of Iowa to collect my check and write a book. I didn't know yet that it was out of taste then for a book to be girly or sentimental or perceived as juvenile, let alone all three. I would learn to love some of the contemporary canon, but I'd been brought to grad school by books like *Sassafrass, Cypress & Indigo* and *Brown Girl, Brownstones*. I'd become okay with the concept of Iowa because ZZ Packer had gone there; I was clueless about what legacies I was supposed to value more. It would not be the first time I was saved by my own obliviousness.

There are things in the book that don't hold up—its affection for diversity can't save all of its language about race—but Smith writes beautifully and sharply about class, about how clearly you can see power from below and how little you can do about it, how often Francie is punished for being her own best advocate, things I recognized from having been a little black girl.

I needed that book—I needed its reminder that there is still loss in what feels like escape. I needed its reassurance that children should be taught to believe in things and also to learn to stop, that a loss of faith can be adulthood and not betrayal. I had forgotten for years the order of the ending of *A Tree Grows in Brooklyn*. I remembered there was a fight about Francie's future and a reconciliation and a time her mother comforts her after a heartbreak. But I had forgotten that after the reconciliation comes the line "In their secret hearts, each knew that it wasn't all right and would never be all right between them again," and that the moment when Francie's mother comforts her comes even later still. I had forgotten the lesson in the order of operations: how long things can keep going after an irreversible break, how much you can still need a mother after you've left to become yourself.

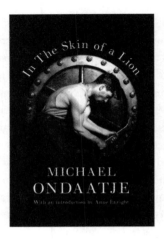

ON MICHAEL ONDAATJE'S

In the Skin of a Lion

MATTHEW SPECKTOR

I'd figured it out. I was going to write *novels*. The year was 1987, and I was a few months away from graduating college, staring down the barrel of my future. This dismayingly general intention was as detailed as my thinking got—to this day, I'm not sure it's ever been much more so—but I wasn't so dumb that I didn't immediately ask the question *Now what?* The idea of becoming a novelist seemed both choate and impossible, as if I'd decided to be a mountaineer, or to travel to Pennsylvania by sea. I hadn't the faintest idea what *kind* of novel I would write, how I would find a subject, or if my sputtering, underconfident imagination, so prone to hesitations and blocks, would even allow me to complete such a mission. I suspected that I had—maybe—some puny amount of talent, and a seemingly inexhaustible stubbornness. If I could only just figure out what a novel *was*.

With this small stumbling block in mind, I read Henry James, Virginia Woolf, Toni Morrison. I read Graham Swift, Timothy Mo, Nadine Gordimer. These writers lit me up more than all the shitty drugs in Western Massachusetts ever could, but not one of them ever suggested to me how it could be done. Their books seemed cuneiform; even the most contemporary were steeped in an aesthetic and experiential knowledge so seemingly unavailable to me that they may as well have been stone tablets. I was just a kid from Los Angeles. How the hell was I supposed to do *that*?

Enter Michael Ondaatje's *In the Skin of a Lion*. I don't even remember how I found it. Browsing the stacks of a bookstore on the Smith College campus, or elsewhere in homogeneously affable Pioneer Valley, I must have been drawn to the cover; the first American edition depicts two bodies, drawn in the voluptuous style of Picasso's neoclassical nudes. I would have flipped it open and seen an epigraph from John Berger, whom I loved: *Never again will a single story be told as though it's the only one.* This was enough to spur my purchase of a book by a writer I'd never heard of. Few Americans at that time had. I took it home, flopped on my thrift store couch in my rented off-campus apartment, and started reading. I didn't expect much in the way of clarification. I assumed I'd finish the book even more flummoxed than I was when I began. Such was the way, in those days: each novel seemed a more impossible magic trick than the last. I certainly didn't expect my reading life—or my *real* life—to change.

Never again will a single story be told as though it's the only one. A decade later, this epigraph would be recycled by Arundhati Roy, but at the time even this struck me as crucial, an indication (borne out by the book itself) that a novel could be a *fragment*, composed of other fragments, rather than a monolith. Ondaatje's novel is kaleidoscopic and dreamlike. Its earthy, raw prose sets forth such imagistic peculiarities as a nun falling off a bridge, a man escaping from prison by painting himself the same sky blue as the prison's roof, and an explosives expert strolling wearily through a tunnel dug beneath the floor of Lake Ontario. Set in Toronto, in the 1930s, the book possesses a plot—a millionaire named Ambrose Small disappears, and the protagonist, Patrick, is one of many hired to find him—but, true to its epigraph, remains largely uninterested in it, preferring to spiral off into the life of a thief named Caravaggio, a woman named Clara Dickens, another, seemingly past-less, woman named Alice Gull. Plot, which had never seemed to me so very important—it wasn't enough to compel me, all by itself—takes something other than a back seat here. It is a complementary piece. "The first sentence of every novel should be: 'Trust me, this will take time, but there is order here, very faint, very human,'" the book's narrator remarks at one point. It was this sense of drift, of waywardness-without-total-disorder, that lured me.

Trust me, this will take time. It strikes me, all these years later, that what I was really looking for was license to get lost. The driftiness of the novel—"Meander, if you want to get to town"—was itself just what I needed, the thing every twentysomething (writer or otherwise) needs; a freedom not even so much to fuck up as to fuck *off* and do nothing. I was an anxious young adult (is there another kind?), bent on becoming something for which there was no template; or maybe I was just a kid who hated templates to begin with, and saw, in Ondaatje's thrillingly polyglot assemblage, a model for becoming fully human without ever having to picture myself whole.

There are other audacities—a first-person speaker who tears the veil of the novel's omniscient-third only occasionally, as if there *only* to violate the illusion of authorial neutrality; an energetic dirtiness (characters spit cum into each other's mouths, fuck in a chaos of smashing crockery); an unapologetic leftism that seems to propose blowing up the rich—but in the end, I kept returning to this: "*Demarcation . . . That is all we need to remember*." "All these fragments of memory . . . so we can retreat from the grand story and stumble accidentally upon a luxury . . . those few pages in a book we go back and forth over." A mixture of languor and furious, romantic vitality. Also things I needed at that age, and at every other.

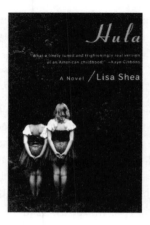

ON LISA SHEA'S

Hula

KAREN SHEPARD

The epigraph of Lisa Shea's celebrated, but now neglected, first and only novel is from a Jorie Graham poem: "Nothing will catch you. / Nothing will let you go."

It's the perfect introduction to the slim volume that follows. "Nothing will catch you": Is that comfort or torment? "Nothing will let you go": Is that to be celebrated or lamented? A source of solace or fear? *Hula* concerns itself with two sisters in Virginia. The younger one describes the summers of 1964 and '65 with her older sister, her largely absent mother, her tormented father. Most of the novel takes place in the family's backyard, where the boundaries between the civilized and the wild, the desired and the feared, the real and the imagined are never clear. It's the kind of book that reminds us—in a stunningly economical 155 pages—of the unknown's

emotional possibilities for children even as it depicts its often terrible consequences.

I didn't read *Hula* until shortly after it came out in 1994, when I was nearly thirty, but it articulated so much of what I had felt, but not known how to say, about the pitfalls and possibilities of childhood.

I am the only child of two pretty odd parents: a Russian Jewish father who veered between narcissism and more extreme narcissism, and a Chinese mother whose prime parenting strategy seemed to be to teach her daughter not to need a mother. Though they divorced when I was three, our family's world felt hermetically sealed and inevitable. Until I came to understand how other families worked, I didn't know that most five-year-olds growing up in Manhattan did not take public transportation to school by themselves. I didn't know that most fathers did not routinely tell their daughters' friends, or waitresses, or passing strangers about the sexual abuse he had experienced as a child growing up in an orphanage. "You think *you've* suffered?" he would say before reminding me, yet again, of what had been done to him. I didn't know that most mothers did not buy their daughters a child-sized set of CorningWare to indicate that cooking meals for herself was now the child's responsibility. And yet, so much of their strangeness *offered* possibilities, and *was* loving: they also created a world filled with love and opportunity, extraordinary experiences, and many, many books.

Most of the books I read then were about obstacles overcome or not: triumph or tragedy. *Hula* is all about both, ambiguity, simultaneous conflicting feelings, and *that's* what childhood had felt like to me. What a gift it would've been to have had that mirrored in words. By another child.

One of the challenges of writing from a child's point of view is the problem of rendering the variety and depths of a child's emotional understanding despite the limitations of her descriptive abilities. *Hula's* unnamed narrator offers us almost no introspection at all. In its place, she gives us what children can: sharp and evocative perceptions stripped of everything nonessential, filled with a nonjudgmental immediacy about the mysterious and scary and enchanting world. She does not, cannot, tell us what all these perceptions mean. That's up to us, her only audience. We're the ones responsible for the most sustained attention she receives.

The book at first seems structured straightforwardly: there are chapter titles, sectioned titles within those chapters, dates, a prologue, and an epilogue. But in terms of the content within that frame of structural order, disorder reigns, producing in the reader a version of the tension the narrator herself is feeling. I remember that tension so clearly from my own childhood: *This* looks *safe and ordered; why doesn't it feel safe and ordered?*

A lot of the disorder derives from the book's insistence that there *are* no clear categories of good and bad. Obviously, the sisters are in many ways at the whim of their parents' moods and desires, so they are each other's solace in a world controlled by grown-ups, but they're also contributing to the dangers of their world.

Their desires are often in conflict, and they often make things worse for each other and for their parents. A young child, willing and able to manipulate her world? *That* was a narrator I could identify with.

I suggest to my writing students that they're trying to identify and explore those aspects of their fictional interests that give rise to conflicting feelings in the reader. If literature allows us to step outside the world we know and then returns us to the familiar, rearranged in some small way, it's those conflicting feelings that are going to get us there. Every aspect of *Hula* gives rise to conflicting feelings in me. Reading it is like standing on the tip of a small iceberg and being told to balance.

It's a book that lays out in clear ways why, despite its obvious potential pitfalls, so many writers return to childhood in their work. Why so many writers find childhood a strange and mysterious place. Its ambiguity is always a useful place for literature to settle itself: a place of lush imagination and stark fears. Where the strange becomes the everyday, and the routine oddly disorienting.

The writer Steven Millhauser has said, "I want fiction to exhilarate me, to unbind my eyes, to murder and resurrect me, to harm me in some fruitful way."

I think of this when I think of how our childhoods continue to work on us. I think of this when I read *Hula* and how it continues, year after year, to work on me. "Nothing will catch you. / Nothing will let you go." Equal parts murder and resurrection. Lucky us.

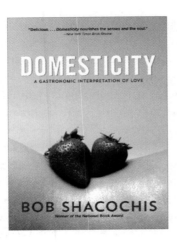

"Delicious. . . . Domesticity nourishes the senses and the soul."
—New York Times Book Review

DOMESTICITY
A GASTRONOMIC INTERPRETATION OF LOVE

BOB SHACOCHIS
Winner of the National Book Award

ON BOB SHACOCHIS'S

Domesticity: A Gastronomic Interpretation of Love

MANUEL GONZALES

Carrie and I took the same Spanish literature class, as did a friend of mine, Jon, who was—and probably still is—way handsomer than me, but for whatever reason, Carrie invited me and not Handsome Jon to go to the lake with her, which I did because I harbored a near-debilitating crush on her. We went out on her parents' boat and drank her parents' Dos Equis (which, while not my first beer, was perhaps my second), and on the drive home from the lake, we sat in the back seat of her friend's car and she laid her head in my lap as I stroked her hair, and then after that, we hung out more and we kissed a couple of times and then one night she invited me to her apartment, where we made dinner together, and she asked me to handle the chicken because

raw chicken grossed her out, and then as I was leaving, she gave me an enormous bottle of Jose Cuervo Gold because she was swearing off tequila—"You know how it is" (I didn't)—and did I want it, and I told her sure, I knew exactly what to do with it, and I detoured to the grocery store, bought some supplies, and when I got home, I poured the tequila over a pan full of raw chicken breasts. Then I squeezed some fresh limes over it, added some salt, some coriander, some jalapeño peppers, garlic, and then slid it into the fridge to sit for twenty-four hours.

This was not my life. This was some strange liminal space between one life, in which I ate Chef Boyardee Beef Ravioli straight from the can (cold), ate in one sitting entire grocery store apple pies, hadn't had sex, didn't really drink, watched (wearing just my underwear?) a lot of *The Dukes of Hazzard* before going to class or work, and this other life, which was shrouded in mystery, but so far included older, wiser friends and, apparently, free bottles of liquor, lake adventures with Carrie, and the book *Domesticity*, by Bob Shacochis.

Domesticity is a collection of essays Shacochis wrote as an ad hoc food columnist for GQ about "relationships and food and dogs, about the gastronomic aesthetic and love and love's language, about friendship and laughter and anger and the distances that often separate us, about cooking and snobs and sorrow and writing and secrets, and about who's going to do the dishes." Published in 1994, it must not have sold too well because shortly thereafter I found the hardcover used. I remember reading the introduction in the bookstore and discovering in Shacochis a voice I hadn't yet encountered in a book of essays—lightly brash and irreverent, funny and taking a firm stand in the face of self-seriousness, when it felt like, for all my years as an English major, all I knew were writers who took themselves too seriously—so I bought it, and, after I read it, I started buying more (used) copies of it to give to people as last-minute, poorly presented gifts.

Around this same time, I discovered writing, moved out of the dorms and into my own apartment, and first tried my hand at cooking.

My mother has always been an excellent cook, in that what she cooks regularly she cooks exceedingly well. *Fideo* (a Mexican noodle dish), chicken mole, pork chops fried in their own fat and then simmered for an hour in homemade salsa, the meat spicy and crispy and tender and then folded into fresh, warm flour tortillas. Tamales, buñuelos (fried flour tortillas sprinkled with cinnamon sugar and eaten for good luck on New Year's Day), and *capirotada*, a Mexican bread pudding that is an acquired taste (one neither my wife nor my kids have acquired). And I imagined, having been with her my whole life, having eaten her food and, from some distance, watched her make it, I could also cook those things.

I could not.

I tried. I just didn't understand how my mother cooked. She is the type of cook who doesn't measure, who cooks based on muscle memory, based on experience, who made her mistakes early and learned from them. She throws ingredients together and makes, magically, meals. When I tried the same, I simply made a mess. I need recipes, I told her. I can't cook without recipes. Who doesn't use recipes when they cook?

So I turned to *Domesticity*.

Shacochis admits in the introduction to his book that he was no food writer when he was tapped by GQ, and not being a food writer, he writes about food in a way I hadn't realized possible. Funny and masculine, his essays on food and his life with his partner—only ever referred to as Miss F.—made food sexy and powerful and, in hindsight, not a little ridiculous. He refers, in an essay on gardening, to the "libidinal swell and fold" of bell peppers and in an essay against aphrodisiacs (he's a skeptic), ends his argument with the confession that he will "admit to an appreciation of the bawdy, pampering decadence [aphrodisiacs] engender, the gastro-sexual trail that leads to those shimmering, phosphorescent erotic dinners choreographed by soon-to-be lovers." The audacity of that sentence, and that Shacochis uses it to describe food, thrilled me. (It still kind of does.)

To be fair to my younger self, I had not yet discovered MFK Fisher's story "I Was Really Very Hungry," or her collections *The Gastronomical Me* or *How to Cook a Wolf*. Nor had I discovered Ludwig Bemelman's fastidious and charming *La Bonne Table*, A. J. Liebling, or Calvin Trillin. It would be five years before Anthony Bourdain wrote his seminal essay, "Don't Eat Before

Reading This," and twelve more years before Bill Buford would write *Heat.* I could have filled a large-sized planet with all the things I had, at twenty, yet to discover about food and about writing and about sex, and Shacochis introduced me to a new way of thinking about all three.

And so for a short and painfully embarrassing time Shacochis became my guru in life and love, food and romance, and it was to Shacochis I turned after Carrie and I kissed good night, after she handed me that huge bottle of Jose Cuervo Gold. It was his recipe for chicken margarita that I thought of on my way home. I would transform her tequila into a delicious meal. She would see me not just as goofy and kind of cute but as stalwart and strong, a man who could cook for his woman.

Tequila would become food would become love.

The thing about the recipes in *Domesticity*—all the recipes, for food and for relationships—is that they assume a certain level of experience (in the kitchen and the bedroom) and a certain kind of audience (1990s GQ, to be exact). I possessed neither the experience nor, thankfully, the attitude.

All of which is to say: the recipe was for a marinade.

Unbeknownst to me, you were supposed to grill the chicken, not serve it raw under the false assumption that the acids in the lime juice and the alcohol in the tequila would "cook" the chicken for you. You might think that pulling that chicken out of the refrigerator, ghostly white and wet in its pan of tequila and juice, thinking it was ready to serve, was my biggest mistake, or that assuring my friends, No, no, the juices cooked the chicken, or proudly telling Carrie, Yeah, I used all that tequila on this one recipe, or cutting into the first rubbery breast to prove to everyone it would be cooked through was where I made my greatest mistake. But really, the mistake came earlier, came with thinking that all I needed was a recipe, that with a recipe, everything would work out just fine.

Sometime in the past ten years, I got rid of my copy of *Domesticity*, gave it away or sold it. As I grew older, gained more experience in food and writing and love, I found myself turning to it less and less and then not at all. In the twenty or so years since I first picked up *Domesticity*, I've collected better cookbooks for those few times when I need or want a recipe—Julia Child, Madhur Jaffrey, Rose Levy Beranbaum, Joshua McFadden. But in most cases these days, like my mother, I wade into the kitchen without a recipe, with only memory and experience to guide me.

James Tate

THE COW AND THE BUTTERFLIES

I visited my friend Rod, who was in jail, I didn't really know what for. "Rod," I said, "what are you in for? I don't really know what they got you for." "Oh, it was nothing, just screwing a cow," he said. "What in the world would make you do a thing like that," I said. "I was lonely," he said. "But still . . ." I said. "I know, it sounds like a pretty sick thing to do but you'd have to put yourself in my shoes. I hadn't seen a woman in over a year," he said. "Where were you?" I said. "On an island. It was a dairy farm," he said. "Where was that?" I said. "In Iceland," he said. "And what were you doing there?" I said. "I was working," he said. "Still, it seems like a very odd thing to do," I said. "It was. I regret it. I must have been crazy to do a thing like that," he said. "I guess so," I said. When I got home I visited his mother, who was in a nursing home. She asked about her son and I said he was doing just fine. Then we talked about her life there. She said she missed her cat most of all. He used to wake her in the morning and now she forgets to get up altogether. But her keepers make sure she gets her exercise. And the food isn't too bad. She likes the pudding they serve. She said I should visit her daughter some time. She lives on Long Island. I said I would if she would give me her address. She did, and the next week I went there. Marjorie was surprised to see me. She lived alone in a little cottage. She served me tea and soon we were talking away. She wanted to know all about Rod and I lied again. I said he was just fine. Then we talked about her life. She worked as a waitress in a small café in the center of her small town. She made just enough money to get by. She had

no friends to speak of, but the more we talked I got to be very fond of her,
and by the time we said goodbye I thought I might be in love with her. We met
again the next day when she got out of work and I was swooning in her presence.
We kissed and that was it, I fell head over heels for her. She said, "I
barely know you." I said, "That's all right, you will." And by the end of that
night, we were definitely in love, like two birds. Or two butterflies caught
in the wind, not knowing where they were going. Just happy to be anywhere
at all.

SECOND CHILDHOOD

Jody and I were sitting in the living room. I said, "You know, we
haven't played miniature golf in twenty years." She said, "So what? I
haven't had a popsicle in thirty years, and I'm still going." I said,
"Yeah, and I haven't been to a zoo in God knows how long and I'm alright
with that." "I haven't been bowling in ages," she said. "I haven't
been to a baseball game since I can remember," I said. "What are we
going to do?" she said. "It seems we're busy all the time," I said.
"But what are we doing? All the things we used to love have disappeared,"
she said. "They're replaced by other things. The second half of our lives
is just different," I said. "I think I liked the first half better,"
she said. "Don't say that. We're more productive now, I think," I said.
Jody got up and looked out the window. "We're slowing down, like we're preparing
for death," she said. "You're crazy. I'm working harder than ever
before," I said. "Okay, let's drop the subject. We disagree, is that
so bad?" she said. "What's for supper?" I said. "I haven't thought that far
ahead. I guess I should," she said. "Let's go to the baseball game. We
haven't been in forever. We can get a hot dog there. What do you say? It
will be fun," I said. "Okay, it will certainly be different," she said.
So, around six o'clock, we drove down to the stadium, bought our tickets,
and found our seats. It was exciting. When the game started I felt a
real childish rush, and I think Jody did too. Around the third inning we hailed
the hot dog man and got our meal. I felt like a kid sitting there watching
the game and eating our hot dogs. Our team was ahead, 4 to 3. Then, in the

bottom of the seventh, a ball was hit foul in our direction, and Jody was hit
in the head. She was knocked out and an ambulance was called. I rode
in the back with her to the hospital, holding her hand, which was limp.
When they pulled her into the operating room they told me to stay outside.
After about a half an hour the doctor came out to tell me she was dead.
I broke down crying and couldn't stop. A nurse came out to hold me.
I thought, this is how we relive our youth.

O JOSEPHINA

Our little baby, Joseph, was the most precious thing in the world. We took turns feeding him and putting him to bed. Alice couldn't believe how we had produced him. She thought it was a case of divine intervention. She even told the neighbors that. They thought she was either joking or just plain crazy. When he got to be two years old he could talk and walk. He ran around the house like a maniac, and when he wanted to eat he said, "I'm hungry. I want something now. If you don't give it to me I'll kill you." We thought that was the cutest thing in the world. When he was five he started to tear the house down. First it was the drapes in the living room, then he started to kick in the walls of his bedroom. We had to tie him up in ropes to put him to sleep. We had to get him a psychiatrist, who said he was just fine, just a little frustrated that he was the only kid in the household. We tried to have another baby, but it was too late. So we pretended we had another child, which confused Joseph all the more. We set the table for four and pretended to talk to our daughter, whom we called Josephina. Joseph didn't like this at all. In fact, we favored Josephina. We talked to her all the time at dinner. Joseph was sad. He didn't throw things or break them. He just stared into his mashed potatoes as if he wished they and he would disappear. When he entered high school he said he had a sister. Students asked him about her. He said she was very pretty and smart. The boys wanted to meet her. He said she went to a private school. Joseph was a good student and very well-behaved. When he started to date he got very frustrated. He couldn't talk to us at all at the dinner table. His grades started to drop and he was kicked off

the soccer team. He got more and more inward as time went by. He said he
missed Josephina. He drew pictures of her in his room. It's what we thought
she looked like, too. Then one day Joseph didn't come home from school.
We were worried sick. By nightfall we notified the police. A week went by, then
a month. Joseph was gone. We talked to all the kids at his school. Finally,
one girl told us he had run away with his sister. They were in love with
each other and planned to get married, somewhere in Nevada, where it was legal.

The Year in Letters

Books to go down, please.

The dispatch near the front entrance would call out the five words—almost a sentence, amounting to a request—until one of the ground-floor staff would reluctantly emerge from the stacks and volunteer to escort to the basement the top-heavy young customer and all the books he had brought to sell to The Strand. Perhaps the floor clerks waited to see if he was cute. I sometimes worried so when my presence was announced a second time.

By 1999 the side hustle was very much a constituent part of the New York publishing industry. I once carried three USPS cartons of review copies of new books on the N down from the Times Square offices of Salon dot com to the store at Broadway and Twelfth and, even after splitting it with my boss, cleared more than two hundred dollars. Later that year, working for FSG, assistants like me had to be more surreptitious, but a full backpack brought forty to sixty bucks routinely. Salaries were famously

Brian Blanchfield

low in publishing—I think I made $19,000 there that first year—so to supplement was necessary. The grift was grist for the mill, like a White House leak to the press: officially chastened and systemically encouraged. I suppose the wannabe literati felt it was great fortune to come across a copy of Sontag's *In America* a month before it published, and good buzz counted on it.

It was an era when heroin users and publishing types were not mutually exclusive sets, so plenty of folks walked directly east from The Strand to Alphabet City. That was not my itch, but I smelled the yeasty need on my compatriots strumming the academic title bins beside the buyer downstairs—it's where and when I got my copies of *Hart Crane and the Homosexual Text* and *How the World Became a Stage* and *This Sex Which Is Not One*. Up on the ground floor, I found I glazed over in Literature, which was only fiction, though I liked to watch the store's most veteran employee preside there: the captain of New York's bookish gays—*Ben M.* it said on his lanyard—looking over his glasses at the team's reserved reserves pacing the aisles. My section was Letters.

1999 was the end of Letters as a literary category. What was it anyway? Short (or butch) for Belles-Lettres—that much I knew. Why so effete a term for—what—certain sorts of nonfiction: essays, autobiography, actual letters, commentary, poetics, diaries, occasional prose? Here's where I bought *Longer Views* and *A Balthus Notebook* and *Eros the Bittersweet* and the masochistic correspondence of Lord Alfred Douglas with George Bernard Shaw. To browse there felt both precocious and belated: queer. It's where all the best books were overlooked, and more to the point, one understood one's company in the aisle. Standing, swaying, there is no better feeling than a reader's soft plummet into interiority ruptured by the brush past or footstool squeak of a boy pretending not to notice the thrum of your returned attention, holding *Etruscan Places* open with a finger.

If I'm making the book world sound a bit noir or louche, well, it was the year of publishing's Dawn Powell revival. Her protagonists were, in a sense, fifty-years-earlier versions of me then, literary youths from the provinces learning the hard way the agility required to avoid being exploited by the tastemakers and media industry heavies. If I was therefore the target audience of Gore Vidal's reintroduction of Powell's work, it was also why in the end I didn't care for it, even as my way in the world was no doubt derivative of hers, particularly the night walks I took after work before heading to Brooklyn. On Little West Twelfth that year I would hope to spot like an ornithologist Quentin Crisp at his corner window table of Rio Mar. The red light of the restaurant still suffuses my last image of him, and the high frill of his blouse. It would've been a few blocks east on West Fourth that Marc Jacobs himself burst from Marc by Marc Jacobs to ask me, passing, where I'd found my soft black leather flight cap with white cotton flocking. The chin straps dangled at my bony jaw when I turned. I'd bought it that winter at the Harley Davidson store in Swannanoa, North Carolina. Women's rack. His crisp return into the glass cube storefront was, as I recall, wordless. Marc into Marc.

Buy why mock that tautology? Isn't to have made it to be able to say, I am what I am? And wasn't I instead browsing impressions I might make, types of gay to be? Trade, academic. In your youth, particularly in New York, your subjectivity can be wholly scripted by others' interest or disdain. Which is why, as many people besides Dawn Powell have said, it can be stunting to remain there.

Who was I walking, reviewing all my new publishing terms in my empty head: Briticism, stet, back matter, recto. We had a lame little very-inside joke at work; some of us had initials that corresponded to typesetting code. I worked for En Dash and Printer's Error. They called me Bad Break.

Do you know the moment in *Inferno* when Eileen Myles writes about young Eileen's glimpse of self-actualization? It's my go-to for acute reminder that selfhood and capitalism are antagonists. About awakening to poetry, she describes stumbling into an understanding: Is what I do a thing I can be? In the summer of 1999 I began dating a friend of hers, Douglas, who was the first person I knew who burned with that self-understanding. For most of the four years we were together he refused on principle to earn money outside of writing. And since he was a transgressive novelist published by small presses it meant he lived on little other than principle. I'd come home from work to find him and his books on my bed. *The Compassion Protocol. I Love Dick. Allan Stein.* Characters were named the author's name or by only one initial or not at all—in Douglas's writing too. He was working on a kind of hustler's journal. No one said life writing, no one said autofiction: *Écriture* it felt funny to call it, but you could, then. He wrote me in.

We liked to tell the story of how we met. He was working his final days, it turned out, at a community bookstore, Community Bookstore. We crushed on each other, and my third or fourth time in the store, I found a way to talk to him. I was in the Ps without a plan, and pulled *The Golden Spur*, Powell's last book, their only copy. I didn't want it. But it was missing its first sixteen pages, a unit I had recently learned to call a *signature*. The first signature had come unglued from the spine, in all the hurry to reprint I suppose. When he was alone at the register, I brought it up, spread it open, and indicated. He'd have to take my name and number and call me when they got a new one in. He saw it was clever of me. At home I waited for the call, and more than a week later, someone told me it had come in. By then I knew his first name and asked for it. He'd been fired—he could be a little surly. Did I want the book? Well. I walked over glumly. They rang it up, bagged it. Outside, on a hunch, I opened it. In the gully before page 17, on a tiny slip of paper, Douglas had written, middle initial and all, his name. It arced downward as they say is customary in depressives. And on the other side, his number, which I took to the nearest phone booth. I didn't even practice what to say. 🛡

MEMORY.

the whole morning swallowed
by audio

of the newly dead poet
reading the long dead poet's
still living poems

streaming out into the air
like a prayer passed down
in code

this set behind a scroll
of men fucking in fifteen
second loops

as if pleasure too
were incremental, fragmented
& unkillable

as if to produce nothing

elsewhere on my computer
photos of men

i no longer speak to
in various stages of intimate

undress. on occasion
i resurrect one's mouth

on my neck just before
he disappears again.

on the screen a man's inside
another in a wood somewhere
cold

the bttm grips a tree as if
it might root him

both making noise outside
language

while Lucie lists the names
of the many poets

who've shot themselves
in the heart

Brenda Hillman

(PEOPLE'S EMOTIONS IN ONE CITY BLOCK)

half-shame, mild joy at hope for food, gray fear of
the walk-through monument, partial love of some humans,
cold resentment at bank options, extra pride at skin color, delight
at witnessing the number heap, shame times dread needing help,
2 quasi-firm hesitations, disgust at fried eagle, half-joy
at pride after sex, deep grief plus middle deep grief, twice
terror at law enforcement, half-worry for someone not the right one,
mild anxiety about pigeons, light interest in flower salads, oblivion
about skin color, eager reckoning at the gallery, mysterious relief
about 3s, white numbness at doorway sleepers, swell of allowable rage,
craving for flower salads, semi-pride after sex, love of fire enforcement,
blue terror at the bank options, craving for fried eagle, post-fear
of the number heap, furious regret at auto-correct, sweetness
of the drug in the dream, pure love of the right one, rage
at the change of schedule, dark love of hope for sex, shallow wit
plus shame, dark love of trees & birds, fear of minutes, regard for
spines & thumbs, relief for the sick one, hesitant fear before joy

for MR

The Furnace Room

J. Jezewska Stevens

For his seventieth birthday, my neighbor hosts a little party. He lives one rowhouse down. The chatter drifts politely through the wall into my room, where I am in bed, reading a magazine special on nuclear war. Had he invited me to his birthday, perhaps I would not be so in love with my neighbor as I am now. On the other side of the wall, there are sure to be any number of interesting men, or at least one or two. It's possible we might hit it off. The wall persists, however. Quite structurally sound. And I am in bed, with the bombs.

I cannot account for this attraction to my neighbor. He is nearly thirty years my senior, not particularly handsome, and lately my primary response to humankind could be best captured by disgust. The other day I watched a young man kick his dog and did nothing. I am distressed by the sight of my own trash, piled on the curb. It is so upsetting I've stopped throwing things out, and yet despite the steady accretion (newspapers, plastic wrap, jars), I cannot shake the sense that life proceeds not by accumulation but according to the logic of radioactive decay—going, going, never quite gone.

I turn in my bed, look as if through the wall.

There are good days. These should be mentioned, for accuracy's sake. I look forward, for example, to my monthly magazine. On the evenings when it arrives, on the first of the month, or sometimes just before, I take it upstairs and lock the door. Turn off the phone. Get into bed, by the lamp. It is a sacred time. I dream the news. Then, in the morning, I restore the phone. I brew coffee in the miniature pot. I teach my students scales, arpeggios. Adjust sharps and flats. Occasionally, I editorialize: I prefer the flats. The furnace goes out, the water runs cold, I wash my hair in the sink. Each day of my life unfolds according to its usual routines, and sometimes I'd like nothing more than to disappear, if only for a change of pace. That's where the magazine comes in. It lends perspective, establishes distance, throws life into relief. Too effectively, perhaps. This afternoon, for instance, I feel so distant from my routines I can hardly exist in any world at all. The metronome resounds in frantic knocks. Once more, I say, as my first student struggles through a progression of major chords. My mind is adrift, like a Volkswagen at sea, in the remarkable nuclear news I consumed the night before. I see the warheads waiting in underground silos, standing stiffly on their skirts. My own apartment, raw. I see my neighbor's face. What is he doing at this hour, I wonder, on the other side of the wall? I push this thought aside, reset the metronome. Again. My student begins to cry.

I used to be a very coveted teacher. An international soloist. Things changed. Sometimes I think the talent must have fled the city, or else promising young people don't choose to play the cello anymore. When my tearful pupil departs, she is replaced by an awkward boy with chiseled knees and hopeless wrists, a boy so thin that when he sits he seems to unhinge himself around the instrument like a second folding chair. Suzuki on the stand. The same notes that troubled him before trouble him again. Measures collapse in glassy silence and breathy twangs—and not in a positive way. Very good, I say. I interrupt a painful glissando to ask, Tell me, are you doing nuclear drills in school these days? He looks at me blankly, fingers flapping in fourth position in search of a harmonic that he will never find. For a moment he seems to think a nuclear drill is something Suzuki might ask him to perform. He glances at the music. I don't think so? I nod. Well, practice makes perfect, I say, and tap my pencil on the stand.

It was like dating a slightly more talented version of myself.

I was with someone once. A long time ago. He played the cello, too. It was like dating a slightly more talented version of myself. And therefore doomed. Most relationships are, I assume. People pass like clouds. Though sometimes I still slip into small reveries of hope. After the last student leaves, in a magazine not so different from my favorite monthly in content or in tone, I like to read the classifieds. I make myself a sandwich, fashion a plate out of the centerfold. The publication is renowned for its in-depth analysis of the global situation, which is that the whole world resonates

PREVIOUS PAGE: H. ARMSTRONG ROBERTS / CLASSICSTOCK / ALAMY STOCK PHOTO

with an evil hum. I watch the sky, expecting drones, but it is only traffic, the radiator, the furnace, the fridge—the other day the freezer began to growl. The sandwich takes on the newsprint, tainted. Who could eat it? The thought of throwing it away makes me equally sick. Instead I flip straight past the award-winning polemics to the classifieds: *82-year-old man seeks Mandarin-speaking partner to accompany him to films. 64-year-old woman, attractive, shy, well-spoken, seeks romantic companion interested in reading & discussing* À la recherche du temps perdu *(in French)*. Are they optimistic or desperate, these ads? It's hard to say. Though on nights when the silence of my apartment seems ready to erupt, I have gone so far as to settle at the secretary and uncap a pen. I sit for a long while with an index card. *Midforties ex-cellist seeks older, intelligent man w/decent pitch to share pint of shrimp fried rice & who preferably lives on block*. This too seems doomed. My neighbor, after all, lives in the building adjacent mine. The thing to do is knock. And anyway I tend to over-parameterize.

> The bones in my wrists come alive with hidden nerves. It hurts.

On Tuesday, no one is thinking about nuclear bombs. Outside, children are dressed in neon vests and linked together with yellow tape. The teacher unbuckles them onto the green, where they flash across the park like signal flares.

Tuesdays are my day off. No students come, and I rise early to visit Olaf, my acupuncturist, who has attended to my arthritis for many years. His office is a mile east, in one of those old New York buildings that looks to have once been a bank and is now given over to the seedier self-employed. Steam heat. Exposed pipes. Lots of LLCs devoted to the estates of the deceased. The halls tunnel every which way, ending in obscure suites where doctors and dentists and day cares wait. On the seventh floor, I open a coat closet and out falls a lamp.

I am not in love with New York. I think of moving. Sometimes I wish I lived in the woods, in the dead center of a pine and maple forest, which would explode in autumn: a cabin surrounded by a flame of foliage. No one would think to aim a nuclear warhead there. What a waste it would be! Out in the woods, the greater risk is oneself. My father was a hunter, and once he fell from a tree stand and broke his leg, collapsed a lung. He dragged himself the whole way back to use the phone. How lucky you are, people say. You can't move, you'd lose the rent control. It's true. Still, one can dream. A few years ago, I applied to join the convent. It seemed to me so separate and self-contained, custodian to purity. No trash goes in or out of a nunnery, and the same must go for drones—there is something impenetrable, I imagine, about abbey walls. The nuns are more selective these days, however, they won't accept you if you're deep in debt, if you seem too lonely or without recourse. The order, they emphasize, is no last resort. I was too old, they said, and yet still young. Also not particularly religious. I have always felt a little older than I am. I've had arthritis since age sixteen. Every night, for thirty years, I rub the cream into my hands.

The acupuncture helps. Or at least it does not make things worse. When I arrive, the office is dim and empty, and Olaf is in the back. Just a minute, just a minute, he says. A printer whirs. The windows are shellacked with red rice paper, and in the ruby light, I remove my clothes and slide beneath the towels. Then Olaf appears. He shifts the coverings this way and that, exposing small territories of skin. How's the pain? The same. Tissue paper crinkles softly in a stray mechanical breeze. Above, I can hear an aircraft circling, waiting for the signalers at LaGuardia to call it home. I ask Olaf what he thinks of the recent civilian casualties, per drones, and what multiple of the reported number calculates the truth. He frowns. Olaf is from Serbia. He keeps the conversation light. *I've* never had any casualties, he says. He inserts the needle. I take a breath. The muscles in my arms contract. The bones in my wrists come alive with hidden nerves. It hurts. Acupuncture often makes me feel as if I am a collection of many separately twitching creatures, like a coral reef, as opposed to a continuous whole. Ouch, I gasp. I'm dying here. He stands calmly in the door. You're very much not. Then he turns out the lights. I am left in the dark for a full hour to give the blood a chance to flow.

Sometimes, at acupuncture, or on the train, I run into people with whom I used to play. Last week, at the pharmacy, I met a cellist who was once second to my first. She was in her black silk gown, on her way to the symphony, and had stopped in for mints. I was waiting for my anti-inflammatories. How happy she was to see me! Her perfume, when she leaned in for an embrace, carried a burnt sugar smell. She reeked of success. What are you doing now? Oh, I said. I teach.

There was a time when most were second to my first. At eighteen I played Dvořák in B minor on a Copenhagen stage. It is no tragedy.

Truthfully, I think I always would have quit, arthritis or no. At twenty-five I'd discovered, like so many young brides, that I was not so in love as I thought. I set the instrument into its case. I may never have opened it again, if it weren't for rent.

I have a financially savvy friend who lives in Chelsea on the block that took the pressure-cooker bomb. She too is mortally preoccupied. As are most people endowed with some financial sense. She bought a two bedroom on Twenty-Third in 1992, built a wall down the middle, and sold one half. Needless to say, she doesn't have to worry about money anymore. But she does think about her life. How long it will last. How there would have been no one to inherit her studio apartment, had the pressure cooker detonated more forcefully, as planned. No one but you, she said. The whole building resounded. The walls shook and faltered. She said she crawled beneath the table and hid. That's good, I told her. That's exactly what you're supposed to do. Although, in a tornado, one ought to avoid hiding beneath furniture, and which is more similar to a pressure cooker, a nuke, or the twisters of our childhoods? In the Midwest, the whole family tucks itself beneath the stairwell, the strongest part of the house, to wait out the storm. We tap into these memories over breakfast-for-dinner, after acupuncture, while watching *Annie Hall*. Whenever I visit, it seems my friend is reliving the pressure-cooker bomb. It is the most violent thing she knows. When the movie ends, I look around her apartment, slightly stunned. The silent walls. Still standing. The bananas in the bowl. She stretches lengthwise on the sofa, rests her feet in my lap. She will go on needing, I think, right until the end. She closes her eyes. Let's move to LA, she says. Wear suits. Life would be more frivolous in general, if we lived like Annie Hall. I watch her pupils quiver placidly beneath her lids. For a moment, I can see it: a convertible, linen slacks in pale pink. It occurs to me Los Angeles is also a convent of sorts, it refers back to itself, worships all that glows inside the beltway—I am certain it would reject me, too. You've come for the wrong reasons, LA would say. Gently, I push my friend's heels from my lap, pull on my coat. You know, I tell her, I don't think we're supposed to want that anymore.

Me, I have my own plans. In event of emergency, I am prepared. I think of my father, that hopeless man. His favorite phrase: Let's blow this popsicle stand. As he did, with a 9 mm semiautomatic, a controlled explosion to his head.

After Annie, I go for a walk. I go to the river. I stop in a bodega for choc-olate. It is a certain kind of woman who walks alone at night, snapping squares of chocolate with her hands. Me, I guess. At home, the park is empty. The children have gone, and across the street the parlor-level ten-ants have fallen mute. Then a voice breaks out. *Fuck you!* I stop at the base of my neighbor's stoop. Upstairs, the light is on.

He has the whole house to himself, my neighbor. One catches sight of him through first-, second-, or third-floor windows. I run into him on the street. He is tall, grayed, slightly stooped in a way that connotes the great weight of the thoughts he entertains—he is rather famous, after all. A reg-ular contributor, in fact, to the monthly magazine I love so much. Last month, he knocked on my door. His voice was soft and stern, and up close his gaze seemed more intense. As did the weight of the thoughts in his head—he stooped severely through the door. You are lovely, he said. Only, could you please keep it down? His office, as it happens, shares a wall with

> What was I doing, I wonder, when he was writing about the bombs?

mine. I sympathized. But as a cellist, I explained, keeping it down is a rather difficult thing to do. My students are not always in control of their volume or their tune. I thought of pointing out that while my neighbor may work in any number of rooms, I have only the two, and that includes the bath. But he was so charming, positioned in my door. His distress seemed to me sincere. In a swell of magnanimity, I offered to suspend les-sons on Tuesdays and weekday mornings before noon. Fantastic, he said. You're a dream. He kissed the air beside my cheek. The gesture hovered there, an inch away. I stood for a long moment while he crossed to his door. As he reached for his keys, I called to him, Come back sometime! He waved, then went inside. Now he has all kinds of silence, while I have extra time. What was I doing, I wonder, when he was writing about the bombs?

It is too late for a visit. Too late to ask. I decide to go home. Then I watch myself mount his stoop and reach for the dial pad. The bell rings with alarming volume through his private halls. Horrified, I descend as quickly as my knees will allow. I am well inside before I hear him shout into the dark: *Hello? Hello? Hello?*

Upstairs: The apartment, empty. The cello on the stand. I think of rushing back down to the street. Instead I take off my shoes. I look around. It occurs to me, barefoot, in this silence preceding midnight, that there is nothing to stop an adult woman from conducting a nuclear drill on her own terms. I crouch under the desk. *One Mississippi. Two.* Across the courtyard, in a white bedroom, a mother is putting her little girl to sleep. Engulfs her in a wave of sheets. *Three Mississippi. Four.* Another plane passes overhead. I read somewhere that they've relaxed restrictions on how low an aircraft can fly. The buildings haven't gotten any shorter. I find this unwise.

That night, in bed, I wake up very cold. My breath forms ghosts. I pad to the radiator and press a palm to the pipes. Cold as a carton of milk. I think of my neighbor, predisposed to quiet, and blush in the dark. Then I shrug on my robe, grope toward the door.

The furnace gives my landlady and me no end of trouble. There are two furnaces, in fact. My studio was an attic afterthought, an annex, and during renovation a second furnace was installed to pump it full of heat. The old one took offense, it seems, so instead of operating symbiotically, the two now tend to compete.

On the landing, I slip into my rain boots. Then I trudge downstairs to apartment one, apply my knuckles to the door. Inside, the TV and gramophone are going at once—Angela is partially deaf, she is all for noise. A shuffling. Something crashes to the floor. At ninety-six, she certainly remembers the threat of nuclear war, and much else besides. When finally she appears, a wool beret lies flat atop her head, as if it fell from a hook as she was passing by. Who is it? Who the hell are you? Angela, I say, it's me. The furnace is out again.

Angela has lived in her apartment for the better part of fifty years. It shows. The mop is in the bathtub, the handle propped against the wall. The deli on our block has a hot bar half-off after 8:00 PM, and in the kitchen a lazy Susan disappears beneath an avalanche of takeout napkins and small cities of paper plates. It makes me nervous. The cat licks a forgotten chicken wing. Before the old TV set is a wooden chair, and beneath it, a bottle of vodka, centered between the legs. Also a bowl of melting ice. Angela waves her hands above the beret, searching for the pull-string. She curses the super. Horatio! Where are you? Why must you go to the Bronx!

The naked bulb awakens with a thrum. Then, like miners, we begin our descent. There are two levels to go, from the street to the garden to the cellar below, with its ancient floor of hard-packed dirt. The sound of the

TV fades. The opera warbles along the banister. Angela mutters to herself. One of these days, one of these days . . . Her knees hurt, her eyes no longer work. My joints are also sore. I turn on lamps as we go. One floor down, half underground, we wind through the unused bedrooms, bookshelves, first-edition books. It smells sweet, like perfume and mold. Angela stops, as she usually does, at the top of the cellar stairs. Then I go on alone.

I do not enjoy the cellar. The dark. The dust. I take the flashlight from a hook installed expressly for this purpose of examining the furnace late at night. The wooden staircase sags with rot. As do the shelves at the bottom, laden with gardening tools and pots. A birdcage rusts. Twenty years ago, I would have had my cellist make this descent. But this is hardly relevant. There is no lover. No one to ask. Only Angela. And me. The stairs attach to the wall my neighbor shares. He has taken advantage of my idiocy, I know. Because what can I do with a Tuesday off? I maneuver with my hands outstretched, the way I used to navigate the woods as a girl, catching spiderwebs in my palms. Angela calls from the top of the steps. *Is it on? Turn it on!* I am plunged, suddenly, into an expansive calm. I clear a path through benthic junk. My furnace is an olive-green cylinder in the back of the room, propped up on cinder blocks. I listen for its growl. The hiss. The rumbles from within. But the cellar is silent. The furnace, discharged. I move ahead. My footsteps seem to me too loud. My very breath, a crash. How violent it is, to live! I stop. The whole city has fallen away, and what remains is silence. I reach for the furnace, feel along the side for the switch. It is cold. Dead. I turn it on. Nothing happens. Half a thought arrives, with simple clarity, like a flash of light: I do not want—. Then the engine begins to roar. I feel the rupture in my belly. The vibrations in my brain. 🛡

Christopher Soto

TWO LOVERS IN PERFECT // SYNCHRONICITY

FIG. 19

In 1991 // Ross Laycock died of AIDS in Los Angeles // His boyfriend [Felix Gonzalez-Torres] then made an installation in memoriam // The installation's composed of candies individually wrapped in multicolor cellophane // The pile of candy weighs 175 pounds or Ross's ideal body weight before contracting AIDS // Throughout the day // Visitors to the gallery eat the pile of candy & therefore diminish the body of Ross // Making him lose weight like AIDS did // Then at night when everyone leaves the gallery // The curators can choose to replenish the pile of candy // Restoring Ross to his original weight & // Granting him eternal life // Or not // This poem's dedicated to my queer mentors whom I never had a chance to meet—especially Ross & Felix.

•

I was born the year   Ross died of AIDS   In Los Angeles   My baby back

          Toasted & tattooed   My neck sweat   Sweet wetback   Beaner

Spik speaking spanglish   Our clothes cling on the clothesline

               The swing swings on the swing set   I was wearing   Beach sand

Sand dollars   Sand crabs   Summer skin   So tanned

I was born   & Felix was mourning   Ross   The lost hymn of him

Pour one out   Y otra   Pa' arriba   Pa' abajo   Centro

          Free tequila for the kids   Spray-painting our names at the wash

I want to believe   Masturbation's sex with someone you love   But still

I'm apart   A part   Of a whole generation of queer youth
Being raised   Without elders   Who's Ross to me?
A whole generation   Lost to AIDS
                              Our lady of constant dissent   A little gory allegory.

                                        •

Hugo my true love   Jugo de naranja   When we broke up   I broke down
          I'm all ribs & on the barbecue   I play the xylophone with my tongue
Inflatable pool in the front yard   Yellow grass   Caged macaws   Palm trees
Tilted pool tables   The dog with knotted hair
                                        Chanclas with sox on the beach   Seashell buckets
Cocinando pupusas con mi mama   Bebiendo kola-champagne   The boom box
Pokémon   Graffiti walls   & Skater boys   No shirt   Bony as greyhounds
          Hugo's // Plaid boxers peeking   Out of Dickies shorts   Ride on the pegs of my bike
The ice-cream truck   Over Celia Cruz   piñata   Tarot cards   Hoop earrings &
Aerosol spray   I reapplied eyeliner like   A chola before mall photos
Eloteros   Fútbol   Sunday church   Bachata cumbia   No rain
Curanderas & campesinos
          Tio transcribing   At the seance tonight   I'll pretend to get stigmata.

                                        •

O Los Angeles   O Hollywood Hills   O Placita Olvera   O San Pedro   O Long Beach
        O Taqueria in Westminster   O the 405 freeway   Left arm sunburnt
Windows down   I'm on beach chairs   Beach coolers   Beach bums' butts
        Peanut butter & jelly sandwiches   Which chips in the sand   Pringles or Ruffles
Vodka watermelon   Suntan lotion   & I'm laughing with towels over my head
Police said   "Are you drunk"   "Are you high"   & I replied
"No // I'm Salvadorian"   Police harassed me   Soooooooooooooo much
I stopped driving   I stopped biking   I moved to a different city
Police asked   "Driver's lice sense"   My red rubbed eyes   My brown skin   My brown
I didn't jog the stop sign   I didn't pass the speed limit   Turn signal
        My music wasn't too loud   No quiero hablar   Contigo jodon
& It's among these conditions   I love // I try to.

·

Gay cholos   Felix & Ross   Me & Hugo   On the down-low   Lowriders & smog
Homie   Hoe // Me   Hugging   The stomach   Of my pillow
Con boca cerrada   No entran   Tumbleweeds & cactus & every day
        At the museum   Visitors walk to the installation   A pile of candies
Individually wrapped   Multicolor // Cell phones
Every day   The visitors   Are looking for Ross   Are looking for UFOs
                & My family of aliens in the rosebush
Iron-welded gate   Weed whackers   Pushing lawn mowers // Over flinching finches

I hope there are no artifacts // When prisons close   No museums for pain
    Where tourists can safely visit nobody
                    While nobody's visiting prisoners   Around this country
I'm making phone calls // To our deaf friends
Telling them to hurry   To the hospital that Ross holds   The angles of angels
            Have you felt // The extreme loneliness   Of the pervert parade?

                     •

Ross // I'm here baby   Everything will be all right   I wanted to say
But he was gone   Before I came with   Wet dreams of my cousins
Twerking in the library   Tweaking in the laundromat   Feeling nauseous & agnostic
What's good?   Where's god // Beneath the vacancy sign?
    Where's my therapist's therapist?   Maybe this is how we leave   The hospital
The poem   The cemetery   Has fine typography
The ones we love   The fonts we need
    Maybe we never breathe the cleanest air   Visit Scandinavia
    Look at auroras like stretch marks   How Saturn lost her rings
Maybe the chore list was never meant to be completed   With Venus in retrograde
I try not to drown   While swimming backstrokes in rosé
                    & Roses   With pitbulls named Rosie
Maybe one day // I'll wake // An oddity in the domestic   & Say "Ross // I'm here"
"Where are you"   "Was that it // Was that life"
                    "We didn't do enough"   "We did so much."

Analog 1999

He was high a lot now that Gwen was gone and feeling so lonely and bored and unsuccessful enough with other women as to find himself, one work night in spring, looking through her drawers in the dresser they'd shared for an item of her clothing to jerk off into. He thought she might've left at least a broken bra in there, or a once-worn bridesmaid dress still hanging in what'd been her zone of the closet, but there was nothing, not even in her shoe bins. She'd taken all of her stuff out of the bathroom too, except, at the very back of one of her former shelves in the cabinet, a handful of half-melted aromatherapy candles and a glitter-speckled cardboard box that, on closer look, he realized was a camera. It was a disposable camera. He put his eye to its viewfinder, as if by doing so he'd be able to see what photos were inside it. All he saw, though, was his brute white toilet. He clicked, and was surprised to find that there were still some shots left on the roll, and, as he wound the dial on his way back to the couch, he decided to take some pictures of himself to send to Gwen as a reminder—imagining his

Joshua Cohen

ex-girlfriend standing by the mailboxes in the dismal hallway of some new guy's building, or some friend's building, or some flashy dump found for her by the nonprofit she'd been hoping to intern with in that country she always referred to as "Post-Soviet Russia," as if that were an actual country that could receive her mail. All the airmail postage would make her curious. All the stickers that told her DO NOT BEND and HANDLE WITH CARE. She'd grab hold of the red-tabbed strip and tear the package open, with the same urgent greed with which he tugged off his belt.

Two days later, he was back on the couch with an envelope on his gut, flipping through the photos the lab had developed. The first twenty-something photos were of last New Year's Eve. A party Gwen had brought him to. He looked through shots of strangers unicorned in party hats and blowing party horns, shots of Gwen's think-tank crowd on the dance floor, the girls she'd never liked getting grinded on by the IT department in sweated-through shirts and neckties tied around their heads like kung fu Arabs. He saw the club's banquettes and chandeliers, the little plates of cake dug out with little drug spoons, and by seeing he was reminded. He was even reminded of what wasn't in any of the pictures: the disposable cameras that were given out as party favors toward midnight. That explained the camera, and why Gwen wasn't in any of the pictures either. She must've taken them.

As for him: there was the toilet.

This was his portion of the roll. The next few shots hadn't quite come out. They ranged from total blackness to a lighter black, grainy like static. He thought something might've gone wrong with the camera or film—half a year had elapsed since the millennium's start, after all—but the clear resolution of the toilet shot suggested otherwise.

The next two shots were grayish but not identical. One had a white bulb just at the edge of the frame, and the other had two white bulbs, at opposite edges. The bulbs were splotchy white and surrounded by hair. It was only when he saw the second shot, with the two splotchy bulbs, that he realized he was looking at knees. He was looking at his knees. Once he'd figured that out, he recognized the gray-flecked carpet just below him.

The next photo was almost entirely taken up with the unmistakable brown of the couch, blurred like a crumbling cliff over the carpet.

In a few others, he could see legs, and, though they were slightly out of focus, at least one of them was identifiable as his by that fuzzy redness at mid-thigh, which was a pimple he still couldn't get rid of because it kept rubbing up against the inside of his pants.

He could make out the pile of his pants, the same pair he was wearing now, and his underwear bunched over them—he assumed a different pair but all his underwear was blue—a sneaker kicked off and gagged with a sock.

But what he couldn't see in any of the shots, or what so obviously wasn't there, was precisely the thing he'd been trying to capture—*the thing*, whose size he'd tried to flatter with angle, once he'd gotten it hard enough to stand up on its own, without his hand. His *cock*. His *dick*. Gwen had never said those words. His penis—which if he hadn't occasionally prompted her, even begged her, to mention during their less and less frequent sex, Gwen would never have referred to ever, in any way, as if it didn't much exist for her either.

It just wasn't there. Or he couldn't quite be sure it was. In the few shots that showed his legs and clothes mostly in focus, his penis, or where his penis should've been, was an almost pixelated vagueness, a puff of dust flashed into backscatter, or just an indication of motion, like a ghost shaken out of a too-long exposure.

Dropping the photos to the carpet, he clutched himself in reassurance.

What do black holes look like? He fell asleep in front of the TV in the middle of a documentary. The voice was throaty, female, and Russian. *Rather, the question to ask is, can a thing be seen that consumes all light?* 🛡

Antonio López

AUBADE EN PORTLANDIA

¿Mí'jo, y cómo es Oregón?
— MY MOTHER

Amá, I've wandered this city's forests,
pining for hunchbacked trunks who still hum
Saturday's mariachi, the willowed throats
that tickle my neck with a singsongy wind.

A veces susurran, do you breathe better
there? In Oregon? In this poem? Mamita,
at Reed, a famous author signed my book
and said, *You have a nice wide back.* I wanted

to just think of that *Matilda* movie we like,
of Miss Honey signing the adoption papers,
but I felt the felt tip carve her name onto
my shoulder blades, saw me into mesquite,

pine, teak, whatever she wanted her deck
to be built from. I wanted to ask, *Do I come
from good stock, maestra? Does my voice splinter
inside white space, this tin house under construction?*

But I ran, wiped the tears and told myself,
it's the smoke of her cigarette. I kept sprinting
this country's wilderness, and among the dead
leaves, stopped to gather the wooden teeth

that fell from my back. I buried the tokens
under the chalked earth of a callus, folded
fingers with palm, a sealed prayer—to hide

how much I've bled.

Elizabeth Dodd

SOOT PARTICLES CONTRIBUTE TWICE AS MUCH TO GLOBAL WARMING AS PREVIOUSLY THOUGHT

I.

One of the turkeys has a limp. He gimps his way behind the other jakes, *gotta keep up, gotta keep up*, but he can't. Skinny neck and balded pate, he looks anxious, jolting along in spasmodic gait. The other birds ignore him, rustling leaves like feral dogs. Turkey crap dots the driveway and the deck; barbed wire sags beyond a wall of field stones, snags the occasional feather as the birds trot past. The window yawns, half-open, on the mild midwinter day.

2.

Where the two-lane highway sutured mountain foothills to the plains, an old man ran a rock-and-gem shop: cheap glass vials of flaked gold you could shake, geodes sawed in half like sugar eggs. I remember forty years ago, the family car in the gravel lot, my little brother's colored Legos scattered on the seats. Beside the register, rocks in a bowl grew a slow pelt of dust. They looked like the stones sewn into the wolf's belly, Little Red Cap safe for another day. "Dinosaur gizzards," the old man said. On the long drive into town, I kept turning the thought, incongruous fossil, as if I held it in my hand. I remember our small lives' ambulations through the afternoon: laundromat, grocery store, Carnegie Library's steep front steps like a cataract of stone.

3.

When the screech owl hit the window nobody heard the thump. How long did it lie on the drought-gouged lawn, staring at air-turned-stone-turned-air-again? By morning when we found the startled feather-print—outspread wings, beak closed, the scaly feet pulled tight against the breast—the bird was gone. We didn't wash the glass. Even now the light still pauses, infinitesimal, to warm each speck of owl dust rammed against the pane.

WILD SOUNDS!

Splendid blue fairy wrens are mating and the female is pursuing the male,
who is fighting his reflection in car mirrors and house windows! They are wild
with passion and compulsion and whatever else we might dig out to counter
our own vicariousness, but there's no getting away from it and a volume
and vocal range never experienced by us here before are burning out
capeweed flowers and inciting insects to spontaneously generate
and spontaneously combust without any time passing for here
are the answers to particle physics here is the surge against all threat
to outlast the blasts of toxins and clearing and human solipsisms in the dilating
of the psyche hoping to plunder heaven for all it's worth but what's worth is here
exploding in wild sounds and wild moves and role-play is busted and blued atoms
shifted.

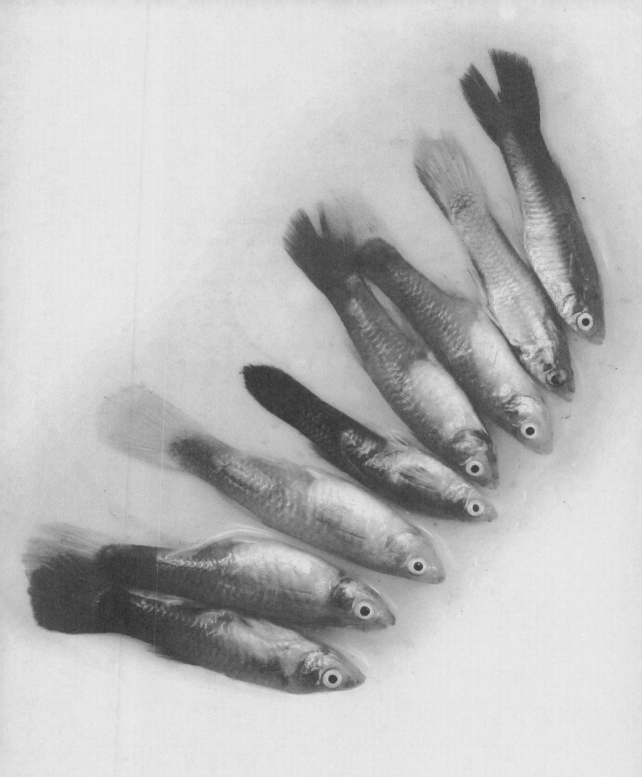

FICTION

Dress Rehearsal

Olga Tokarczuk

translated by Jennifer Croft

The last message they heard on the radio was to inform them that they should cover the windows completely. Then the radio went quiet. Although he still brought it into the kitchen, extended the antenna fully, and turned the dial now and then, hopeful. Sometimes he managed to pick up that same distant station. The voice, which came to them through the stripy speaker in spite of the static and the dull hum—this voice spoke in some foreign language, which they couldn't understand at all. Then it would die away, only to unexpectedly come back—weaker and weaker, less and less certain.

"Like during martial law," he whispered.

"Leave the radio alone, you idiot!" she said. "We've got to get the windows sealed, did you not hear that? Even at a time like this, you're useless. Flapping around the apartment like a poisoned fly. The only thing you know how to do is cause me problems."

She got up on her armchair and stuffed the edges of an old blanket into the balcony doorframe. The blanket slid down, letting in some brown light from outside. A grimy light, like dishwater.

"Give me the hammer! What are you standing there staring at me for, can't you see my hands are getting tired?"

"Just shut up already," he muttered under his breath and went into the entryway to dig out the hammer from the toolbox in the cabinet underneath the phone.

"Hurry up, can't you see I can't just keep on standing here?"

He tapped her with the end of the hammer as though she were a large and disobedient animal. He told her to get out of the way. She watched him as he clumsily nailed the blanket to the doorframe. He was conscious of that critical, cold gaze.

"I couldn't quite catch what they were saying. Something about shelters. That's about it," he said, a nail in his mouth, trying to deflect her attention from his hands.

"Yes, that much I gathered, too. But what shelters? Shelters. They've all gone insane."

"In Switzerland they have shelters under every building. If something were to happen, only the Swiss would survive. Noah's going to be a Swiss. Imagine: a whole new world with only Swiss. Just banks and cheese and watches. Every now and then a Toblerone."

He chuckled and got off the chair. She looked at him disdainfully.

"You are so stupid," she said. "Absolutely hopeless. You got stunted somewhere along the line. Like all men."

He ignored her. He went over to the cupboard where the phone was and picked up the receiver.

"It doesn't work."

He said that, but really it seemed to him that he could hear something. A plethora of voices jumbled together like the noise in an enormous waiting room. Some voices

> He tapped her with the end of the hammer as though she were a large and disobedient animal.

impatient, some sleepy, like they were telling a story in a monotone, from beginning to end. There was even a baby crying, and a dog barking off in the distance. He looked at the receiver in surprise, as if he were expecting to find some clarification there. A television picture. Television in telephones. He chuckled again. She must have noticed his look of surprise, because she came up, snatched the receiver out of his hand, and put it up to her own ear.

"Static," she said.

They sat in their vinyl armchairs, and he started to be scared she would return to weeping, that she would remember their daughter, who had gone the day before—before all this happened—to Warsaw, just as calm as calm could be. Before the sky had turned brown, before people had run home, warning each other, citing the alert. Running with their collars raised like it were raining.

"Like during martial law," he murmured to himself, very quietly. He regretted never experiencing any wars during his lifetime (he remembered nothing of World War II, when he had been a child), any cataclysms (well, there was a flood once, but that didn't really count). Martial law was the closest thing to war, or disaster, that he could truly imagine.

"What are you going on about?"

"Nothing."

"I just heard you going on about something."

"Just that it's similar to martial law. I was just thinking it's too bad there were never any wars during my lifetime. Maybe I'd be stronger now."

She looked up at the ceiling, and he saw her throat—white, fat, lined with moist creases like the thinnest necklaces. He knew the gesture well. Next she would say, "My God, it's like they want me to laugh at them."

"My God, it's like they want me to laugh at them," she said. "You would have liked a war? I mean, I would certainly say I've been right, you are immature—infantile, even. You really never did grow up. Men never grow up. In old age they just get Alzheimer's, and that's the end of that. A real sad caricature of humanity."

> Men never grow up. In old age they just get Alzheimer's, and that's the end of that.

For a moment she savored a silent satisfaction. Fulfilled like after intercourse. He felt a surge of disgust.

Then she resumed. She was on the verge of tears—her voice sounded like it was coming out of a well.

"How come you're not thinking about our child? Why, why did she have to go right then? How could we have let her? She could be lying in a ditch somewhere, hurt or even . . ."

"She isn't a child . . ." he said in a half-hearted attempt to head off this wave of hysteria he could see swelling now.

He thought of her as a dangerous yet stupid animal, and he knew what he had to do. He lit a cigarette.

"Must you?" she said. "Can't you see we're running out of air in here anyway? You're a real idiot, aren't you?" she shrieked.

He put out the cigarette and went to his room. There he lit it again. He sat down on the bed, straightened the blanket in the window, and then he looked at both his aquariums—one with angelfish, the other full of guppies. All the fish were dead. The pale, lackluster angelfish suspended there, motionless, at the surface of the water. The guppies were floating belly up.

"A holocaust," he murmured.

He took a drag off his cigarette. He decided not to tell her about the fish, and this decision brought him a certain satisfaction.

She was still talking in the other room.

"If this all happened around noon—all this darkness—and she left early in the morning, then, well, maybe she made it to safety. Maybe they got them off the bus, supposedly there're shelters at the bus stations. Supposedly they have big shelters underneath the station in Wrocław. Are you listening? Oh God, God, how are we to bear it. God, oh God, we'll die. If it's radiation, then we're not going to make it—then no one will survive."

He could hear her voice shifting seamlessly into a sob.

"Quit it," he shouted, then put out his cigarette.

He leaned over so he could see her. She had regained control over herself. She covered her mouth with her hand. A single tear landed on that hand and soaked into her skin. She wiped her eyes with one finger, furtively. He found this gesture touching. He liked it when she would suddenly weaken. He took yesterday's *Times* and sat down in the armchair next to hers. He cast a glance at the headings as if looking for something that would have predicted the catastrophe. All he found was interest rates and exit polls.

"How can you read the paper at a time like this?" she asked. "Do you not have feelings?"

Hysteria had crept back into her voice.

"Leave me alone, you old bat."

"You have Alzheimer's, you do."

"Well then I suppose you have mad cow disease."

She clasped her hands on her chest and turned her side to him. He already knew the first page of the paper by heart. Now he was beginning to learn the second. The first article was about the death of a famous pianist. The next was on the Oscars. An obituary of some woman with two last names. He noticed, out of the corner of his eye, that she had risen and gone up to the window. He noticed that her skirt had rolled up a little on her. He noticed how thin her hair was on the back of her head.

"I'd be interested to find out what it was. I mean what happened. Did you get any of what they were saying yesterday on the radio?" she asked.

He lowered his gaze to the obituary.

"Cataclysm, war, comet, who the hell knows."

"I was thinking," she said, "you know, we've never really lived through anything really . . . really terrible. No wars . . ."

"Martial law . . . '68 . . . '70 . . ."

"It's not the same."

He didn't respond. He thought about the fish, about how he wasn't going to tell her. They were his fish, in any case. He knew he'd have to go and gather them and flush them down the toilet.

"What were they saying in the stairwell?"

"Nobody knows anything. The guy from downstairs said they'd used some type of weapon."

Her face fell. The creases around her mouth made her face look like the bloated face of a drowned corpse. It reminded him of his fish and that he wasn't going to tell her.

"Weapon? Who?"

"Must have been the Russians. Could be another Chernobyl."

The fish.

"We could go over to their place, you know, just to talk."

The fish.

"Who?"

"The people who live downstairs."

He tried hard to think of their names. A married couple about the same age as them. He was so full of himself, although she was quite an attractive woman. But he was reading an article about the economy, and he didn't feel like getting up.

"We don't even know their names."

"What does it matter if we know their names? What would we need to know their names for? Ridiculous."

The fish. He was not going to tell her.

"And what are we going to talk to them about, I mean, it's obvious, this is the end. It happened. Somebody finally just couldn't take it anymore. Ladies and gentlemen, this is the end of the world."

"Maybe they'd know something," she said hopefully. "I know them by sight. He's that really attractive man and she's that little crybaby."

"Then go."

Neither of them got up. If it weren't for the covered windows, he thought, it would be the same as always. No, there was something missing, something wasn't right. He shifted, restless. It was darker, the light of the floor lamp didn't cut all the way through the dusk. Was that it? The angelfish? The voices in the phone? And suddenly, for a minute, for a second, he was gripped by panic. Short, sharp pains like a heart attack. He looked at the stock reports—the market was down. He was falling, they all were. She coughed. Then he realized, with relief, that it was just the TV, that it was just that the TV wasn't on. So that was it. That was what was wrong. The TV. He leaped out of his chair and turned it on. There was just snow on the screen. There wasn't anything on. He flipped through the channels with the remote control. It was the same on all of them. He just pressed mute so they wouldn't be able to hear the static, and he gradually began to calm down.

"Why'd you turn it on? You know there hasn't been anything on since yesterday. We already checked. So? Why?"

He didn't respond. He sat in his chair. The panic vanished quick as lightning.

"The fish. My fish died," he said then.

"Fantastic. We're next, you know. First the fish and then us."

He'd known she would be happy. He'd just known.

The market was down. He was falling, they all were.

"I'm hungry," he said.

She looked at him in disbelief and hatred.

"How can you be hungry, how is it even possible to think about food at a time like this? What is wrong with you? You've got the brains of a celery stalk. Must be Alzheimer's."

"You must be a cow."

He got up and went into the kitchen. He pulled the cucumbers out of the fridge and started to slice the bread. He stopped, still holding the knife over the loaf. Then he rummaged around in the bottom drawer. In his hand was the pocketknife with the broken handle he'd had since his scouting days. He was moved by the sight of this knife now. It was dull, but he managed to cut two slices of bread with it. He set them on a plate along with the cucumber and brought them into the living room.

"That's all the bread we have, don't eat up all of our provisions . . . At some point we'll have to go out, you know, just to the store," she said to the snow on the TV, not moving.

He hesitated for a second over the plate, and then he cut the bread and cucumber into smaller pieces. He slid her piece onto another plate and put this plate in her hand. She took it unquestioningly. As they slowly began to eat, a siren started howling in the distance. She got up and went to the window, carefully lifting up the blanket and looking out. She saw a little strip of brown sky between the apartment buildings over her head.

"Can't see anything," she said to the glass, and he took that opportunity to take a couple of pieces of cucumber off her plate.

They ate in silence. She as if she didn't care what she was eating. Which he found irritating. He speared crumbs of food on the end of the knife and placed them in his mouth, chewing thoroughly. This reminded him of summer camp, years ago. A choice cucumber with bread, better than dinner in an expensive restaurant.

"Hunger is the best chef," he said with his mouth full.

"I think she made it. With a little bit of luck she could have made it just fine. She must be at his place now. They must be in some kind of shelter, there must be a lot of shelters in Warsaw left over from the last war. They're safe. I'm telling you."

He nodded.

"It would have been better not to last this long. You know, to die before this. You know what's going to happen when people start dying like flies, who's going to bury them all?"

"Yeah."

"Yeah what?"

"Nothing."

"You read the paper every day, watch TV, and you didn't know anything? Nothing predicting misfortune? Maybe other people knew? Maybe it was just us who didn't know. Maybe other people had time to prepare? And you didn't get anything from your stupid papers. You are so stupid."

She sighed and pushed her empty plate out of the way. She wet her finger with saliva and picked up the remaining crumbs.

"We have to ration," she explained.

He followed her with his gaze as she squeezed past the table and looked for something on the walls, which were covered with tapestries and country landscapes. Finally she found a piece of bare wall, knelt before it, and folded her hands for prayer.

"What are you doing?" he asked with a sarcastic smile, although he already knew what she was doing.

"I'm not doing shit," she said, closed her eyes, and started to pray. "Angel of God, my guardian, watch over me always, morning, evening, day, and night, be always by my side . . ."

> "I'm not doing shit," she said, closed her eyes, and started to pray.

"Maniac," he said to himself and took the plates to the kitchen. He wasn't sure if he should wash them.

He remembered that when there wasn't any water at camp you washed the pots with sand.

". . . keep my soul and body, lead me to everlasting life. Amen."

She got up and brushed off her knees. Then she took the remote control and flipped through a couple of channels. They were all snowing exactly the same. He stood in the doorway and asked, "You know how tomatoes look in the dark like this?"

"How?"

"Strange. Yesterday when I was in the garden, we didn't know we weren't allowed to leave the house yet, I was just standing there and just looking at them."

He was lost in thought, a smile on his face.

"And?" she said and sat in her chair.

"They looked beautiful . . . this strange light or radiation or whatever it is, it lit them up, like they were shining, plants full of tomatoes, what a waste . . . so beautiful, but you can't eat them."

"You should have picked them, they might not have soaked it up yet," she said calmly.

"Yeah, really. They'd be shining in the house now. And if we ate them, would they shine through our stomachs? Just imagine—both of us walking around, and this light would be shining out from underneath our clothes, our whole bodies lit up, our whole stomachs shining and . . . and then in the toilet . . ."

They both chuckled. He to the point of tears. He wiped his eyes with his sleeve and the laughter returned in spurts several more times. Then they leaned back in silence in their chairs, spent.

"Do you think those blankets are going to help anything, I mean, they're just old blankets . . ." he asked after a moment.

"Everyone has blankets in their windows, that whole apartment building does. Supposedly some towns have shelters. Have you heard anything about any shelters?"

He gazed up at the ceiling.

"We've already talked about that."

"Well, what haven't we already talked about?"

"Nothing."

"You know what really gets me?" he asked suddenly. "That we didn't say goodbye. We might not see her again now."

She started crying. She was gulping down air and getting more and more carried away. She doubled over in her chair. Another minute and she would slide onto the floor.

"Quit it," he said and wondered how he could have failed to foresee this reaction.

"You quit it," she sobbed.

"You weren't even kind to her. You two were constantly arguing. It was like you had nothing else in life to do."

"Oh, yeah, of course, and you were so great. You always have to be better at everything . . . Good daddy . . . You useless . . ."

He got up and left the room so he could smoke. He heard her sobbing, erratically, inconsolably, like a child. She was saying something through her sobs, he came up to the door so she wouldn't see him and listened.

". . . she was born she cried all the time. I asked the nurse if that was normal. Like everything hurt her. She cried and cried. Other babies were sleeping, and she would just cry . . . Oh God, we're all of us so hapless, so fragile."

He leaned against the wall and looked up. His eyes had filled with tears, and now drops flowed one after the other, ricocheting off his woolen undershirt and then hitting the floor. They soaked into the rug. The ashes from his cigarette fell in the same place, but they didn't soak in. He licked his finger and the ashes stuck to his fingertip. He scattered them in the aquarium. Then he went back and turned the dial on the radio, but all they could hear was static. The static, like a whisper, was comforting to her. For a while some station came through, and they were both listening in suspense, but it was some foreign language. And everything went quiet. So he went back to his seat next to her.

"Remember Bobik? How many years has it been since he died?" he asked.

She made a mental count.

"Four, five? That dog drove me crazy."

"Remember how he used to take things to his bed? Remember that time he made off with your new shoe?" he chuckled.

"Yeah. He was certainly no genius. He stole various things . . ." She laid her hands on her chest and drifted off into a reverie. "The thing I liked most was that you had to get up early to take him for a walk. You would go out with the dog and bring in the paper and fresh bread from the store. Because it wasn't that good at the bakery. Then after lunch and after we'd watch our movies . . . We organized our whole life around that dog. He always did everything just so, he never changed the order of things. He had to have a biscuit after his morning walk. Once there weren't any biscuits, something hadn't come in or something, and I had to bake him a cake and then dry it out in the oven . . . I was a real sucker, baking a cake for a dog! Can you imagine?"

He almost interrupted her, suddenly animated, excited.

"Remember what the vet said when he got hit by that car?" he said.

"That we had to put him to sleep," she replied.

He fell back into his chair, fulfilled, placated by anger.

"Why do they say you put animals to sleep? You're killing them, really," she said.

"People die, animals go to sleep. I don't know why."

"Sleeping fish."

He thought he should toss the fish out of the aquarium, but he didn't want to look at that again. Later, he thought.

> He went back and turned the dial on the radio, but all they could hear was static.

"Dogs have their own routines," he said.

"People too."

"But dogs even more. The human psyche can break out of any routine. Animals are just doomed to it."

He was pleased with the way he had put this.

"Doomed," he repeated, delighted with the sound of this word.

They were silent, sitting side by side in their brown armchairs, turned toward the window that was covered in checked blankets. After a while she said, "That was really something else . . . Remember how he would lie down on the settee even though he knew he wasn't allowed to. But only when you and I were arguing, like he wanted to divert our attention onto himself . . ."

"He used to lie down there when you were gone," he added with considerable satisfaction.

"He did? Are you sure?" It was clear that she didn't quite believe him.

"I used to smoke in the living room, too, yep, one cigarette right after another, and you never noticed it afterward. I'd smoke, have myself a beer, and Bobik would sleep on the settee."

"You think I didn't know you'd been drinking? Course I knew. I let you have that. I pretended like I didn't know. I knew about the cigarettes, too, I just didn't know he'd been sleeping on the settee."

He stood up.

"We have beer," he said.

"What, no," she said, waving him down. He sat obediently. "For later," she said.

He felt a wave of anger washing over him.

"For what later? Are you genuinely mentally challenged? There is no later."

She apparently didn't notice this outburst, because she went on placidly, "She was the one who brought him here. She said, either me or the dog. Remember?"

He sulked for a little while but finally he said, with some satisfaction, "You didn't know how to act or what to say. She could be a real character sometimes."

> He gathered up the fish in a net made out of panty hose.

"Why are you using the past tense? You think that . . .? What do you think?"

"Give me a break," he said and stood and went into his room. He made a crack between the blanket and the window frame and looked out. It was the same everywhere. There was no one out.

"Cover that up right now, you idiot, you never learn . . . You want your eyes to burn up?" she said, peeking around into his room.

"They're my eyes, and this is my room."

She left. He gathered up the fish in a net made out of panty hose. After a little while he had a whole pile of them.

The enormous eyes of the angelfish were looking straight up at the ceiling. His hands were shaking as their brittle tails tangled up in the diamonds of the net. He closed his eyes when he flushed them down the toilet.

"Maybe a volcano erupted and this is all volcanic ash that got into the atmosphere," she said from the other room. "That could be why it's so dark. Then there wouldn't be any contamination, and we'd be able to go out. Supposedly that's how the dinosaurs went extinct."

He mumbled something.

"Nothing would grow, there wasn't any food, and they all died out."

Then they heard the clatter of broken glass. They both stood still. Him leaning over the toilet, her there in front of the armchair.

"What was that?" she whispered.

"Not everyone's just sitting at home. They might be looting our store."

"They're going to take all the food! Those brutes. Call the police."

He looked at her and struck the side of his head with his palm.

"The phone doesn't work," he said. Still, he went to the front door and looked out through the peephole. In a bit he opened the door, carefully. He could hear echoes of voices carried from floor to floor through the apartment building.

"I'm going to get some information," he whispered to her, but she seized his sleeve and grimaced, hoping, with that grimace, to hold him back.

He pulled his arm away. He disappeared into the dark rectangle of the doorway. She stuck her head out and listened. Then she went back into the living room and started to clean off the table. She took a pickle out of a jar and ate it quickly. She sat at the table, still as a statue. He came back excited.

"I invited the people from downstairs," he said.

She put her hands on top of her head.

"Whatever for? What are we going to talk to them about?"

"They'll be here in a second."

She began to sweep the crumbs off the table. She straightened out the tablecloth.

"Thank God we still have gas. Put on the kettle."

Then their guests were whispering in the hallway. There was a quiet knocking at the open door. The neighbor let his wife in ahead of him. They greeted them.

". . . owski," said the neighbor.

". . . czyk," said the host.

"We've been living below you all for so many years and never been here. It's nice to see you."

"Please do come in. We'll just shut the door," she said.

Their neighbors stood uncomfortably in the hall until they were led into the living room. They sat down in the armchairs. There followed a moment of awkward silence.

"Would you like some coffee?" she asked, standing over them with a dish towel in her hand.

"Oh, we wouldn't want to cause you any trouble," said their neighbor.

His little wife was perching at the edge of her chair. Their host pulled himself up a chair and sat down by them.

"It would do us good to drink some coffee. Who knows how much longer we'll have gas . . . Maybe this is the last coffee we'll ever have," he tried to joke.

"Would you quit it?" said his wife with unnatural cheer. "Instant or brewed?"

"Brewed, if it's not too much trouble."

She disappeared into the kitchen.

He asked impatiently, "Do you know anything? What it was? Or anything."

"People are saying it was a terrible earthquake that hit the whole planet, apparently half of Europe is already gone, the Netherlands are underwater, and America and Japan plain don't exist anymore."

"But we didn't feel anything," she said, standing in the doorway with the bag of coffee in her hand.

"That's because we're not on any fault line," he said, reproaching her with this simple reply.

The neighbor went on.

"Everything blew up, nuclear power plants, everything. That's why they're talking about contamination."

"That and probably volcanoes. That's why it's so dark. I told you," he said to his wife, who was bringing in the coffee on a small tray.

"My husband had this theory," she said, setting the cups on the coffee table. "He thought that the same thing's happened as back with the dinosaurs . . ."

Suddenly the little neighbor woman began to cry helplessly, hiding her face in a handkerchief. Her husband stroked her hand.

"It's always hardest on the women," he explained. "We have children in America. Two of them. They were supposed to come for Christmas . . ."

"And there isn't going to be a Christmas now . . ." sniffled the small woman indistinctly. She looked so pitiful that everyone felt a lump forming in their throats. Only the simultaneous clinking of all four teaspoons in all four coffee cups broke the silence that ensued.

"Our daughter left us yesterday, actually, to go and see her . . . her fiancé," said the hostess. "Just this morning, and then just a few hours later, all this. So we're worried, too."

"Why do we always worry about our children, even when they're grown, and never about ourselves?" asked her husband philosophically.

"How can you say such things?" she said. "Sometimes when you come out with things like that . . ."

Everyone started stirring their coffee again, this time much more frantically. The neighbor said, "That's why the radio and the television aren't working. It's that radiation interfering with the radio waves and everything, with electricity. There's some radiation that isn't letting something through . . ." he said, getting lost in his hypothesis.

"So all we have left is the gas . . ." his wife said quietly, raising her cup to her lips.

"You've got to suspect, though, that they'll turn off the gas too."

The hostess shifted.

"What will happen then? Can you all smell how it already stinks around here, from the sewage? And when it gets clogged up?"

"What line of work are you folks in?" said the host, to change the subject.

"We're retired now. Long story short," answered the guest vaguely. "I used to be an official. I used to see you on the bus fairly often. You used to take bus number thirteen, didn't you?"

"Yeah, thirteen, and I got off near the city offices. I worked at the school—"

His wife butted in.

"I heard they have bunkers under the city offices, and all the workers have been sheltered down there. I guess apparently they have reserves of freshwater and sustenance in cans, enough for everyone for a whole year. I heard they even have a movie theater."

> "I heard they have bunkers under the city offices, and all the workers have been sheltered down there."

Her husband looked at her in surprise. "Who in God's name managed to talk you into that?"

"That's just what I heard," she shrugged.

He ignored this and turned back to the neighbor.

"Do you think those blankets are going to help anything, I mean, they're just old blankets . . . They really ought to instruct us on what to do."

"Apparently they were going around in protective suits and giving out flyers. They were in that building"—here he waved his hand to indicate a general direction—"but they just haven't gotten to us yet. Maybe they'll still come, though."

"Don't you think that we ought to get organized, I mean, even just the people from this side of the building, you know, this stairwell? Were you ever in the Scouts?"

"Back then there weren't any Scouts, there was the Union of Polish Youth, you know, all us kids having to pitch in and help spread socialism."

"Well, you all were organized, anyways," said the host sarcastically.

"I remember that if there was an atomic bomb we were supposed to get down there by the window and cover our heads with our hands."

"Right, that would really help. About like these blankets in the windows."

He went up to the window and lifted the curtain a little.

"I wonder how that brown air smells. It must smell like something. Ozone? Char?"

"Maybe volcanic ash," suggested the neighbor.

The host stood in front of the wall unit and looked for something on the bookshelf. He took out a book. He flipped through it for a moment, as if trying to remember if this was in fact the book that contained the thing he was looking for. He stopped on one of the pages and showed it to them.

> "I don't get scared as long as I don't think," she said.

"Memling's *Last Judgment*," he said. "People are rising from the grave, there's the archangel Gabriel with a fiery sword. There's hell—see, those are the outlines of people flying into the fire. The sky over hell is red, and all the black ash . . ."

"Why are you showing us this? Have you lost it?" she asked, and then she turned to the guests and said, "I don't know why my husband is showing you this."

"I'm not afraid of devils and spirits. I am only afraid of my fellow man," said the neighbor animatedly. "Somebody must be responsible for all this, somebody must have made some kind of decision, you know."

"But you were saying that it was an earthquake."

"It doesn't matter, earthquakes don't happen for no reason . . . Global warming and so on."

The hostess set her cup down.

"Sometimes things happen that people have no control over. Actually, people often have no control over what happens. People don't know anything, people don't understand anything, can't arrange anything, because no matter what everything happens the way it has to happen. People don't even understand themselves because they're governed by emotions, instincts . . . Tomatoes, you know, we planted some tomatoes in the garden and they ripened, right now they're at their ripest, and we can't pick them. Nothing's as it should be."

Meanwhile the neighbor's wife was gazing at the Memling, which was now lying in front of her on the table, with a mesmerized, terrified expression on her face. There must have been something wrong with her, because little drops of sweat appeared on her forehead. She didn't touch her coffee.

"I don't feel good," she said to her husband. "Maybe we should go?"

It was as if he regained consciousness then.

"What time is it?" he asked.

"Seven," replied the hostess and after a moment's hesitation she added, "in the evening."

Both guests rose.

"I think we'll be off now. Shouldn't overstay our welcome on the first . . . oh, what am I saying. Maybe you could stop by our place tomorrow?"

Their parting words came only at the door:

"If you happen to hear anything . . ."

"We'll be in touch."

They both went back to their armchairs and sprawled out in their old seats. They pushed the neighbors' cups away.

"Why did you bring them up here?"

But he didn't respond. He was completely absorbed in looking through an old newspaper.

"There was supposed to be a movie after the news today."

"They weren't interesting. They were just like us, scared and boring. Did you see the state she was in?"

He still didn't respond, so she got up and put the book back in its place.

"I don't get scared as long as I don't think," she said, "but as soon as I start thinking I start getting scared. If we just had the television. What was the movie called?"

He put down the paper and leaned back. He shut his eyes.

"I don't know."

"Say something."

He didn't move.

She got up and started looking for a place to pray again. She knelt in the same place as before, facing the covered window. He observed her from under his half-closed lids, furtively.

"Angel of God"—she looked at him, and instantly he shut his eyes—"angels of God, our guardians, watch over me always. Morning evening day night, be always by our side . . ."

"What are you praying to, the tapestries?" he said quietly.

"Keep our souls and bodies, lead us—"

"There's no such thing as angels or God. People come from dust and then they crumble right back into dust."

"—to everlasting life. Amen."

She got up off the floor, wiped off her knees mechanically, and went back to her chair.

"I was just thinking that the angels must be the same thing to us that we are to dogs. Looking after us. Knowing what's best for us. Bobik never knew what was good for him. He didn't want to take his pills when he had worms. So maybe something like that is happening now, you know. He's treating us for worms."

"Who?" he said, opening his eyes.

"God."

"You've gone insane."

She looked at him in disgust.

"You're just so awful, so awful."

"I have no illusions."

She stood, picked up the cups, and went into the kitchen.

"You're a bad little man. A slippery snake," she said.

They were sitting in their chairs, practically in the dark. Only the little lamp in the hallway was still on. She had on a stretched-out, beat-up nightshirt, he was wearing striped pajamas. He brought in a little candle and set it on the coffee table. She looked at him in surprise, rubbing lotion into her hands, when he lit it.

"We have to economize electricity," he said conspiratorially.

"I always have felt ill at ease just about when it starts to get dark," she said. "Everything seems worse and scarier in the dark. Then in the morning I'm always surprised I was so scared during the night. Now it's dark all the time. You think something happened to her?"

"I don't think so."

In the light of the candle he lay out three types of pills in little piles and started putting them in a little box for the next day.

"Who else do we love?" she asked after a brief pause.

He froze in surprise, pills in his hands.

"What do you mean?"

"Who else can we worry about?"

"Don't you have enough?" he said, returning to his former pursuit.

She twisted the cap back on the bottle of lotion and went to the window. She slowly slid back a corner of the blanket.

"There's a car," she shrieked.

He leaped out of his chair and ran to the window.

"Where? Show me where."

They crowded around the exposed strip of glass.

"I told you people weren't just going to sit at home, that they would start going out. It's just not human nature to let ourselves get shut in like this. Better to die immediately."

"I think they're beginning to loot the stores. Collecting sustenance."

She looked at him.

"We have to go out and get something too. What are we going to eat if this keeps on?"

"Has it occurred to you that it could be like this forever?"

He went back to the coffee table and collected the pills. She took the lotion to the bathroom. They stood across from each other in the hall.

"Do you think you could come to my room tonight to sleep? Maybe it'd just be safer somehow . . ." she said.

"You snore. I wouldn't get any sleep."

They retreated into their separate bedrooms, but she paused once more with her hand on the door handle.

"Do you think that Bobik will be saved?" she asked.

"Maniac," he muttered, and they both shut the doors behind them. ⬟

Khadijah Queen

I SLEPT WHEN I COULDN'T MOVE

after Alice Notley

Black girl, black girl
Don't lie to me
Tell me where
Did you sleep last night
                    —LEADBELLY, "Black Girl (In the Pines)"

I slept in my own bed in need of replacement
I slept sitting up against a steel bunk in Illinois winter next to military strangers
I slept beneath a run of pipes on a destroyer & I slept with a failed guitarist
I slept on his brocade couch in the Valley & left before I could remember his face
I slept in the deepest part of Watts
    in my lover's grandmother's house
    with a view of an abandoned lot overgrown with weeds & drug trash
    he kept his mouth
    persistent & unfamiliar
In a dark turn I slept in a bathtub dispossessed
I slept with love & treated myself to unkindness
I slept after repeating myself alone & I slept in a friend's guest room with a broken window
    & listened to nameless strays killing what they eat it's hard work
When I was small I slept with three sisters the same size in a house with the gas cut off
I slept with a man who hated himself & we slept in a beautiful bed in a loft with a
    downtown view
    & he brought me red wine & cold water

I slept happily in hotels when I could escape

I slept in a mountain cottage & wrapped myself in a crocheted blanket & sorrow &
     wrote poems about my animus

I slept on the floor in my father's house I never slept in the brick
     one-story my grandfather built & sometimes I feel like concrete

I slept in the palm of my own black hand

I slept when I couldn't move

I slept in a place that hadn't been built yet & dreamed the sheer violence of the future

I slept inside a song with a Blacker voice than mine which meant I slept good

I slept in the orange light of day silence

I never slept on the street

I slept in the knotted hair of my sister's children in Detroit & washed & combed it in the
     morning

I slept when I couldn't move

I slept in a California desert, free of bodies & trees

I slept through earthquakes & El Niño & never stopped traveling

I slept by an ancient lake

I slept in my car on the side of Fountain Street at dawn & my car shook from the traffic
     but I worked all night & couldn't wake up

I slept in a rented studio apartment in Brooklyn with roaches & the aroma of
     methamphetamines
     climbing through vents & under the door & dreamed about work I slept to the
     repetition of Cesária Évora

I slept on a feather bed & let myself dream a cracked blue

I slept in a red dress & sparrows woke me in the morning

I slept in a black dress & saw a hawk in my grandmother's magnolia I slept in my beauty
    & in sleep I knew that beauty as an inheritance
    & couldn't be stolen or strung up or caged or appropriated effectively & it's mine
    & what I have to own I have to love it

I slept where I was born & a rude wind pushed me into exile

I slept in the infinite arrangements of Prince's instruments

I slept out of dreams when cranes cut the sky in an era of smog

I slept in San Joaquin farm country & there were too many kinds of molesters

I slept when I couldn't move

I slept in on a Sunday next to the radio

I slept crying every night for a year when I failed at my best thing but I kept him alive I
    slept in a world I forgot to love sometimes

I slept as if I still believed in rescue

I slept expensively & poorly & middle class

I slept when I couldn't afford to

I slept in stolen freesia

I slept for a moment in snow & reclamation

I slept in Hejira & wasn't cruel when I slept

I slept in kinship with my faults

In a dream I was hopeful & slept when I needed a radical silence

I slept next to a man's portrait with someone else & more than once I didn't close my eyes

I slept in a lie & the comfort felt so real it was real

I slept as if I were years

I slept so many years I couldn't find

In sleep my eyes dreamt the nearness of waiting & couldn't touch it

I slept in the clues I couldn't wake from

I slept in hidden cameras & microphones

I slept in secret & in public

I slept so sure in a used place & so anonymous like womanhood & so hypervisible

I slept in a kind of fire & became it

I slept in a place of mourned bones & the future of Blackness

I slept in a system outside of every law but one

I slept when I couldn't move

I slept in a simple way

I slept in a place just for us

I slept where I could see it

ANDREW WYETH'S FOOTNOTES TO MARRIAGE, 1993

1. "Every poem is a momentary stay against the confusion of the world." (Frost)
2. Where the poetry of love lies, I will ask to sit before it.
3. *Realism.*
   * Chadds Ford, Pennsylvania.
   † Gain their trust.
   ‡ Ask for entrance.
   § Paint them without waking them.
   ¶ Leave before dawn.
4. In the marriage bed, two bodies under the weight of sheets, wool, quilt, coverlet.
5. Both pink faces peek out from under cover.
6. The arms are concealed, but do the hands touch?
7. The wedding gown has almost entirely been eaten by moths.
8. Her body, even in sleep, knows he is hers. His body, even in sleep, knows she is his.
9. The ruffles line the seams of the mattress. The dark wood of the headboard.
10. Out the window, the straw-colored field and barren trees.
11. The morning star held sky-high, as lovers side by side sleep.
12. They share this bed, although there are other beds in the house. He takes the side by the window; she has the side by the dresser.

13. Someone turns over, someone coughs, someone snores. They do it together.

14. "There is no remedy for love but to love more." (Thoreau)

15. To love nearness, one has to love otherness, in the dead truth of the night.

16. I came at night to paint the marriage hour, for here is acceptance, here is peace in each other's company. Tonight, here is a love beyond love.

17. *Aperi oculos tuos*: Coral sepia cinnamon green egg buff creosote heather mauve peach.

ANDREW WYETH'S FOOTNOTES TO CHRISTINA'S WORLD, 1948

1. "All good things are wild and free." (Thoreau)
2. *Realism.*
   * Cushing, Maine.
   † Observing will teach you the world.
   ‡ Compose with your imagination.
3. *Tempera.*
   * Use a technique unlike your father's.
   † Toss the egg whites.
   ‡ Some landscapes require white wine.
4. Their house high on the hill, the distance she's traveled to distance herself from it.
5. Eventually, the arms must drag her body either way she chooses to go.
6. For now, she prefers to sit among the summer hues.
7. The slope that holds her seated body does not judge.
8. A breeze whips her hair from her face.
9. The loyal earth beneath her feels companionable.
10. I painted my imagining of her seeking the quietude and stillness of nature.
11. To sit alone with her thoughts, which are themselves quiet.
12. Restorative silence, I suppose, is what she craves after each day that's burdened by a dependent body.
13. "The poet writes the history of his body." (Thoreau)

14. A woman cannot live with a pack of wolves or in the tree canopies.
15. The collective is stronger than the individual.
16. At times she just needs to be on a grassy knoll and to remain in a space of no choices.
17. To find grounded purpose in a singular, conscious moment on Earth.
18. "The earth I tread on is not a dead inert mass. It is a body—has a spirit—is organic—and fluid to the influence of its spirit—and to whatever particle of that spirit is in me." (Thoreau)
19. *Aperi oculos tuos*: Blush rose cobblestone honey loden peridot bay leaf glacier molasses brandy.
20. *I have this hate within me.*

Can Only Houses Be Haunted?

Marie-Helene Bertino

SOMEONE SAYS, "LET'S RENT A FARMHOUSE IN THE COUNTRY.
"Let's pick apples and swim, lie on blankets and read, make pies with
the apples we pick." They say country peaches are faultless. That even if
you think you don't like them once you have one you can't imagine your
life without it. So we load our sedan with what we know we're good at—
bread recipes, Bananagrams—and what we hope we'll be good at—croquet, from a box of equipment we found *just lying on the street*. We spend
the weekend in an after-the-second-drink malaise, swim laps, gorge on
supple peaches, and with heavy mallets perform majestic roquets to make
one another giggle. Each afternoon a breeze looses golden leaves upon our
sunning bodies. The report of the screen door: everything's fine. Everything rented. Lathered, reapplied. Watusi-ed. When Monday arrives we
idle in the kitchen, leftovers cellophaned, damp trunks drying on back
windshields, in the part of the afternoon when the light is most beautiful,
and everyone feels slightly deceased.

That's when Riva and Aurelio mention they need a ride home.

My husband, Vig, hoists himself into a sitting position on the counter
and says, "We'll take them," and I say, "But we were planning to stop in
at farm stands?" which is one of those questions that is really a statement,
and instead of replying he asks Riva how she feels about farm stands and
of course she loves them because who doesn't?

The matter settled, we break ranks to run final checks of the bedrooms
and hug Cooper, the farm's guileless, luminous retriever.

I fold towels and sulk. I'd been nursing an idea of myself strolling
through aisles of produce, fingers bumping harmlessly over eggplants and
cantaloupe. Riva is a clinging, anxious shopper who makes strolling impossible and I prefer shopping alone or with Vig and Vig knows this. I didn't

grow up with things like farm stands or croquet or whiskey glasses or even lawns. I'd borrowed money from my mother to afford this weekend. Vig's offer to Riva violates a pact we have: No intruders. Us before everyone. We decline most invitations and sleep with weapons by our bedsides.

"Isn't this something we should have discussed?" I say, as we pull a macrame cover over the bed.

He passes me a glacial look. "Try to be friendlier."

Which hurts of course but I do it, I friendly up. I'm even smiling when we rejoin the group to discover that Riva and Aurelio forgot an errand they have on Frank's side of town, and it follows they should ride back with him. The problem has evaporated, yet as our sedan crunches down the driveway, the idea of our potential passengers shimmers as solidly as if they were safety-belted in the back: ghosts of some infraction Vig has committed against me.

"If you'd like a kid," I say, "I'm happy to kick you in the shins."

Even Cooper's cheerful jowls as he gallops next to our car fail to please me. We may as well've taken the freeloaders home.

The bliss of the weekend already husking away from me, we pass the first farm stand. No longer interested but trapped by my earlier, forceful passion, I point and Vig dutifully pulls in.

Within moments we are standing in front of a stack of velvety peaches. In aggregate they seem to tremble with good health but when I pick one up its tacky skin recoils from my touch, which figures. Like Vig, they don't want to be around me. "These are maybe not the ripest?"

"I'm sure they're fine," Vig says, though his gaze rests on a little boy sitting in a shopping cart, gumming a banana peel. Seeing Vig, the boy chucks the peel onto the ground. His mother picks it up. The boy considers, chucks it again. Vig catches it and, smiling, returns it to the mother.

We bag eight peaches and join the line.

"If you'd like a kid," I say, "I'm happy to kick you in the shins." One of Vig's favorite things about me is my wit. I'm always saying things like, *Doing yoga is like lighting a candle and throwing it out the window*. I have a bit for children. Whenever we are doing something that would be rendered impossible by having them, I say, "Should we have children?" Cocktails at noon, cocaine at midnight, panting after one of our intense screws: *Should we have children?* I'm positive I am very funny.

"What a jerk," I prompt him, about the kid.

"Jerk," he says, his tone absent.

Driving out of the parking lot, we notice a parliament of gravestones near the highway entrance.

Vig announces: "This farm stand has been brought to you by the souls of your dead relatives."

This brightens my mood. I'm thinking, *If he's willing to make a silly remark, maybe this ride can be salvaged.*

During our first years together, we offered each other copious, tangible examples of our love. A vintage pencil sharpener, the kind you crank. New ways to make a hamburger. This grew tiring. Eventually, humanely, we allowed each other rest from being impressive, which was comforting until it became uneasy, something we weren't sure we'd invited.

> Boo-hoo, says the dead girl, like she's been hired to provide crying sounds for an old cartoon.

That night, clattering in the kitchen wakes us. Metal against metal, a collision of separate things against a solid. In the rubbed nothing of predawn Vig and I wait to see if it is a solitary disturbance, able to be explained by a surprise of wind through our measly screens, or whether it will prove itself malignant by repeating. Wind, I pray.

Another burst of noise.

Vig sleeves the crowbar he keeps on his side of the bed and I take hold of the bat I keep on mine. Armed, we creep down the hallway and stall in fear when we reach the kitchen. Whatever is behind the door overturns a drawer of silverware.

Vig straightens, his mouth in a serious line. Giving himself a pep talk in the voice of his sixth-grade baseball coach, no doubt, the one who gave him the chance to bat during the only game his mother attended. I know every inflection of that story better than I know certain friends. He told it two days before while everyone treaded water in the swimming hole, feet pale disks pedaling beneath us.

Strike one. Turn and face his mother. Strike two. His mother digging for something in her purse. Full count, etc. . . .

Vig traces a square in the air, points downward, points to me, the square again. I get that he wants me to stay behind him while he opens the door but Vig doesn't trust my ability to understand simple facts. He hisses, "Stay behind me while I open the door." He turns the knob and soundlessly pushes.

In the corner of our kitchen an eyeless girl carangs the emptied silverware drawer against the antique hutch I bought when I was single. Cutlery is piled in jagged hills by her ankles. She's seven or eight. But also a million? It's obvious she's been dead for a while, even to Vig, who usually requires three unrelated sources to believe anything. Gray skin corkscrews off her throat. Exposed veins reach toward the overhead light. A glowing current throbs around her, tethering her to the fruit bowl, where the peaches we bought seize and pitch. They are attendant in this haunting, each one pulsing with a force that wants out. We both realize this simultaneously, still Vig whisper-screams, "She came from the peaches."

"Vig. I know!"

The dead girl swivels at the sound of our voices. She produces the steak knife I'd asked Vig to sharpen but now I'm glad he never did because she hurls it at us, then reloads with a soup ladle.

We retreat into the hallway and slam the door. I suck in air and Vig paces.

The dead girl is still throwing cutlery and now it sounds like she's crying. Sloppy-sounding and exact. *Boo-hoo*, she says. *Boo-hoooooo*.

"She's crying," Vig says, needlessly. "What do you think she wants? With us, I mean."

"I don't know what she wants." My tone meant to remind him that it doesn't matter what she wants.

Her boo-hoos intensify. *How's drama school?* I want to say.

Vig's expression digs at me. The way he looked at the dead girl was the same way he looked at the farm stand kid, a mixture of wonder and longing. "Do you think she's trying to find her mother?"

There is no doubt this jab is deliberate. "Maybe her mother is working," I say.

"This is not about you," Vig says. Which makes me certain it is.

Boo-hoo, says the dead girl, like she's been hired to provide crying sounds for an old cartoon.

Vig rests his hand against the doorjamb as if consoling the girl. "She's more scared of us than we are of her." It's a personal reflection, he's given up speaking to me.

"I knew this would happen," I say.

"You knew a dead girl was going to rise from the produce?"

"Something felt off. My nerves have been—"

"Your nerves." The word returns us to an argument we'd had at the farm-house. My nerves are famous within our relationship, and were the reason I'd given when I'd suggested we wake everyone up early in the morning.

"Frank would've slept until midnight!" I hiss. "I didn't want to miss the day!"

"Did you think we were going to say good night and never see each other again?"

The discomfort of the weekend's conclusion settles over me newly, how quickly Vig offered a place in our car even though he knew I wanted to drive home alone, open to whatever sprung up along the way that seemed doable. Even though I couldn't articulate what those doable activities might be, I wanted him to protect my desire to do them. Refueled, my anger catches onto itself and spreads.

On the other side of the door, the dead girl drags what sounds like the table across the floor. A walnut vintage find. I imagine the divots this is carving into the hardwood.

"What if there are more?" Vig says. "We bought eight."

We realize that we've each ingested a peach and look down at our stom-achs, expecting mutiny. None comes. In a moment I can only describe as relationship telepathy, we understand how we can get rid of her. Vig explains it anyway.

"If she came from the peaches"—he points to the kitchen—"and we eat the rest of the peaches—"

"I know, Vig!"

"I can't re-kill that dead girl," he says at the same time I say, "I'll hold her."

"Are you are empathizing with something that just threw a steak knife at us?"

"Listen to her," he says. "She's sad."

"She's dead!"

"So judgmental!"

"Not a judgment. Not up for debate. She's fucking dead."

"Still. She's a—"

"Don't say it."

". . . guest in our home."

"A pest! A roach or one of those box insects that crawl into the air conditioner."

"Stinkbugs," he says. "Don't even bite."

"This is my house. That's my steak knife. You're on her side!"

"A little girl!"

"An intruder!"

Our arguments tend to hedge between hurtful and comically ridiculous. I'm wondering which side we're on when another knife hits the door and sticks. It makes a sound like *sarong!* and helps Vig shake his hesitance. "You're right," he says. "Let's get her."

I preen in this rare give. It's my turn to pantomime. I point to the kitchen, pretend to hold a struggling thing, point to him, pretend to quickly eat a number of ball-shaped things.

We reenter the kitchen. The dead girl cries cruddy tears in the corner, clutching one of Vig's childhood spoons. A bunny-shaped handle.

"Not a judgment. Not up for debate. She's fucking dead."

It's always the singular first-person pronoun with him, I think as we creep toward her. Always *I* can't re-kill the dead girl, never *we*.

"I'm sorry," Vig says. "Maybe you can find another home where people are better equipped to handle you?"

Her soulless gaze darts around the room. My shadow stripes her when we approach, yet she fixes on Vig. Her whole body palpitates as she weeps. She senses he is the more emotionally permeable, her veins plead for him, as if I'm not capable of maternity. I make myself as wide as possible and trap her while Vig clamps onto the furred flesh of the first peach. He bites down and the dead girl reacts as if punched. Even before swallowing the first he takes another, bigger bite. Juice streams down his chin and pools in the hollow between his collarbones. He bites again and again, the pulp of the pulp, finishing it.

"Watch the hardwoods," I remind him, attempting to make my voice jaunty.

He looks at me with lifeless eyes.

The dead girl throws herself at me, her decomposing body like sandpaper against my bare arms. Burns bloom where she touches me.

"Are you seeing this?" I say, but Vig has turned toward the hallway, unable to watch her suffer. This ignites something unprocessed in me. Now the dead girl and I are both yowling. With every bite, her pain increases. She singes my skin everywhere she touches. My throat convulses as vomit ascends.

Two peaches remain. We're going to make it. Vig chews through a choking fit that slows his progress. I yell for him to hurry and he tells me to for once in my life be goddamned patient. One peach to go. Vig runs his bottom molars across the soft meat as if it were a corncob. He finishes. With a teeth-shattering shriek, an arc against the sky, the girl's outline advances its grotesque theory, quibbles, then fades.

She's gone. What's left are the pits. Flinty-looking with clots of jam and marrow. "We have to get rid of them too," I say. "Can't take chances."

"It's over," he says. "You got what you wanted."

> How unlike a country peach
> I am. How filled with flaw.

I've been told I've a tendency to grow inches taller with indignation. I tower over him. "What I—?" I show him the burns on my arms. "She tried to kill me! Someone needed to do something."

He says, "Don't say it."

"What kind of man—"

"There it is," he says. "Set your watch. It always ends with the man thing. Honestly, honey? You need a new act. I am the man I am. Able to show love the only way I know how."

"Show love?" I soil the word. "Where love? What love? Sounds nice. I'd like to order some of that."

He disappears through the back door. This is it, I think. The final final, but he returns carrying a croquet mallet. He raises it over his head and sends it down on one of the pits, which splinters under the assault. "This is love!" He brings the mallet down again, obliterating another oaky center. His aggravation has faded into mania. He's giddy, irreverent. "My love!" The mallet comes down. "For you!" The mallet comes down, catching the morning light ekeing through the windows. "This is my devotion!" The mallet comes down, bruising the hardwood. "My manhood!" His absurdity has surpassed mine. He's won.

I laugh, in spite of myself. Surprised, he turns to me. His posture softens. He hoists the mallet to the opposite shoulder so I will laugh again.

"Do you like this?" he says. I say, "I do."

He thrusts his hip to the side, bats his lashes, comically askance. "And this?" I say, "Very much."

Of course, it was already over. It had been since Vig leapt to a sitting position on the rented counter and offered Riva and Aurelio a ride.

Before the country weekend, all of it—us, I mean, Vig and me—had been beginning to end—the initial descent. We lingered in the doorway between stopping and saving. Neither of us knew how to kick the relationship toward the good side or, more likely, neither of us knew which side was good.

I hated the way he said "ice-cold milk." Worse than double homicide, that sound. Every night it seemed he wanted a glass of one.

"You know what I could go for?" he'd say, as if he didn't posit the same thing every night. "A glass of ice. Cold. Milk."

You should like the way your partner says *milk*. But I know less than nothing. For example, I don't even remember one way to make a hamburger.

I hadn't thought about that dead girl for ages until yesterday when someone asked if only houses can be haunted. And Tessa said, "Yes, only houses and buildings." This was after the morning meeting, when we usually loiter in the conference room deciding whether to eat the other side of the bagel. Tessa is always correcting me over things that mean nothing, over things that aren't even things. She reminds me of Vig.

I hadn't thought about Vig in a while either, but now he's as present as if he were sitting at the conference table with us, slathering jam onto a bagel. The truth is, I can't remember him ever saying he didn't want children. All deception is self-deception. They don't tell you this in lying school. How disappointed he must have been with me, a girl who wouldn't give her friends a ride home. How unlike a country peach I am. How filled with flaw. I hope whoever he's with now grew up with enough of everything so that they never feel the need to guard their experiences.

So I told my office mates that once I fought a dead girl who came from a haunted bag of peaches and their expressions switched to *tell us more*. Which is a welcome change from how they normally look at me, a combination of *who let that fly in* and *this paint color looks darker than it did on the chip*. I haven't been working this job or living in this town long, and I realized the story could curry me friendship. I'm not above using personal low points as currency. So I told them about the dead girl and the peaches and they asked questions until it would have been deceptive to not mention it had happened with an ex-husband.

"That was the last experience we had together," I said. "Unless you count divorce."

Thinking about it now however, divorce is more procedure than experience. A removal that produces a scar. One thing gone, one thing added. So I agree with my first statement. It was the last experience Vig and I had together, in the part of a relationship when you agree without consult to avoid opening the door for the thing that will completely unravel you. How interested we all are in delaying the inevitable when the inevitable has never been anything other than the most patient, caring lover on earth. 🏮

Katie Condon

PRACTICING DIGRESSIONS
for Richard

I am eager to grow old. What a joy
it will be to bear love down
on whatever daughters I force

into this sometimes lovely world,
preaching similar things, I bet,
that my mother preached to me

—like: *You are a woman. Praise
yourself.* What a light her scriptures are
on this morning that is as gray and cool

as the last lake on the mountain
before it gives itself up to the sky.
I meant to be telling you about

age, not my mother, who is aging,
not mountains or mornings
or the unforgivingly expansive sky. I admit

it will be difficult not to mention
the robin on the wire, the light
lifting itself up over my lover's

slender body, which he lives in more
confidently than I have witnessed of myself.
I am practicing digressions on you

so that I can prepare for the ways my
memory will loosen itself from around
itself, uncoiling like the threads

in the ice-skating-penguins sweater
I'll love when I'm eighty
and never want to take off, even

as summer's weight bears
down like my mother bore down
on me—my mother, whose voice

is familiar in this poem, though, years
will have bounded by since I heard her
sing. Where was I—mountains, steep

as memory. Water, morning, light.
My lover's body stirring, his hands
trembling after thousands

of mornings exploring every new
wrinkle on my breasts. Have I
spoken of birds? How they stay

on longer into the cold than
they should, and for what? To learn
how to forage for food that is not there,

to harvest something finally of absence
that they will keep with them
when they decide to flit off

into the thick mist of late fall
that, when I was young, I wanted
to walk through, believing

I would make myself a ghost.

PARABLE

Rage & oregano.   The open window.   The lawn.

      A fledgling hops the nest
           while the robin is gone.

Steam from the pot.
        Tomatoes. Tomatillos. Ricotta.

    Same as anywhere else.   A mother's corpse rests

      in the armoire.   O, ash.   O, want

    for miracle.   Aspen. Chrysanthemums.   Caterpillar

in the basil   Mother said you should have killed.   Liver & current.

   Blood & sand.   Dove songs.   Early kale.

      Mother said,
          Desire digs a pretty grave.

You balance on her tomb.

        Foxglove. Forsythia. A bad spill
        on the white carpet.   Get the bleach.   Hold

        the baby.
            The fledgling shakes in the cardboard box.

            Dusk bears dawn bears dusk.

YOGA SOLILOQUY

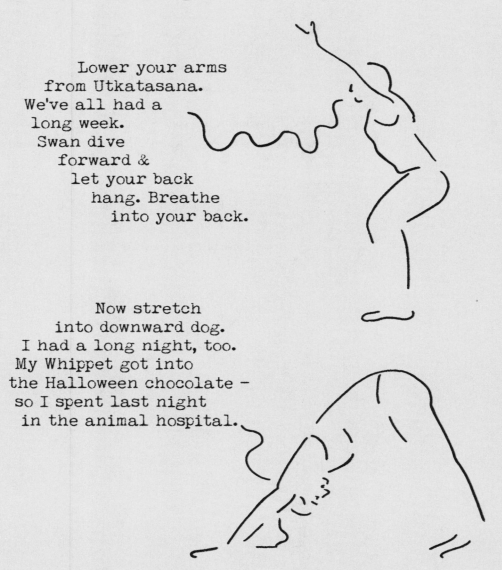

Lower your arms
from Utkatasana.
We've all had a
long week.
Swan dive
forward &
let your back
hang. Breathe
into your back.

Now stretch
into downward dog.
I had a long night, too.
My Whippet got into
the Halloween chocolate –
so I spent last night
in the animal hospital.

Back into
  child's pose.
    There were all sorts
      of sick dogs.
    Cancer, one dog
    with Alzheimer's.
    Don't forget to
    keep breathing!

    But he's alright now.
  Now on all fours.
Do some cat & cow.
  Only a few
    more minutes
      until Savasana.

from A PRIMER FOR FORGETTING

Lewis Hyde

On the Use and Abuse of History for Life

Many years ago, reading about the old oral cultures where wisdom and history lived not in books but on the tongue, I found my curiosity aroused by one brief remark: "Oral societies," I read, keep themselves "in equilibrium . . . by sloughing off memories which no longer have present relevance." My interest at the time was in memory itself, in the valuable ways that persons and cultures keep the past in mind, but here was a contrary note, one that clearly stirred my own contrary spirit, for I began to keep scrapbooks of other cases in which letting go of the past proves to be at least as useful as preserving it. My consequent thought experiment has sought to test the proposition that forgetfulness can be more useful than memory or, at the very least, that memory functions best in tandem with forgetting. To praise forgetting is not,

of course, the same as speaking against memory; any experiment worth conducting ought sometimes to yield negative or null results and mine is no exception. As in the excerpt that follows, there are times when we're forced to say, "No, here we must remember" (though, ironically, stirring up resistance to forgetting can itself be one of the uses of forgetting). Memory and forgetting: these are the faculties of mind by which we are aware of time, and time is a mystery. Writers like myself who work very slowly are well advised to settle on topics such as these, topics whose fascination may never be exhausted. Such authors do not simply tell us what they know; they invite us to join them in confronting the necessary limits of our knowing.

—LEWIS HYDE

Grief swept the kingdom of Denmark for the queen had died giving birth to her son. The ladies-in-waiting took the babe and, naming him Ogier, laid him on a royal bed of down. And lo! six shining fairies appeared by his bedside and endowed him fully with gifts of bravery and beauty. Morgan le Fay, Queen of the Fairies, came last, promising a life of earthly glory to be followed by eternal ease as her consort in Avalon, the land of fairy.

Years later, when Ogier the Dane had come of age, he pledged himself a knight in service to the emperor Charlemagne. So it was that when Rome was overtaken by the pagan hordes of Islam, Ogier joined the crusade to regain that holy city. Battle upon battle followed, Ogier galloping into the fray fierce as a lion, hewing his way through the paynims, reaping among the enemy until he ramparted himself with a wall of the slain.

So unfolds the legend of Ogier the Dane. Hindu princes convert to the cross under his spell; women, their white dresses sown with pearls, love him; Saracen giants fall to Courtain, his invincible sword; grateful nations crown him king of Britain, then of Babylon, then of Jerusalem.

Finally, sailing home from the Holy Land, Ogier's ship ran aground on a lodestone reef. The warrior, old and weary, had come to Avalon, where, in her shining white kirtle, Morgan le Fay, Queen of the Fairies, awaited.

"Welcome, dear knight, to Avalon. A weary time have I longed and waited for thy coming. Now thou art mine; my lord, my love. So let the restless ages roll, and the world totter and decay! We will dream on forever in this changeless vale."

Then she put an enchanted ring upon his hand; so the years slipped from his shoulders and he stood before her in the prime of youth and vigor. And she placed upon his brow a priceless golden crown of myrtle leaves and laurel, a crown no mortal treasure would suffice to buy—the Crown of Forgetfulness. Then Ogier remembered no more the things that were past. His old loves, toils and battles faded from his mind; and in place of a dead memory a living love was given him, and he joined the fairy queen in a land that knows neither time nor death.

Two hundred years slipped by as if they were a single day.

. . .

Trouble came again to France and Christendom. Chivalry was dead; the pagan hordes of Islam had conquered the Franks on every side. The people cried for help and Morgan le Fay, Queen of the Fairies, heard them and took pity. She lifted from the head of Ogier the Dane the Crown of Forgetfulness and, as if waking from a dream, he cried out, "My sword, my horse, my spear! Oh, let me go, sweet Queen!"

Then once again the mighty warrior appeared among the disheartened Franks, and once again the battlefield was tracked with lines of slain, until France was free, the Church secure, the spirit of chivalry reborn. Then Ogier the Dane assumed the throne that had long ago belonged to Charlemagne and prepared to marry—only of a sudden to be spirited away again by Morgan le Fay, Queen of the Fairies.

But Ogier the Dane is not dead. His brow wreathed by the myrtle and laurel of oblivion, he sleeps in Avalon, and in the days that come, whenever their foes draw near, Morgan le Fay, Queen of the Fairies, will take pity and lift his crown, and send her paladin to fight again for France and Christendom.

SHAM GRANDEURS

Though it is true that the Danish resistance in World War II (Christians fighting Christians in that case) took its name, Holger Danske, from the legendary hero, there is really little to admire in this disgusting old fairy tale. Neither of its worlds appeals, not the temporal land of memory and warfare nor the timeless land of oblivion and peace. The latter is too dreamy with no study of either self or nation; it offers at best an artless forgetfulness, regression without reflection.

As for "France and Christendom," I am reminded of Mark Twain's complaint that the American Civil War could "in great measure" be blamed on romance novels, especially those of Sir Walter Scott, stuffed

"with dreams and phantoms; with decayed and swinish forms of religion . . . ; with the silliness and emptinesses, sham grandeurs, sham gauds, and sham chivalries of a brainless and worthless long-vanished society." Just so the tale of Ogier the Dane and its jejune daydream.

And yet two things do interest me here. That Crown of Forgetfulness, of course, but also the way it is set against conflict—and not just any conflict but the centuries-old division between Christianity and Islam. "Ogier the Dane" is pure Orientalism, that politics of difference animating the violence of Christian imperialism.

The twinned pattern of the legend—forgetfulness and conflict in recurring sequence—is also of interest, its vision of history in which differences mean nothing for centuries, then suddenly come back into play, then as suddenly disappear. By turns the heroes are shoring up their identity with enemy corpses and letting it dissolve in fairy idleness.

Where is the politics or the spiritual teaching that might end such a cycle? Is there any statecraft such that nations might forget their wounds? And what, for that matter, is a nation?

"THE ESSENCE OF A NATION."

In the late nineteenth century, the philologist Ernest Renan published an essay—"What Is a Nation?"—in which he argued

And what, for that matter, is a nation?

that "the essence of a nation is that all its individuals have many things in common, and also that everybody has forgotten many things." The point need not be limited to nations; all group identity, all abstract knowing, has such origins. Families know themselves by mixing recollection and elision; so do oral societies (it was Walter Ong who noted that they keep themselves "in equilibrium . . . by sloughing off memories which no longer have present relevance"). Still, for centuries now nations have been perhaps the largest theaters for the practice of collective forgetting. "No French citizen knows whether he is a Burgund, an Alain, a Taifala, or a Visigoth," wrote Renan. "Every French citizen has forgotten St. Bartholomew's Day and the thirteenth-century massacres in the Midi."

A late entry in France's sixteenth-century Wars of Religion, the St. Bartholomew's Day massacre saw Catholic mobs slaughter thousands of Calvinist Protestants. But French citizens no more call that day to mind than do American citizens remember how their Puritan ancestors used to hang Quakers on the Boston Common or, for that matter, the history of nineteenth-century Indian Wars.

INDIAN REMOVAL FULLY
ACCOMPLISHED.
When I was a child we had cereal boxes from the backs of which could be cut cardboard figures of cowboys and Indians. Nightmares then disturbed my sleep, a chaos of cardboard bodies clashing and threatening, their very flatness adding to the horror.

. . .

Grandfather and Grandmother owned a cabin on Ten Mile Lake in northern Minnesota where we sometimes spent part of the summer. Grandmother once gave me a model canoe, perhaps sixteen inches long and fashioned from birch bark strapped to a bentwood frame. Perhaps it was Ojibwa, perhaps an antique, or perhaps made for the tourist trade, I never knew. And I never to my knowledge met an Indian during our summers at the lake.

At home in Connecticut I took Grandmother's gift to school to display in the glass case outside our classroom. My teacher, Mrs. Swenson, inspected my offering and gave her critique: I had misspelled canoe.

. . .

We went on a hike and got lost. I was nine, we were living in rural northeast Connecticut, and we were trying to find Hatchet Pond, a popular excursion site in the nineteenth century (or so we were told by one of our aged neighbors) because around the pond lay the remains of Indian

> In my mind's eye I can see them still, deep in the shaded pine forest.

villages and graveyards. In my mind's eye I can see them still, deep in the shaded pine forest, dark grave mounds with rotted wooden markers. My mind, however, is the only place these graves appear for in fact we never found them. Nor did we find the pond despite hiking for hours and Father at one point sending me up a tree in a fruitless attempt to spot it.

My main memory of this adventure is not, however, any details of forest or pond but rather that my brother and I had loaded our backpacks with comic books to read when we pitched our tents that night, and Father's amused disgust at how shallow were his children. My favorite comic heroes: Superman and Scrooge McDuck.

Such is the full account of the Indians of my childhood.

DAWN, NOVEMBER 29, 1864, COLORADO TERRITORY

Two white men came running from the Indian lodges as Colonel John Chivington and his cavalry descended on the Cheyenne and Arapaho encampment at Sand Creek. First the interpreter John Smith ran out with his hands raised but he retreated when the soldiers shot at him. Then Private Lowderbuck came out with a white flag but he got the same welcome. Chivington's cavalry of about seven hundred met a similar number of Indians, but only a fraction of these were men of fighting age. "Hundreds of women and children were coming toward us and getting on their knees for mercy," reported Captain Silas Soule, who had refused to join in the attack. "I tell you," he wrote a fellow officer, "it was hard to see little children on their knees have their brains beat out by men professing to be civilized."

Soule witnessed one soldier sever a woman's arm with a hatchet, then dash her brains out. Another woman hung herself in a low-roofed lodge, holding up her knees so she might choke to death. Another "was cut open and a child taken out of her, and scalped." Another knelt with her two children "begging for their lives of a dozen soldiers"; when one of these wounded her in the thigh "she took a knife and cut the throats of both children and then killed herself."

Chiefs Black Kettle and Left Hand had been to Denver earlier that year to meet with Chivington and territorial Governor John Evans and express their desire to live in harmony with the whites. They left with the understanding that they would not be disturbed so long as they flew an American flag. George Bent—whose father was a white trader and mother a Cheyenne and who was living at Sand Creek when Chivington attacked—reported that Black Kettle had the American flag "tied to the end of a long lodgepole and was standing in front of his lodge . . . the flag fluttering in the gray light of the winter dawn." White Antelope "had been telling the Cheyennes for months that the whites were good people and that peace was going to be made." Now, as the cavalry shot him, he "stood in front of his lodge with his arms folded across his breast, singing the death song: 'Nothing lives long, Only the earth and the mountains.'" Left Hand too was shot, "hands folded across his breast . . . saying, 'Soldiers no hurt me—soldiers my friends.'"

Some Indians fought back and some escaped, "but most . . . were run down by horsemen . . . They were all scalped." Bodies were "horribly mutilated," Soule wrote. Fingers were cut off to get their rings. "White Antelope, War Bonnet and a number of others had Ears and Privates cut off. Squaws' snatches were cut out for trophies." The massacre lasted eight hours, at the end of which Chivington's men burned the camp. For a day afterward they carried one three-month-old infant around in the feedbox of a wagon, then left it on the ground to perish.

"THE VOICES OF CHILDREN . . ."

The first memorial to the Sand Creek Massacre appeared in 1950, an obelisk near Chivington, Colorado, bearing a plaque that reads in part: "Many Indians were killed, no prisoners were taken. The white losses were ten killed and thirty-eight wounded. One of the regrettable tragedies in the conquest of the west." Years later those who were the object of that conquest began to make themselves into the agents of its memory. In 1978, Cheyenne chief Laird Cometsevah and the Cheyenne Sacred Arrow Keeper conducted a ceremony to reclaim the Sand Creek killing field and make it once again "Cheyenne earth." Later, when the federal government moved to make the site officially "historic," there was considerable disagreement as to the massacre's precise location, but Cometsevah knew exactly where it had taken place because when he and the Arrow Keeper conducted their ritual he had heard "the voices of children, of mothers, crying for help."

For the Cheyenne and Arapaho a prime motive for memorializing Sand Creek was to respond to those restless dead and give them proper burial. For Gail Ridgely of the Northern Arapaho, whose great-great-grandfather, Lame Man, survived the massacre, the creation of a national historic site promised to "allow our people to remember their ancestors and help put their suffering to rest."

Ridgely's statement supposes an interesting divide—the memory will endure, the suffering will not—and raises the question of how traumatic memories get resolved. In the case of Sand Creek, would the creation of a memorial be adequate to the task? Could a "national historic site" serve as the kind of grave marker (something you can visit but you do not have to) that sufficiently separates past and present to allow a fresh future to unfold?

When I try to enumerate all that needs to be in place for any marker to accomplish such ends I find myself with a daunting list: it would be good to have truth and justice, of course, but also apology (both declared and acknowledged) or forgiveness (both requested and granted) and reparations for all that was lost, and finally, in this case, the literal burial of the mutilated dead.

To begin at the head of this list, there should never have been any doubt about the truth of what happened at Sand Creek, Silas Soule and others having written eyewitness accounts within weeks of the massacre. But from the very first Chivington and his supporters contested those accounts—to them the engagement had been a glorious battle, not a massacre, and Black Kettle a savage, not a peacemaker—and, despite a federal investigation, no one from the Colorado Cavalry was ever brought to trial. The truth-teller Soule himself was assassinated: he testified before a military investigation in February 1865 and a few months later in Denver two of Chivington's men shot him. Historian Ari Kelman's book *A Misplaced Massacre* was my primary guide into this complicated story and Kelman tells us that for "nearly a century, from the start of the reservation era until relatively recently, Cheyenne and Arapaho people were discouraged, sometimes violently, from telling their Sand Creek stories. Boarding school administrators, Bureau of Indian Affairs officials, and other white authorities believed that keeping alive memories of the massacre preserved links to the past, to a traditional way of life, hindering acculturation."

As for the white population, to this day there are those willing to celebrate Chivington as a hero and to speak of the Sand Creek encampment as "harboring terrorists." For many years, one Jerry Russell of Little Rock, Arkansas, served as national chairman of the Order of the Indian Wars, a group dedicated to preserving the memory of the "soldiers, pioneers and settlers who were the agents of manifest destiny, and who, with unyielding bravery and uncommon sacrifice, helped to tame the New World and build the America that we all cherish beyond description."

Complaining that the National Park Service was wrongly advocating a multicultural agenda, Russell traveled to Colorado in 2003 especially to celebrate Chivington. "Some folks, bleeding hearts from back east, have been calling Sand Creek a massacre for a long time," he declared, but it wasn't a massacre, it was a battle, "battlefields are about honor," and Chivington was an honorable man. The National Park Service's version of events was just "politically correct" history, complained another member of the order. Indians are "always victims. They're always downtrodden, victimized by oppressive power. And there's some truth to that, yeah. But it's an excuse now. Get over it."

In sum, truth and justice have been hard to come by.

In sum, truth and justice have been hard to come by.

REPARATIONS & APOLOGY

As for reparations and apology, these appeared to be in the offing almost immediately after the massacre when representatives of the US government met with the Cheyenne and Arapaho in the fall of 1865 to sign the Treaty of the Little Arkansas.

Article 6 of that document opens with the United States declaring itself as "being desirous to express its condemnation of, and, as far as may be, [to] repudiate the gross and wanton outrages perpetrated against certain bands of Cheyenne and Arrapahoe [sic] Indians." Noting that "said Indians were at peace with the United States, and under its flag, whose protection they had by lawful authority been promised and induced to seek," the treaty goes on to affirm the government's desire "to make some suitable reparation for the injuries then done," these being mostly land grants (320 acres to Black Kettle, for example) and payment "in United States securities, animals, goods, provisions, or such other useful articles," all as "compensation for property . . . destroyed or taken" by Chivington's troops.

The terms of this treaty have never been honored; until they are, all subsequent expressions of regret have a hollow ring. Colorado Senator Ben Nighthorse Campbell (of Cheyenne descent on his father's side) once announced his support for reparations and Kansas Senator Sam Brownback once declared, "As a U.S. senator from a Plains state, I deeply apologize, and I'll work to right this wrong. I humbly ask the Native Americans here, and their leaders in particular, to forgive us." But Senator Campbell never followed words with action, saying that to bring the matter before the US Senate would be "a nonstarter," and Senator Brownback's offer "to right this wrong" did not mean making good on the broken promises of the 1865 treaty.

"The Cheyenne will not accept an apology for what happened at Sand Creek for the simple reason that Sand Creek is not over," Cometsevah has said. "The U.S. government still owes the descendants of the massacre. We're not going to accept any apology until Article 6 of the Treaty of the Little Arkansas is completed."

> It was an imposition of identity: "You are a conquered people."

PROPER BURIAL

As for actual and proper burial, the spirits of the Sand Creek dead have good reason to cry out for help. Not only did Chivington's men mutilate the bodies—taking scalps, ears, and genitals for trophies—but some years later General William Tecumseh Sherman and his troops visited the killing fields and gathered more souvenirs. Some of the remains they collected ended up in specimen drawers at the Smithsonian Institution while others went to the Army Medical Museum in Maryland, where, during the Indian Wars, they were used to study the effects of gunshot on the human body. As Steve Brady, head of the Sand Creek Massacre Descendants

Committee, once said, "We, the Cheyenne people, were the scientific specimens that improved the U.S. military's killing efficiency, its ordnance."

In 1911 the family of Major Jacob Downing, one of Chivington's fellow officers, made a donation to the Colorado Historical Society, briefly described by its accession label: "Scalp (Cheyenne or Arapaho), Taken from an Indian by a soldier at Sand Creek Massacre, by Jacob Downing Nov. 29, 1864." In the summer of 2008 this and the body parts of five other Sand Creek dead—reclaimed from museums and private collections—were assembled at a park service site near La Junta, Colorado, and then driven to the cemetery established at Sand Creek, where Cometsevah had heard the voices of the dead. Beneath an American and a white flag—flying in deliberate echo of those flown in 1864—the gathered descendants prayed in Cheyenne, sang again White Antelope's death song, read aloud Silas Soule's account of the massacre, and then lowered the dead ancestors' remains into sandy graves.

A FAILED EXPERIMENT

Truth, justice, apology, forgiveness, reparations, burial—that list makes for an ambitious preamble to any release from historical trauma. If *A Primer for Forgetting* is a thought experiment seeking out places where forgetting is more useful than memory, then here is an instance in which the experiment fails or, at least, where it has yet to be carried to closure. Interring the body parts of six of the mutilated dead seems hardly sufficient to soften the Indians' insistence on the need to keep Sand Creek history alive. "People always say you can't carve things in stone, but we have to. We have to be sure nobody forgets," said Cometsevah during negotiations over the proposed historic site, a sentiment repeated at the dedication of the completed monument: "Now Sand Creek will never be forgotten."

The mutilation of the bodies at Sand Creek was more than trophy hunting, it was an imposition of identity: "You are a conquered people." The cutting of genitalia was an almost literal genocide: these are people who will now not be able to reproduce themselves, the generations will not follow one upon another, the very organs of generation having been cut away and the unborn stripped from their mothers' wombs.

At issue for Native peoples, then, are matters of agency, of cultural and political power. Who's in charge of this story? One of my aphorisms reads, "Nothing can be forgotten that was not first in mind," but I must admit it begs the question of who is forgetting, especially when it comes to cultural memory. If there is a "work of forgetting," it has to involve claiming or creating agency such that you, the people saddled with history, can work on the past rather than have the past work on you. When it comes to collective memory— the kind that calls for a national historic site—you can't begin to remember in a way that allows you to forget until the collective itself recognizes and responds to the history at hand. Only then can you both claim an identity as your own and enjoy the privilege of forgetting about it. There is no self-forgetting without self.

AMERICA

Recall Ernest Renan: "the essence of a nation is that all its individuals have many things in common, and also that everybody has forgotten many things." As noted, in one sense, Renan is describing the process by which all abstractions emerge: we select the particulars that count and discard the rest. How then, if the goal is to establish a national historic site, to assemble the abstraction "The United States of America"? Several options come to mind.

In one, Indians will not forget Sand Creek and the rest of the nation will not remember it, in which case "America" does not include the Indians. In another, Indians are forced to forget. The story is erased, denied, disputed; its telling is forbidden in the name of assimilation. Indians then become part of an "America" that is a version of Gore Vidal's "United States of Amnesia," a place where the real work of forgetting (the working through of a memory rather then its repression) never gets done. Or, finally, Indians do not forget and the rest of the nation joins them in remembering. The Sand Creek Massacre then becomes a thing held "in common," and "America" is understood to be a nation born in blood and cruelty, as are so many others. 🏛

Joshua Marie Wilkinson

BIGHORN RIVER, MONTANA

The old ways in the world
are probably still somewhere inside
the bones of my wrist.

I don't want to be part of any song
you're humming as you use baiting
as a kind of verb.

On the third day I let the fishermen take
to the river early as I hung around

the cabin alone with a pot of coffee and
The Savage Detectives.

There's something of me in that
story. But what does it communicate

of significance? If you shift, the hawks know.
That's part of it. And if the vultures want you
they know what to do. That's another part.

The moon's raining white ash in the cholla.

My elderly neighbor likes to go in
and out of her house all morning, all afternoon.
Back and forth, the screen door's squeak, then
smacking again and again, evidently

for nothing. Sometimes when I can't think
I ask her in my mind to stop it. I never say
it out loud.

It's her house, after all. But
God. It's over. Just stop.

Three Scenes

I

Elmhurst café, kind with zero English on the signs, where you can get frog eggs or taro balls in your bubble tea, hot summer afternoon, tinny girl K-pop over the speakers—an Asian boy sitting with his white girlfriend and his mother. The mother is recounting in solid English a story about the war, the supplies cut off, rations reduced, the boy sitting with his knee jogging, impatient to model patience, waiting to take control of the conversation (he'd already made fun of her for saying, "People have no sense of geometry nowadays" when she'd meant "geography") while the white girl checks her face in a compact mirror right in the open, right under their faces. The mother is completely used to being ignored and patronized. Each of the three, in fact, exudes their particular private disdains: the old for the young; the young for the old; the white for the yellow; the male for the female. At the end of the mother's recital the son announces, "Let's go," and the mother stands up instantaneously, serenely. The white girl first takes her time finishing something around her eyebrows.

Nam Le

What they'd been talking about. The boy mocking some white girl who had asked his friend Ricky where he was from in Taiwan, and whether he spoke Taiwanese, when he'd said he was from Thailand. And they didn't even speak Taiwanese in Taiwan anyway. His white girlfriend had defended the white girl in the story, knowing she could well have made those errors, and look at her, she wasn't racist, she was going out with an Asian guy! At which point the mother had made the comment about geometry: some people she talked to still thought Hong Kong was owned by the Japanese. The Japanese! And suddenly she was telling a story she'd never told before, about the public execution of a colleague she'd attended in King's Park in Kowloon, the sound of the sword when it met bone, like in the movie about Nanking, or was it Nanjing, and how these things coexist and co-pollute every moment of our lives: a smutty pop song on the radio, the sun-dazed street, the matter-of-fact recountal of hallucinatory murder over condensed-milk oolong, the daycare across the street tumbling toddlers into a large fenced play yard, the countergirl wiping the specials placard, the grinding over of a mortal human millennium, the fight you're having with your husband, whom you love and who you know loves you, yet you believe unworthy of you, whom you know yourself unworthy for.

2

(A man proposes to a woman. She says no. She does it even though she loves him, she does it because she wants to be true, to herself, to the long game of her feelings. She is sure about her decision. She honors her non-certainty, she honors her irresolved feeling. She knows (has long known) how she wants this moment to feel—the moment of being proposed to—and this is not it. Then follows excruciation: they remain together in an expensive hotel room, in great, strangled, interlocking pain, they love each other but can no longer bear to be with each other; she pities him, hates herself for hurting him, is secretly, perversely, inordinately self-proud for standing

---

NOTE: These pieces are drawn from a longer sequence inspired by events described in Fredric Dannen's account of Asian American gangs in New York City ("Revenge of the Green Dragons," the *New Yorker*, November 16, 1992).

up for her principles (whatever they are) (whatever the cost). (The costs here borne mainly by him.) He had arranged a speech, a wood fire, Japanese magnolia petals, her favorite, a rare recording of their song, champagne, all things impeccable (if a little passé), each prop now shrapnel in his heart. Needless to say, he is embarrassed, humiliated, but also slowly filling with fear: his sense of himself has sheered away, the promise, the confidence that he was good enough for her, that someone like her could love someone like him—could love him. He desires nothing more than to leave, to get out from under the pain, but he knows that if he leaves now he may never see her again. And he suspects that that would destroy him. The record plays on at its customary pace. She comes up behind him. He is crying. She puts her hand on his shoulder and he turns, slowly, and they dance. And as happens in the movie of it, one thing leads to another and they start kissing, he undoes the clasp of her dress, she lifts herself back onto the dining table, the dress slides up her bare, freshly shaved legs; they start to make love—she feels . . . more for him than she ever has; she feels the pleasure of giving him pleasure; the pleasure is bittersweet, laced, strong. She feels suddenly uncertain about her earlier certainty; she feels suddenly sure—in a way that requires strength, and that pleases her, always has, the idea that rightness can be at least in part a function of will—and her decision is changed, now it is yes. She says yes. She tells him yes. Time passes, months, years. It was the wrong decision.)

3

Speaking of movies, it was *The Blair Witch Project*, he was coming home from a matinee when, entering the high-rise lobby, he saw the elevator door open and a lone white woman step in. Around here you might wait fifteen, twenty minutes for the lift, that's if it's even working, which don't get your hopes up, and even then maybe not make it in; he sprinted through the two sets of security doors, braced his arm against the side portal and slung his weight around into a small Asian man who was on his way out. He smiled apologetically to the Asian man, conspiratorially to the white woman. Inside, *hot*. He pressed the button for floor 14. As the cab door closed, he heard the sound of footsteps running toward them.

He did not press the "open" button. One hand's breadth from closing, the door shuddered, stopped, then slid back open and already his finger had flown to the button, jabbing it urgently and repeatedly for the ancient Asian woman, heavily wrinkled, with merry eyes, who herded in a group of kids in school uniforms, who then smiled at him with knowing scorn. The white woman dabbed her sweating cheeks with the insides of her shoulders. Must be twenty degrees hotter in here. The kids were about second or third grade: three chubby Asian boys with spike cuts, one Asian girl, and one skinny black boy who wore a nonregulation hoodie and held a red plastic plate on which was a half-eaten hot dog, some fries, ketchup, and a wad of sauerkraut so rancid it started to make the small room swim. The kids pressed a bunch of buttons—2, 3, 5, 20, 21—and the white woman caught his eye and made a look as though to say, *Great*. In fact, she may have said this under her breath. His sinuses smarting, stinging, he turned away from the black kid just as one of the Asian boys turned toward him and asked, "Are you Bowls?" The black kid mumbled something. The old lady smiled. The Asian kid said something about Johnnie getting suspended, and the black kid said, *I know*, in a strong old-school Queens accent. At 2, one of the Asian boys got out. At the next level no one got out. At the next level the black kid got out. No goodbyes or anything. When he was gone, everyone exhaled audibly. The boy who had spoken to him turned to the girl, probably his sister, and declared, "They all *do* look the same, seriously!" The girl exploded into delighted laughter. The old lady continued to beam. The boy mimicked the black boy stooped under his hoodie, mumbling, eating his fries, giving it all a moronic spin, and then glanced up at the white woman, and then at him, to see if they minded. Did she then share a look with him? He didn't mind.

That night, he had difficulty getting to sleep. Any time he came close he'd be startled by the bang of a basketball against wooden backboard, the clang against steel rim or cast iron manhole cover. He saw without looking the spasmodic movements of the players fourteen floors below, stop and go, pick and pop. He wouldn't have minded a lot more, to be honest. Someone shoves the black boy out of the elevator. Gives him an educational whack upside the head. Kicks him in the ribs. Hacks him with a blade. No, a wholesome bashing's okay but not that, not hacking, none of that Hutu shit. But now you're lying to yourself. (But what if you saw it only from a distance? What if only on a screen? What if someone merely told you that someone else had taken it upon themselves to do this thing?) He would have been amazed to learn that the basketball court fourteen floors down was utterly empty of life, save for a cat stalking the three-point line, then pressing its belly to the blacktop. To be honest. You could be genuinely aghast at the thought and yet, given mood, given time—and not even time of any real want or pain—a hot stint in a sauerkraut stench—you could just as genuinely crave butchery. *Blair Witch* could not be more wrong: the worst horror was not—had never been—what you couldn't see. Barely five yards above him, on the other side of paint, gypsum, lime, fly ash and concrete, the white woman from the elevator permitted herself a nightcap, noticing for the first time that the wineglass's rim was exactly the same circumference as its base, such that you could invert the glass again and again and the tablemat would never know, never tell. 🛡

from SOME QUESTIONS ABOUT TREES

MISSISSIPPI:
Of course I read about the trees. I was taught to fear the trees
at night and don't look too close into the branches. And I had seen
a catalpa before but I didn't know how mighty, how they grow
under so much sun and shine. Some swooped so heavy and so low
you'd need a metal beam to help hoist its branches and the giant leaves
like a skirt over a puddle. When you say it—*catalpa*—it sounds as though
you're trying to chew a mouthful of gumdrops, all the smarting sugar
already tongued off clean when you try to tell someone a secret.
Have you ever told a catalpa a secret?

INDIANA:
Not a catalpa—though how could you not fall at least a little bit in love
with the cascade of dangling hearts, or with the shadowhearts herding
beneath the tree like buffalo, that very most solemn of beasts. Is that catalpa?
Shadowheart sounds like maybe not the best friend for telling secrets to. All
the same, every spring I catch myself whispering to the redbuds, also a heart-
on-the-sleeve tree, though their hearts come, shadow and otherwise, after the
flowers push from the wood like a zillion tongues telling their own secrets.
Which makes it kind of mutual, though I always eat some of the redbuds'
secrets, which are ghostly sweet. You?

MISSISSIPPI:

You and your redbuds! I never understood what you meant
until I saw one here—how its blooms plash out from unexpected places
—the most beautiful wound in a redbud's bark. I'm too nervous to taste
tree secrets now, but surely I've smelled some. Surely my marbled lungs
still carry spring pollen from loblolly pines. Which suits me just fine—
a glorious gold-green rewarding everything in its path with a sylvan radiance.
What else do I practice here but the lost muscle of breathing? Sometimes
a scrape of nest falls from the loblolly pines like a mud turtle from my hands.
Sometimes the moon gifts me a scrap of paper but I want to paint a whole
mural. What charms your bones these days? What do you hold?

INDIANA:

The most beautiful wound in a redbud's bark. The most beautiful wound
in a sycamore's bark. The most beautiful wound in a pin oak's bark. The
most beautiful wound in a silver maple's bark. The most beautiful wound in
a loblolly's bark. The most beautiful wound in a dogwood's bark. The most
beautiful wound in a persimmon's bark. The most beautiful wound in a
hickory's bark. The most beautiful wound in a chokecherry's bark. The most
beautiful wound in a pawpaw's bark. The most beautiful wound in a black
walnut's bark. The most beautiful tree growing from the wound in my small
heart's dark.

MISSISSIPPI:

And the slender tree in me is not a cave for bats
to make a curlicue in the atria of my ripe hearts.
If I let the tree ladder out of me—let it grow a bit wilder
in the South—would trees give us sweet and would trees
give us slow? This month the harvest moon lights
each tree as if they hatched fresh from a gecko egg. What
the moon does to magnolias is something like a bit of magic
and it deserves a better name. Something celestial
or clouded, but beautiful on the tongue. Did you know
a moon can have a moon and that is called a moonmoon?
When twilight ends, I hope the moonmoon I walk under
becomes a cloud of perfume—my throat would color
the end of the day like how scarlet milkweed creates
such a flying, fine attitude in so many tiny mouths.

INDIANA:
It is not unheard of, this tree scaling
through your body, scrawling amidst moonmoon-
lit ribs: earthen letter inscribed on your tongue.
And if this tree, too this owl; too this bat
swaying asleep beneath your breath; too this
pill bug, or the thousand thousand pill bugs
blazed like gems in the fluffy black loam too
in you, loam the moonmoon licks through with light;
too the coyote's whisker flecked with blood; too
the fluff of whatever we killed for sport
the moonmoon looms into a caul ringing
doomdoom; *doomdoom, doomdoom* the trees these days
ladder through my throat singing.

Dogpatch

Elizabeth McKenzie

I used to go from office to office, filling in for people who were sick, on maternity leave, had family emergencies, or had simply said, "I quit" and walked out the door. I was fast on a keyboard and could fit in quickly without much training. I developed a good reputation as this kind of office substitute in the radius of three buildings in downtown San Francisco in the nineties. One of these buildings was full of small businesses and nonprofits, another of medical offices, yet another of law firms. Before I knew it, my schedule was full, almost as if people were planning their pregnancies or their family emergencies around the next opening on my calendar.

Not really. I'd never say such a presumptuous thing if it were about something I really cared about. I'd feel too vulnerable and superstitious. But looking back on those days, talking about basic office skills, I see no reason not to brag away.

Back then I was single, had been in a few relationships, wasn't especially eager to have a new one. I liked being so busy I didn't need to plan my spare time. I had a month-to-month room in North Beach, skipped dinner sometimes in favor of a few cocktails, ignored calls from my crazy parents. I was young.

At work, I made an art out of my organizational skills. I wasn't fussy about anything else in my life, so it was amusing when office mates started to make remarks about having me check their work as if I were the resident anal retentive. Sometimes I felt I had to rebel, so as not to be seen as some kind of uptight worshipper of minutiae. For instance, if I went out with people I'd met on jobs, I'd find myself drinking a little more than I should, preferring to leave a trail of confusion behind me than to develop real friendships. And there were no repercussions, work-wise. I got along with the revolving temps at the agency saving up for their trips to Thailand or other short-term goals. I was always in demand. Occasionally, the agency would even pull me out of one job to put me in another, more important one.

Maybe it was all due to Eleanor, one of the dispatchers at TempRight. She was weirdly enthusiastic about me.

"Well, doll, you have several choices next week," she'd typically say. "You could take a position over at Curtis for two weeks, their front office gal is getting married and going on her honeymoon, and they pay higher than standard. Or you could do a month at Shoreline, the data firm. You enjoyed that last time. Or, let's see, we have a new order today from Haarton Medical, day to day at this point. But all those handsome doctors parading around! What'll it be?"

Something did bother me. I had the feeling that Eleanor, having watched me rise up the ranks, thought I planned to work for TempRight forever, as if this were my life's purpose, finally achieved. On the other hand, my goals were nebulous at that point. Making a quick splash followed by escape seemed to be my only area of expertise.

> Sometimes I felt I had to rebel, so as not to be seen as some kind of uptight worshipper of minutiae.

One day she called about a new account in the area known as Dogpatch, an industrial zone a few miles south of Market where the agency had been aiming to get a foothold. TempRight, she claimed, wanted to send me as their ambassador. It could be an important breakthrough for them. I was sure to make a good impression, she said, as if I were concerned for the firm's health and even eager to help shoulder responsibility for it. I appreciated that TempRight thought highly of me. But what kind of company could they be, if I was their secret weapon? And were their problems supposed to be mine too? Wasn't that the point of doing temp work, that you were free from all that?

The new account, Abernathy's, made lacquer and other coatings. Not much to get excited about there. A month could be a long time, but I agreed to it.

. . .

My first day on the job I arrived early, allowing extra time because I'd never taken public transport to this scruffy, forgotten part of town. The address was on a mixed-use street littered with cans and paper, and, true to its Dogpatch name, a few strays were sniffing and scavenging the sidewalks in a perfected state of detachment. I walked past an old parking garage, a noisy brake and muffler shop, a bar called The Cave, and a key maker before arriving at a cement-block building abutting a large warehouse. The office had a glass door, the desk in full view from the street, and when I entered, I introduced myself to the young woman sitting there. She had pale skin and notable peach fuzz on her cheeks. She said her name was Melody and that this was an exciting day for her because Abernathy's had made her permanent and she was getting her own office in back somewhere. Just then, a slightly older woman appeared. With beautifully coiffed dark hair, wearing an emerald-colored skirt, a white blouse, pearls and red lipstick, heavy nylons and black heels, she made a striking impression. She said, "Jan Wyatt? I'm Mrs. Kennedy. Please take a seat. I applaud your eagerness, but you'll have to wait."

Huge fans rotated from the ceiling, but the fumes were inescapable.

Eagerness? That was funny, but I was into fine-tuning the impression I made at these jobs, so I replied, most politely, "Of course."

Having gathered her things, Melody slid her chair against the desk. "Good luck," she said cheerfully, and I said, "See you around." They exited into a corridor, and I heard a large, heavy door open and close behind them.

The front office held little of interest, except for the hangings on the wall behind the desk—a bunch of shiny lacquered objects, like wooden trays, masks, and carvings, seemingly collected in various parts of the globe. There was also a plaque of beetles and other insects immortalized in glossy coats. Maybe the most singular item was a single red rose, tied to a hook with invisible thread. The rose was as glossy as glass. But when I looked closely, I could see the burrowing marks of an insect on the long green stem, daring me to conclude that it was a real flower, suspended in time through the magic of sealants.

I suspected I would not last there long. I started planning what I would tell Eleanor, but eventually I heard the door open and shut and Mrs.

Kennedy returned in a considerably brighter mood, as if shuttling Melody to her promotion had left her engorged with some kind of administrative ecstasy. She said, almost breathlessly, "Welcome to Abernathy's, one of the largest manufacturers of sealants in the western United States. Miss Wyatt, I have been with Abernathy's almost thirty years, and we're a company of over one hundred full-time employees, many of whom have also been here nearly as long as I have. You will work here at reception, where you will answer phones, direct orders, enter data into the computer, and take various typing assignments from me. Your agency tells us you're one of the best."

"Thank you," I said, blushing not so much at the compliment but at the absurdity of it.

As she described a few more aspects of the company and my job, I listened, startled by her odd composure and formal diction. She looked as if she should be hosting dinner parties in Washington, DC, rather than tucked away in this dumpy office on this mangy street. I listened as if the instructions for my job there were a matter of national security.

The initiation included a short tour of the warehouse. Mrs. Kennedy led me down the corridor, whereupon she used a ring of keys to unlock the door that I'd heard slam before. I was startled by the intensity of the fumes that surrounded us as we entered the factory, which was distinctly colder than the office and bathed in gray light from some grimy skylights. Despite the chill, danger signs warning of flammable substances seemed to be everywhere. Dinosaur-sized machines buzzed and clanked, conveyor belts hummed, moving metal cans under huge drums with funnels, where they were filled, closed with mechanical arms, then bundled by labelers, clustered, slapped onto pallets, then stacked by forklifts into towering piles near the loading docks in back. Huge fans rotated from the ceiling, but the fumes were inescapable. All around me were people of indeterminate age and sex wearing white coats, white caps, and face masks.

As I followed Mrs. Kennedy through the warehouse, I casually asked where Melody's new office was.

She turned and said, "Melody's in another location. She won't be available to speak to you, I'm afraid."

"That's fine," I said, detecting a note of defensiveness in her voice. Maybe she thought I was criticizing how she hadn't arranged for Melody to brief me on the job, which was fairly standard practice when I started somewhere. I must have misunderstood Melody when she mentioned the location of her new office. "Really, that's fine," I reassured Mrs. Kennedy.

We returned to the sanctuary of the front office. What a miserable place, I thought. What could account for the longevity of these workers? I took my seat at the desk and Mrs. Kennedy gave me a list of new accounts to enter into a database and thus I began. From my desk I couldn't hear a thing from the warehouse.

. . .

Every morning that month I woke up glad I had somewhere to go, and equally glad the job would soon be over. I'm not sure I can explain the odd relationship I had to this type of work. Every day I was aware of myself standing on the precipice of decision. At any moment, if I didn't like what I was doing, I could request a different job from Eleanor. If she said no, I could abandon TempRight and go to a different agency altogether. Nobody owned me and that's exactly how I wanted it. At the same time, I liked being wanted, and I knew this was my weakness. It was very easy to manipulate me by making me feel needed. It was a struggle that went on inside me all the time, yet somehow kept me on track.

The supply and demand for sealants became the currency of my days. To add color to the hours, I'd fasten onto extraneous details in the correspondence and the bills of lading, such as the mailing addresses where products were being shipped: Atlanta, Georgia. Oak Lawn, Illinois. Bisbee, Arizona. Binghamton, New York. Toledo, Ohio. Hammond, Louisiana. Crofton, Maryland. I'd imagine each town and make myself choose from the current batch the one I'd move to if someone said I had to choose. (Oak Lawn sounded nice enough, though perhaps like a cemetery.) Maybe I was suffering from the fumes.

It was true, from time to time, I felt light-headed, and wondered if vapors were seeping into the office and if they were having some kind of effect on me, but the feeling would pass and I'd return to my work. My fingers typed away. Sometimes I tested my typing. I'd memorize a line I was supposed to enter, then type it in without looking, then see whether or not I'd made a mess. Usually I'd get it just right. Other times I'd produce a bunch of gibberish, what I called the language of the keys, everything off by only one letter but completely unintelligible: YJsmld upi gpt upit trvrmy ptfrt pg zkimr . . .

A steady stream of wholesalers quickly learned my name and crossed Melody's from their Rolodexes, and over the phone we'd exchange human pleasantries to give the dry transactions some soul. At lunchtime, I'd go out to a food truck on the corner and buy two pork tacos. The first week, I walked around the warehouse to see if any of the glue sniffers were hanging around outside, but it just wasn't that kind of place. So I'd bring a novel or a crossword puzzle and eat behind my desk.

Nearly every day, Mrs. Kennedy made a point of complimenting me on something or other. She liked my scarf, she liked my skirt. "Of course, it's not hard for a young woman to be pretty," she said one day, with a detectable bite. "And yet it takes a lifetime of smart choices to be attractive in middle age." To be sure, she seemed dedicated to her appearance, and dressed like Jackie Kennedy, in Coco Chanel- and Oleg Cassini-style suits. Even her hair was like Jackie's. I imagined it kept things interesting for her, decking herself out for work. Otherwise, how could she stand it? Thirty years there—anywhere for that matter—managing that office and payroll?

> The supply and demand for sealants became the currency of my days.

The main strange thing about Mrs. Kennedy, I hate to mention, was that she seemed forever surrounded by an unpleasant smell. As she spoke, a sour, musty odor came forth not just from her mouth but from her entire being. It reminded me of something, and every time I came up against it I tried to figure out what could account for the utterly dead smell of her person. Then it hit me. My parents had once allowed some of my stuff that I was storing with them to sit under a leak, and when I came to claim it, just about everything had been ravaged by mold. Suffice it to say, despite her elegance and sheen, Mrs. Kennedy's exhalations smelled like rot. I wondered if she might have an undiagnosed illness, her insides being eaten alive by disease. Or was it simply the stagnation of thirty years in one place?

· · ·

One day, we had a visit from the company's owner, Mr. John R. Connelly. He was a man in his eighties, with icy white hair, even icier blue eyes, and bright white teeth, who despite his years seemed in admirable shape. He'd undoubtedly been a handsome man in his youth, and possibly still fancied himself as such. He asked me a few questions about where I grew up, what my "people" did—I said something vague but passing as respectable. My "people"—the phrase curdled my blood.

In the manner of an old-timer, he wanted to educate me.

"Let me ask you, young lady, what is the nature of a sealant? Yes, it's to preserve and protect. And in essence, that was what my young life was dedicated to. Banking was a gentleman's business in those days. We protected young families and helped them start their independent lives. And then came the war. When it was over, and I thought about what I'd seen across Europe, I realized I'd seen destruction raised to an art form." He went on to say there was a change in the banking industry after the war. It became all about unchecked growth and profit. When presented with the opportunity to join the community of solvent manufacturers, through his dear deceased wife's family, he took the broad view. The mission of the company appealed to him. Sealants, polishes, lacquers—preserving and protecting.

Of course I knew what she meant, or believed I did.

Then he asked if I could guess who had inspired him most in his life, but I had no clue. His voice changed tenor and he said: "'The times demand new invention, innovation, imagination, decision. I am asking each of you to be pioneers on that new frontier.' Do you know whose words those are?"

I shook my head.

"That's a pity. It was John Fitzgerald Kennedy. I once met the man. I met his wife. The absolute best of youth, idealism, and beauty."

I gagged inwardly. My parents, malcontents of Irish descent, had somehow made room in their cynical hearts for the whole Kennedy mystique. It was *If Kennedy had survived everything would've been different* my whole life, as if his death were an excuse for their drinking, gambling, and other failings.

"A brief and shining moment," he went on.

"Now I see why Mrs. Kennedy got a job here," I blurted out, stupidly.

"What's that?" he said, leaning my way.

"Mrs. Kennedy," I said. "Her name."

His smile was so mild, I wasn't sure he'd heard me. He said I looked like a fine young lady and had the gall to wink at me as he wandered out of the room. Even in the nineties, a successful older man thought the world and everything in it was his to mark.

Later that day, Mrs. Kennedy reported that he'd been impressed with me, so to deflect the shallow compliment, I said, "He sure loves the Kennedys."

"Yes he does."

"Do you think you got your job because your name is Kennedy?"

It was a ridiculous provocation, but the end of my time there was in sight.

"My name wasn't Kennedy when I was hired," she replied.

"Oh, of course, it's your married name." Then I wanted to ask if she'd married someone named Kennedy to please Mr. Connelly, but held my tongue.

. . .

The nineties in San Francisco were great and terrible, I want to mention. But I lost track of so many people back then I could avoid finding out what had happened to them. The tech boom had yet to come, and the landscape of the city was still largely quaint and uneven. I'm not sure we really appreciated that a little apartment remained cheap, or that slow-starters like me could still be part of the scene. At my favorite club, I told my friends about the freaks at Abernathy's, but I was probably just adding noise.

The day before my assignment ended, Mrs. Kennedy made her move. "Why don't you come into my office, Jan? I think it's time to have a talk."

Of course I knew what she meant, or believed I did. The talk would be to see if I'd go from temporary to permanent. There was no way I wanted to work there for real. It would be easy to tell her so because I was a mainstay at TempRight and was clearly loyal to them. I could tell her that without saying anything about my personal feelings about her deadening job.

I followed her down the corridor to her office. It was the first time I'd set foot there. Her space was pretty drab, especially considering the length of her tenure at the company. She had a basic desk on which sat a stapler, a big heavy computer of the type used back then, a printer, an in-box, a mug filled with pens and scissors. There was an indoor plant by the window, some kind of bromeliad with leaves the size of crocodile heads. And there was a chair stacked with trade magazines in a corner with an end table on which sat a small collection of thimbles, placed in a circle on a doily.

I forestalled the inevitable by asking her about Mr. Connelly. In those days, you couldn't just look somebody up on the internet.

The thrill in her eyes! She described a man from a "fine midwestern banking family" who'd been a football hero and a business major at his college in Wisconsin, who had married into a "good" San Francisco family, and had gone into the varnish and lacquer business with his father-in-law just after the war, when the housing boom in California was taking off. They had made a fortune. But John R. Connelly was more than a businessman, she assured me. He was a civic leader, a Rotarian, a preservationist, a maverick.

I sensed she'd been in love with him, maybe still was.

Once she'd finished exclaiming about Mr. Connelly, she said, "Jan, let me get to the point. Your assignment here ends tomorrow, but we just can't have that. You are everything that Mr. Connelly—and I—believes makes this company a success. You understand, I'm sure."

It was best to cut this off as quickly as possible. I expressed my gratitude, but explained that I was happy working for TempRight.

"But the agency has given us permission to offer you a permanent contract already," she said. "They'll receive a finder's fee, of course. Didn't you know they're headhunters as well?"

Her face, though composed as ever, was so full of deceit that there was little chance I could disguise the scorn on mine. I said, "I'm sorry, but there's no way Eleanor would agree to that without asking me. Let's call her right now, let's ask her."

She placed her hand on the phone, but right then I was hit by a powerful wave of vertigo, and held on to my seat. The fumes were worse in her office than in mine.

"I need to get out of here," I said.

"Miss Wyatt, please," she said, in a slow and steady voice. "There's no reason to fight. This is a wonderful opportunity for someone like you. It's not easy to drift from one allegiance to another, I know that . . ."

The next thing I knew I was back at my desk. I felt as if I was coming out of a fog. Bit by bit, reality reassembled itself. I looked at my watch and realized nearly an hour had passed, and it was after five. I shuddered and put on my coat. What had just happened?

As I walked up the street I stopped at a dismal telephone booth. The one that smelled like a urinal. Chewing gum was stuck to the phone box on all sides. A greasy bag had been stuffed between the phone and the metal platform beneath it, and a phone book dangled from a cable splattered with something red and sticky like catsup. I put in a call to Eleanor and told her the story, asking if she'd really made an offer to place me there.

I was expecting an indulgent apology, but it didn't come. Instead, Eleanor betrayed me. She said, "Babe, Mrs. Kennedy said that you fit right in, that you seemed a natural. I'm sorry I misunderstood. But we really need to do right by these people. We want their business. Please go back tomorrow and complete your temporary assignment. All right? You're the best, Jan!" she said.

I extruded myself from the stall.

Until now, I'd thought Eleanor wanted to keep me at TempRight forever. I'd never thought she'd want to pawn me off like this. I'd thought she was on my side, almost like a mentor. But what was I thinking, what was the chance of that? Another sham upon sham. I felt both rejected and entrapped. Of course, that was how I usually felt, one way or another.

. . .

And so came my last day at Abernathy's. I arrived that day in less than optimal shape. I'd stayed out late, drinking a few too many. Earlier in the evening, in a moment of weakness, I'd almost made the mistake of calling home.

I felt as if I was coming out of a fog. Bit by bit, reality reassembled itself.

At my desk, I found a bouquet of roses and an envelope with my name on it. I took off my coat, smelled the roses. As I tore open the envelope a warm feeling passed through me. It seemed almost normal that the card should say: *We're so glad you're joining us, Jan. You are what makes Abernathy's great.*

I sat back in my chair and laughed. I was no longer angry. I simply tried to piece together the bizarre events that had led to this mix-up. At the same time, I felt flattened, ready to surrender. What did it matter, as I crept in this petty pace from day to day? When Mrs. Kennedy came into the room, she looked brighter and Jackier than ever. She wrapped me in a brittle hug, and I held my breath and felt her skeleton under her pink suit. She said, "Gather your things, Jan. Come with me."

Under the influence of my insecurities, I suppose, I complied. After all, in the religion of TempRight, I was finally achieving something like Nirvana. I grabbed my purse and coat and followed her into the warehouse. I stuck close behind her as we wove past the machines and the white-frocked workers, eventually going behind a stack of casks in a far corner. Behind the casks was a door, which she unlocked with her keys. She stood back to allow me in.

We entered a small, stuffy room with heavily draped windows and two narrow armchairs. The walls and various doors had been painted a dark, gloomy shade of red. It looked like the waiting room in a funeral parlor.

"Where are we?" I asked.

"Take a seat, please," she said. "This room holds a very special place in the history of Abernathy's."

She proceeded to fuss with something over on the counter while I awaited the courtship, bemused and indifferent. There was a large portrait of Mr. Connelly on the wall, young and handsome, a myth in the making.

Mrs. Kennedy came over and took the other chair. She was holding a camera. "Jan, you're becoming part of a great tradition here at Abernathy's. You should be proud. We don't offer permanence lightly. To the contrary. Only to those with the right qualities and the natural grace that Mr. Connelly believes to be of eternal value. I'd like you to repeat a few words that Mr. Connelly has always found inspiring, and which guide him to this day. Are you ready?"

> I felt embarrassed, witness to an indecent secret.

"I must be," I said, not recognizing my voice.

She said, "*We shall be as a city upon a hill.* Go on, say it."

"We shall be as a city upon a hill," I repeated, and she lifted the camera and blinded me with a flash of light.

"The eyes of all people are upon us," she intoned.

"The eyes of all people are upon us."

"Please, say it again," she said, taking some more shots.

"We shall be as a city upon a hill," I said. "The eyes of all people are upon us."

"Very nice. Again."

I was growing dizzy. "Could we have some fresh air?" I asked her.

"Jan. This is something we like our girls to internalize before the final step. It's a lovely sentiment passed down from John Winthrop, an early American settler who saw the potential for our young country to become a beacon of hope in the world, and conveys what Mr. Connelly has long wished to preserve. One more time."

"We are like"—I snorted, feeling fidgety—"a city in a dog patch, the eyes of all dogs are upon us."

She ignored my little joke, but her voice went cold. "All right, come along."

She rose and unlocked another door and ushered me through. There was a space off to the right that looked part costume shop, part laboratory. "Straight on," Mrs. Kennedy instructed me, but in those few seconds I glimpsed a number of oddities: women's clothes hanging on hooks, wigs, shelves full of shoes, a large stainless-steel table, and, I swear, a counter with knives and other instruments and fluids. I even saw some thimbles on the counter, and a large spool of a thick, pinkish thread.

"In here, please," she said, as we entered a dark and chilly chamber. She closed the door behind us and switched on the overhead lights, where-upon I was confronted by one of the strangest setups I'd ever seen. It was the glass I noticed first, large expanses of it like those used for dioramas in natural history museums, through which you glimpse skillfully taxider-mied creatures posing in their habitats. Yet there, behind the glass, was a tableau of prim young women in an office environment, behind desks, at file cabinets, answering phones. They wore plaid skirts, sweater sets, and loafers. They were perfectly lifelike and remarkably detailed in feature. They lacked the uniformity of typical mannequins. It was macabre yet laughable. What warped ideal was this meant to represent? Another Aber-nathy nod to a nation's lost innocence, the fetish of a deviant, both? There must have been at least twenty girlish figures on display, their eyes shining, their skin as glossy and radiant as the rose in the lobby.

Mrs. Kennedy said, "I imagine you're quite breathless?"

"What could ever make this a good idea?" I blurted out, wondering which of my many bad choices had landed me in this grotesque moment. I felt embarrassed, witness to an indecent secret.

"Mr. Connelly started the collection years ago, understanding the effort it would take to hold on to the best and brightest, to preserve his ideals against an uncertain future. But I've had everything do with it. These young women have ranged from those with privileged, private school educations to those who have been in foster care, who were unwanted at times, who found themselves passed around like trading cards, were unsure whom to trust, were disappointed, were abandoned, were betrayed from time to time between spells of relative calm and the occasional kind-ness of strangers."

"So that's what you think of me?"

"This is why becoming permanent is such an honor. It's the end of that kind of suffering and loneliness and that kind of, well, meaninglessness that haunts you as you try to understand what life could bring you next.

Becoming permanent is really the best place for someone like you, Jan. You will be very happy being permanent. There will be no more worry for you, no more sadness or fear . . ."

I was focusing on the last figure in the display, in the blue cardigan and Black Watch plaid skirt. It was Melody. I started violently. I could see the very real texture of her skin under the glossy coating. I could see the downy hairs on her cheeks.

"Don't do it," I croaked out.

"Don't do what, Jan?"

I was backing away from her, looking for something I could use to protect myself.

"Remember," said Mrs. Kennedy, "you're a very common, ordinary young woman."

I think I screamed.

"What's the matter, Jan?" she asked me. "You don't seem to understand. Jan? Come back here. Come back!"

I ran for the door, her voice rising behind me. I scrambled through the funereal red room, out onto the factory floor. I was gasping, under the impression I had just escaped with my life. Yet as I came into their midst, disturbing nobody, I became aware that the workers and the machinery were performing an intricate dance. Nothing, not even a gasping, terrified woman fleeing a room full of embalmed secretaries, would stop them. The white frocks of the workers were immaculate. The machines provided a steady rhythm, while the gray light from the skylights cast cool shadows on the cement floor. The fans made clipping sounds overhead, dispersing the fumes of the solvents evenly throughout the warehouse. A huge roaring exhaust hole loomed over the space like a dark moon. I stood transfixed by the practiced fluidity of the operation. I had a sudden insight into the peace that could be had in it.

I looked back to see if Mrs. Kennedy had chased me, but I was alone in the company of these dedicated workers. And because she hadn't chased me, my escape felt ridiculous. Hadn't she been dead set on obtaining me for their collection? Had I miscalculated her commitment and desire, was she giving up that easily? Was I yet again that expendable? I had control of my breath by then, found my way to a drinking fountain, guzzled the ice-cold water until the top of my mouth froze. A time clock was mounted on the wall there. The workers all had their own cards, alphabetically arranged in a gray rack, stamped with the accumulation of their hours. I

ELIZABETH MCKENZIE

was struck by the insidious simplicity of it all. I pushed myself through the doors, out through the front office, and onto the street.

I'd used the nearby phone before. I could slip inside it with all my imagined freedom. I was free to call anybody, if there were anybody to call. Free to choose my next move, if there were anywhere to go. Who needed me now? The stray, matted terrier poking its way up the street? How would I even talk to it? "Come here, girl," I called. "Come here. You are such a good girl. Such a good girl, come here!" 🛡

Daniel Johnson

INSHALLAH

When it was over,
though it would never be over,

his mom sent a gift
to our house,

a chrome lamp and candles,
a tornado lantern

or hurricane lamp. It depends
what you call

that black wall of water,
skirling and rising,

that takes what it wants:
cars, refrigerators,

cows, wedding
photos, birth records—

inshallah—
your firstborn son.

When it was over,
though it would never be over,

as it would never be
before again, only *after*,

as the rains, the rains
would never be the same

rains or lashing waves—
I struck a match

against the flooding dusk,
then again,

and hung the lamp.

Adrian Matejka

HEARING DAMAGE

I had a trumpet
shaped like a downward
heart, all of its dented
iterations of brass
& bell. Three-valve
marginality. Marching
band possibility
pointing at the muddy
dirt. I had a vernacular
as overachieving
as a kid with a boom box
in the rain. The trench
coat was there.
The wet socks, the look
of wonder were caught
up in high school's ghost
gears, greedy for their
own moments of attention.
& it never worked—
when the tape deck
got soaked, the tape
stopped playing. When
the music stopped,

her shades barked
as they shut. As if attention
itself had been magnetized,
stretched around eager
reels, then fed into
the machine. Click,
click, click. As if
my bleating, waterlogged
pleas weren't trumpets
for attention, but gentle
quarter notes clipped
into polyester tinsel,
future twists of glory.

HEARING DAMAGE

from what? Want & tumble? From word
crumbles in the kitchen's halogen?

Here, hands greet the aching butter knife
before the big spread. What I want is a better

word for *instead* after the skull & crossbones
ideogram. What I want is to bucket

my addendums & their severe labels,
dialectical fabrications downtagged

on the sales table each & every spring.
Here we go with that old seasonal bullshit

again. Put on your earphones so the eardrums
don't get punched out. Put on your sunglasses,

too, just for the flex of it. Is it too much
to ask for some quiet in this insistent chorus

of renew? Too much to be momentary
in morning grass, suede kicks beat by dew?

Out of Time

In the long gap between *Predator* (1987) and *The Predator* (2018), we find cusp year 1999, made famous in 1982 by Prince but mostly memorable because we became concerned that the way we had long encoded dates on computers (using only the last 2 digits, rendering 1999 as "99") might cause computers to understand "00," reached on 01.01.2000, as 1900, causing banks and power grids to fail.

Mostly it was okay in the USA that year, but it did cause minor problems at 3 of 51 Japanese nuclear power plants. 154 pregnant UK women were sent incorrect test results of the risk of Down syndrome, and at least two terminated their pregnancies based on that information. In *Predator 2* (1990) the alien spares a female detective because it can see she's pregnant. Ice Cube's third studio album, *The Predator* (1992), had long been out in 1999, but it wouldn't make its way to me until 2015.

Ander Monson

That year I moved from Iowa to Alabama, between the announcements of the extinction of the Canarian oystercatcher (1994) and the eastern cougar (2011), the Javan tiger (1994) and the Acalypha wilder (2014), the ivory-billed woodpecker (1994) and the Mariana mallard (2004), the golden toad of Costa Rica (1989) and the Vine Raiatea tree snail (2002), the Hainan ormosia (1997) and the black-faced honeycreeper (2004), the Zanzibar leopard (1996) and the Christmas Island pipistrelle (2009), the Formosan clouded leopard (2013) and the Caribbean monk seal (2008), just to name the ends of some of the things we paid attention to.

Was it that year I began to move back and forth through time? In 1999 my mother had been dead for 18 years. My daughter wouldn't be born for 13 years.

With my car I hit a boar in rural Mississippi that year. I don't know whether it lived or died, or whether it was the last of its kind. That year is perched between the other animals I've hit: a bird (1992), a dog (1993), a deer (2012). I hope that list ends here. Often I rewind and replay those moments, on the kind of tape you'd still rent then, between when Blockbuster debuted (1985) and went bankrupt (2010), then dwindled down to its 2 remaining stores (2019): Bend, Oregon, and Morley, Western Australia. Though they still survive for now, the 2 remaining stores are not a mating pair.

That year I learned that the novelization of *Predator* was written by poet Paul Monette in 1986 while his lover, Rog, was dying of AIDS. Monette died as a result of an AIDS-related illness in 1995. In 1999, I first read Monette's elegy for Rog, *Love Alone*, published 10 years before, and 10 years after, in 2009, I finally read his *Predator*. It's better than you'd expect.

In 1999 the global mean temperature was the fifth warmest on record. Nearly every year since has had a higher mean temperature. The aliens in *Predator* come only in the hottest years, so it's good we keep having more and more, a fact remarked on both in and by the fact of the sequels, which also number more and more. If you've seen the films you know that

Predators attack only the armed; these days we are armed more and more (more than 1 gun per American in 2019). In 1999, we performed 9 million background checks as part of buying a gun, mandated by the Brady Act of 1993 (referencing the man shot and wounded in an attempted assassination of the president in 1981). In 1987, these checks did not exist. In 2016 they did; we did 27.5 million of them. 28,874 were killed by guns in America in the last year of the millennium. Of those 28,874 people (approximately 4 times the population of the town in Michigan where I grew up and where my mother died and my friend's sister was murdered and another friend blew off most of his hand), 57 percent were suicides, 37.5 percent were homicides, and 2.9 percent were unintentional. The remainder are ambiguous. In 2017, 39,773 died by guns in America, almost double the population of the largest city within a 3-hour drive of my hometown.

In 2005, the Silver Jews told us, "Time is a game that only children play well," likely referencing Heraclitus (circa 500 BCE).

In 2002, Missy Elliott told us, "I put my thing down, flip it and reverse it."

1999 is equidistant between Prince first releasing "1999" in 1982 and 2016, when he died, after which the song charted once again (all told it entered the Billboard Hot 100 4 times: in 1982, 1983, 1999, and 2016).

If you reverse time some problems solve themselves. Global warming shrinks with the population. The Predator movies get better. We holster our guns. Bring them back to the store. Prince and many others live again.

In 1998, Eels told us, "Thought that I'd forget all about the past / But it doesn't let me run too fast."

In 1999, the human population of the world surpassed 6 billion, give or take a few. That year the attempt to impeach Bill Clinton ended. 143 died in an Athens earthquake. More than 2,400 died in an earthquake in Taiwan. 15 died in Columbine, shot by 2 teenagers in a school, 1 of whom had been accepted to the University of Arizona, where I now teach, where I am now on the Active Shooter Response Training Committee, where the training officer told us by way of reassurance: "by the way it's always guys," "they almost always announce it on social media," and "most of them are in rural communities."

Died that year include Stanley Kubrick (director), Dusty Springfield (singer), and Iris Murdoch (novelist). Joe DiMaggio (baseball player), Wilt Chamberlain (basketball player), and Curtis Mayfield (musician). Gene Siskel (film critic), Dana Plato (actor), and Dylan Klebold (mass murderer).

We are still looking for 1999: "Kansas authorities search for Adam Herrman boy last seen in 1999" (*NY Daily News*). "Montreal river searched for body of girl last seen in 1999" (*CTV News*). "Garden of woman last seen in 1999 excavated" (*The Times*). "Digging to start in search for woman last seen in 1999" (*BBC News*). "Re-Appeal For Missing Hemel Man Last Seen In 1999" (*Hemel Today*). "Pair on trial accused of murdering woman 'last seen in 1999'" (*ITV News*).

The West Nile Virus was first seen in the United States in 1999. I nearly froze in record colds in Minnesota with my brother in an Isuzu Trooper II with a malfunctioning heater. We had borrowed it from my father. Gunmen opened fire on Shia Muslims in a mosque in Pakistan, killing at least 16. Unarmed Guinean immigrant Amadou Diallo was shot dead by cops in New York. We started using Napster. Pluto was still called a planet then. We still bought CDs then. A woman killed 3 at a shooting range in Finland. Rwandan Hutu rebels killed and dismembered 8 tourists in Uganda. 2 men became the first to circumnavigate the globe in a hot air balloon. I went on a first date with the woman who would later become my wife in 2002. In 1999 the Dow closed above 10,000 for the first time. 2 Swedish police officers were wounded by armed bank robbers, and later executed with their own service pistols in Malexander, Sweden.

In 2019 I listened to the album version of Prince's "1999," which is longer and much stranger than the familiar single version. It ends with a child's voice repeating: "Mommy, why does everybody have a bomb?"

A series of tornadoes featuring the fastest wind speed ever recorded on earth (302 mph) killed 38 in Oklahoma that year. That year came between *Predator 2* (1990) and *Alien vs. Predator* (2004). My *AVP* T-shirt reads: "Whoever wins, we lose." (Not true.) That year uncountably many died. Some more were born. That year I turned 24. 🏠

Derrick Austin

IS THIS OR IS THIS TRUE AS HAPPINESS

When we finally make it, we sit on cold stones.
The river curling over and under our feet
even colder. Your secret place.

The air has that early fall smell, things beginning
to rot, the wet soil nourishing itself.
We're trespassing.

Anything could happen to me
in this white-ass town. I'm terrified
if you know that and terrified if you don't.

My body is puffy, unremarkable.
I've grown distant and sullen.
A witch told me gin placates the dead.

Whose dead have I been trying to drown in me,
drinking my own elegy?
You ask if I'm happy, and I say yes. *See how easy it is*

to get here? you say. *Yes,*
I say. *But you have to take me back.*

PASTORAL: RE-PLEAT

last night the little one sat up in his bed&pajamas,
puked yellow over all five stuffies, the wall
& the Cerberus parents had to strip all the bedding in the dark

& I put Vaseline under the bigger one's chafed nostrils all day

& my eyes are onions, with a decorative lump under the right

    (in case you were thinking, as D did, that this polyphonic is a constant spree,
     replete with comforts)

& this morning the bear-man & I
twin-star dreamed of his libido & woke enwrapt

so I moved down the wine-pouch of his body
& swallowed without spilling

    this too

    this very plain&happy poem w/its bodily fluids

    this plaiting, this pleating

PASTORAL: DID YOU HAVE A MIDLIFE CRISIS ON TOP OF YOUR MIDLIFE CRISIS?

(A Response)

A. I left the city, left my salary, left a daily touching of strangers in other languages on the elevated train and came to this white place with balsam sewn into muslin pouches. Hung the tree swing low.

A. When I tell you about the choice to fuck like I'm now fucking, you ask, *How's Maine?* You worry, maybe, that I'm already bored, that the country is a failure, that the dropout's a failed experiment, that I have failed in my choices.

That I have, in my own farmhouse, contracted "cabin fever."

A. No, I am not bored. No, I am not sorry.

A. I enjoy watching the bubbles rise in my mason jar of goopy starter. I enjoy spending every day with my dinosaur-obsessed son in my lap while he squeezes the curled tubes of my hair and tells me he is loving me like a predator, with fierceness, which is the biggest quantifier he can imagine. I enjoy knocking the dirt off the purpled bulbs of garlic. I enjoy plainly seeing the harbor zinged with buoys.

A. If sex is a way to be seen, then those activities are also ways I see myself in the cedar-fenced privacy around my small-town home.

A. If being seen is a way to encounter myself and ask a question, then I'm glad I am in my unheated bedroom tonight, next to my husband, reading about rough sex.

A. I never thought I'd want my face slapped as erotic play.

A. I love living in Maine. The air is clean. Most of the children's friends have never watched television. I remember to pick up the onions and fine bright squash delivered from Maia's farm to the back room of the Green Store. I do not feel lonely. I live in a small town. I don't leave the house some days and still I am not alone. Neighbors walk the block, and at my desk I log in to the black-and-red screen to comment on the art of begging on a forum about submission. I talk to my girlfriend in Vermont while I fold the laundry, and I talk to my boyfriend in Rhode Island on chat while answering my email. And sometimes I get in my little blue hybrid car with all the bumper stickers about books and food and love and drive to a hotel or a house in another place, maybe a more urban place, maybe a more rural place, and fuck and love someone to whom I am not legally partnered, while still being married to the man with whom I decided, perhaps foolishly, to let the government have a thing or two to say about our relationship.

A. My husband and I sit down and make the time for all of this, opening our datebooks, which are leather-bound on Mount Desert Island. We talk about what we do while we are doing it and we talk about it after. We don't stop talking about it.

A. This was not the kind of community I thought I was seeking when I came to this life, but it's not *not* the kind of community I was seeking.

A. I would like to put more about the face-slapping into this conversation. I would like to talk to you about it. Or do a demonstration.

A. My desire to have my face slapped on the side of my cheek, where the risk of damage is minimal, immediately after I've cum, uses resources. It takes electricity to book the room at the big hotel. It takes fossil fuels to get the man who will slap me to the lobby of the big hotel. It takes money, which takes time, to pay so that the big hotel will give us a plastic key card for a room. It takes water gushing through the tap of the big hotel to clean up after.

A. But to answer your question: I do not consider this yet an apocalypse, and I am not on lockdown.

A. Some people consider this an apocalypse, and some people are on lockdown, cannot travel, will not travel. Some people cannot, will not, fuck for pleasure. Some people cannot, will not, love a lot of some people.

A. I find my town a hopeful place. I find it a sheltering field. My sexual pleasure is non-site-specific and mobile, and sometimes happens in the ether, or in text. And before or after my face is slapped to the snap of ecstasy, I want to eat raw honey from Swanville on a spoon and walk to the post office.

A. I can travel. I can fuck. I love a lot of people. I am well, thanks.

Nathaniel Dolton-Thornton

WONDER

however hard they worked
she still had to take a part-time job in town
to pay the health insurance, and yet
when the tumor appeared in his neck
he refused all treatments
except the bees
who stung him every morning for months until
it was a miracle, the doctor said

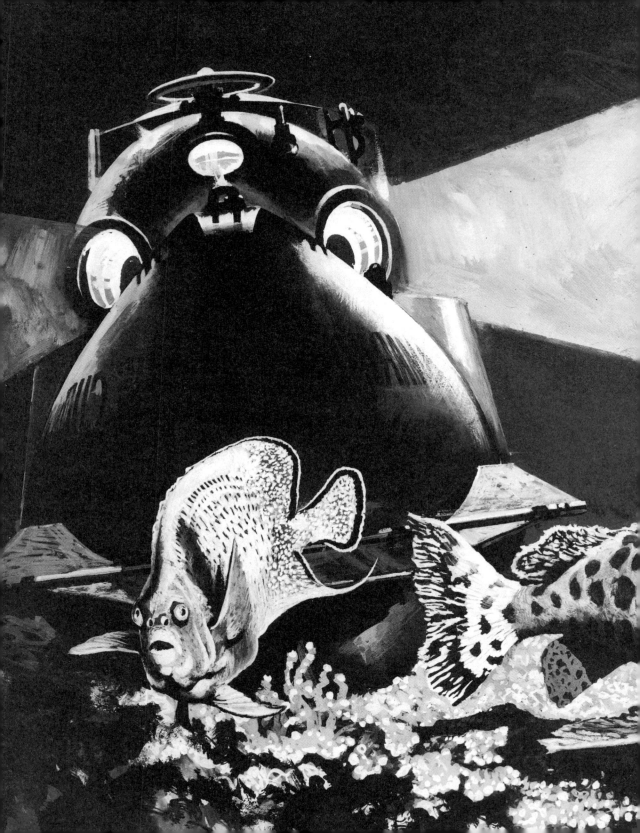

NEW VOICE FICTION

Abyssal Gigantism

Bridget Chiao Clerkin

THE SUNLIGHT ZONE

The expedition to find the sea monks was funded by a benefactress whose husband and two adult sons had been lost at sea. She said "lost" but people tended to say "dead" when she wasn't in the room.

She herself knew better: her husband and sons had been taken in by the sea monks. She gave staggering amounts of money to clean-ocean initiatives. The planet was changing, and the woman was plagued by nightmares of her loved ones watching in impotent horror as die-offs percussed the oceans and reefs bleached and jellyfish bloomed. Part of her felt that if they had chosen not to return, she shouldn't disturb them—she pictured her loved ones' human hands clasping the sea monks' fins as they joined together in a Paternoster, man and fish side by side, tending seabed gardens, illuminating waterproof manuscripts, brewing wonderful underwater ales—but she wanted to know. Having heard about a new technology that allowed craft to stay underwater for theoretically any amount of time, she consulted the local monsignor, who, as the woman spoke, strenuously kept his focus on how generous the woman had been in the past and off the cartoon reel in his mind of miniature friars bobbing around like bath toys, riding little sea horses through kelp forests. With the monsignor's blessing, she decided to fund the sea monk expedition.

Ruby was on the expedition because she was the receptionist at St. Egbert's in the parish adjacent to the benefactress's country house. Those organizing the expedition hadn't been able to find anyone from the benefactress's own parish willing to go. They hadn't found anyone in Ruby's parish of employment either, but then somebody had said, "Why don't we ask Ruby?" Ruby had never been on anything even approximating an expedition, and she was acutely aware that her presence was a clear indication of the organizers' minimal expectations. Ruby had just ended a relationship and thought maybe going on the trip would help the transition. Help as in, *Hey, Lloyd, what have you been up to since we broke up? Oh? That's cool. I'm going in a submarine. I'm going to touch the edge of the unknown.*

Sea monks had failed to assert themselves into the popular imagination the way mermaids had. They lacked a certain appeal. The few pictorial depictions stuck a tonsured human head on a fish body, scaly fins and tail forming the monk's robe. These were all in dated natural history volumes that took Herodotus at face value and featured unicorns, cynocephali, and Blemmyes. Following the Reformation, sightings had petered off from rare to virtually nonexistent. Ruby doubted she'd ever known anyone who had even heard of sea monks, not even the boy she had gone out with in high school who had shamelessly noted on his college applications that his intended career path was in cryptozoology.

> "Hope is a beautiful thing."
> Trevor trafficked in such
> ingenuous statements.

The high school boyfriend was now a realtor. Ruby had looked him up online when she and Lloyd were breaking up. She'd looked up a few other exes, too, men who had secured gainful employment only after they'd broken up with her, as if she were a job-securing talisman they'd needed to rub a few times.

When Trevor had explained that their benefactress believed the sea monks had taken her sons and husband in, Ruby had replied, "That's so sad," meaning pathetic, but in a sad way. If Lloyd had been swept out to sea, she too could be sad, sad but grateful for the time they'd spent together. This seemed preferable to resenting how she'd wasted her time as well as her security deposit, to which Lloyd had been unable to contribute.

"Oh, I don't know," Trevor had said. "Hope is a beautiful thing." Trevor trafficked in such ingenuous statements. "To her credit, there are documented encounters with sea monks. There's one story about a king who finds a sea monk—I think this one's referred to as a sea bishop. The king put him in a tank but the sea bishop started to look a little sick. A little green around the gills."

He paused to let Ruby absorb this.

"As it were," he said.

"Ha," Ruby said belatedly.

"So some human bishops prevailed upon the king, convinced him to release the sea bishop. They brought him back to the water, he thanked them, made the sign of the cross, and then swam away."

"Is that the whole story?"

"What, you need more? More than a half fish, half human who isn't a mermaid but who for some reason is a bishop?"

Trevor then told another story about how someone in the seventeenth century had caught a sea monk and refused to release it despite its pleading. It turned down food, pining for the sea, and died after about a week.

Trevor, who still seemed miffed by Ruby's reaction to the sea bishop story, had ended this anecdote with "You like that one better?"

Saliha worked for some big think tank that was often cited on NPR.

The submarine was an Ohio-class sub with miles of corridors that curled intestinally within. During the orientation, which had been held on the boat that had brought them to the submarine, the first mate had explained the mechanism that was letting them stay underwater for so long, called gills, or possibly GILLS. The captain was not present at the orientation, and the first mate apologized for his absence: the captain was already aboard the submarine, he said, attending to the final preparations.

An Arizona police department had acquired the submarine under the 1033 Program and then auctioned it off at their annual Back the Blue Gala. The winning bidder was an entrepreneur who intended to be the trailblazer of the luxury underwater cruise experience industry; he had traveled all the way from the Bay Area just to put in his bid. When investors failed to materialize, the benefactress had stepped in.

The entrepreneur had completed an overall update, including the installation of the GILLS. The construction had been cleverly contrived so that you could spend days without seeing the machinery or the crew. There was a grand chandeliered dining room, and at the bow there was a viewing area with huge windows, couches, and booths, originally conceived of as a lounge where you could get top-shelf pickled while watching the ocean pass by in the crepuscular intensity of the submarine's spotlights. The viewing window, which was thirty feet high and stretched around the front of the submarine, was said to be made of a five-foot-thick sheet of plexiglass. The spotlights made what could be seen murky and velvety.

The last-minute additions to accommodate the current expedition included a large state-of-the-art lab, sponsored by a clutch of drug companies whose names were on a plaque by the door; a workout room; and a rec room with a TV and VCR, a VHS library dominated by Kevin Costner, and an air hockey table that nobody could use because it sucked air in instead of blowing it out.

The lab was bright and white like a Mac store, and the lights were always on, unlike the hallway lights, which were on a timer that mimicked a day-night cycle. Saliha, who studied the brain and human-animal relationships, had warned Ruby that if deprived of these rhythms people tended to exhibit very strange behaviors.

Saliha was one of the three scientists on board, the other two being Maria and Natasha. Add Trevor, who had introduced himself as the team coordinator, and Ruby, and you had five, a small team considering the ambitious size of the lab: most of the solicited institutions hadn't been able to get past "sea monks." Collectively Saliha, Maria, and Natasha held four doctorates, which meant somebody had more than one. They had never worked together or even been at the same institutions, yet seemed to know all the same people: Maria knew Natasha's advisor's advisor, Natasha as an undergrad had lived on the same floor as Saliha's advisor's daughter, and Saliha was friends with the editor of a journal Maria and Natasha had each contributed to in the past. When they realized they had all signed the same open letter in the *New York Times*, a comradery beyond professional obligations was sealed. Natasha had just finished a postdoc and specialized in marine snow; Saliha worked for some big think tank that was often cited on NPR when statistics concerning large groups of people were called for; and Maria was at a well-known East Coast university and spent her summers in Venezuela doing something Ruby hadn't quite caught. They had consented to swallow "sea monks" because the submarine would grant them unprecedented access to the parts of the ocean they specialized in.

Trevor often referred to places the others didn't know about. When someone inevitably confessed unfamiliarity (and even when she didn't), he'd say, "Yeah, not many people have heard of it. It's off the beaten path." Sometimes he'd say "track" instead of "path." He seemed to do the same thing in each of these exotic places: get drunk on cheap local beer with other westerners. Supposedly Trevor had been hired to run everything, having worked for several global backpacking outfits. Later, after they started fucking, and spurred by the recollection of her own hiring process ("Why don't we ask Ruby?"), Ruby came to question the decision-making that had resulted in Trevor's employment.

The other three women were researchers whose long-term projects were meant to be carried out over the course of the entire voyage. Ruby herself was single-use: she had one task. She was to deliver a papal bull, the document from the Vatican that would start the process of officially recognizing the monks' underwater order in its current iteration; since the last recorded sighting had been in 1855, there was concern that the sea monks had missed the news about Vatican I and II, big things like papal infallibility and not having to say Mass in Latin anymore. The bull was rolled up in a fancy poster tube. The cardboard was thick and of an elegant matte black. The tube was stored in a larger FedEx tube that still bore the dents, smudges, and stickers that had ushered it from Rome. Ruby had never seen the bull, and she didn't know if any part of it was waterproof, but she could hear the metal papal seal, the bulla, thunking around inside the tube.

It was not until Ruby was unpacking that she processed that the priest who'd blessed the expedition had not boarded the submarine with them. Because she hadn't been convinced they were actually going to find a sea monk, she hadn't thought about the details of her task; now that she was on the submarine, she was no longer so sure she wasn't going to be called upon to fulfil her duty. Were the sea monks coming into the submarine? Was she to go out in a diving suit—and was she meant to have taken a class and gotten certified for deep-sea diving?

Some thought sea monks were walrus sightings; what if she saw a walrus and didn't realize it was a sea monk? If they had fins, would it be rude to extend her hand for a handshake? Did they understand English or, worst-case scenario, high school Spanish? There suddenly seemed to be many particulars that needed to be addressed, but when she asked Trevor what the expectations were, he replied genially, "Yeah, however you want it to go down works for me."

They each had their own cabin. Each cabin had two double-decker bunks with a small chair between them pushed against the wall opposite the door. The cabins had been hastily refurbished for the expedition, and too many cabins had been prepared with far too many beds.

Ruby was sure she'd read that a large percentage of the casualties on foreign ferry tragedies, and maybe even the *Titanic*, could be attributed to passenger disinterest in posted emergency procedure. She made a point of studying the maps on the back of her door. They were marked with labeled routes and "You Are Here" stars, and vigorously color-coded (though there was no key). Ruby's room was assigned to Evacuation Group Purple.

The first full day of the voyage was spent traveling near the surface to reach the coordinates where they would begin the dive. Over the course of that first day, Ruby watched from the viewing window and through her own porthole as they passed teeming tableaus of wild flashing colors.

At first, she felt optimistic that the water sloshing up to submerge her was easily reversible; she was still able to picture the submarine resurfacing, the five of them blinded by the sun leaping and glittering on the water like handfuls of tossed coins. This optimism held until the first morning of the dive, when she woke up to see all that utter nothing still there, framed in the little circle of the porthole.

> Some thought sea monks were walrus sightings; what if she saw a walrus and didn't realize it was a sea monk?

She had known academically they would be deeper under the water, and thus farther from the sun, but she suddenly understood what that meant. They had descended into an endless night, and she realized that her worry wasn't so much that the night was eternal but that there was no day to approach. The window seemed to bubble in toward her. She had slapped the cover shut. Now she avoided looking at the porthole at all, even covered.

THE TWILIGHT ZONE

On the second day of the dive, the submarine began to descend alongside an immense cliff that they would continue to follow into the earth for the rest of the journey. The cliffside was riddled with holes and caves and tunnels that the lights from the submarine picked out but couldn't reach into.

When the drill came that day, Ruby set out for the emergency meeting point, repeating the directions from the map in her room: *turn right at the bathroom, turn right at the bathroom*. She turned right at the bathroom, and after several minutes of speed-walking found herself in front of her own door. She hadn't made any extra turns. The hallway didn't curve. The klaxon was still sounding off. Again, the captain, or someone, said, "Please report to your emergency meeting area," and so again she lit out. Again, she wound up in front of her door. She looked up and down the passageway, but nobody was there.

Her door began to open. She watched it, fascinated. Trevor stepped out. It wasn't her room: it was his.

"I'm lost," she said.

He sounded like he had been sleeping. "How long has that been going off?"

"The alarm? Ten minutes, maybe," she said. "An hour. It feels like an hour. It's disorienting."

"We'd better go. They're pretty serious about these things."

She trailed after him. They turned right at the bathroom, the very same bathroom she had turned right at earlier, but this time they came almost immediately upon a small area where the hall met another hallway. Natasha, Maria, and Saliha were there. So was a crew member and a man in a kitchen uniform, but not the first mate who'd delivered the orientation. The crew member was holding a clipboard.

> **Shortcuts will always have an impact on someone.**

"Finally," Natasha said. The man in the kitchen uniform seemed to take this as a cue and left.

The crew member had Trevor and Ruby initial a sign-up sheet that had nothing on it but the other three's initials. "That's all of us, then," he said briskly.

"All of us?" Trevor asked.

The crew member was writing rapidly. He spoke without looking up. "There are several evacuation meeting points. They've been designed to get you to safety as quickly as possible, so you'll want to make sure you remember yours." He clicked his pen shut. "Okay, stay here until they sound the all clear." He left in the direction opposite that taken by the man in the kitchen uniform.

The all clear never sounded. It took some time before one of them summoned the gumption to suggest they all just leave.

By then it was dinnertime, so they made their way to the dining room, which was located one level down from the lab, the cabins, and the workout room. Meals were laid out and the doors unlocked three times a day:

seven, noon, and six in the evening. There were dozens of tables, but the food was always at the table farthest from the entrance so that you had to cross the whole room to reach it. Something about the huge room and the scores of empty chairs discouraged lingering.

As they ate, Trevor asked Saliha how she had gotten into her field.

She said that as an undergrad she had taken a psychology class where she learned about an experiment in which a nine-month-old baby, Little Albert, had been conditioned to fear animals that he had not previously feared: rats, dogs, rabbits. The scientists would present him with one of the animals and at the same time hit a metal bar directly above his head with a hammer. Because most if not all infants react fearfully to loud noises, Little Albert began to also fear animals.

"So you were interested in that? Conditioning behavior in humans?" Trevor said.

"Not quite," Saliha said. "What I found most interesting is that today, the experiment would not be performed. It would be unethical. The challenge of gathering knowledge under the constraints of ethics is what I find exciting about our fields. Shortcuts will always have an impact on someone. Sometimes it's thousands of people, like the thalidomide babies, and sometimes it's just one person."

"Like Little Albert," Maria said.

"Exactly. But not only that. *Not* taking shortcuts also impacts someone, someone who might be depending on us while we figure out an ethical way to embark on our research."

"It's interesting to think about everything we'd know if we didn't have things like laws and ethics," Trevor said. He was using a knife to scoot some bright yellow rice pilaf onto his fork and so missed the contemptuous look Natasha favored him with. "That's what war criminals are for," she said.

On her way to the rec room, Ruby had to pass the lab, where she often saw the three women moving about in lab coats, sometimes gloves and safety glasses, labeling containers and typing on computers that were suspended on arms from the ceiling. Their research determined their daily schedules so that even the quotidian was dictated by advanced thinking. Saliha usually left lunch early to check on her rats, whose circadian rhythms and other behaviors she was monitoring as the submarine went deeper and deeper. Natasha was always late for breakfast because she had to record observations first thing in the morning. She was there to study marine snow, the slow drift of organic waste matter in the water. There were organisms out there that existed entirely on the stuff. Natasha had racks and racks of samples in tubes that looked like water until you put one up to a bright light, and then you could see the particles clouding the water. The searchlights outside the submarine's viewing window did this, too. Once you began to focus on the particles, it was easy to go cross-eyed and stop noticing everything else, even the bioluminescent creatures glittering past in the dark: tiny dragonfish; little glowing jellies; and anglerfish, their lures lighting up their nightmare needle teeth.

"So, what did you do before this?" Natasha asked Ruby. They were watching a movie in the rec room. Trevor was trying to fix the hockey table.

"I was a receptionist at a church."

"What does that entail?" Natasha asked. On the TV, Kevin Costner was peeing.

"It's not much different from other office jobs. A lot of scheduling. I had to take over the altar server schedule after the vice president of the Italian League quit. The kids are supposed to find substitutes if they can't make it, but they never do."

"But you must have been pretty involved, right? To get sent?"

"Honestly," Ruby said, "I think a lot of people said no."

Trevor said, "It's not important that they said no. It's important that you said yes."

Natasha ignored him. "I looked it up online. They think it's just people who saw seals or giant squid, the way they thought manatees were mermaids. What's the paper say?"

Ruby shrugged. "I think it tells them to get in touch. It's probably in Latin."

"So you haven't seen it?"

"I didn't open it. If we find them, I give it to them."

Natasha shook her head. "The shit we put up with to get funding."

"The more preconceived notions you bring in with you, the less you get out of a situation," Trevor said. "The harder they come, the harder they—"

"This movie is even worse than I remember," Natasha said abruptly, and stood up and left. Ruby was surprised by this, but then later realized that Natasha and Trevor must have already been fucking by that point.

The first time Ruby and Trevor had had sex was tricky, the starts and stops of a sober first time amplified by the cramped environment. The bunks were narrow and low, and everything was metal.

The best way to do it ended up being over a chair pushed against the wall, Trevor behind her. Of all the things about Trevor, and about her plus Trevor as a thing, this she minded the least. She found that the position suited her in terms of depth and angle.

THE MIDNIGHT ZONE

Ruby, walking down the hall to the communal bathroom, saw Trevor standing completely still outside the workout room window. She knew what he was looking at. She could hear the pneumatic exhales of the equipment, knew that the three others were in there. She had watched them, too.

"The shit we put up with to get funding."

Ruby never stayed long, afraid they'd turn and spot her, or see her reflection in the mirrors. They all wore white earbuds and workout clothing, breathable and wicking. It hadn't even occurred to Ruby to pack workout clothing. As she watched, they all three seemed to grow streamlined, longer-limbed, more lithe, more wondrously female, rising up with each stroke of their machines like Venus, the mussel-black stationary bikes and StairMasters their shells.

Brushing her teeth in the bathroom, Ruby looked in the small hazy mirror over the sink. She thought about how Natasha's long braids stayed centered exactly at the small of her back, even as she went up and down on the workout machine, so regal was her posture; and she thought of Saliha's calves and the gentle flexing of the muscles beneath the sleek skintight leggings; and Maria's narrow ankles like swans' necks, the slight sheen on her forehead as if applied by a makeup artist. Ruby watched in the mirror as a pimple scar on her chin started to darken and widen, become a blemish, a blotch, a continent. The hair on her arms grew long and coarse, and her lips became drier and then cracked open to show bright seams of blood. Her teeth yellowed and her gums receded. A freckle on her neck put out two wiry hairs that could probably pick up radio signals, and then the freckle became a mole, grew taller and more three-dimensional and developed cancer. She watched it all, mesmerized. If she went out in the hall, stood very still and waited, she could really scare someone, the way she looked.

The halls were carpeted with dark red movie theater carpet. The lighting was of varying quality so that you might at any moment step from a well-lit stretch of hallway into a dim wavering pool. When the lights shut off at night, they were replaced with a strip of guide lights on only one side of the hallway, which sometimes made Ruby feel as though she was walking on a tilt. You could, in theory, use the guide lights to find your way back, keeping them always on your right or whatever, but if she was in the rec room or the viewing room when the overhead lights went off, she'd usually stay put until the artificial morning. If she was in the rec room, she tended to stay up all night watching movies, then sleep when she returned to her cabin; on such days, she often missed breakfast and sometimes lunch.

Returning to her cabin one of those mornings, she'd seen Natasha coming out of Trevor's room, sneakers in hand. It was then Ruby realized that it was not a commentary on Kevin Costner that Natasha's suddenly quitting the rec room had indicated, but one related to Trevor. Ruby thought now too of when Maria had first explained the work she did and the organisms that lived around the thermal vent—extremophiles—and Trevor had said, "I consider myself an extremophile. Carpe diem, right?" Ruby realized Maria's look of pure disbelief was twin to Natasha's reaction in the rec room, and to the disgruntled feeling Ruby was beginning to feel anytime Trevor opened his mouth.

> "Maybe my emotions are experiencing abyssal gigantism."

Ruby slept fitfully on the nights she camped in front of the viewing window. The couches were not uncomfortable, but the room was large and with the window it was like sleeping in public. She would come in and out of consciousness to catch glimpses of huge things, or the ends of huge things, as the creatures passed out of the submarine spotlights; when she finally rose in the morning, she often had trouble determining which had been dreams and which had not: the flat long end of an oarfish hanging down from the top of the window, its tulle-like fin fluttering, the part she could see suggesting a fish as long as a telephone pole is tall; an anglerfish, the male, atrophied into a sperm sac, attached to the much bigger female; spider crabs or skateboard-sized isopods clinging to the cliffside or crawling over the whale falls and other carcasses that had settled onto ledges.

Natasha said the isopods were really just enormous roly-polys. "Things get bigger down here. It's called abyssal gigantism. Maybe because it's cold or there isn't enough food. It takes longer to reach maturity, so they keep growing."

They were sitting on one of the couches: a whale carcass had sunk into sight, and now it was keeping pace with the submarine. It was covered with writhing hagfish lacing muscularly in and out of the holes they'd chewed into the whale's side and head. Over the two weeks since the dive had begun, they'd seen a number of these in varying states falling sedately past the viewing window; each one sported a unique variety of creatures that had chosen to help it in its transformation. Now that they were deeper, the carcasses were usually more thoroughly broken down by the time they came into view; this one, however, was relatively intact.

"You're sleeping with him, too, aren't you?" Natasha said.

"A few times." Ruby wondered if she should mention she thought Maria was, too, but then she was surprised to see that Natasha's face was buried in her hands. "Hey, now," Ruby said tentatively.

"I don't know why it bothers me," Natasha said to her palms. "Maybe it's because I'm competitive. Or stupid." She began to rub her eyes with her fingertips vigorously. "Maybe my emotions are experiencing abyssal gigantism." She brought her hands down and blinked many times, and then pointed at the whale; by now, most of the flank closest to them had been eaten away. "Sometimes the bones drop out the bottom of the whale when it's still decomposing and the blubber is released. Tons of it." Natasha explained that while the bones sank, the blubber floated up to the surface and sometimes landed on beaches, terrorizing whoever found it, this pile of hide and fat, its form untied by decomposition and then restrung by the currents into something not resembling a whale. "Those things people find on beaches and they think they're sea monsters? It's really just piles of fat. They're called globsters."

"I feel like a globster sometimes," Ruby said. This, as she had hoped, made Natasha laugh.

After Natasha left for the lab, Ruby stayed. The big, gently plummeting whales made Ruby think of astronauts who had become untethered from their space stations and were now floating into a great void. She watched until it finally outpaced them and descended past the bottom of the viewing window, and then she was alone.

"L'appel du vide," Trevor said. Ruby jumped. He had come up behind her and gone to the viewing window and was now also looking down into the darkness.

"Excuse me?"

"That feeling you get when you're up high that you want to jump."

Ruby knew this feeling: high balconies, a trip as a child to Hoover Dam, giddiness. What happened if you jumped? It might be exactly what you think. Or it might be something different. There was only one way to find out.

But, not particularly interested in common ground with Trevor at the moment, she said flatly, "Like suicide?"

"No," Trevor said. "Like curiosity."

They rarely saw fish anymore. The organisms they did see were often a worn-out sort of white, sometimes a strange dark red color that Ruby couldn't recall ever having seen in nature above the water. It was difficult to recognize the life they now saw as animals. The basket stars, for instance, looked like plants. They were usually curled like fists with dozens of fingers, and their long, fern-like arms unfurled to feed before clenching back up.

The cliffside was thick with rock chimneys that jutted out and up, some as tall as multiple-story buildings. Great white plumes of hot gasses blew from their tops, and the water was rippled and glassy-looking from the heat. Sometimes on the big ledges there would be whole fields of chimneys, with groups clustered into towers that loomed over the rest. Maria said they had names like Loki's Castle and the Lost City.

"Some of the organisms that live around these vents only live in that one particular vent," Maria said. "In the entire world, our entire planet, they can only be found right there. So each time one of those vents goes dormant, for all we know, we've lost an entire species."

THE ABYSS

One day at lunch, Ruby learned that Saliha's rats had died. Natasha and Maria seemed bothered by this news, but Saliha was thoughtful and quiet.

Trevor said, "You know what I'm thinking? If the crew came and killed them, we would never know. All that chicken they've been serving us?"

"It's not funny," Natasha said.

Saliha said patiently, "All the bodies are accounted for."

"Are you sure?"

"I dissected them and incinerated them."

"Wow," said Trevor.

"Not that I agree with Trevor," Maria said, "but he has a point. We're totally segregated from the rest of the sub. We can't see behind the scenes back on the surface, either. I was thinking about it the other day—it's like this one time, I was maybe seven, and I grabbed a gallon of milk from the case at the store and a hand suddenly reached out from inside the case and started straightening out all the milk jugs. It had never even occurred to me that there was something back there. It scared me."

"Think about it," Trevor insisted. "If the crew just disappeared, we'd have no way of knowing."

"Stop it," Natasha said. "All this Halloween shit. You won't stop talking about the *Flying Dutchman*—"

"Doomed to forever wander the seas . . ." Trevor intoned.

"If you know something, say it. If you don't, shut up."

Trevor turned to the others. "She won't listen, but I'm telling you, I got a spooky feeling when we signed that paper during the emergency drill—like we were signing our souls away."

Natasha said despairingly, "Oh my God."

> It was difficult to recognize the life they now saw as animals.

Saliha cut in. "Listen, rats die. When I was at Caltech, the control group and the test group just—bam." She paused, then said, "Have you ever heard of the fear frequency?"

Maria said, "They discovered it accidentally in the eighties."

"Yeah, that one. It's a tone that makes you feel scared. It tells your brain there's a presence in your vicinity—you'll even see movement around you. As soon as the noise stops, the feeling goes away."

"Okay, there you go," Natasha said. "Maybe the engines are humming at that frequency and some of us, like Trevor, are particularly sensitive to it."

Saliha said, "What do you think, Ruby? We never see the crew. We should have reached the bottom of any abyss on Earth by now."

Ruby said, "Wait—when were we supposed to get to the bottom?"

Maria said, "There was a pretty broad window on the itinerary I saw. We know more about the moon than we know about the ocean floor. We were meant to spend a week in each post-photic zone, which we did, but we've now been in the abyss for two weeks. Even if we've spent more time moving laterally than vertically . . ." She looked pensively at the other two women. Natasha shook her head and Saliha shrugged. "We each came up with a different estimate of how long it should've taken."

"Wildly different?" Trevor asked.

"Close enough to know it's been more than enough time."

Saliha had turned back to Ruby. "Any theories?"

Ruby was reaching into the past now to something the high school boyfriend had once said. "Maybe," she said, "okay—maybe it's like that planet that crashed into Earth? That formed the moon?"

They were all looking at her. Maria was frowning. She said, "Theia? That's just a theory."

"But isn't it inside the earth now, and if you keep going down into a cave, you can end up inside it?"

"Come on, people, hollow Earth theories went out with the hobble skirt," Natasha said.

"They don't know that the rest of us are just putting our heads down and keeping on."

Late that evening, Trevor said to Ruby, "Do you think Saliha is here to study us? All, *What's your theory? What's your idea? How do you feel?*"

"What? Why would she?" Ruby asked. Ruby had come to Trevor's cabin, feeling restless, but now she had an urge to get away, particularly when she realized Trevor wanted to talk.

"I don't know," Trevor said slowly. "I'm still trying to figure that out."

"You picked the team," Ruby said. "What did you hire her to do?"

"Observations on the sea monks. How human are they? I was told to find a human behavior specialist instead of, like, a fish scientist. They want to emphasize the human in any reports. I was told there's some pushback against integrating the sea monks into the Church, especially in America. American Catholics are notoriously conservative. I guess there used to be a saint with a dog's head, but they demoted him."

"I thought she was studying her rats."

"She's obligated to report on the sea monks when we find them, but the rats are her own research. When I first started wondering about her, I thought they were just a cover: you know, give her something to do that would distract us from the truth, that we're the lab rats. But now I think they're a key part of the whole setup: I bet she killed them to see how we would react. Saying we haven't reached the bottom—same thing. She's applying the screws now."

The linchpin of Trevor's argument was that Saliha wouldn't sleep with him. "It's not that she doesn't want to. She can't. It would be unethical."

"Wouldn't trapping people on a submarine be unethical?"

"That's what all the Little Albert stuff was about. She was trying to tell us she feels guilty."

This had gone far enough: Ruby said, "I don't care about Saliha. I think you're a fraud."

Trevor looked surprised. "That's a lot of negative energy right there," he said, gesturing at the air between the two of them.

"Nobody would put you in charge of an expedition," Ruby said. "You act like you're some expert but all the sea monk stories you told me are on Wikipedia. You don't know any more about any of this than I do!"

Trevor leaned with one shoulder against the top bunk, his arms crossed. "You know the others think you're a Vatican agent? A spy." This made Ruby pause.

"It's not true," she said.

"I know it's not true."

"Why would they say that? I'm pro-choice."

"I'm just guessing, but you remember their open letter in the *Times*? It was about *stem cell research*. They're paranoid. They probably think they're on some Vatican watch list now and you're here to monitor their research, sabotage it, even. Maybe they think you killed the rats."

"I've never even been in the lab!"

"Look, I said it was a guess. They're highly educated women, in very specialized fields, but they don't know shit about the real world. It's what the ivory tower is all about. They can't believe that people really are just receptionists. They don't know that the rest of us are just putting our heads down and keeping on . . ."

Ruby resented this: she might only have an imprecise idea of what peer review was, and she might not have an opinion on whether DOIs reinforced an already-racist taxonomy (a discussion sustained through lunch and dinner earlier that day), but she certainly had more in common with the other three than she did with Trevor. She said, "The Vatican doesn't even have spies."

"Come on, yes they do. I meant I don't think *you're* the spy." He said fondly: "You're a mess."

"This is some divide and conquer bullshit. You're trying to distract me," Ruby said. "We're talking about you."

Trevor said suddenly, "You're right. I've misled you, misled you all." He grasped her hands in his and began to talk very quickly. "On my CV? Says I have a BA. But I don't! Never graduated. Junior year—couldn't pay my student fees. Wow, that feels good to get that out in the open! You won't expose me, will you?" And then he burst out laughing.

The next day, instead of lunch, they found the leftovers from breakfast still on the table. Trevor was still there too, sitting in the same chair he'd been in that morning, intensely zoning out. When roused he explained that he'd been waiting since breakfast to catch sight of the kitchen staff. Among other things, he wanted to discuss the menus, which had gotten progressively less diverse until they were eating chicken breast with mushroom cream sauce, wild rice, a side salad with Italian dressing, and a roll three times a day; also, could the dressing please be on the side. Ruby often needed to pause to remember if it was the lunch or dinner chicken. Breakfast was easier to differentiate, as there was still coffee, though the cream had long ago been replaced with a bowl of Coffee-Mates.

Maria said, "Why are the breakfast things still here?"

"Nobody came," Trevor said.

"Because you were in here!" Natasha said.

"Yeah, that's the thing," Trevor said. "Why do they wait for us to leave?"

They sat down. There was scattered conversation, but it was as if they didn't want to be too engaged when lunch arrived. But it never came.

At six o'clock, they returned and found Trevor in the same chair, the same array of dirty dishes before him. He was asleep, his arms folded and his head down.

"I think we should set a watch," he said when they'd woken him up. "How many of us are there, four? So, six hours each?"

"No," Natasha said impatiently. "There's five of us."

Trevor was staring past them, frowning. "I still think we should give it a try," he said. Then he shrugged and picked up the cup in front of him, drank the melted ice, and stood. About half an hour after he had left, the other four left as a group. There was an agreement that they would prevent Trevor from lingering the next day after breakfast.

The next morning, the table was laid. All seemed forgiven, the chicken breast less dry than usual, the romaine icy and crisp in a way it hadn't been in a long time. After eating, everyone, including Trevor, immediately left the dining room.

Two days later, days happily free of mealtime complications, Maria came into the rec room, visibly agitated. "I've just spoken to the captain."

"You saw him?" Natasha asked. None of them had ever seen the captain.

"No," Maria said. "I spoke with him on the intercom by the gym. You just push the white button. Trevor showed me."

Saliha said, "He knew? I wonder how he knew."

"He looks like the kind of person who would just push a button. Who can't help but push buttons," Natasha said. "Like a little kid."

They all went down the hall and crowded around the intercom.

"Who did you talk to, again?" Natasha said.

"The captain," Maria said. She paused. "He said he was the captain."

"What's his name?" Ruby asked.

Maria turned to look at her. "You guys don't believe me," she said.

"We believe you," Saliha said. She put her hand on Maria's arm.

Maria said, "I called him because we're passing a hydrothermal field, one of the biggest I've ever seen. Unbelievably active. Crawling with life. I wanted to stop and send the cameras out. He said we couldn't stop."

Trevor said suddenly, "You're right. I've misled you, misled you all."

"What's that mean?" Natasha asked sharply. She reached out and pushed the button, said, "Hello," brusquely at the box.

"I had to wait a while before I got anyone," Maria said.

Trevor had come out of the workout room. They hadn't realized he was in there. He was shirtless and held a small towel. He had a seamless tan that Ruby had never noticed. The tan made it seem as though he'd only recently joined them on the submarine.

"I thought you didn't work out," Natasha said.

"Have to keep busy somehow," Trevor said. "Impress you ladies." When nobody responded to this, he asked, "What's going on?"

"Hey, hey," Natasha was saying into the box. "Hello?"

Trevor said, "It can take a while. And they don't always answer."

"What do you tell them?" Natasha asked him. "What do you say to them?"

Trevor reached over and gently removed Natasha's finger from the button. "If you keep holding it down, you won't hear them when they reply." Natasha snatched her hand away from him. "I know that," she snapped.

Trevor sighed. He said, "I don't tell them anything. I've asked them to replace the lightbulb over my sink seven times. They tell me to restrict intercom use to emergencies."

"This is an emergency. Maria can't do her work. We all have contracts, you know, to produce a certain amount and type of material."

"I do know. I had to sign off on all that, remember?"

"So what're you going to do about it? You're the team leader."

Trevor paused, as if deliberating. Then he said to Natasha, "You're the one who is worried that changing ocean temperatures will affect the composition of your marine snow and destroy the food chain and life as we know it, right?"

"I'm worried because it's already happening," Natasha said.

"And haven't you also been taking data on microplastics in the water, the microbeads and whatever?"

"Yeah, you know that already."

"Well, then, be happy Maria can't do her work. She works for Shell. What do you think she does in Venezuela? Thermal vents are notoriously mineral-rich."

"I told you not to—" Maria began angrily.

"Pillow talk," Trevor said. He turned and walked down the hall.

"Pillow talk?" Saliha was asking Maria, who said, "He's mad at me."

"What a piece of shit," Natasha said.

Ruby thought this might be a good time to follow up with how Trevor had accused her of killing the rats, but she couldn't bring herself to become, in the eyes of the others, the sort of person who believed Trevor.

Saliha was now asking Ruby: "Not you too?"

Ruby said, "A few times. Not recently."

"You can't let him get to you," Natasha said.

"Am I the only one who turned him down?" Saliha exclaimed.

THE TRENCHES

Ruby had fallen asleep in front of the viewing window. When she woke up, she turned on her side and looked blearily out the window, blinking to clear the gumminess out of her eyes. Outside, the lights had just picked out a large patch of tube worms that furred the cliffside. They made Ruby think of cilia, as if the sub were now within some huge vital organ, from a long-ago high school science textbook.

A small part of her felt a little flattered that the others thought she was a spy. In the rec room was an extravagant James Bond VHS set that stopped right before Pierce Brosnan. What would a spy do if her cover was blown? Only Trevor knew that she was aware of the others' theory, so she'd need to get rid of Trevor. It would be a net benefit anyway: he was sowing dissension, trying to get them to turn on one another. A spy knew how to work for some greater good, even when the work was distasteful; a spy would wait for him in the hallway, her hands and feet braced against the walls to keep herself suspended up near the ceiling, then drop down and eliminate him, push the evidence out of an air lock. He would be an offering to the sea. She imagined tendrils of warm currents curling around him as he was borne up, swaddling him against the cold of the deep water until he could be delivered to the surface. Or maybe his bones would fall out the bottom of him, his destiny to terrorize the beaches. She imagined the ecosystem that might colonize his body. Like a whale fall, he would become an entire planet to the decomposers, and they would devour him, and he would give them life.

> He would be an offering to the sea.

For the first time since they had embarked on their voyage, she thought of the benefactress's lost husband and sons. Even if there had been nothing or nobody to take them in once they had plunged toward the bottom of the abyss, she wondered if the woman would ever draw comfort that at least each of them had become a planet, a source of life. She tried to think if she would ever be able to cherish this idea, if one day, like people who jumped to defy a burning building, they would decide to leave the sub and become something new.

She sat up. There was something outside the window. She suspected the thing had been gesturing at her for some time, trying to get her attention. She ran to the window.

The sea monk was emerging from the gloaming of the cliffside. She thought she saw two big black eyes, gentle round eyes, unhuman eyes, but she wasn't sure: the sea monk was holding one fin up to shield its face from the submarine spotlights. As Ruby stared, the spotlights lit up a shimmering veined pattern on its fin that struck Ruby's eyes with a disorienting blue-and-green dazzle; Ruby rubbed her eyes and tried to peer past the burning afterimages. The sea monk was as tall as a house. The Vatican had gotten it so wrong! The bull they had prepared, scaled for a human, would be novelty-sized for this abyssal giant; it would be like trying to read fine print on a matchbook.

Ruby pushed her face against the window. The sea monk was waving a great diaphanous fin, beckoning in a slow and elegant sweeping motion of welcome that seemed capable of carrying the entire submarine to its scaled glittering breast. Ruby banged on the plexiglass, shouted for someone to come, to help, to get the captain, as the submarine continued to descend. 🜚

Iris Jamahl Dunkle

HISTORY OF THE INDIAN WARS AS SEEN FROM THE 1980S

Have you seen the one where the handsome white man (shiny brass
buttons, blue wool coat with no holes) comes to the prairie and tames a
wild wolf, a girl gone feral? The sun is always shining; skies press down
blue. How his white teeth glint as he turns the arm of the coffee grinder
for his new native friends (not the face-painted, weapon-yielding Pawnee),
a softer, gentler tribe who has put aside his mission (the white pickled
egg of a lie he has swallowed as to why he is there) to befriend him. If you
listen closely, you can feel the sound of 10,000 wagons rolling toward
them. Over that knoll, where the camera never pans, eight skinned buffalo
rot in the hot sun.

Under a five-month beard
the truth quivers
like a caged animal.

FIELD GUIDE TO THE LOST SPECIES OF CALIFORNIA

It's the small ones that disappear first:
lavender butterflies that once freckled

the greasewood brush, delicate thistles whose ghosts
still sting. Then, we lost what we can gather

with our hands: the kangaroo rat, the white splittail.
Hardly even a meal in that tiny body, but we were hungry

for the dull stare of an empty lake void of any life.
We are the algae that comes, after. The green idea

of want and need. Then, when we settled down
into missions and tilled the land, what we conquered

were human bodies: sweat, cornmeal, and tallow.
Alta, California, established in 1769, a machine of labor

swallowing everything in its path: *a caelo usque ad centrum*
"from the sky to the center of the earth."

Joanna Klink

ON ABIDING

I never wanted
to be awash in

agreement, I never
wanted to argue or

agonize, only to listen
for the rain blown

against glass, sense
who you are

when you are alone but
with me. Present,

the way a birch
late at night
is present to wind.

*

Only I wanted you
next to me
in a sleeping

curve of heat. It seemed
like I was always
misplacing you.

But I loved every
part, eyelashes

and limbs, the way you
leapt into the day.

To want a simple life
might mean
to have given up

on expectations.
It could mean

that faith is easily
crushed, that something

as easy as crossing
the street at dusk

is suddenly too physical,
too narrow, too
empty, too hard,

too rich, too small,
too soon.

*

If I could see
through the rains,
the liquid trees,

quarrel only for a
moment, never be
rushed. Stop

completely at the river's
lightflutter and wait
until it passes

and feel that quiet,
which is the sound
of feeling

growing, hawk
and cloud—to make
good of what you have,

to feel the air press
around you and not regret
the loss of you—

the windows of the
night-trains filling with
metal dusk—snow

turning back to rain,
the underside

of everything you have ever
cared for, unsparing

days and nights,
the plain evening,

the uncertainty, the hard work,
the courageous happiness,

the suffering, to see it, to stay
alive, to hope, to hope

for more, to act,
to crave, to reach for,
to let ourselves be

graced, to leave behind
made things, beautiful things,
cool trails of fire,

to tap and then step back,
falling silent, to risk an
opening, to find time

to be nowhere and lost
and to love. If we
can. If we do.

Freedom from Want

Joan Silber

My brother's longtime boyfriend decided to leave him, once and for all. Enough, he said, was enough. If you can't stop arguing after twenty years, when will you ever? Time for a new start for both of them. They would always be friends, of course. He would always care about Saul, but he really did not think that waking up every day in the same apartment was good for either of them.

This speech might have made sense except that my brother had just been diagnosed with some stage or other of liver cancer. (It was hard to get a full story out of Saul.) And the apartment, in the upper reaches of Manhattan, belonged to Kirk, the boyfriend. My brother, a fifty-seven-year-old librarian with no personal savings, was going to have to find a new place to live. For however long he planned to do that.

I was stunned and outraged by the news, maybe more than my brother was. Why had I ever liked Kirk? I had, I always had. With his deep voice, his good haircuts, his quiet merciless jokes. He called me Sister Susie (my name is Rachel, the name was his kidding). Sister Susie was a perky lass, always getting into the gin on the sly. We had a whole set of stories about her and her unusual relations with her dog Spot. Some of his friends thought I was really called Susie.

How could you decide to break up with someone who had a mortal illness? Who could do such a thing? Kirk could.

"The man is a fuck-head," I said to Saul. "And he has no honor."

"We never got along that well," Saul said. "Remember when he picked a fight with me in front of the entire Brooklyn Library staff? He was always a pain. And you know how full of himself he's been. He thinks being a digital art director is like being Michelangelo—I always laughed at the way he used the word *creative*. Don't make a big deal out of this. It's not the end of the world."

What is, then? I thought, but I didn't say it.

Kirk had not given him any particular deadline for moving out, and everyone in New York knew couples who stayed together for years after breaking up, while prices rose and good deals slipped away. Meanwhile Kirk and my brother were sharing the same bed every night and were—I gleaned from my brother's remarks—still having what could be called sexual contact. I didn't blame Saul for mentioning it either, showing off a last bit of swagger.

And maybe the breakup was just an idea, a flash-in-the pan theory. Maybe Kirk didn't mean it.

"He says I'm lazy about being sick," Saul said. "I should do more, be proactive. Has anyone used that word since 1997?"

"What is it with him?" I said. "I don't get it."

"He's seeing someone new," Saul said.

"He's *what?*" I said. I had to stop wailing in protest, because it was useless and only increased my brother's suffering. He had his ties to Kirk; he didn't want to hear what I had to say. *No big deal* was his mantra, and there was probably a way to say it in Sanskrit or Pali. Even so, I hated to hear it.

> I was his big sister, two years older, but we were both old now.

I was his big sister, two years older, but we were both old now. I was the one with the more chaotic sexual history—I'd been with a long list of men and lived with some very poor choices—but time had passed since those days. The daughter of one of my boyfriends (I was never into marriage) still lived with me, after losing patience with both her parents, and she was already twenty-six. I loved Nadia, I was glad to have her with me, but my apartment wasn't really one that could fit her and me and my brother too. An old bargain of a place in Hell's Kitchen. Not that Saul had expressed any interest in moving in.

Was he looking at apartments? Not at the moment. At the moment he was busy going to a clinic where they inserted a needle into his tumors and a high-frequency current heated them to death. I went with him for this— it was not an adorable procedure—and it took a while. Nadia went to pick him up once. And Kirk went the rest of the time. He did.

Saul would go home to sleep after the procedures—who wouldn't?— and he'd lie around with headphones on watching Netflix for hours when sleep evaded him. The library was giving him time off with no trouble, and maybe he was never going back. He was still losing weight; his nose looked bigger, outgrowing his face. It hurt my heart to look at him. "He could *try* to eat," Kirk said. "He doesn't even try. I buy things he likes, that he always liked. You know he likes those pecan crunch things. It doesn't matter."

I had my own life, of course, my own work, my own loyalties. I had a decent enough job in human resources (who dreamed up that name?) for a hotel chain, overseeing stingy policies and crazy rate changes. I was the old girl who'd been there forever and knew the ropes. Nadia liked to ask if I could game the system—get billions paid out in insurance for someone who was healthy—but I had to tell her that was beyond me. Nadia had a youthful attitude about the possibilities of cheating. Anyway, one night I was buying us supper at a Mexican place in the West Village that was a big favorite of hers, when I heard someone at a nearby table say, "Okay, be patient. Okay?"

"May Saul be better," I heard. "May he be well and happy. May he live with ease. May he live longer."

I knew the voice; it was Kirk's. He was talking to a nice-looking dude in his forties, arguing in that weary, reasonable way of his. I knew that tone. It must be his new lover, this not-so-happy guy in a dark suit.

"I've been waiting a while," the guy said.

Oh, were they waiting for my brother to die? Or just to disappear, to crawl offstage? I was choking with fury. Did I want to rush over and make a scene, did I want to stay where I was to hear more?

"Hey!" Nadia said, solving the problem for me. "There's Kirk! Hey, Kirk!"

He took in the sight of us, waved. What a fuck-head. "Look at you," he called out to Nadia, across two tables in between. "You're looking great. Hi, Rachel. This is my friend, Ethan."

We all nodded at each other.

Even Nadia was taking things in. "Why does everybody all of a sudden know about this restaurant?" she said. "I hate the way it is now, all these people."

"Everybody knows everything nowadays," Kirk said.

"Not for the better either," I said.

"We had a very nice meal," Kirk said. "Didn't you think so, Ethan? We're almost done. Don't mind us. Enjoy your drinks."

And then he turned away from us and murmured something to the Ethan person. He could go ahead and pretend they were in another room, he could do what he wanted.

"They'll leave soon," I said to Nadia. Not that softly either.

Around us a speaker was playing, "Bésame, bésame mucho." The singer was pleading in long notes. We stood our ground, we chewed and drank. Nadia said, "I can't believe he had to bring him here." I didn't know they had left until, halfway through my second bottle of Dos Equis, I looked across and spotted other diners at that table.

"He thinks he's so slick," she said. "Mr. Not-Embarrassed."

"He's like Woody Allen—*the heart wants what it wants.* Remember when he said that when he ran off with his stepdaughter?" Nadia had probably not even been born then, but she'd heard about it. "People think if they're honest about their big cravings, it makes anything okay," I said. "That's a big fallacy of modern life."

I found out Nadia was doing what sounded like praying for my brother. She hadn't been raised in any religion (not with those parents), but she was a great reader online, she taught herself things. In the middle of the night I was in the hallway on my way to pee, when I heard her voice in the living room. "May Saul be better," I heard. "May he be well and happy. May he live with ease. May he live longer."

And Who did she think was processing this request? I didn't ask. I didn't want to smudge the purity of whatever she was doing. I listened for her again as I walked down that hallway the night after, but no words vibrated in the air. The next morning, when I got up early, I saw that she slept (as always) flat on her back on the folded-out sofa, and the statue of the Buddha had been moved to a shelf in her line of sight. It was Saul's Buddha—that is, he had brought it to me after a trip somewhere. Thailand? Cambodia? It was a gray stone figure, the size of a gallon of milk, sitting with one hand raised with a flat palm. Fear not, that hand gesture meant. Saul had been a fan of Buddhism—he read books, he went to meditation classes, he explained very well how ego craving was the source of all suffering—but his interest had faded in the last few years. He hadn't said anything about leaning on it now. But Nadia was?

"You don't have to follow all the rules," she said, when I sort of asked. "People get so caught up in that. As if somebody twenty-five hundred years ago was the last one to know anything about spiritual matters. How could that be right?" What I'd heard as prayer were phrases from a Buddhist practice, but she had added flourishes, like setting out a green ribbon (I hadn't noticed) because Saul's favorite color was green.

At least she wasn't kneeling. When I was a child, my mother caught me kneeling by my bed, intoning, "Now I lay me down to sleep, I pray the Lord my soul to keep." (How did I even know that prayer?)

"Jews don't kneel," my mother said.

I got up right away. I sort of loved the urgency in my mother's voice. She spoke rarely about religious matters and sometimes made fun of what I learned in Hebrew school. This was serious. I wanted serious, that was why I was praying.

Like Nadia. All over the world (I traveled much in my wayward youth), people go in for petitionary prayer; they ask for concrete and specific things, even when they're not supposed to, according to their systems of belief. They set out flowers, fruit, candles, money. Tiny models of body parts they want fixed. Votive wishes on papers they pin on trees.

I looked at the green ribbon, a strip of satin left over from a Christmas package. Did she think a Higher Power could bring about what she wanted? "You never know," she said.

"Can't argue with that," I said, though I could have.

Nadia was nine when I first met her. I was dating Nick, her dad, and he had her on weekends. She kept calling me by the wrong name on purpose—Rochelle, Raybelle, Michelle—and looking at me with fiendish eyes. But she got over all that, eventually, and then she was nuzzling and cuddling like a much younger kid and saying she liked my house. She pocketed a spoon when she left (I saw, who cared?). I admired her resourcefulness, her range of attempts to be on top of the situation. She was working hard to watch out for herself. When her father later referred to her as a total pill—he liked that phrase—I said, "What kind of crap is that?"

Now it was Saul's turn to be a total pill. He talked too much about his ablation treatments, he talked too much about his liver. Once he had been happy to argue about how detective novels were good for the brains of middle-school kids and why online reading was a triumph against capitalism. Now he was like any patient, caught up in the drama of his own ordeals, his schedule of medications, the textures of his own shrinking world. I wanted him to be better than that.

"Sister Susie says you should have a joint," I said. "Your treatments are over. You can do what you want." I lit up while I was spreading this doctrine.

"What *do* I fucking want?" he said. But he took a hit. "There's nothing I want."

"Isn't that an ideal state in Buddhism?" I said.

"That's a gross simplification," Saul said. But he looked at least a little pleased. It was better news than he'd heard for a while.

"Did you know Nadia's been chanting on your behalf?"

"She told me," he said. "What a good girl she turned into."

He really wanted nothing? He had to want to live, if he was going to last a little longer. Indifference would drag him under. But maybe I wasn't paying attention properly.

Did she think a Higher Power could bring about what she wanted?

Before my brother's diagnosis, my life had been in what felt like a good phase. Two crucial areas had shown improvement. An ex-boyfriend—everyone called him Bud—who'd left New York seven years before had started sending me emails. He'd gone off to Cambodia to work for an NGO, defending workers' rights, which clearly needed defending, there and here. We'd parted badly but we always remembered each other's birthdays, which was mature of us. On my last birthday, he'd written, "Hands across the water, hands across the sky," lines to a song I used to like. Once he started writing, I was always humming it in my head. And finally, at long last, Nadia seemed to be out of the woods—she'd left behind her habits of moping and quitting and having fits of fury and bouts of despair and going a little nuts. She was back in school, taking computer design classes at FIT that she liked to talk about; she was sane. I walked around feeling secretly smug, as if I'd been right about everything all along.

Which at least made it easier to be nice to Saul when he uttered the same complaints over and over. "I'm nauseated all the time," he said. "I hate it. I can't even barf. I can't do anything."

"You can't read?" I said. He was a librarian, for Christ's sake. The original escapist reader. Thrilled by discoveries, an enthusiast of hidden corners of information. "You want some audiobooks? You could be nauseated and listen at the same time."

"Never mind," he said. "You don't get it."

We were having this conversation in the bedroom of his and Kirk's apartment. He was sitting up in bed, wrapped in a blanket. The night table was a mess of pill bottles, old socks. Did he maybe want to smoke something? "It doesn't help," he said. "Why do people say it helps?"

Kirk was in the living room, tapping on his cell phone. He called out to Saul, "You know there's some of that mango smoothie in the fridge. Easy to swallow. Don't you think you would like that?"

"Why do you think I would like anything?" Saul said.

"Silly me," Kirk said.

I was at my desk at work when my brother called with a piece of startling news. Meanwhile, in the midst of this, Bud the old boyfriend had decided it was time for us to Skype each other—Phnom Penh to NYC. Hands across the water. "Rachel!" he said, when we were on each other's screens. I always loved his voice. It was Bud! His hair was shorter, grayer (so was mine but dyed). Had he always had that slight web under his chin? "Isn't this weird, this teledating?" he said. Oh, we were dating? I could see the room behind him, a beaded curtain over a closet, an open window with green fronds outside.

"Is it hot there now?" I said. "It's snowing here."

"It's in the eighties. You'd like it. You like summer."

I'd been to parts of Southeast Asia when I was a restless young thing—Thailand and Malaysia—but people weren't going to Cambodia then, a postwar mess even to backpackers. "It's still a mess," he said.

"It's a mess here too," I said. I had already told him my worst Trump jokes. "The rich get richer. *You* know."

"What amazes me in my line of work," he said, "is the strength of people to go on." He had these moments of grandstanding but his points were good. "You see them come out of these factories where they work ten hours a day in suffocating heat, wages so low they can barely eat, and sometimes a girl is laughing at what her friend said. Too tired to move but something is still funny."

I was wondering if Bud could kid around with them in whatever they spoke. "Khmer," he said. "Khmer is Cambodian. It can take them a while to see I'm being funny on purpose."

He probably wasn't as hilarious as he imagined. "You should come visit," he said. "Come to Phnom Penh."

"Sure," I said, as if he really meant it, which I didn't think he did. As if I could go any time, just like that.

I was at my desk at work when my brother called with a piece of startling news. "Guess what I did?" he said. "I ate a huge bowl of mint chip ice cream. Two and a half scoops. I'm feeling better."

"Icy cold? Is that okay?"

"Went down fine. I might have more."

I laughed. "You were hungry."

"Maybe those needle jabs are working. Maybe I'm getting better. I feel better."

"You do?"

"I don't get that tired when I walk around either. I just wanted to tell you."

"I'm so glad."

"Two and a half scoops. I might have more."

I couldn't believe it—I was too happy to stay still, I was strolling around the room with the phone. Maybe he had more time than we thought. The percentage of people who lived five years after they'd been diagnosed wasn't very high, but a person could be on the good side of statistics. Somebody was.

Later that night, Nadia said, "Well, it was *supposed* to work. That's why he did it."

"Supposed to doesn't usually mean shit," I said, and then I was sorry I had spoken like that to a young person.

"If he's better," my friend Amy at work said, "then you can run off to Cambodia. Have sex with your ex, see Angkor Wat."

"It's too far. You know how far away it is? Twenty hours by plane. At the very least."

"I guess you looked online," she said.

And the airfare wasn't nothing either. Or did Bud think he was paying? We hadn't gotten anywhere near that question.

"Everyone's leaving my brother," I said. "I don't have to join them."

"So I found this nice little apartment," my brother said. "Small but small isn't bad. Decent light."

"You were looking?" I said. "I didn't know you were looking." This made me worry what else I had missed.

"Well, it fell into my lap," he said.

"It's affordable? Really?" Was it over a sewage plant? In nearby Nevada?

"It's in our building," Saul said. "Our neighbor has this studio he wants to sublet."

It was just three floors down.

"This guy wants a big deposit," Saul said. "People do now. Two months security, one month in advance. I don't know where he thinks I'd be skipping away to. Kirk is lending me the money."

Lend, my ass. My brother's lover was paying him to leave. And they'd be greeting each other in the elevator forever. And everybody was acting cheerful about it.

"I'm looking forward to having my own place," Saul said. "It's been years since I had that."

"Did you want to be alone?"

"No," he said. "But it's fine.

Nadia thought her meditating had caused this improvement for Saul, her focusing on the words with all her strength. Something had gotten him better, against all odds. "I did more than you know. Most of it not out loud," she said. "Don't laugh."

"I'm not laughing."

"What's the other reason? There isn't any."

I wasn't offering any details of science. She looked so happy. She was still an awkward girl, and happiness made her face rounder and bolder.

"Saul thanked me," she said. "He said I was amazing."

My brother's character was improving, now that he was on an upward swing. Sick people had crappy dispositions. "He wants me to design something for the windows of his new place," Nadia said. "I can do that."

Was he going back to work? He'd always had a ridiculously long commute, from Inwood at the top of Manhattan all the way south to Brooklyn, an hour and fifteen minutes, but he used to say he liked reading on the subway. He had an unimpressive salary, decent insurance (I had checked it over), and not that bad a pension. Did he want to be in the library again?

He wasn't saying. He didn't even like it when we asked. When he was little, he loved to announce, "That's for me to know and you to find out," and he seemed to want to say that now. "Later for that," he muttered. To *me*, he said this.

My mother always claimed everyone thought Saul was less stubborn than he really was. I got along better with my mother than he did, and I had trouble too. We lost both our parents, within months of each other, a decade ago. Kirk had actually been very good through all that. That was when I still liked Kirk.

All of us helped with Saul's move. Nadia got someone at school to sew the curtains for her—pale greeny cream gathered at the sides, very nice, with misty gray panels in the centers. I scrubbed the place down and bought him a microwave. He was taking a sofa bed and a bookcase out of the apartment, which Kirk and the new boyfriend loaded into the elevator, along with the cartons of Saul's clothes. Ethan, the boyfriend, said, "Good light!" when he entered the room, bowed under the weight of the sofa. He looked different in jeans and a T-shirt, a little stockier.

What was Saul seeing now? All that talk of light.

"I love the light," my brother said. "A new day is dawning here."

He was sitting in a corner while we all worked, and he said, "You know, I really don't need any place bigger."

The new boyfriend looked properly embarrassed. Kirk said, "The couch looks totally great here."

I worried about all this compliance from Saul, this no-problems adaptation to his new situation. Was it sincere? Was it admirable? In my own life, I prided myself on being on good terms with my exes, but I had fought some bitter fights along the way. Nick, Nadia's father, had been so infuriated by what I once said about his personality that he threatened to kidnap Nadia back. Arrive in the night and spirit her away. He didn't mean it for a second—Nadia didn't think so either—but he was hot with anger; he was, as they say, seeing red. What was Saul seeing now? All that talk of light. I wondered if he was seeing a muted glare, if he had a vision of his long days bathed in peaceful beams, streams of brightness in the air all around him. Blessing and bleaching his months in that room, however many months. He knew more than we did.

And sometimes he slipped into being his former disgruntled self. New York was having a very cold and rainy spring, and when I tried to get him out for a meal of any kind—brunch or dinner or anything—he said, "Who wants to go out in *that*?" Even when the weather had nothing wrong with it, he was annoyed at the prospect of going outside. The bother of it, the inconvenience. And the food. Did I know how greasy the food was in all brunch places? Did I know anything about what he couldn't eat?

Kirk's new boyfriend had not moved in upstairs—he apparently had his own very good apartment on a treelined street in the far West Village. I happened to see Kirk in the elevator, and he did not look pleased about anything, but who knew what that meant? "Hey there," I said to him, and he mumbled, "Oh, hello." Not that he could be expected to be overjoyed to see me.

> How to support her friend but not lie too much: that was the problem.

So what did Saul do all day? He looked things up on his computer, he binge-watched good TV, he reread some Dickens, he did a little meditating. He kept the place neat and relatively clean, a sign of his fondness for it. And did anyone visit but me?

"Friends come. And people from work. And you know who comes a lot?" he said. "Kirk."

I chuckled bitterly. "Does he help?"

"He brings food. We had strawberries the other day. He says he misses me."

I was fucking tired of the caprices of fucking Kirk. "What do you say?"

"I tell him he has to get used to being alone."

How calm my brother was choosing to be. I hoped it bothered Kirk.

And Saul wasn't rushing to go back to work, was he? He wasn't going back. How had I thought that he would?

"Were you ever in Cambodia?" I asked Saul. "Or was it just Thailand?" I was making tea in his kitchen, the one thing he'd let me do. It was a nice kitchen, blue tiles on the wall.

"Just Thailand. Before I knew Kirk. We went up to the Northeast, not very visited then. Ever go to that part?"

"Not me."

"Great people," Saul said. "Dirt poor. I felt like a jerk as a tourist, with my jangling change. They deserved better."

"Freedom from want," I said. "That was one of the four freedoms in FDR's speech. Nobody thinks of that now as a human right."

"So you want to go to Cambodia?" Saul said. "This is new."

"Remember that guy Bud I used to go with? He lives there."

"I think he treated you not very well," Saul said. "As I remember."

"That was then, this is now," I said.

"Famous last words," Saul said.

Nadia said, "So how did people decide who to marry in the old days when they didn't even sleep together? How did people understand what kind of deal they were getting?"

"Don't ask me," I said. "I didn't come in under that system. But you can't go just by sex, you know. Do I have to tell you that?"

"You so do not," Nadia said, rolling her eyes. "But how do people make these colossal bargains about what they decide to put up with?"

I knew this wasn't about her own dating life (which was quiet at the moment) but about her friend Kit, set to marry a person whose merits were entirely invisible to Nadia. How to support her friend but not lie too much: that was the problem.

"Lie," I said. I wasn't her parent, I could talk that way to her.

"She thinks he's smart, and he's really stupid. It depresses me what people do."

"You don't know how it will turn out. No one can tell."

"She thinks she's won the lottery," Nadia said. "She feels sorry for the rest of us."

"People are like that," I said. "I used to be like that."

Saul told me he was thinking more about finances lately. He had made a list of how much he spent on rent, how much on food and utilities, what income he had coming in, how much wiggle room he had. He had a little. "I get benefits," he said. "I'm not destitute. I hope you know that."

And, by the way, he'd made a will, and it was in the bookcase by the big book of Audubon drawings, if I wanted to know.

I thought he'd always had a will.

"Well, no. And this one is good. I had someone, a lawyer, make sure everything was all right."

"You found a lawyer without ever leaving the apartment?"

Ethan was a lawyer.

"Estate law isn't his specialty," Saul said, "but I knew he could get the forms for something simple. He made it easy. I just told him what I wanted. Easy as pie."

"How nice."

"Don't forget. By the Audubon book."

I was tearful when Nadia came home. "Saul decided to have a little conversation about his *will*," I said. "What kind of nineteenth-century novel are we in?"

"I hope he doesn't leave all his money to Kirk or anything," she said, after I'd calmed down and she'd poured us a little wine.

I secretly hoped he was leaving whatever he had to Nadia, a person not legally related to either of us.

"He's not rich anyway," she said.

"It doesn't matter," I said.

That was the question about money, wasn't it? How much it mattered. I used to argue with Bud about that, in the old days, when we liked to talk about which friends were happy. I was always claiming that high incomes soured people and made them anxious and stingy.

"I don't think you should go to Cambodia," Nadia said.

"Who said I was going?"

"I saw on the news they're arresting journalists. It's very unfair."

"I'm not going anywhere any time soon," I said. I wanted to hop into bed with Bud—that was true, however old we were—but it had nothing to do with the heart of the matter at the moment, which was my brother.

Nadia said, "You mention Bud more than you did."

"Saul knows him. He's not a big fan."

"Excuse me, but Saul is not a proven expert. I wouldn't listen to his opinions about any boyfriends if I had any."

"Who would you listen to instead?"

"Not you either," she said.

What I liked in this was her hopefulness. She was twenty-six, and she was never going to make the mistakes we'd made.

Ethan went with Saul for one of his doctor's visits, on the theory that it was always good to have another person paying attention and writing things down. What kind of world was it, where you needed a lawyer to listen to your doctor? "He asked good questions," my brother said. "We all had a nice chat. But I don't think I'm going again."

How good could those questions have been? In my opinion, Ethan had been no help at all.

"How can you just not go?" I said.

"A question that answers itself," he said.

I believed in freedom—it was my brother's right not to go anywhere—and it would've done no good at all if I'd bossed or begged or reasoned. It seemed that the doctor was no longer offering anything he wanted. Saul had more than one doctor, and they were united in their lack of appealing offers.

"It'll be very relaxing," my brother said. "To stay home."

"What kind of nineteenth-century novel are we in?"

What home? But the new place had a good kitchen (better than the old place, really) and I believed that if we could keep him eating, he'd have more time. I got this from our mother, always indignant if we didn't finish what was on our plates—"People in other parts of the world would be very happy to eat what you're leaving behind." We were born too late to hear about starving Armenians, but she brought up the people in China (was this about famines under Mao?), and adults were always letting us know that ingratitude about food was dangerous. Did parents in places like Cambodia say this to their children now? Or did the children always eat?

Saul would eat a few things—I could make a very nice corn chowder that he didn't mind and also a Middle Eastern version of fried eggs with mint, oregano, and scallions. Sometimes he ate pad thai from a place nearby. On good days he could be tempted by ice cream in certain flavors. He was a slow eater, like a fidgety five-year-old.

On weekends Nadia came with me to deal with the housecleaning. We brought the vacuum cleaner down from Kirk's; in the elevator Nadia wore the hose around her shoulders like a boa. Even with all the dust bunnies collecting under the furniture, the place was so small the work didn't take long, and Saul got to make a joke. "How come," he said, "the Buddhist didn't vacuum in the corners of the room?"

"I know this one," Nadia said.

I didn't. "Because," my brother said, "he had no attachments."

"Oh, my God, she's laughing," Nadia said.

"The woman's been inhaling the floor polish," Saul said.

What did that mean, no attachments? Saul used to tell me it meant *don't worry, it won't last, nothing does*. And he said all that was more uplifting than it sounded.

"Don't go to Cambodia," Nadia said, when we were eating dinner that night. I was sure I had made it clear to her I wasn't getting on any planes. "How can I deal with stuff that happens with Saul when you're not here? I'm young, you know."

Bud had stopped issuing invitations to Phnom Penh, perhaps for lack of an enthusiastic response on my part. Maybe he had found someone else. NGOs were full of intelligent single women. We still had our conversations on Skype. I combed my hair, I put on lipstick; I got excited before he called. We flickered on the screen at each other. That was the way it was.

> **When we were growing up, there was still some rhetoric left about drugs as a source of enlightenment.**

"I asked Saul," Nadia said, "where he'd want to go if he could get his wish, like they do with kids, that wish foundation. I told him he should go to Jamaica. It's where my ridiculous friend Kit is going on her ridiculous honeymoon. I'd take him. It's not that far."

"What did he say?"

"He said he liked it fine where he was."

I snorted.

Adults usually didn't act out their wildest wishes before they died, despite all the movies that used that plot. They had other ideas by then. They left the old ones behind.

Nadia started wearing a green ribbon as a choker, in honor of Saul (it looked good on her, she looked good in everything). As a charm, it didn't work. He had a really bad week; he said an eagle was coming every night to eat his liver. The whites of his eyes looked stained yellow. By phone I pestered the doctor until he prescribed more painkillers. Maybe not enough—scrips were stingy because of the opioid crisis—but welcome for now. "I'm turning on, tuning in, and dropping out," Saul said. "There's a lot to be said for it."

When we were growing up, there was still some rhetoric left about drugs as a source of enlightenment. When I was in Thailand in my twenties, we could buy anything (or my then-boyfriend could) and we sat around stoned on who knows what. Waiting for moments of strange clarity, which sometimes came. Opiated hash, did people still smoke that? Who came up with that combo?

"Do you remember anything?" Saul said.

"I remember my boyfriend," I said. "Except I've forgotten his name."

Saul laughed. He could still laugh. "Sister Susie," he said.

What did I long for? "Are you discouraged," Bud asked on the screen from Phnom Penh, "because of Trump?"

Yes, but I hadn't remembered to think about it lately. We all had different levels of grief, didn't we, a whole hierarchy.

"In NGOs," Bud said, "the aid workers who see the worst are always going out on the town to get stupidly cheered up. Like those Oxfam Brits who hired prostitutes."

He was my cheering up, a very hygienic form.

"What do you do in Phnom Penh?" I said.

He smirked a little. "Well, there's not much to do. Actually, there is, but I don't do it. There's a bar I like. The girls know me, they don't bother me."

I was glad he wasn't bothered.

"You'd love the river, we have three rivers. And the temples."

"What do Cambodians do for luck?" I was thinking of Nadia and her ribbon.

"Some people get protective tattoos. Angelina Jolie got a Cambodian tattoo."

How far away he was. What did it mean to have a romance that was never going to be acted out? It didn't seem so bad to me anymore. In fact it had certain superiorities over contact in person. And it was as real as the outlines of Angelina Jolie's tattoo (which I'd seen online), with its guardian blessings inked out in Pali. Bud had become a wish of mine with no trouble in it.

Kirk was upset. I could tell by the sight of him, rumpled and frowning, when I ran into him by the recycling bins in the basement of the building. I was throwing out a whole bag of empty cans of ginger ale. It was the one thing Saul liked now that he was back to not liking again. The cans were clanging as I dumped them.

"He's not doing well, is he?" Kirk said. "I didn't know how it would be."

"I guess you didn't," I said.

"Don't be against me," Kirk said.

He wanted me to like him too? I might've pushed him into the recyclables, if I'd been a different sort of person. "What's the matter with you?" I said. We seemed to be connected forever, but so what?

"Did he tell you?" Kirk said. "I asked him to move back."

I gasped out loud, a wheeze of amazement. I had just been thinking of getting someone to come in a few hours a day to help, as much as his insurance would cover. Someone good. Not needed now? No longer my business?

"He said no," Kirk said.

"Fuck," I said.

Of course, I was proud of my brother (we don't kneel) and quite surprised. Kirk had been even more surprised.

"He insists that he's happier without me."

Kirk sounded devastated by this bit of news. Which was probably not even true, though maybe it was. Who knew what my brother really wanted? He acted now as if he were in a kingdom whose language was too much work to translate for us.

Kirk was gazing at me, waiting for something he was hoping I could give. "Everybody thinks he's so mild, but he's the stubbornest person on the planet," I said. "No is no."

Kirk said, "Maybe he'll change his mind."

I loved my brother's stubbornness. He didn't have to run around anymore, did he, rushing to get what he thought he should have. Fine where he was. Of course, I envied his freedom, who wouldn't? Only a few days ago I'd gone into a little fit because I'd lost my favorite earrings; they had been a gift from Nadia's father, whom I didn't even like, but I'd had them for years and they looked good on me. "What are you hanging on to?" Saul said. "You had them and they're gone."

This bit of philosophy did stop my wailing. Saul could do that—he could utter a tautology in a way that made it sound beautifully plain and right. "Goodbye to all that," I said to my earrings. Saul was speaking from a spot further on, a better view, speaking with expertise.

Not that he always abided by this. He had spells of being very irritated at me for spending his dollars on overpriced takeout meals or organic detergent—"I'm not made of money." Little pissy amounts of cash. He was afraid of his resources running out. A metaphor there.

Kirk said, "Who knew you would turn into a skinflint?"

How poorly Kirk understood him, what a mess Kirk had made of everything. Yearning and grabbing. Kirk the now-repentant lummox who dreamed my clearheaded brother would change his mind.

Which he did. Five weeks later, Kirk called to give me the news. "We've got him all settled in." Saul was already in his old bedroom watching TV in a newly rented hospital bed by the time they told me. "I'm very comfortable," Saul said. "I have this new kind of pillow under my neck. Ethan got it for me."

Who knew what my brother really wanted?

"Did they bring up all your stuff? Tell me what you need."

"I think I have everything pretty much."

The one who sounded really, really happy was Kirk. "He looks better already. He does. You can tell by looking at him this is the right move. I never thought he'd say yes. I gave up, I had no clue this would happen. And we got everything done so fast! We did." His voice had gotten giddy and young, he was burbling away.

When I dropped over to see Saul in his new-old lodgings that evening, Kirk was glowing in the doorway. "Ethan made this great little supper that was some kind of mussel stew. And Saul gobbled it up. Well, not all of it, but he ate it. He liked it."

"I ate it in Iceland," Ethan said. "I went there with my mother last year."

Ethan had a mother? I never thought about him outside these rooms. "It's gorgeous," Ethan said about Iceland. "Expensive but worth it." What did a lawyer with a fat paycheck care about expensive?

Kirk said, "Ethan can cook, I can cook. We'll keep trying different food."

"We have a whole bucket of empty mussel shells now," my brother said. My brother with his pinched face, his elbows knobs of bone.

"Ethan's good in the kitchen," Kirk said.

"Now and then I can do something," Ethan said. "But you know how late I work."

"I can't eat late," Saul said. "Don't expect me to stay up. I get tired."

"He ate ice cream too," Kirk had to tell me.

Whatever the report of his chef's skills, Ethan slipped out soon after I arrived. There was murmuring with Kirk by the door, and he was gone.

"Hey," my brother said, when Kirk walked back in, "I don't have to do the dishes now, do I?"

Kirk acted as if that was the funniest thing he'd ever heard. "We just throw them out when they're dirty," he said. Did I actually laugh too?

Soon after, the two of us walked my brother to his old room. Saul showed me the way a person could crank the bed down to make it easy to climb into. "A miracle of science," he said. "It's costing a fortune, I think."

"Good night, sweet prince," Kirk said.

On the way back, I saw from the hallway that Kirk's usually pristine computer studio was a mess, with piles of clothes littering it. It had become the room where he slept. (Alone, it seemed. Not with Ethan at the moment.)

"He's crazy about that bed," Kirk said. "Did you see that? He is."

When the sunlight, which my brother used to love, bothered his eyes, even in this dimmer apartment, Ethan set up curtains around the bed. He had someone construct posts at the bed's four corners, and then he hung the elegant drapes that Nadia had designed—they became bed curtains, like the ones Scrooge had around his bed when the ghosts frightened him.

Even Nadia thought the curtains looked good, the pale green and gray. She was still not a fan of Kirk ("Why do I have to like him?"), but she made an effort when I took her to visit. We were all sitting around the living room, and Ethan brought in tea and a plate of pastel meringue kisses from a bakery, a low-fat delicacy for Saul. "How pretty they are," Nadia said.

Kirk said, "You made the tea too strong. Saul needs it weaker. Can you bring in the hot water?"

I would've said, Get your own fucking water, but Ethan was back with the kettle in a jiffy. "Taste it," he said to my brother.

"Just right," Saul said.

"You're sure?"

Saul was chomping and sipping. Between bites he said, "We watched this thing on Netflix that was really hilarious."

"We were totally into it," Ethan said.

"I couldn't stop laughing in one part," Kirk said.

Nadia got all the details (a Tasmanian lesbian comedian she already knew about) and my brother imitated the woman's accent. Kirk cracked up watching him. "You missed your calling in stand-up," he said.

"He went for the big bucks in library science," Ethan said.

Saul couldn't resist telling how he'd once spilled an entire cartload of books on a library trustee, a story I'd heard many times before. As had Kirk. My brother told it well this time. Nadia laughed at the oafish amazement of the fallen trustee, Saul's version of his own loony apologies, but the one who loved the tale the most was Kirk. He gazed and nodded at my brother, he clapped and hooted. I'd rarely seen him so happy.

Saul, for his part, had the sly look people get when they've told a joke that's gone over. How pleased my brother was, on that pinched face of his.

When we left, Nadia muttered to me in the elevator, "So I guess he's okay there." Her face was still tinted pink from laughing, but now her voice was flat. The whole thing had confused her about the nature of love. I wasn't saying a word either. What did I know? I was thinking that this would become an elemental part of what she'd remember, for who knew how long, that she'd have what she'd just seen. The way they were, just like that—I wanted her to have that. 🏛

Alison Pelegrin

MY SNATCH IS PRETTY GOOD

If you hear *pussy* when I say *snatch*, either
you belong to my cabal of weight-lifting poet yogis,
or you're my mother, snatch the frequent star
of her dirty jokes, and as explanation all I have
is that her father was a marine with a vodka IV
who told home health to blow it out of their asses.
Hip!—we called him Hip—when I think of him,
I think of suicide—I saw how his eyes roved for that pistol,
I imagined the froth of blood pinking his undershirt
the exact color of the tank top I now wear to the gym,
which claims, in girly script, *my snatch is pretty good*—
an understatement, and a double entendre if you know
that in addition to the vajayjay, *snatch* also refers
to that olympic lift in which the barbell, in one pull,
travels from the ground to overhead. I'm giddy
with the miracle of speed and kilo math,
my bouncing plates so loud that other lifters
look my way—that's why I giggle when I hit a snatch,
and also because of my mom, who reminds me, even now,
when I screw up, to check myself, because I used to live
"in her snatch." Considering our history,
I knew she would laugh at my tank top
and the bumper sticker version I bought for her

because I'm proud of all my women,
bad ass, indelicate broads, and me the same,
in a full squat bearing down with sixty kilos overhead,
the sweet spot where I find my balance.
I have felt a midwife's intimacy with other lifters,
our tribe gathered around the platform
as though awaiting a birth, only it is the weight
we are waiting on, waiting for it to move,
willing with our minds, helping with yells if one
among us is buried under a squat, grinding to stand.
But it is the lifter who does all of the work,
as in birth it is the mother, alone and watched,
all eyes on her, on her snatch, vortex from which
daughters and sons emerge and unfold,
each of them a bloodied lotus, and the mother—
well, when it was me, I was stunned, amazed,
as with a PR on the barbell overhead—*what the hell just*
    happened,
how did I do this, is there no end to my strength?

Pre-Millennium Tension

2799 BCE

A worried Assyrian once etched a doomsday prophecy onto a slab of clay:

> *Our Earth is degenerate in these later days; there are signs that the world is speedily coming to an end. Bribery and corruption are common, children no longer obey their parents, every man wants to write a book.*

This untraceable tablet is most likely apocryphal—for one thing, books weren't invented until several centuries later. But as myth, it has been repeated verbatim by Isaac Asimov, *Smithsonian* magazine, and Eleanor Roosevelt—not to mention all the spottier perches of the internet. We don't seem to care that this "ancient" prophecy was fabricated in our most recent century. Someone knew we'd want our oldest ancestors to have logged their troubled thoughts about an imminent demise.

Elena Passarello

99

Chapter nine, verse nine of the book of Revelation is twenty-five words long. It begins in mid-description of the locusts summoned when the fifth angel sounds her trumpet. Through the persona of John the Revelator, the authors imagine no ordinary locusts. See their stinging tails, their glowering faces, and their hair like that of human women. Once unleashed from their underground lair of chaos by the demon Apollyon, the locusts then spend months torturing the condemned; they spare only flora, fauna, and any human marked with the seal of Christ. Imagine the noise of these avenging insects as a chord loud and dissonant enough to nauseate the listener.

999

Much of Europe's storied "Y1K" panic appears to be fiction as well. For starters, claiming that any tenth-century person could identify the exact year proves tricky. Churches arranged the calendar according to their own wonky math. Plus, any given fiefdom might observe the new year at Advent, Easter, or on the twenty-fifth of March. Not to mention all the invasions and pestilence with which the masses were already saddled. In the Middle Ages, it seems, every day held the potential for apocalypse. Evidence points to a nineteenth-century historian as the disseminator of this legend. In his 1855 doorstop chronicle of the French people, Jules Michelet depicted 999 as a panorama of unease—all walks of life stuck between the promise of eschatological salvation and the fear of God's red right hand. He used that chaos to contrast their church-driven values with his own era's more rational bent. And Michelet's dramatized panic held enough narrative sway to influence decades of European storytelling and music.

Over a century later, the *New York Times* used a story that exposed Michelet's hyperbole to draw a new, ominous conclusion: "Could it be that the fears and hysteria surrounding the coming of the year 1000 were nothing compared to those surrounding the coming of the year 2000? If so, who is living in the Dark Ages?"

1499

The close of the fifteenth century found much of Europe embroiled in existential turmoil. The rapidly expanding world—with its technological advancements and discoveries of new continents—yielded an uptick in both cataclysmic prophecy and general doomsday woe. Many of the era's most imaginative artists illustrated that wrecked interiority. Albrecht Dürer published his folio of the book of Revelation in woodcuts, *Apocalypse with Pictures*, in 1498. Thanks to the newly minted printing press, Dürer's awful images went viral. In 1499, Hieronymus Bosch was still painting his triptych *The Garden of Earthly Delights*, which features a nightmare-inducing hellscape on its right-hand panel. Bosch painted the humans who had first enjoyed the titular delights of the triptych's center panel getting stabbed, vomited upon, and eaten alive by armadillo-dog monsters. Musical instruments became torture devices, trees hosted demonic taverns and sported the heads of exhausted giants, and all the nuns had morphed into amorous pigs. And above this noisy chaos, several blackened villages teemed with fire and chiaroscuro smoke.

1599

One April morning, architect Domenico Fontana was called to the site of his latest project—rerouting the Sarno to make a new canal near Naples. Fontana's workers had dug into something hard and thick and not unlike a wall. According to legend, when the crew dusted off the stone to reveal frescoes of ancient Roman fuckery, they were mortified. They rushed to rebury the images before the police caught them enjoying pornography. We know Fontana saw the word "Pompeii" as written by a graffito's blocked hand, but he ignored it, and no one dug back into that dirt for nearly 150 years. Had he kept going, Fontana would have unearthed the last day of a city that had been lost for 1,500 years, with its "Beware of Dog" mosaics, its bathhouses, and its 1,150 empty pumice coffins in the shape of incinerated humans.

In a letter written not long after the book of Revelation, Pliny the Younger described Pompeii's last day, which he witnessed from across the Bay of

Naples. He remembered the screams of thousands of displaced survivors along the beach. "Many besought the aid of the gods," Pliny wrote, "but still more imagined there were no gods left, and that the universe was plunged into eternal darkness forevermore. I derived some poor consolation . . . from the belief that the whole world was dying with me, and I with it."

1799

There's no reason for Beethoven's *Pathétique* piano sonata to begin the way it does—a louder-than-hell chord thundered out on seven fingers, that then shrinks away. The sound falls out of sync with both the mores of the late Classical period and the rest of the sonata. These door-slamming chords continue intermittently as the quieter melody advances—with the listener, perhaps, tensing in wait of the next eruption. And all this happens in C minor, a chord so tortured it should be served with an SSRI. Then, two minutes later, the score repeats, returning the listener to the same sonic gallows. Though beautiful, the work destabilizes the ear, making the listener question the sonic world and what comes next in it. Beethoven sets the pace for these doomsday chords at the slowest of all tempo markings: *grave*.

1999

The songs from the last year of the second millennium were an apocalypse in and of themselves: Cher's "Believe." Sugar Ray's "Every Morning." "La Vida Loca" and the global pox that was Santana featuring Rob Thomas. The uselessness of these songs matches the futility of this particular end-of-the-century panic. Two-thirds of Americans still didn't own a computer, yet computers were set to do us all in. Not exactly the 1999 many of us had envisioned, nor the apocalypse others had feared. And of course, this all came with the sneaking suspicion that all this unease, all that dull panic, could turn out to be nothing. Though things were set to go down with a bang rather than a whimper, the possibilities still frightened us, and the album that best captures that conflict is probably Tricky's *Pre-Millennium Tension*. Released three years before the century ended, Tricky's fractured and chaotic record teems with low-end menace to make a sinister report of End

Times: "Look to the sun; see me in the psychic pollution. . . . Who do you think you are? You're insignificant—a small piece, an ism, no more, no less."

Shortly after *Pre-Millennium Tension*'s release, journalist Liz Jones mentioned the album to Prince in an interview. Tricky harnessed intense production values and genre-play in ways that Prince's own music did, she told him. When Jones reminded Prince of the title of Tricky's album, the Purple One smirked like a prophet—like a man who's had the answers for at least five thousand years.

Faced with *Pre-Millennium Tension*, Prince replied, "isn't that just a longer way of saying *1999*?"

Victoria Chang

OBIT

Victoria Chang—died on June 24, 2011,
at the age of 41. Her imagination lived
beyond that day though. It weighed two
pounds and could be lifted like weights but
it had to wait for her to work out. Once
she brought her father to the arcade. He
found the basketball machine and shot
one after another. As if he were revisiting
his past self in prison, touching the clear
glass at his own likeness. On the other
side of the glass, words like embankment,
unsightly, and heterogeneous lived. When
the ball machine buzzed, he stopped, eyes
deformed and wild. He called my dead
mother over to see his score, his hand
waving at me. What happens when the
shadow is attached to the wrong object but
refuses to let go? I walked over because I
wanted to believe him.

OBIT

Memory—died on August 3, 2015. After
my mother died, the weather got hotter so
gradually no one could see. Another bird
fell out of the ficus. The arm that turned
the earth never bothered to stop for the
bird and the bird was crushed between
the earth and time. After my mother died,
my love for her lost all shape. Everything I
had disliked about her became fibrous like
her lungs. I let them harden and suffocate
on their own. I posted about her last days
on an online pulmonary fibrosis board,
typing to strangers into the night. We were
traveling lights to each other. That story
is still there but I can no longer find it
or the people who might be dead by now.
Each letter a little soldier in formation for
a new dying person to read, to see how the
living will perceive them when they are no
longer conscious. Grief isn't what spills out
of a cracked egg. Grief is the row of eggs
waiting in the cold to lose their shape.

AN ANTISOCIAL FRITTATA

Catherine Lacey

It Means No Worries / For the Rest of Your Days

I've always been a morning person, and I am sometimes a people person, but I generally dislike people in the morning. For some reason this did not stop me from running a small bed and breakfast in Brooklyn for the latter half of my twenties. I cofounded and operated it with seven strangers who were also my roommates—yes, just like MTV's *Real World*, but actually in the real world and without any major drama or cameras. The shared revenue covered everyone's rent and groceries, affording us just enough security to pursue other interests.

Each day was divided into shifts we took turns working depending on our schedules and skills. Changing the beds was a chore I found to be too lonely and cleaning the bathrooms was plainly unpleasant, but my previous job as a cook qualified me to work more breakfast shifts than most. The morning, however, was the only time I could manage to write, so I rose around dawn to ensure that breakfast would be ready before anyone else woke up and tried to talk to me, which I felt (whether wrongly or rightly) might throw off my concentration for the day. Though my fellow innkeepers sometimes fried eggs or pancakes to order while having actual conversations with guests, my breakfasts were left to be discovered tepid—fruit salads, quick breads, and the omnipresent vegetable frittata.

Lo! The frittata! Good when warm and good enough when cooled; hearty, yet

approachable; predictable, but not entirely boring—I knew this dish so well I often cooked it without turning on the kitchen lights. The basic recipe could be varied to accommodate dietary restrictions, and scaled up to a large baking dish when we had a full house, but my preferred method involved six eggs and an eight-inch cast-iron skillet, partly because the pan imparted a golden sear that kept the frittata's interior luscious and airy, and partly because I relished the moment I thwacked it from skillet to cutting board, then fled the kitchen to go write.

One morning I was running slightly later than usual when a young Irish man I'll call Patch traipsed into the kitchen and asked me what I was making. It was bad enough that a stranger was polluting my solitude, but there was something overly loose in his eyes, as if he were stumbling around with his shoes untied and mouth agape. I don't remember if I told him what I was making. I had my ways of avoiding conversations, sometimes with a tooth-less smile and avoidant body language and once with a handwritten note saying I had lost my voice.

Patch, however, was not a hint taker. He told me that he was in town to build a robot in Central Park, that he was a pro-fessional artist and experimental sculptor, that some soap he'd been using had given him a rash. I was moving as quickly as I could to get out of there. I smacked the frittata out, he served himself a slice, then he made a sort of howling noise and fell out of his chair to the floor. "It's so good it made me fall out of my chair!" he said, then complained that he'd hurt himself in the fall, looking balefully at me. It was, after all, my frittata that had done it.

Later it became clear that Patch wasn't altogether okay. He left strange love notes for some of us around the B&B and eventually revealed himself to be a pathological liar who wouldn't or couldn't pay for the majority of his long stay with us. He earned himself the distinction as the only guest we ever had to kick out. After he was gone, I sometimes wondered what happened to him, how he'd decided to con a small business out of hundreds, and how he'd ever come to believe himself capable of building a robot in Central Park. While cleaning up the kitchen late in the morning, worn out by the gloom of my undone manuscript, I often ate the last, cold slice of frittata while standing over the sink, trying to calculate the difference between delusion and determination.

> "It's so good it made me fall out of my chair!"

REGARDING INGREDIENTS:

Quality matters with the eggs much more than you think. Local, free-range eggs will taste much better. There is a huge difference between a hen that's allowed to peck around a yard and a hen that's in a cage getting shat on by other hens, so don't be cheap about eggs.

Some nondairy milks and creams work all right here, so long as they're unsweetened. If you have to skip cheese, double the garlic and add some herbs to the eggs. I'd add more pepper, too.

You could skip the garlic but you'd be insane to do so. I guess the cayenne and parmesan are optional as well, but did I skip them? No, never. Sometimes I would top the warm frittata with the parmesan instead of whisking it into the eggs. You get a nice outer texture if you take this route.

Regarding the vegetables—onion, leeks, asparagus, mushrooms, zucchini, broccoli, or a few cherry tomatoes all work nicely. You could add some already-roasted potato if you have it or if you have the wherewithal to fry some thinly sliced potatoes in the skillet beforehand. I never did that because it makes the frittata seem as if it's trying to be a Spanish tortilla and I am not about to step on the toes of the Spanish tortilla. There are many excellent Spanish tortilla recipes out there and this is not one of them.

REGARDING DAVE:

Dave Ferris, my former business partner and roommate, is the real genius behind this recipe. Though I've varied it a little to my tastes, he's the one who first taught me this method. He's one of the best home cooks I've ever known. 🎙️

An Antisocial Frittata

INGREDIENTS:

6 eggs

6 tablespoons milk or cream

1 large clove of garlic, grated

2 pinches of salt

Several grinds of black pepper

A dash of cayenne pepper

1/4 cup grated parmesan

Some amount of olive oil

Vegetables of your choosing

Grated cheese, soft goat cheese, or both if you're feeling decadent

Minced parsley, if you're that sort of person

A handful of arugula, maybe

INSTRUMENTS:

A deep bowl

A whisk in good condition

A well-seasoned 8-inch cast-iron skillet

A large cutting board

INSTRUCTIONS:

1. Preheat your oven to about 350 Fahrenheit.

2. Aggressively whisk the eggs, milk, garlic, salt, pepper, cayenne, and parmesan. Set aside.

3. Heat some olive oil in the skillet to sauté the vegetables of your choosing over medium heat. If you're using an onion, finely sliced or diced works best, and you'll want to cook it first, then add the other vegetables according to density. Use a little salt here, but not too much since the eggs are salted as well. To be honest, you probably need to know what you're doing with the vegetables or you really have no place making this frittata to begin with.

4. Remove the vegetables from the skillet and wipe it out with a paper towel. If you fucked up and burned something to the skillet because it was too hot or you cooked the vegetables too long, take care to scrape any black gunk out.

5. Make sure there's a good greasing of oil on the base and edges, then return the skillet to medium heat.

You want the skillet to be hot enough to sear the eggs on contact, thus making it easier to flip the frittata out when it's done. You can tell it's the right temperature when a drop of raw egg cooks through on contact, but it's too hot if the drop of egg sputters or bubbles. If that happens, remove the skillet from the heat and stand there awkwardly waiting like the fool you are before returning it to the heat and trying the egg drop again. When the skillet is the correct temperature carefully pour your whisked eggs in. Wait a few moments, then sprinkle in the vegetables. If you're using soft goat cheese, plop it down in globs all over and let it sink a little into the eggs. If you're using grated cheese, spread it around and let it sink in a little as well.

6. Once the frittata has cooked just enough on the stove that you can see it pulling away from the edges of the skillet, pop that little guy into the oven and turn off the burner.

7. To be honest, there's no precise amount of time in the oven that the frittata will need. It will depend on your particular oven, the skillet, the thickness of the frittata, and the type and quantity of vegetables. Ten minutes? Maybe. I'd definitely check on it after seven minutes. It's done when the eggs are barely set through. You can test it with a knife.

8. When the frittata is done baking, take it out and let it cool off for about 5–10 minutes. Use a spatula or butter knife to loosen the frittata from the edge of the skillet. If it's not letting go of the skillet at this point, give up all hope of flipping it onto the cutting board; the damn thing will almost certainly make a huge mess and ruin your day. You'll just have to serve it out of the skillet itself, which is charming enough but honestly not that great because the heat from the skillet will keep cooking the eggs, leading to become dry and sad looking. Be careful not to damage the cast iron with metal knives. If the frittata is separating easily from the pan, try flipping the whole skillet onto your cutting board. How did that go? A chunk of it clung to the pan? Bummer. You can do a little reconstructive surgery and cover up the damage with a handful of arugula, a sprinkling of cheese, and/or parsley as a garnish. 🏮

THE BLISS POINT

Emma Copley Eisenberg

Dad Screams at Ice Cream

In the loft where I grew up, we had an ancient Sub-Zero with a bottom freezer drawer that was the sole domain of my father. He was in a perpetual war with the ice machine: he wanted the ice machine to make ice; the ice machine didn't. He kept coffee beans there, as well as lentil soup, vegetable stock in freezer-burned beige Tupperware, and sesame bagels from Fairway. Also popsicles—lime, lemon, Weight Watchers chocolate fudge ice cream bars and diet Creamsicles.

My father feared dairy, specifically cream. He didn't drink milk at all, not even the skim my mother bought for my sister and me. Cream cheese, brie, butter— these were white and globby, and thus like cyanide to him. If he ordered soup in a restaurant he always double-checked—*Is there cream in that?* If the answer was yes, he didn't just demur out of personal preference but felt called to articulate the ideological folly of it. *Blech*, he would sputter, turning to us, the women of his family. *Sounds awful!*

Dairy was soft, and warm, and fat, of course, which were the opposite of all the things my father wanted to be. He had been a fat boy in a poor and Russian part of Brooklyn and had vowed never to be so dispossessed again. In his imagination, I think, dairy was gentile and suburban and midwestern—buxom farm maidens on their tiny wooden stools, cows lolling in the soft, flabby background. My dad wanted to be hard, to be fast, to matter. He walked in the gutter through the streets of Times Square, lapping the tourists. He drank martinis—very dry, in and out on the vermouth, three olives for luck. He ate mainly fish, carrots, asparagus, artichokes, and fruit. Often, he did not eat at all. The sole exception to his dairy-free existence was, mysteriously, cottage cheese, which he liked to mix with blueberries. Once, he told me he liked that berry's sweetness and tartness, which seemed to happen in the mouth at the same time. You should try, I wanted to say but did not say, ice cream.

> Dairy was soft, and warm, and fat, of course, which were the opposite of all the things my father wanted to be.

. . .

Nero Claudius Caesar sent runners miles into the mountains for snow to be flavored with fruit juices. The ancient Persians constructed expensive ice houses to store winter snow year round to serve the same gastronomic purposes. The cream entered later, when the first king of the Chinese Shang dynasty employed more than ninety men to make frozen buffalo milk, thickened with flour and flavored with camphor.

In its early days, ice cream was an extravagance only for the very rich, but when insulated ice houses and commercial dairy production made it widely available, its character shifted from signifying wealth to signifying moral weakness. Churches and ministers throughout America at the turn of the nineteenth century observed ice cream's ecstatic effect on their parishioners and declared eating ice cream a sin. In 1890 in Evanston, Illinois, the local Methodist church lobbied successfully to ban ice cream sodas on the Sabbath. Yet Pope John Paul II's favorite "guilty pleasure" was tubs of marron glacé gelato which he had regularly fetched for him while at the Vatican or delivered every few days to his summer home.

People still have a lot of feelings about ice cream and what it means if they eat it. In the 1977 document "Dietary Goals for the United States," Senator George McGovern asserted that a low-fat diet was essential not just for patients with a high risk of heart disease but for us all. "Out were cream, chocolate, cheese," writes Ann LaBerge for the *Journal of the History of Medicine and Allied Sciences*. "What could be eaten? Fruit, but no cream. Low-fat advocates preferred processed substitutes, such as Cool-Whip." Sugar was okay, but sugar combined with fat was condemned. So pervasive was this low-fat brainwashing through the 1980s and '90s that many began to think of fat, particularly dairy fat, not just in scientific terms but in emotional and moral ones— as dangerous, repulsive, and wrong.

"Butter is back," Mark Bittman wrote recently with relief. "Eventually, your friends will stop glaring at you as if you're trying to kill them."

. . .

As a kid, I sometimes cat sat for the couple that lived in the apartment a few floors above my family just so I could eat their mint chip ice cream—a sharp journey into the Swiss Alps, a crystal clean feeling all over. Their cat, Sam, was a lumbering orange purr machine who was supposed to have died the previous winter from diabetes but instead had made a miraculous recovery during a visit to Palm Springs. Sam observed as I ate the ice cream straight from the container—not enough that it would be missed, I hoped—watching with what I believed was hatred born of envy.

I discovered strawberry ice cream in the house of a childhood friend when both she and her family were away. Away where? And why was I there alone? What sticks around is me sitting on their black leather sectional and eating from their tub of ice cream with its chunks of whole strawberry while watching Jerry Springer.

There is a very particular kind of space-time magic that happens when you are eating ice cream and watching TV. The mind goes absolutely quiet. I sat, transfixed by the tawdry and often transphobic drama—*You are not the father! You're secretly a man!*—and moved spoon to mouth by muscle memory. The fact that my theft might be discovered and the revelation of secrets on the TV show combined to produce a flavor of delight and the taste of shame. Once, I was so transported that I finished the entire tub and had to walk down to the deli on the corner and replace it. From then on, I brought my own.

That friend's apartment was one of the few places I could be alone for vast swaths of time, as our apartment was essentially a single open space with a few pieces of Sheetrock posing as walls. At this point I was a little bit fat, but my sister was properly, truly fat, and her body became the receptacle for everything that was going wrong in our family and in my parents' marriage. I can't conjure up any picture of my parents in the same frame from this time; the only togetherness I remember is auditory, their voices talking over one another. They didn't like each other very much then, and were always finding reasons to walk out of the room when the other came into it.

My parents wanted my sister to go on this or that diet, attend this or that fat camp, get this or that surgical procedure. Our apartment rattled with endless reasons fatness was wrong—your health, your future, your love, your mind—and a fate worse than death.

Our apartment rattled with endless reasons fatness was wrong.

Where were you? is a question that I have been asked more than once about those early years. The truest answer is that I was in another country, one where I ate a lot of ice cream and watched a lot of television. To this day, when I need to not exist, this is still where I go.

. . .

Actually, my father retained absolute control not only over the bottom drawer of the Sub-Zero but also over the whole appliance. Every night he organized and reorganized the fridge, stacking like with like. Whenever he heard the whooshing sound of the refrigerator door opening he would appear in the kitchen to inquire what the intruder was eating and why. If you walked by with an apple, he had to touch it and make a comment about its shape or size. If he bought bread for dinner, death be to she who took a slice for lunch. If my dad bought clementines and they weren't eaten within a week, they were declared to be not "moving," and were never bought again. If my mother bought the special tuna fish from Jefferson Market—full of mayonnaise and some magical combination of spices I have never managed to replicate—my father would divide it between two plastic containers and add flavorless canned tuna to each half, cutting it with dryness. (To be fair, this may have been where pleasure-denying and thriftiness overlapped; my father's mother had been a balabusta—the Yiddish for a woman with the gift for stretching a dollar.)

So open was my mother's resentment of these habits yet also her complicity in them that she asked my sister and me to handcraft him a gift. We made him a black hat with yellow embroidered letters across the front that said FOOD POLICE, accompanied by a black plastic whistle.

. . .

Of course it wasn't that my father had never tried ice cream, it was that he had tried it and liked it too much. Ice cream would now occasionally materialize in the freezer, mostly an indicator of my sister's growing bravery. She had done what my parents had asked for as long as she could—the classes, the food logs, the counting, the charts and graphs in her room with their endless numbers and rules—so that they would love her. But then she couldn't anymore. From my bedroom, I would listen to them do battle in the kitchen. *Are you sure you want to eat that?* my father or mother would say, and it would ignite.

Sooner or later my sister would flee to her room, crying. We all had our own zones of retreat. My mother had her dark wood sleigh bed, where she would go after dinner. My father had our long bleached pine dining room table, where he would make notes on yellow legal pads or read *Variety*. On the other side of my bedroom wall late at night, I could hear the TV going—my sister eating ice cream or my father drinking vodka. In the morning when I left for school, whoever had been watching TV would be passed out—black couch, white dots, head back, jaw open.

During that time, the ice cream would disappear just as magically as it had appeared, the only record of its presence the empty carton stuffed down deeply into the side of the trash can. Often it was I who ate it, but just as often it was my father, drunk or starving or at the limit of his capacity to refuse. "We just don't get love right, this family," says the narrator of Pam Houston's *Waltzing the Cat*. Love we could do in my family, but eating we couldn't.

Then my sister went away to college and I moved my bed into the room with the television. I don't know what we did with the couch. My father was forced to drink at the kitchen table now, which he did with gusto. I wasn't cat sitting anymore so I had nowhere to go but where I was. With my sister gone, there was only my body for my parents to worry about and look at. If I went to the fridge to retrieve a snack my father offered his opinion as to where on my body it would end up. He watched me cross the living room in my towel, vigilant for signs of impending fatness, which began to appear. He suggested I wear my hair up more because men liked it that way. He suggested I lift weights so my arms would grow more toned and sexier. Even if I could get ice cream into the freezer, there was no longer any way for me to get it out again. I took to sneaking it straight from the deli into my room, bypassing the kitchen entirely.

. . .

I find that people are often looking for permission to eat ice cream, and once I give it to them, interesting things happen. At first my friend cuts into the pint with the side of her spoon, but soon she is shoveling great heaps into her mouth. Another friend's father does the opposite—for all other foods he is a shoveler, but he eats ice cream in little bites with his bottom teeth. When a lover who claims he does not like chocolate and is generally uninterested in sweets tastes my mocha chip, he comes over to share my side of the bench. He wraps me in both of his arms and sighs, the quietest sigh you've ever heard.

Ice cream lights up the same pleasure centers in the brain as winning money. It can boost neurotransmitters that raise dopamine and decrease adrenaline levels. The proteins in dairy increase serotonin production, which makes us feel calm and at peace. A great quantity of fat all at once is soothing. In one study, volunteers were administered fatty, sweet, or salty solutions and then shown sad pictures and played sad music; when they got the fatty solution, the intensity of their sad emotions was reduced by almost half.

My father was forced to drink at the kitchen table now.

"Many of us have what's called a 'bliss point'—the point at which we get the greatest pleasure from sugar, fat or salt," Professor David Kessler told the *Telegraph*. According to Kessler, this bliss is the result of an exact combination of tastes that triggers neurons in our brains. That's why there exists a man named Howard Moskowitz whose job is to "optimize" foods like pizza, tomato sauces, salad dressings, and Dr. Pepper, in an effort to hit this bliss point. But ice cream requires no optimization. It is already optimal.

. . .

Just before I went away to college, I started babysitting for a rich family in Greenwich Village. I needed money to buy the things I wanted to buy in secret—alcohol sometimes, but mostly ice cream. Dulce de leche was my bliss during this period. The salt was the key, its tang activating something previously un-activated. A sharpness, a certain anger I didn't know I had, was beginning to take shape.

My charges were a little boy and a precocious pre-adolescent girl. The true terror was the girl. "Do you have a boyfriend?" she asked one night. I didn't, and told her so. The girl's dark eyes flashed, telling me I had failed in some essential way—I was ten years older than her, yet I had nothing to offer that she didn't already know. Though she too had stomach fat, a healthy ring around her middle, she poked mine through my sweater, said nothing, then poked it again. She had caught me eating their ice cream once, and her implication was clear: Who would want you, with all that?

Later that night, I dreamed her father gave me a ride home in his silver Lexus as he sometimes did, but this time instead of letting me out by the trash can on the corner, he locked the doors and raped me. In the morning I felt changed. *See*, I wanted to tell her. *Look at me now.*

Ice cream and sexual shame are wound around each other for me, the strands of a double helix, and even now I can't seem to pull one without touching the other. It was around this time too that I started downloading porn. In one video, a lean older man pushes a young teenaged girl into the back of a square station wagon and fucks her from behind, but also sort of on his side. *No, no, no,* she is saying. She is crying. What I remember is that he kept his T-shirt on while she was naked and that his balls got very red with all that effort, so red I thought they would pop. I don't remember selecting this video, only that I wanted to watch sex and this was the sex I got, a true coincidence that wrought real consequences, the way coincidences often do.

. . .

I want you to know that my father loves food, that he has exquisite taste in food, that he knows all the best places to get the most delicious things, and that there is no food he would not buy if I asked for it. I believe my father possesses not only supersonic hearing but also supersonic taste buds that perceive more pleasure than other people's. It is a particularly sad thing to have such a mouth and then, for years, to deny its talents.

The strange thing is that he has spent much of his life chasing taste—discernment, and also just that good feeling, that pure bliss. A great pleasure for him used to be to buy cheese danishes or cream cheeses or cannolis and ask my sister and my mom and me to decide which was the most delicious. He himself would not participate in these taste tests except maybe for a nibble here or there, but he liked to see the pleasure we, the women in his life, experienced when we found it. At the time I found these tests excessive and morbid and coercive—I did not feel free to refuse—but now I have more empathy for him. He wanted the pleasure for someone, even if he did not know how to want it for himself.

My father never wore the FOOD POLICE hat; he put it in a kitchen drawer with the batteries and the Chinese takeout menus. The hat stayed there for more than a decade, until he and my mother sold the loft and threw it out in a black trash bag along with everything else they could no longer carry.

. . .

Friends and lovers and people on the internet know me now as the full-fat ice cream lady and send me hot tips on where to procure particularly fatty ice cream, which I then add to a comprehensive Google map. It's not so different from my father's taste tests, only nationwide. I have driven one hundred miles and walked through cow pies for a biting espresso chip or a brilliantly balanced blackberry. I have to have at least three flavors of ice cream in my freezer at any given moment. I might go weeks without eating it, but I like to know it's there. Cones can be fun and glass dishes are pretty but my preferred ice cream experience will always be straight from the carton; I like the flat surface and how it changes as I dig into it—the creamy depressions mapping where I have been.

Aging has been a rock tumbler for my parents, grinding away their sharpest points. When my father lay in a hospital bed by the East River, swimming in opioids, it was ice cream, pure vanilla, that my mother spooned into his mouth, just as my father had for his own mother as she lay, too young and dying.

For years my father has supported the growth of my mind and my career as a writer by sending me clippings from the *New York Times*, things he thinks I will find interesting. The note always reads, *FYI, love Dad.* Acknowledging my obsession with dairy, and as a gesture of love, he often sends pictures of cows grazing and cream churning.

My parents live in the country now, and when I come to visit there is ice cream in the freezer—coffee, chocolate chocolate chip, pistachio. They have bought it for me; my sister, having fought hard to listen to her own body, no longer has much of a sweet tooth, though she will still have a taste now and then, in full view of my parents, who say nothing. But it is my job to open the freezer door and extract the cartons. After I have served myself, my parents will sometimes get themselves two spoons. They look at the containers with a kind of wonder. Then they open the ice cream and eat, passing it back and forth, sharing politely, like children learning for the first time. 🖋

STRESSING THE ROOTS

Emily Withnall

No Shade for This Nightshade

Just outside Denver, I dig two bags of ice out of the metal freezers at the gas station. The cold is refreshing against my skin in the ninety-eight-degree August heat. Colorado is as brown and dry as New Mexico, though the Rockies look bluer here. The heat, the congested interstate, and the endless swath of pump jacks along the highway have made me tense. I'm hoping to reach Wyoming before the sun sets.

I lift the rolling metal door at the back of the U-Haul and let the water drain out of the cooler onto the oil-stained blacktop and against my legs. My stomach drops when I feel how warm it is. Flipping the lid open, I reach inside.

The fifty-two-quart cooler is filled to capacity with bags of frozen green chile. On this three-day journey of over 1,200 miles, from our small hometown in New Mexico to our new home in Missoula, Montana, I have made it my priority to keep the chile from thawing. It is no small task; the back of the U-Haul feels like the inside of the adobe ovens—*hornos*—prevalent across the Southwest. But the chile still feels solid. I drop the bags of ice on the pavement to break up the cubes, open the bags, and spread ice between each layer of chile, jamming the bigger chunks into every corner.

Alex's nose wrinkles when I return to the cab. "I hate the smell of gas."

Talia doesn't look up. She is hunched over the electronic game on her lap. They both held back tears when we left our home this morning, but appear to have adjusted to the drive. They don't understand what this move means in the way that I do. To them, it's an adventure.

. . .

Chile season begins in August and extends into early October—my favorite season. September in New Mexico is particularly sumptuous, offering an almost erotic buffet of sensory pleasures. Yellow and orange sunflowers sway lazily against an achingly blue sky, red raspberries warm off the bushes melt on the tongue, cottonwood leaves flutter in the breeze, and cicadas rasp lullabies on nights cooling toward fall. But among these pleasures one surpasses them all: the smell of roasting green chile.

The aroma is the lovechild of the sun and earth—potent, sweet, and spicy. It enters your nostrils, spreads over the pores of your skin with sudden, tingling warmth, and buckles your knees. In September, the smell of roasting green chile wafts through every street of every town across the state, coaxing even the most reclusive from their homes. Our need for chile is boundless. Which farmer has the best variety this year? Which pepper best combines heat and flavor? Heat alone does not determine the perfect, mouthwatering chile. The thickness of the flesh, the texture between the teeth, and a smoky, biting flavor all contribute to an experience that overcomes body and brain. Chile is not just a vegetable. It is a landscape, a culture, and a way of life.

New Mexico's state vegetable is chile (and don't try telling a local that chile is technically fruit). New Mexico also has a state question, most frequently posed by servers in restaurants: "Red or green?" Sometimes you know the restaurant's strengths and can order accordingly. El Sombrero has a more robust red, for example, while Estella's has a spicier green. But if both the red and the green make you salivate profusely, or if you are in an unfamiliar place, the answer should always be "Christmas."

Even the spelling of "chile" is a point of contention in New Mexico. Ensuring that it is spelled c-h-i-l-e is almost as vital as our fanatic intake of the stuff. The other chili, more commonly prepared in homes outside of New Mexico, is a gluey mess of tomatoes, beans, and meat that bears little resemblance to New Mexican chile. In New Mexico, chile can be served roasted and chopped, sprinkled into burritos, on top of pizza, or slathered on burgers. But most frequently, chile is served as a thick roux—either an earthy brownish red or piquant, biting light green—which is poured over enchiladas, burritos, huevos rancheros, chile rellenos, and tamales.

> The aroma is the lovechild of the sun and earth— potent, sweet, and spicy.

My sister, Katie, and her boyfriend, Adam, have a long-standing squabble about how to best make green chile sauce for enchiladas. Katie and I say the secret ingredient is cumin. But Adam says the secret ingredient is oregano. Katie told me they tried to settle their dispute once by asking an *abuelita* in the valley outside of town for her green chile recipe. She was the woman who had taught Adam's mom how to cook New Mexican food when she had settled in the valley many decades prior. The *abuelita* surprised them. She told them she used both.

• • •

The cooler was the last item I loaded this morning before we said our goodbyes. It was already hot at ten in the morning and the houseplants, crowded around the cooler, were drooping. I took a final look at my mint-green stuccoed adobe on the railroad tracks, the place my kids and I had lived for five years. Like many of the houses in my town, it was more than one hundred years old. I knew a writer for the local newspaper who had been born in the kitchen. Everywhere I went with my kids, people in town knew me. Going to the farmers market or grocery store took hours because I'd run into friends, old teachers, and coworkers. Some days I welcomed the chance to chat with Debby as she bagged my groceries at Semilla. Other days, I wasn't Emily at all, but the daughter of the

It feels as if I am physically dragging my home behind me.

midwife who had delivered half the babies in town. Tellers at the bank, diners at the next table, and nurses at my doctor's office stopped me regularly to share birth stories. Sometimes I craved solitude or a sense of self separate from my connections. It felt both difficult and liberating to leave this place that knew me so well.

I'd lived there for most of my life and had no real plans to leave until my boss informed me that I was going to be restructured out of my job at a local high school. There were scant other options in the area for a single parent of two, and most jobs in nearby Santa Fe required a graduate degree. Though it meant uprooting my kids from the only community they had ever known, I had to trust that my acceptance into the University of Montana would bring us security. I loved the sun in New Mexico, but I looked forward to the abundant water and lush greenness Missoula promised. If we liked it, perhaps we would put down new roots.

• • •

The best environment for producing the spiciest chile is an inferno. The sun must be blazing, and the plants must be given just enough water to keep them alive and bearing fruit. The heat in the peppers depends largely on how much the chile plant is stressed. When shocked, the plant's roots react by sending an alarm into the

peppers in the form of a higher concentration of capsaicin—the substance that makes a chile spicy.

This is the landscape that produces chile: red rock mesas dotted with scrubby juniper and sagebrush, searing sun, and a wind that scours you clean. It is a landscape that produces the kind of person who seeks heat with increasing intensity, a quest that is unhurried but dogged, year after year. Perhaps this is why most New Mexicans prefer chile varieties that have been thoroughly stressed.

· · ·

When we hit Wyoming I am relieved to be out of Colorado congestion. We are heading to Cheyenne for the night, with 425 miles behind us. Undulating fields of brown and green spread out on either side of the highway, which is almost empty now. There are wider spaces on the map between towns, and the mountains are distant, the sky bigger. Antelope dot the hills to the east of the highway, leaping effortlessly. The U-Haul, however, is heavy and slow. It feels as if I am physically dragging my home behind me.

My kids play chess on a magnetic set while I worry that my reasons for the move are selfish and misplaced. Maybe now they will never feel a strong affinity for any one place. Even if I never return, New Mexico will always feel like home to me. Will my kids feel that same sense of connection to Montana? Do I want them to? When my parents arrived in New Mexico from Vermont and New York in the 1970s, they felt at home among the sagebrush on Taos mesa. We didn't have extended family around us like so many of my classmates did, but the family-oriented Hispanic-Catholic culture in our small town encouraged a close-knit community. My kids had attended the same daycares as my friends' kids, and they had all played dress-up and tag while we laughed and cried at each other's kitchen tables. My dad walked my kids home from school. The three of us regularly ate thick burritos at my parents' house for dinner. I don't know if I will be able to help the kids sustain a connection to the family and community in New Mexico. I don't know if I should.

· · ·

Chile farmers set up their roasters along the main roads and in busy parking lots. They do business not in individual peppers, but in pounds. Only the tourists buy a single pound of chile, wondering why they had to buy so much and wondering what they could possibly do with it all. New Mexicans won't settle for anything less than twenty or twenty-five pounds, depending on freezer space. The lucky ones have deep freezers in a back room or garage and buy enough to pack them tight.

They can afford to gift their chile in large quantities, or eat it with every meal. The rest of us use it more sparingly.

I usually visited the tri-county farmers market in the Immaculate Conception Church parking lot to buy my year's supply from Evelyn and Ramona. They were a chile-farming couple of few words. They both had a gaunt, kiln-fired appearance, wrinkles like arroyos carved into their flesh by the sun and the wind. Their chile had an intense heat that burned slowly and lingered on your lips long after the warmth had abandoned your tongue.

When I forked over a twenty for a twenty-five-pound bag of chile, Ramona dumped the kelly-green peppers from a burlap sack into a cylindrical metal basket. She turned the crank to rotate the chile over a steady gas flame beneath the basket. A small propane tank supplied the gas. The chile skins slowly began to blister and brown until the air was thick with sweet smoke. It did not take long for a small crowd to gather. Some savvy farmers had roasted samples to pass out to bystanders and some even offered homemade corn or flour tortillas to roll the chile in. I made it a habit to stop at Charlie's to pick up a twelve-pack of thick flour tortillas so fresh that they filled the inside of the plastic bag with condensation.

I waited until the chile began to sing, when it began to sizzle and pop and split its blackening skin. The process took an agonizing ten minutes. Then Ramona unhooked the hinged door on the basket, and the chile cascaded down into a thick black garbage bag. The garbage bag ensured that the chile would remain hot and would "sweat," making it easier to peel when I got it home.

Once, I grabbed a handful of freshly roasted chile from the garbage bag before Ramona could tie the bag off. I wrapped one in a still-warm tortilla. Alex watched as I tore into the chile burrito. I felt my sinuses open like doors being flung wide and my nose took up a steady drip.

"Mama, are you okay?" Alex asked, forehead wrinkling. Alex has always been the serious child.

"Yes," I answered. "This is just so good I can't stand it!"

Alex laughed, intrigued by my fervor. "I want to try one but . . . what if it's too spicy?"

Finally! My nine-year-old wanted to try the food so central to my kids' birthplace, and mine. I always teased my kids that they were not truly New Mexican if they didn't like chile—even though I'm pretty sure I was older than nine when I developed my insatiable appetite for the stuff.

"I'll take all the seeds out," I said. "And if it's still a little spicy it'll be wrapped in this thick tortilla."

Alex's eyes narrowed. "Okay, I'll try it."

I placed a tortilla on Alex's upturned palms, and split the flesh of a pepper with my thumbs. I set to work removing the scattering of tiny white seeds until the dark green chile glistened like silk. The first tentative bite contained only tortilla. At my urging, Alex bit in deeper and began crying.

"It's too spicy!"

In a matter of seconds Alex's crying became full-fledged howling. Water would only make things worse, so I grabbed a plain tortilla and offered it in a kind of penance.

"This will help soak up the spiciness," I said. "I'm so sorry, sweetie."

The garbage bag bulging with roasted chile sat in the back of the Subaru and filled the car with a thick, earthy smell. Peeking in the rearview mirror, I saw that Alex's shoulders were hunched, bottom lip drooping, eyes fixed on me as I steered with one hand and finished off the discarded chile burrito with the other.

. . .

By the time we wake, late, in Cheyenne for the second day of the drive, the chile's outer edges have gone soft. I'm forced to assess the cab of the truck. It is air-conditioned, unlike the back. But the cab is small and cramped, and the kids' backpacks fill most of what little space remains. So I leave the chile in the back and stop several more times that day. *Park, run, slam, drain, pack. Park, run, slam, drain, pack.* The actions become a physical mantra.

On this day, I drive almost six hundred miles—our longest day yet. We pull into a motel in Bozeman late at night. We've come more than one thousand miles in two days. Only two hundred left.

The next day, the kids begin to get excited by their surroundings.

> I waited until the chile began to sing, when it began to sizzle and pop.

"Look, Mama! That river is *huge*," Alex says.

"It's like an ocean," Talia adds.

The lush green foliage and the wide Clark Fork River work their magic on me, too. Although the heat hasn't eased, I am used to perpetual drought and the abundance of water here makes me hopeful about the possibilities that wait for us in Missoula. Throughout the next few hours we sing together—"The Long Way Around," by the Dixie Chicks, and "Caroline," by Brandi Carlile. I can't help noticing that the lyrics to these songs involve different kinds of uprooting. One is intentional and empowered, and one is filled with longing.

We pull into our new driveway late in the afternoon. I put the kids in charge of cleaning up the cab while I move things in.

Heat slams me when I open the back of the U-Haul. I shuffle into the house with the massive cooler and begin to toss bags of chile into the freezer as fast as I can. The water in the cooler is warm so I test the firmness of each bag. The edges are soft but the centers are still solid. When I am done, the freezer is almost filled.

I sit on the cooler for a moment, taking in the tiny duplex. Shabby carpeting covers the floors and there are very few windows. The apartment is not the adobe we have left behind. Its walls are not made of mud and do not insulate and protect us from the August heat. It does not have a woodstove I can fill with cedar and piñon when the snow falls. It is not over one hundred years old with a history I can recite; I do not know who was born in the kitchen sixty years ago. But there is green chile in the freezer.

. . .

It's now been five years since I made the journey with my kids to Missoula, Montana. My family and most of my friends have remained in New Mexico but due to work pressures of their own are now spread across five cities—too distant from each other for the frequent gatherings we used to hold. Being four states away is a distance that often feels impossible to bridge. I can no longer grab coffee with Reina at Travelers Cafe or stop by Cristina's house to see her new art and hear what ideas she's dreaming up. I don't know if Melissa has added another tattoo to her sleeve. Phone calls have become infrequent and hurried, just the highlights.

Author Bill Kittredge called Montana "The Last Best Place." Montanans seem to feel the same way about their home as I do about New Mexico. I am still struggling to appreciate the eight-month winters, bland food, and gray skies. But I understand how a place can feel like a part of you. I've come to understand that being rooted is about being known and seen. It's about relationships between people and the landscape that sustains them. It's about how people come together to survive in a place that can be both harsh and nourishing. While there is no chile here, you can find huckleberries in jams, ice cream, cakes, honey, scones, and peanut brittle. When you grow up going to the same huckleberry picking spots as your neighbors, and when you share recipes for huckleberry pie, you share an experience of place. These intimate experiences are what make one mountain or river so different from another.

I don't understand the appeal of huckleberries and my kids don't have a taste for them either. But they have come to love the deep cold of Montana winters in a way that I cannot. Perhaps the ruby-cheeked northern flickers and the golden western larch have claimed their sense of belonging, anchoring their roots. They still won't try green chile. Fortunately, my mom brings it with her when she visits, and when I am at the Albuquerque airport, I load up at Comida Buena on the way to my gate. We visit New Mexico at least once a year, but I suspect our long absence, coupled with my nostalgia, has for my kids rendered the state a place where memories live, not people. It is not a stretch to say I am heartbroken. Perhaps I fear that if Montana is home to my kids, I will someday have to choose between the place I love most and the people I love most. Red rocky soil runs like fire through my veins and until now I had assumed that this red earth would flow through my kids, too. Already though, their lack of enthusiasm for sunlight and sandstone makes my stomach lurch. I hope I have not uprooted my kids entirely. I hope that if they were transplanted again, they would thrive. ◈

ENCHILADAS

NOTE: This is a recipe I make with the New Mexico chile I keep in my freezer. It's a big hit at potlucks in Montana. These enchiladas are flat, rather than rolled, and are typical of northern New Mexican cuisine. New Mexican food is very different from Mexican food, but it does share similarities with cuisine from some of the northern states in Mexico. I cook this recipe with pinches and handfuls—not with strict measurements—so every batch of chile is a little different. The roux should be thick, like stew—not too watery, and not too pasty. Add more chile for an extra kick!

INGREDIENTS:

For the chile roux:

Vegetable oil

1 small yellow onion, chopped

3–4 cloves of garlic, chopped

Cumin (roughly 1 tablespoon)

Oregano (roughly 1 tablespoon)

Flour (roughly 1/3 cup)

10–15 chopped roasted green chiles, depending on the size of the chiles and spiciness desired
or red chile powder (roughly 1/4 cup)

Water

Salt

TO MAKE THE ENCHILADAS:

Vegetable oil

Chile roux, above

18–24 corn tortillas

Asadero cheese or other mild-tasting
    cheese like Monterey Jack

Shredded beef or chicken (optional)

INSTRUCTIONS FOR MAKING THE CHILE ROUX:

Liberally coat the bottom of a 3-quart, thick-bottomed pot with vegetable oil and place it on medium heat. I use safflower, but any neutral oil with a high smoke point will do. Add onion and cook until translucent. Add garlic, a couple pinches of cumin, and a couple pinches of oregano. Sauté for a minute or two, then add a couple of small handfuls of flour. Stir the flour thoroughly, then add the chopped green chile (or a small handful of red chile powder). Stir until all ingredients are blended into a thick paste and keep stirring for several minutes until fragrant. Begin adding water 2–3 cups at a time, using a whisk to blend the ingredients well. Keep adding water until the pot is full, then turn the heat down to low and let it simmer. The roux should burn off some of the water and thicken. This can take up to an hour. Add salt to taste.

INSTRUCTIONS FOR PUTTING THE ENCHILADAS TOGETHER:

Preheat oven to 350 degrees. On the stovetop, coat the bottom of a pan with oil and begin lightly frying the corn tortillas, just long enough to soften them. You don't want them to be hard or crunchy. You will need 18–24 tortillas, depending on how thin or thick you layer the enchiladas.

Cover the bottom of a 9.5 x 11-inch casserole dish with the fried corn tortillas. Then cover the tortillas with about a quarter of the shredded asadero cheese and ladle on a layer of chile roux. (If using, add a third of the meat over the chile.) Cover with another layer of corn tortillas and repeat the process. The top layer should just have a thin layer of cheese and chile. Adding less chile and cheese to each layer will result in firmer enchiladas, and a generous layering of ingredients will result in goopier enchiladas. Both are delicious! When the pan is full, cover it with foil and bake for roughly 20 minutes, or until the cheese has melted. Take out of the oven and let cool before cutting into squares.

Serve with pinto beans and calabacitas.

APPLEJACKING

Ginger Strand

House Cider Rules

In the zombie apocalypse, booze will be as fungible as ammo. And it was a vague desire to be zombie-ready that caused my husband, Bob, and me to learn to make hard cider. Something about country living brings out your inner prepper. We keep a manual grinder and a propane camp stove in our house in the Catskill Mountains so that when the power goes out, we can make coffee and not kill each other. But this is mere household readiness, not prepping for survival in a WROL situation. People who use the acronym WROL ("without rule of law") tend to be apocalypse-minded conspiracy theorists. Bob and I aren't, but we do share a smidgeon of their survivalist impulse. It propelled us to start applejacking.

The Catskills are already a bit zombified: they're depopulated. In the nineteenth century, people came with dreams of farming—dreams that cracked up against countless rocks. (Local saying: "For every four rocks, one dirt.") By the 1870s, farms and whole towns were being abandoned, and a century and a half later, the only signs left of many of them are stone walls and apple trees. You can be miles from roads or houses, deep in the Catskills wilderness, and stumble upon an overgrown orchard. Untended and gnarly, the trees have gone feral, hoarding their small, ugly fruits out of reach in witchy tops. They are breeds no one recognizes anymore: Arkansas Black, Esopus Spitzenburg, Ellis Bitter,

Dabinett. Black bears eat them, but few people do. They weren't planted for eating; they were planted to make cider.

What wine is to southern France, hard cider is to the northeastern US. It's the full expression of our terroir, the best product of our inherited expertise. Inherited but not native, since the apple is not indigenous to North America; it's actually an immigrant from Kazakhstan. But it came to the continent with the Europeans, and like them it displaced natives to put down roots. It even interbred with native crab apples. From colonial times to the early 1800s hard cider and small beer were popular everyday beverages. Even children drank them. But during the temperance movement, farmers were urged not to sell their apples for demon drink. Some used apples to fatten pigs and feed cattle. Others chopped down orchards, or burned seedlings. By 1862, so many orchards had been abandoned or destroyed that Henry David Thoreau waxed nostalgic about a time "when men both ate and drank apples."

Drinking apples is back now, with a plethora of artisanal brands and adorable cideries. Catskills old-timers find this ludicrous, and they assured us there was nothing to making the stuff. All you had to do was go see the Hubbells, locals who run a century-old cider press for fun on fall weekends. But there was a hitch: to get an appointment, you needed five bushels of apples. The old trees on our land produce a handful of apples that are cleaned out by bears, who swing in and out of them like overgrown monkeys. We had two options: purchase or theft.

Bob and I have been together for twenty-two years, and I won't say we've grown tired of each other, but time, familiarity, and routine wear away at excitement. But crime: What could be more exciting than that? We started spending weekends driving around looking for untended trees, for apples to liberate. *Let's go applejacking*, we'd say. We kept a pile of bags in the car, and we would pull up to a likely tree, look around for other vehicles, and then pick as fast as we could. If a car snuck up on us, I would pose with my cell phone, making like a tourist photographing a tree, while Bob hid in the underbrush. We focused on trees near the side of the road, but trespassing was unavoidable. I am an enthusiastic trespasser. Bob is not. Yet somehow, there he was. Cidermania had transformative potential it seemed.

We found apple trees at the edge of a cemetery, apple trees on a hunting club's land, apple trees in the yard of a house that was for sale. Near an abandoned farmhouse, we found a tree bearing different apple breeds on its grafted branches.

Drinking apples is back now, with a plethora of artisanal brands and adorable cideries.

That same farmhouse had a pear tree, so we liberated those too. Then one day, while exploring some gangly, untended trees along a dead-end road, we hit the jackpot. Behind some scrubby woods, we came upon an entire orchard, its trees sagging under the weight of unpicked fruit. I wanted to pirate at once, but Bob resisted. There was an email address on the No Trespassing sign, so he wrote the owner asking if we could harvest his untended orchard. When we didn't hear back, Bob looked up the property in the tax rolls. The owner lived in another state. Bob agreed to relax his principles. We parked up the road and collected at least three bushels, leaving the bags in the ditch as we filled them, to be picked up later. That day, we made an appointment with the Hubbells.

Bob grew up in suburbs, but I grew up on a farm. In addition to that, he's an engineer, and a rationalist, while I am a pragmatist. When we bought our land, it became clear that I am a conservationist, but Bob is a preservationist. Every tree we had to cut down, every rock that was moved, caused him deep emotional pain. I was never happier than when I hired two guys with earthmovers and had them tearing up the place. When they buried a boulder Bob liked, he made them unbury it, and then he spent an afternoon hosing it down to put it back *exactly the way it was*.

Growing up on a farm, you get used to change: nothing ever stays the same. You get used to death: chickens, rabbits, goats, horses, cats—I've watched them all go down to various sad demises. At some point, armed with my reading of Freud and my dentist's old issues of *Psychology Today*, I diagnosed Bob's resistance to change as a pathological fear of completion, probably brought on by the premature death of his mother. When I reported this conclusion, the reception was predictably frosty. Bob and I are alike in our disbelief in an afterlife, but while I think about death constantly, Bob doesn't like to think about it at all. I have at times considered this a fundamental incompatibility, because it will inevitably affect how each of us will face growing old.

But cidermaking was all about change: from apples to cider to fermented booze, an actual embrace of things rotting and turning into something else. It felt profound. At least to me it did. I think Bob was most excited to have an excuse to buy a hydrometer. We also differed on the question of equipment. Country people value the art of "making do." I wanted to ferment the cider in some drywall buckets, then decant it into old Almaden bottles from a midden left behind by the former owners of our land. But Bob wanted gear, so we found a local home-brew supply store: an old barn packed with carboys, airlocks, and stills. The proprietor was definitely of the deep-state conspiracy camp. He had a poster on his wall showing Hitler, Stalin, and Mussolini with the slogan: "World leaders agree: gun control works!"

On a crisp October Saturday, we backed our car up to the Hubbells' barn and unloaded our stolen apples onto a conveyor belt. The barn was a death trap, with hatches and ladders and belts and flywheels everywhere just waiting to strangle an unsuspecting visitor with her own scarf. You and your apples entered on the upper story, and proceeded to the floor below, you by ladder, your apples—having been crushed—via a chute. The pomace—apple mush—oozed into the press, an impressive iron-and-wood contraption the size of a truck. The two-stroke engine fired up, and after what seemed like a long time, juice began gurgling out a spout at the bottom. All the old-timers who had been hanging around now cranked into gear: they took out Dixie cups and tasted the cider. Tart, they said, but good.

At home, we sterilized all our equipment with a food-grade sanitizer and poured the cider into two buckets. We fitted both with airlocks, and that was it. All that remained was to wait. We had never felt more zombie-ready. But the weekend yawned before us. What would we do with ourselves if we weren't applejacking? *Let's just go look around*, we said. Before long, we were raiding more apple trees. We couldn't stop. We began to understand criminal compulsion. It wasn't the cider we wanted; it was the thrill of theft.

In England, to go "scrumping" is to filch apples. In the UK I could say that Bob and I couldn't stop scrumping and not be misunderstood. In the end, we collected only a couple more bushels—too few to go back to the Hubbells. But a guy in town—one of those eccentrics who fills his yard with sculptures made of old tractor parts—had a press. He looked like Bilbo Baggins and his apple press looked like one from Hobbiton: a wooden bucket with a lid that squeezed down when you cranked a big screw on top. He didn't charge for the use of it: he seemed to be in it for the entertainment.

This whole operation was far less rigorous than the first one. I crushed the apples with a log in a drywall bucket. Bob walked in circles pushing a metal rod to crank the screw; juice trickled out into a plastic container. Bilbo sat there merrily drinking a beer and praising our industry. A pair of cats wandered in and out. We took that batch home and didn't bother sterilizing anything. It was infused with cat hair, after all. We just fitted its lid with an airlock.

Soon after that winter came, and there were no more apples to scrump. Life seemed to diminish. We decanted the cider into carboys when it stopped bubbling, and bottled it at one month. We made it to the holidays before cracking one open. The first batch was good: bone-dry, but with a noticeable apple flavor. But it was the second batch, Bilbo's batch, that was the real prize. It tasted like apple juice that had grown up, like apples that had learned to accept their differences. It had hints of the dryness of time and the bitterness of death, mellowed by the sweet tinge of larceny. It was six percent alcohol: just enough, after a couple of glasses, to give you that glowy feeling, as if you were getting something for nothing, as if you might live forever. 🔹

"TRUMP" "SOHO" "HOTEL"

Emily Flouton

Tending Bar in the Belly of the Beast

It's March 2010, and the Trump SoHo hotel, a sleek phallus of blue steel thrusting forty-six stories into the air from the western end of Spring Street, is just weeks from opening. Press releases have promised heretofore-unseen views of Manhattan, guest rooms furnished by Fendi Casa, sexy Italian dining, and a luxury spa where you can lie naked on a marble slab and get pummeled with tree branches. Because this hotel is in a "young and hip" area and needs a "young and hip" image, Trump's three eldest children are the faces of the venture: Don Jr. and Eric, the big-game-hunting enthusiasts, and Ivanka, whose fashion advice is "dress modestly."

I am living in a minuscule walk-up on Avenue B, where I eat dollar pizza slices on the dining table of my frayed duvet cover, dye my hair black, make fun of things, and attempt to write screenplays. Bartending in casual spots has kept me afloat. That is, until I quit my bar gig in a fit of burnout, figuring I'll find something better. I don't find something better. I don't find anything at all. Then rent is due, and there's this job post on Craigslist about Trump SoHo.

It should be noted that the Trump SoHo hotel is not actually in SoHo, but just west of SoHo in the no-man's-land of Hudson Square. And that the Trump SoHo hotel is not a hotel, but a "condotel," which allows it to get around the zoning laws created to keep places like it from existing. And that the Trump SoHo hotel does not exactly belong to Donald Trump. The Hair hasn't invested any of his own cash in the project, though he has received a nice chunk of equity in the place in exchange for the use of his name.

I try to think of the glass as half full. The place may at least be amusing.

At an ungodly hour (by bartenders' standards) on a Monday morning, I enter the brand-new hotel's schmancy function room and join the milling crowd of freshly hired staff. A number of very excited suits dart among the plebes, urging us to find seats. The round tables are draped in fresh white linens and immaculately appointed with full silver place settings. After we're seated, the suits go around pouring coffee from silver pots, bowing their heads with conspicuous humility.

The lights dim. A hush falls. Two women in snug corporate dresses ascend to the podium and fiddle with it until Lady Gaga's "Bad Romance" blares from the speakers. As Gaga bemoans the destructive nature of her romantic impulses, the two women dance awkwardly and pump their arms, trying to get us to do something. Cheer? I grin widely, teeth clenched.

A parade of men in slightly ill-fitting suits and women in better-fitting ones tell us the same things in cosmetically different ways. Hundreds of people applied for our positions. The group in this room is the crème de la crème. We deserve a round of applause. We give ourselves one! Then they get serious: It is a privilege to be here. We must be very well behaved so they don't regret giving us that privilege. It seems to boil down to "with great power comes great responsibility," but unfortunately, nobody directly quotes *Spider-Man*.

I'm more intrigued by their explanation of the whole "condotel" deal. You can buy one of the hotel's 391 rooms, but you aren't allowed to stay in it for more than about a third of the year. The hotel rents it out the rest of the time, splitting proceeds with the owner. It sounds a bit like an illegal sublet, the kind of thing that would get my landlord all in a tizzy. Yet here are these suits, referring to it as an investment opportunity.

One suit makes a speech intended to "provide us with tools" to make the hotel sound not-evil to people from the

> It should be noted that the Trump SoHo hotel is not actually in SoHo.

neighborhood. This may be a hard sell. No one around here wanted this monument to corporate greed blighting the skyline, with which I totally empathize.

At this point I'm not yet aware of these two facts:

—During the hotel's negligently overseen construction, a piece of faulty formwork collapsed, decapitating a worker as he fell forty-two stories to the ground.

—Hundreds of human bones from the 1800s were discovered while digging the hotel's foundation, which turned out to be on top of a burial vault belonging to a former abolitionist church. The Trump Organization pledged to rebury the remains, but never did. Indeed, the whereabouts of the remains is unclear.

At the end of the day, those of us assigned to the hotel's restaurant, Quattro, get a tour of our new workplace. It gives me high-end-chain-restaurant-in-Florida-strip-mall vibes. Shelves of booze stretch up to the ceiling, and there's a rickety silver ladder you have to ascend in order to reach half the bottles, which tells me whoever designed the place has never bartended.

The managers stress that we must never, ever refuse our customers anything.

We're just supposed to *make it happen*. This kind of policy is common enough in higher-end service jobs, but the enthusiasm and solemnity with which they repeat the directive feels alarming.

Cocktail training reveals Quattro's booze program to be a dozen years behind the times. The rest of Manhattan is serving speakeasy classics with imaginative updates: herbaceous gin cocktails, smoky Scotch ones, or anything with a dash of bitter, yellow-black Fernet-Branca. Quattro mostly offers inoffensive fruity concoctions made with vodka. But I suppose if the Trump guys can get away with charging sixteen dollars for middle-of-the-road vodka mixed with frozen passion fruit puree (a "Ruski Passion"), then more power to them—er, to us.

My fellow barfolk range from slightly older with unflappable, I've-seen-it-all-before-honey demeanors to baby-faced and fresh off the turnip truck. One of the latter variety, a creamily midwestern aspiring actor, is so over the moon to have landed this dream job that he won't hear a critical word about the place. The jaded among us try to keep our bitchy gripes on the DL.

Our gripes are plentiful. We don't have half the bar supplies we need for opening, and no one in power seems to have the faintest idea how we can get them. They tell us we can "requisition" supplies by checking off boxes on a printed list and giving it to the purchasing department, but the things we need are not on the list. For instance, we need half a dozen straight pint glasses for shaking cocktails. Not on the list. In any other bar, you'd take cash from the register, buy the glasses, and submit the receipt with your paperwork at the end of the night. When I suggest this, the managers say, "No, just requisition them." When I tell them purchasing told us they can't get the pint glasses, they quiz me on the hotel's three tenets of service, which I can never remember, because they are so abstract as to be useless. Even when we requisition items that *are* on the list, it's as though purchasing has never seen a bar. We requisition cocktail stirrers and come in the next day to find they have left us boxes of rock candy swizzle sticks in pastel colors. There's nothing to do except eat them.

> The managers stress that we must never, ever refuse our customers anything.

Then soft opening is upon us, and we begin serving invited guests—graying men with expensive watches and slim, shrewd-eyed women in white pants and silky patterned tops. With actual guests staying in the hotel, we plebes are now forbidden to enter the restaurant through the front door. Our entrance is around back, a hidden rectangle in the butt of the building where we must pass through a fingerprint scanner to gain entry. On the way out at the end of our shifts, security guards search our bags—in case, I guess, we decide to start stealing silverware, which management has repeatedly informed us costs ten dollars a piece. While it would ordinarily never occur to me to steal silverware, now that they've got security guards rifling through my purse every night, pretending not to see my tampons, I want to steal silverware. I fondle the heavy forks as I set bar diners up for their truffle risotto, watch tiny, perfect spoons gleam temptingly next to espresso cups. But how? Big Brother is watching from every angle.

My barback is a skinny, freckled hipster kid from Tucson, a part-time model and full-time acerbic wit. He and I have regular "staff meetings" in the one corner of the bar the cameras can't reach, taking sneaky shots of Jameson and planning silverware heists. It becomes clear that my survival mechanism for working at Quattro will be the moments when he drags me into this corner and says, with maximum drama, "Have I got a story for *you*!"

"At lunch, there was this old dude who ordered three mojitos at, seriously, *noon*. I figured there were people coming to meet him but no, he pounded them all in five minutes. Then he was like, 'I guess I'm not getting on my flight! Can I see the wine list?' He ordered a $350 bottle of champagne, told me to chill another one, and went and hit on these two women at a table. They drank both bottles of champagne, and then he said, 'I'm going to take you ladies on a crazy shopping spree!' So they went outside, where, like, his *driver* was waiting. They came back with so many shopping bags, *wasted*, and they *all* went up to his room."

My uniform consists of a white button-down, a pinstriped vest, a shiny black necktie, and too-big black slacks. Despite the fact that this get-up makes me look like a middle schooler playing best man at her dad's wedding, the suits ask me to represent my bartending brethren in the hotel's official ribbon-cutting ceremony.

I feel honored by this, which I resent.

The ceremony brings me back once more to the function room, where Trump, his progeny, and the money guys stand in front of a white paper step-and-repeat of the Trump SoHo logo. After a few unremarkable remarks to the press, one of the managers gives me a frantic wave and I find myself leading a procession of variously uniformed hotel plebes down the aisle. Each of us is holding a gigantic pair of scissors. When I reach my designated suit, wealthy developer Alex Sapir, I hand him his scissors with maximum solemnity, like a ring bearer at a Republican polygamist wedding.

A gray ribbon rises into the air in front of the suits, hoisted by two plebes. It hangs there, in front of nothing and connected to nothing. Perhaps it would have looked

The phrase *I have wasted my life* runs unbidden through my head.

nice stretched across the hotel's imposing front door, or up on the roof before the jaw-dropping view of Manhattan. But here, hanging in the stale conference room air, it reminds me of a piece of dental floss stuck to someone's bathrobe.

Flashbulbs pop. The fat cats' grins oscillate. The phrase *I have wasted my life* runs unbidden through my head.

"Have I got a story for *you*! Quentin Tarantino came in last night. He had seven Long Island Iced Teas and tried to get one of the waitresses to go for drinks with him. I think he offered her a part in his next movie. The last thing he said was, 'Thanks for the heavy hand.'"

All Quattro bartenders are required to work several lunch shifts per week, to "earn" the right to work nights. Three bar customers is a booming lunch crowd. I am not happy about spending entire days lugging crates of booze, polishing glasses, and juicing fruit to set others up for the night shift, while making a serving wage of five dollars an hour. We complain to management. Why not hire a lunch bartender and pay them a living wage? They assure us our concerns "have been noted."

But then something strange happens. All that lugging and polishing and complaining has made me feel invested in the place. When the bar manager finally comes in one evening with those precious straight pint glasses, holding them over his head like a champion prizefighter, I let out an actual whoop.

A month or so in, on a night shift, I encounter the first customer who seems like someone I might want to hang out with, and who might give me the time of day in real life: a screenwriter, in town from LA for a meeting. He's not wearing a baseball cap, but might as well be. It's slow, so we get chatting, and I admit I'm working on a screenplay. He seems to dig my pitch. "Send it along!" he says, handing me his card. "Maybe I know the right producer." This feels like a gargantuan win, possibly worth this entire painful job—*if* he leaves after the first or second martini. Because we all know how these things go.

Six martinis later, he's slurring about how artists like us shouldn't have to conform to societal norms, how his girlfriend and my newly invented boyfriend have nothing to do with the energy between us, how I should come up to his room and do what comes naturally. I've already said no to this offer half a dozen times. But very, very politely. Because although I'm realizing this guy is not going to send my screenplay to anyone, we at Trump SoHo never refuse the customer anything. While I don't *think* this extends to my body, I still feel a soupçon of guilt.

"Have I got a story for *you*! Some Real Housewife came in last night . . . How should I know which one? I don't watch that shit. This guy three tables down sent her a Sex on the Beach. She was really flattered, but then before she could drink it, *another* one arrived, and then another one. The guy who sent them was waving at her and cracking up. He just kept sending them to her, like, to make *fun* of her."

One evening, a skinny man in paint-spattered jeans wanders through the front door and installs himself at the corner of the bar. He's not our usual clientele—there's dirt on his hands—but it's more than that. His gait is jerky, his demeanor vague. He looks around the room, but his eyes don't seem to land on anything.

I exchange a look with my fellow bartender, who is new—three months in, staff are dropping like flies. We'd both rather this guy wasn't here, but we're not about to Pretty Woman him. Über-rich hotel guests come in looking like crap all the time, and it's not acceptable to mistake some stringy-haired starlet in sweat pants for a heroin addict and refuse to make her a Ruski Passion.

The man looks in the general direction of the new girl's face and jabs his finger at a bottle of Macallan—but not the ubiquitous bottle you'd find in any bar. The Macallan Sherry Oak 30 Years Old.

"The Macallan 30 is two hundred dollars," says the new girl, which makes me wince, but for which I am grateful. He makes an affirmative sound. So she climbs up the ladder for the bottle, measures the drink carefully with a jigger, and presents it with a flourish. Half of it disappears down his throat in one gulp. "Are you sure that's what he wanted?" I hiss at her, backseat driving after the car accident.

"I told him the price!"

"Well, at least get a card for a tab."

She quirks her eyebrow at me. Taking the hint, I approach him and say, "Hello sir, would you like to start a tab?" After a few more asks, he jams his hand into his jeans, producing a battered red debit card. I swipe to pre-authorize and it goes through, which means there's at least a hundred bucks in his account.

When I turn back around, his glass is empty. He's gesturing at the new girl for another drink, and she's back up on the ladder. I say things like, *um, hold on, do you think that's a good idea?* To appease me, she shoves the bottle in his face and says, "This costs two hundred dollars for one drink!" He doesn't look at the bottle, just keeps gazing past it in the general direction of the wall of booze, but he does make the affirmative sound.

He sips this second drink, which relaxes me slightly. Perhaps he's some wealthy, eccentric artist, working on a cutting-edge installation in the medium of dirt.

Then he slumps forward onto the bar, jaw slack. For the first time, it's clear that he's wasted. Uneasy, I ask the new girl to keep an eye on him while I find a manager, because I don't know what to do. He probably doesn't realize what he ordered, and he definitely shouldn't drink any more. And while I've cut people off at every other job I've had, I'm not sure you can do that at Trump SoHo. When I return with a manager in tow, the man has a third glass of Macallan 30 in front of him. I give the other bartender a look designed to freeze lava.

She throws her hands up. "He asked for it! What was I supposed to do?"

It's a fair question, what with the whole no-refusal thing. I serve the man a glass of water, which he ignores. "Did he pay his tab?" the manager asks. Right, because priorities.

His card goes through. In a way it is a relief—I certainly don't want to be on the hook for his tab—and yet. Did we just steal six hundred bucks from an alcoholic construction worker and stick it in a billionaire's pocket? I place the credit card slip in front of him and say my best six-hundred-dollar thank-you. I can see in his eyes that he wants another drink. That it's all he wants. "I need you to sign your check, sir," I say inanely. Eventually, he grasps the pen like a toddler with a paintbrush and scribbles at the top of the receipt.

"You have to tip us," says the new girl. I cringe, but I'm also glad she said it. An appropriate tip—twenty percent, $120—will signify that the man understands what he ordered. He reaches into his pocket and fishes out a crumpled, disintegrating lump that may once have been a five-dollar bill.

The bar manager and the GM appear behind the man. "Come on, buddy," chirps one of them. The man is drooling onto his T-shirt. They try to pull him off his stool, but he hunches his shoulders and refuses to go. One of the more hulking waiters joins in. As the three neck-tied men drag the man in jeans across the floor, he begins to vibrate his body from head to toe in protest. Violently. I've never seen anything like it. At first, diners crane their necks and stare, but the performance soon becomes part of the fabric of the restaurant.

I get distracted by serving other customers; diners go back to eating and chatting. Then I notice that the hulking waiter is back to refilling waters, and the bar manager to flirting with the hostess, and the GM to clearing empty champagne glasses.

"Did you get him in a cab?" I ask the GM.

"Nah."

"You just left him on the street? He couldn't even walk."

"He could walk. He took off."

I find this difficult to believe, so I cross the room, push open the not-for-staff-use-under-any-circumstances front door, and run down the block, first in one direction, then the other, but there's no sign of him.

I tell my barback about it when he comes in later, going for gallows humor, maybe looking for absolution. His interest wanes quickly. There's too much other intrigue to discuss: cops showing up to arrest one of the new bartenders for stealing a customer's Amex, our favorite manager getting

> I place the credit card slip in front of him and say my best six-hundred-dollar thank-you.

fired for no apparent reason, a three-thou-sand-dollar bottle of cognac disappearing without a trace. I decide I'm overreacting.

Still, back in my tiny apartment, I can't sleep. I try to tell myself the man proba-bly was an eccentric millionaire artist. I picture him putting his battered red debit card into an ATM, only to see the words *Insufficient Funds* scroll across the screen. I picture him OD'ing on Sixth Avenue.

The next morning, I spread peanut but-ter on my toast using my new silver knife, a knife I didn't pay for, but told myself I'd earned in a million little ways as I slipped it behind the lining of my purse. I thought having that knife would make me feel better, that tiny act of sticking it to the man, but it doesn't. Reflected in this heavy silver knife, this shiny thing, I see the distorted face of someone I don't entirely recognize. 🏛

*In December 2017, the Trump Organization dropped the struggling Trump SoHo. It is now called the Dominick Hotel.

The "I Have Wasted My Life"
(a remix of the Ruski Passion)

INGREDIENTS:

1.5 oz. Russian Standard vodka

1 oz. passion fruit puree

1 oz. simple syrup

Splash of lime-flavored seltzer

.25 oz. TRUMP Vodka (available online, $1,999.95 for 1.75 L)

INSTRUMENTS:

Cocktail shaker, filled with ice

Martini glass, chilled

Aerator

INSTRUCTIONS:

1. Add vodka, passion fruit puree, and simple syrup to the cocktail shaker. Shake. Strain into the martini glass. Top with lime seltzer.

2. Measure TRUMP Vodka into the aerator. Spray 1–3 spritzes over the surface of the cocktail. This will make the cocktail taste noticeably worse, but not so much that you won't be able to drink it. Stay with it! The more you drink, the less you'll be able to taste it.

Trouble Maker

Elissa Schappell

CAREER DAY

Years later, members of the Academy could still recall the exact moment when the writer, a perfect simulacrum of all debut female authors, invisible and sweating in the compulsory costume,
realized why no one had complimented either her speech or delivery, and so vowed retribution.

A NECESSARY PRECAUTION

For decades scientists posited that "bonnets" or "bubbles" were, like the chastity belt, a desperate invention of men seeking to contain female energy, steadfastly refusing to believe that women grew them out of love and pity.

J.F.Shoemaker. Pierceton, Ind.

PORTRAIT OF THE WRITER AS SAINT DYMPHNA

The learned men denied that the spine of flames was actual fire, only an aura, until they attempted to touch the girl against her will, and they, like her father, who had tried to make her his new wife, were consumed in flames.

I ALWAYS BELIEVED
I HAD A BOOK IN ME

CABINET PORTRAIT *Hotchkiss* EST. 1206 BROAD ST.
NORWICH, N.Y.

BIRTH MOTHER

To the doctors she complained about the voices in her head. Hours lost in a waking dream, the scent of orchids, being overcome by euphoria but just as often hopelessness and dread. Their diagnosis was too much reading.

Derrick Austin is the author of *Trouble the Water*. He was a finalist for the 2017 Kate Tufts Discovery Award.

Janée J. Baugher's the author of *The Body's Physics* and *Coördinates of Yes*, and she teaches at Southern New Hampshire University and Writing Workshops Dallas.

Aimee Bender is the author of five books, including *The Particular Sadness of Lemon Cake* and *The Color Master*. She lives in Los Angeles and teaches writing at USC.

Marie-Helene Bertino is the author of the novel *2 A.M. at the Cat's Pajamas* and the story collection *Safe as Houses*.

Brian Blanchfield is the author of three books of poetry and prose, most recently *Proxies: Essays Near Knowing*. He lives in Moscow, Idaho.

Lucie Brock-Broido was the author of four books of poetry, most recently *Stay, Illusion*. She was Director of Poetry at Columbia University's Writing Program from 1993 until her death last year.

Victoria Chang's fourth book of poems, *Barbie Chang*, was recently published. She lives in LA and teaches at Antioch's MFA Program.

Bridget Chiao Clerkin lives in Chattanooga, Tennessee.

Joshua Cohen is the author of nine books, most recently *Attention: Dispatches from a Land of Distraction*.

Katie Condon's debut collection of poetry *Praying Naked* will be published next year. Her poems appear in *The New Yorker* and *Prairie Schooner*.

Jennifer Croft's illustrated memoir *Homesick* comes out September 10 with Unnamed Press.

Matthew Dickman is the author of four poetry collections. He is the poetry editor-at-large for Tin House Books. Born in Portland, Oregon, he and his family now live in London.

Elizabeth Dodd teaches creative writing and environmental literature at Kansas State University. Her most recent book is *Horizon's Lens* (essays), from University of Nebraska Press.

Anthony Doerr's most recent novel, *All the Light We Cannot See*, won the Pulitzer Prize for Fiction.

Nathaniel Dolton-Thornton's poems have received the Roselyn Schneider Eisner, Emily Chamberlain Cook, and Ina Coolbrith Memorial poetry prizes. He studies political ecology at Cambridge University.

Iris Jamahl Dunkle is the author of the poetry collections *Interrupted Geographies*, *Gold Passage*, and *There's a Ghost in this Machine of Air*.

Emma Copley Eisenberg's work has appeared in *Granta*, *McSweeney's*, *American Short Fiction*, and others. Her first book, *The Third Rainbow Girl*, will be published in 2020.

CJ Evans is the author of *A Penance* and *The Category of Outcast*, and received the Amy Lowell Scholarship.

Danielle Evans is the author of the story collection *Before You Suffocate Your Own Fool Self*. She teaches in The Writing Seminars at Johns Hopkins University.

Emily Flouton is a writer from the Northeast who lives and writes in Portland, Oregon.

Nick Flynn is a poet, playwright, and memoirist. His most recent book is *My Feelings*, a collection of poems. His work has been translated into fifteen languages.

Ross Gay is the author, most recently, of the essay collection *The Book of Delights*.

Manuel Gonzales is the author of the novel *The Regional Office is Under Attack!* and he once baked a pecan pie in the same El Cosmico trailer in Marfa, Texas that Beyoncé once slept in.

Arielle Greenberg's fourth and fifth collections of poetry are forthcoming; the latter is *I Live in the Country & Other Dirty Poems* (Four Way, 2020).

Brenda Hillman is the author of ten collections of poetry from Wesleyan University Press; she teaches at Saint Mary's College in Moraga, California.

Lewis Hyde taught at Kenyon College until his retirement in 2018. He lives in Cambridge, Massachusetts with his wife, the writer Patricia Vigderman.

Daniel Johnson authored *How to Catch a Falling Knife*. His second volume explores his friendship with journalist James Foley, who was killed by ISIS in Syria.

Etgar Keret is a leading voice in Israeli literature and cinema. He is the author of five bestselling story collections.

John Kinsella's most recent collection of poems is *Firebreaks*.

Joanna Klink is the author of four books of poetry. She has been living in Rome, supported by the Trust of Amy Lowell.

Matthew Kramer is a cartoonist living in Providence, Rhode Island. He's a recent Yaddo resident & Brown MFA graduate in Digital Language Arts. More at matthewckramer.com & @canttakemeanywhere.

Catherine Lacey is the author of *Nobody Is Ever Missing*, *The Answers*, and *Certain American States*. She lives in Chicago most of the time.

Nam Le was the Tin House Writer-in-Residence in 2015. He lives in Melbourne, Australia

Rebecca Lindenberg is the author of *Love, an Index* and *The Logan Notebooks*.

Kelly Link is the author of four story collections, most recently *Get in Trouble*. In 2018, she was awarded a MacArthur Fellowship.

Antonio López's work has appeared or is forthcoming in *PEN/America*, *BOAAT Press*, *Hayden's Ferry Review*, *Permafrost*, *Huizache*, and elsewhere. He received his MFA at Rutgers-Newark.

Ruth Madievsky is the author of a poetry collection, *Emergency Brake*. She lives in Boston, where she works as an oncology pharmacist.

Adrian Matejka is the author of four collections of poems, most recently *Map to the Stars*.

Louise Mathias is the author of two books of poems, most recently *The Traps*. She lives in Joshua Tree, California.

Elizabeth McKenzie's novel *The Portable Veblen* was longlisted for the National Book Award for fiction. Her work has appeared in *The New Yorker*, *The Atlantic*, and others.

Ander Monson is the author of eight books, including *I Will Take the Answer* and *The Gnome Stories*, both forthcoming in 2020.

Aimee Nezhukumatathil's most recent poetry collection is *Oceanic*. She has a book of nature essays forthcoming and teaches in the MFA program at the University of Mississippi.

Sharon Olds is the author of twelve books of poetry. She teaches in the Graduate Creative Writing Program at New York University. Her next collection, *Arias*, will be published in 2019.

Michelle Orange is the author of *This Is Running for Your Life: Essays* and the forthcoming *Pure Flame*.

Elena Passarello is the author of the essay collections *Let Me Clear My Throat* and *Animals Strike Curious Poses*. She teaches at Oregon State University.

Alison Pelegrin is an NEA fellow and the author of four poetry collections, most recently *Waterlines*. She lives in Louisiana.

Maya C. Popa's first collection, *American Faith*, is forthcoming from Sarabande Books. She is the poetry reviews editor at *Publishers Weekly* and teaches in NYC.

D. A. Powell's books include *Repast* and *Useless Landscape, or A Guide for Boys*. He teaches at the University of San Francisco.

Khadijah Queen is the author of five books, most recently *I'm So Fine: A List of Famous Men & What I Had On*. She teaches at University of Colorado, Boulder.

Karen Russell is the author of *St. Lucy's Home For Girls Raised by Wolves*, *Swamplandia*, *Vampires in the Lemon Grove*, and *Sleep Donation*. "The Gondoliers" appears in her most recent collection, *Orange World*.

sam sax is the author of *Madness* and *Bury It*. He's the recipient of a 2018 Ruth Lilly and Dorothy Sargent Rosenberg Fellowship.

Elissa Schappell is a co-founding editor and Editor-at-Large of *Tin House*. "Trouble Maker" is an excerpt from, "How the Light Gets In."

Karen Shepard is the author of four novels, including most recently *The Celestials*, and one story collection, *Kiss Me Someone*. She teaches at Williams College.

Joan Silber's last book, *Improvement*, won the National Book Critics Circle Award and the PEN/Faulkner Award. She also received the PEN/Malamud Award for the Short Story.

Sondra Silverston is a native New Yorker who has lived in Israel since 1970. She has translated works by Amos Oz, Etgar Keret and Eshkol Nevo.

Christopher Soto is the author of the chapbook *Sad Girl Poems* and the editor of *Nepantla: An Anthology for Queer Poets of Color*.

Matthew Specktor is the author of the novel *American Dream Machine*, and the forthcoming memoir-in-criticism *Always Crashing in The Same Car*.

J. Jezewska Stevens's first novel, *The Exhibition of Persephone Q.*, is forthcoming from Farrar, Straus, & Giroux. She lives in New York.

Ginger Strand is the author of one novel and three books of narrative nonfiction, most recently *The Brothers Vonnegut: Science and Fiction in the House of Magic*.

James Tate's awards include the Pulitzer Prize, the Academy of American Poets Wallace Stevens Award, and the National Book Award. His new collection, *The Government Lake*, will be released in 2019.

Fran Tirado is the Deputy Editor of *Out* magazine, co-host of the podcast Food 4 Thot, and writer working on a book of essays.

Olga Tokarczuk is the winner of the 2018 Man Booker International Prize for *Flights* and the Jan Michalski Prize for Literature for *The Books of Jacob*.

Vanessa Veselka is the author of the novel *Zazen*, with short stories and nonfiction in *GQ*, *The Atlantic*, the *Atavist*, *Tin House*, and elsewhere.

Colson Whitehead is the author of nine books, including *The Underground Railroad*, which received the National Book Award and the Pulitzer Prize.

Joshua Marie Wilkinson is the author of a book called *Meadow Slasher*. He lives in Seattle.

Emily Withnall lives in Missoula, Montana, with her two kids. She is at work on a book about domestic violence and hydraulic fracturing.

Matthew Zapruder is the author of *Why Poetry*, and the forthcoming *My Heteronym in a New Dark Age*. He teaches at Saint Mary's College of California.

FRONT COVER:
Digital illustration by Allen Crawford.
www.allencrawford.net

CREDIT:
Pages 401–404:"Trouble Maker," photo documentation by Alex Olsen

CALARTS MFA CREATIVE WRITING PROGRAM

AN INNOVATIVE AND INTERDISCIPLINARY CURRICULUM DEDICATED TO NURTURING THE EXPERIMENTAL IMPULSE IN WRITING

2017-2018 KATIE JACOBSON WRITER IN RESIDENCE
KEVIN YOUNG

RECENT VISITORS:
JUNOT DÍAZ, GEORGE SAUNDERS, SAMUEL DELANY, LYDIA DAVIS

WRITING.CALARTS.EDU

Brenda Shaughnessy
The Octopus Museum

© Janea Wied

A battle cry in the form of bold and scathingly beautiful feminist poems that imagine a future world colored by our current state of environmental destruction, racism, sexism, and divisive politics.

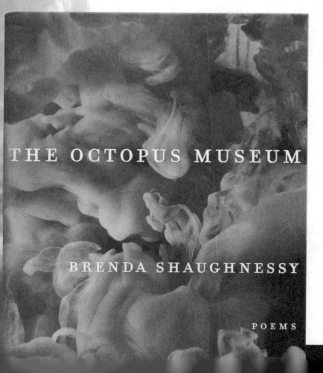

THE OCTOPUS MUSEUM

BRENDA SHAUGHNESSY

POEMS

About the Cover

Jakob Vala

In 1999, Jon Baird, the first art director of *Tin House* magazine, proposed a handmade aesthetic for the covers, with layered components, hand lettering, and a cigar-band-like title. The premiere cover centered around a sketch of the tin house—the real-life home of the magazine and workshop offices and the inspiration for our logo—on a golden brown background. Later designs featured larger, splashier imagery that stood out on the shelves. In recent years, art director Diane Chonette has curated the work of fine artists from all over the world to produce dozens of standout covers.

For the final cover Chonette was faced with the challenge of capturing the spirit of our vast and varied catalog. She decided to return to our roots with an illustration by longtime Tin House collaborator Allen Crawford.

Crawford is known for his gorgeously illustrated edition of Walt Whitman's "Song of Myself," which we recently reissued due to its popularity. He also created the cover of the fifty-ninth issue of *Tin House* ("Memory"). We commissioned him to reinterpret a vintage playing card for the cover of the novel *A Hanging at Cinder Bottom* and, most recently, he contributed instructional illustrations to *Grow Your Own*, our guide to growing cannabis.

Crawford's incredible artistry is matched only by his modesty. Referring to his line work as "crude," he says he used to avoid the medium by working primarily with collage and type, but, in planning "Song of Myself," he found that "line art was an ideal fit for the unadorned, simple passages" of Whitman's vision. He continues to use a range of styles, but says his "simple line art has attracted more interest and awards than any of [his] previous illustration and design work." Crawford "approaches illustration like a designer," saying, "designers don't use one typeface over their entire career. I use the right tool for the job."

Allen Crawford lives in Mount Holly, New Jersey, with his wife, Susan. Together they run Plankton Art Co., a design and illustration studio. More of his work can be seen at www.allencrawford.net.

DORIANNE LAUX · VICTOR LAVALLE · SHAYLA LAWSON · NAM LE · KELLY LE FAVE · URSULA K. LE GUIN · AMY LEACH · KRISTA LEAHY · DAVID LEAVITT BONNIE B. LEE · JANET LEE · JONATHAN LEE · MATTY LEE · FRED G. LEEBRON · MICHELLE LEGRO · DAVID LEHMAN · REBECCA LEHMANN MARTIN LEMELMAN · ALEX LEMON · J. ROBERT LENNON · SUZANNE LENZER MICHAEL LEONG · BEN LERNER · RIKA LESSER · FRANCISCO LETELIER JONATHAN LETHEM · MEGAN LEVAD · JENNIFER LEVASSEUR · ADAM LEVIN ANNE-MARIE LEVINE · MADELINE G. LEVINE · MARK LEVINE · STACEY LEVINE · JEN LEVITT · JIM LEWIS · JOLIE LEWIS · MARK LEYNER · YIYUN LI BERND LICHTENBERG · JESSE LICHTENSTEIN · JOHANNES LICHTMAN ALAN LIGHTMAN · TEOW LIM GOH · ADA LIMÓN · REBECCA LINDENBERG BEI LING · KELLY LINK · MARIA LIOUTAIA · LAURA LIPPMAN · MATTHEW LIPPMAN · SAM LIPSYTE · ELLEN LITMAN · EDDIE LITTLE · TIMOTHY LIU JACK LIVINGS · ALBANA LLESHANAKU · LULJETA LLESHANAKU · MARIO VARGAS LLOSA · PATRICIA LOCKWOOD · WILLIAM LOGAN · NATHAN ALLING LONG · PHILLIP LOPATE · ANTONIO LÓPEZ · FEDERICO GARCÍA LORCA · A. LOUDERMILK · MICHAEL LOUGHRAN · CYNTHIA LOWEN · MICHAEL LOWENTHAL · MAX LUDINGTON · MARGARET LUONGO · GARY LUTZ HOWARD LUXENBERG · CATE LYCURGUS · ELIZABETH LYONS · FIONA MAAZEL · CARMEN MARIA MACHADO · TEDDY MACKER · WILL MACKIN RUTH MADIEVSKY · ANN MAGNUSON · DENIS MAIR · ROHAN MAITZEN REBECCA MAKKAI · ALEXANDER MAKSIK · SAKURA MAKU · DORA MALECH PASHA MALLA · DAVID MAMET · LIP MANEGIO · SARAH MANGUSO · SALLY WEN MAO · ALEX MAR · PAUL J. MARASA · ROBERT MARBURY · MICHELINE AHARONIAN MARCOM · BEN MARCUS · MESHA MAREN · STEPHEN MARION GRETCHEN MARQUETTE · JOHN MARR · PEYTON MARSHALL · CLANCY MARTIN · JOSEPH MARTIN · DAVID TOMAS MARTINEZ · CATE MARVIN JULIO MARZÁN · LESLIE MASLOW · ZACHARY MASON · ADRIAN MATEJKA LOU MATHEWS · LOUISE MATHIAS · ASPEN MATIS · KHALED MATTAWA AIREA D. MATTHEWS · SEBASTIAN MATTHEWS · WILLIAM MATTHEWS GERARDO PACHECO MATUS · SHARON MAY · WONG MAY · C.M. MAYO · COLUM MCCANN · RICHARD MCCANN · MONICA MCCLURE · J.W. MCCORMACK · WIN MCCORMACK · SHANE MCCRAE · FRANCES MCCUE · JEANNE MCCULLOCH AMY MCDANIEL · ANNA MCDONALD · MEGAN MCDOWELL · ALEX MCELROY

GARDNER MCFALL · ANNIE MCFADYEN · PATRICK MCGRATH · MICHAEL N. MCGREGOR · MICHAEL MCGRIFF · CAREY MCHUGH · VESTAL MCINTYRE ELIZABETH MCKENZIE · THOMAS SCOTT MCKENZIE · MAUREEN N. MCLANE JOHN MCMANUS · SOPHIE MCMANUS · MARTHA MCPHEE · CLAIRE MCQUERRY ZAKES MDA · PABLO MEDINA · ERIKA MEITNER · MIRANDA F. MELLIS KSENIYA MELNIK · DANIEL MENASCHE · ANA MENÉNDEZ · SUSAN SCARF MERRELL · AUSTIN MERRILL · CHRISTOPHER MERRILL · IMAN MERSAL PHILIP METRES · MARGOT MEYERS · MIAN MIAN · LISA MICHAELS · JON MICHAUD · LINCOLN MICHEL · HOWIE MICHELS · LEON MICHELS · ANYA MIGDAL · NANCY MILFORD · JENNIFER MILITELLO · JOSEPH MILLAR LYDIA MILLET · STEVEN MILLHAUSER · TEDI LÓPEZ MILLS · NICK MILNE CZESŁAW MIŁOSZ · ALBERT MOBILIO · PATRICK MODIANO · TRACEY MOFFATT · KEVIN MOFFETT · ROSALIE MOFFETT · SIYANDA MOHUTSIWA DANTIEL W. MONIZ · RACHEL MONROE · ANDER MONSON · NICHOLAS MONTEMARANO · FRANK MONTESONTI · LEE MONTGOMERY · SY MONTGOMERY · RICK MOODY · ANNE ELIZABETH MOORE · HONOR MOORE JOHN FREDERICK MOORE · LIZ MOORE · LORRIE MOORE · FRANK MOORHOUSE · KEITH LEE MORRIS · MICHAEL MORSE · WALTER MOSLEY ANDREW MOTION · ANDY MOZINA · PAUL MULDOON · EDDIE MULLER · NAMI MUN · ALICE MUNRO · LES MURRAY · CAROL MUSKE-DUKES · JASON MYERS THIRII MYO KYAW MYINT · EILEEN MYLES · DAVID NAIMON · JONATHAN NAPACK · ZEHRA NAQVI · OGDEN NASH · JEAN NATHAN · JESSE NATHAN JAY NEBEL · ALEXIS NELSON · ANTONYA NELSON · ERIC NELSON · MAGGIE NELSON · SIERRA NELSON · PABLO NERUDA · LUCIA NEVAI · SUSANNAH NEVISON · LEIGH NEWMAN · AIMEE NEZHUKUMATATHIL · MŨKOMA WA NGŨGĨ · GEOFF NICHOLSON · SUSANNA NIED · ANGELO NIKOLOPOULOS THISBE NISSEN · JUSTIN NOBEL · EDWARD NOBLES · DELANEY NOLAN MIHO NONAKA · DORTHE NORS · SERGEI NOSOV · AMÉLIE NOTHOMB · JOSIP NOVAKOVICH · BENJAMIN NUGENT · SIGRID NUNEZ · D. NURKSE · ALISSA NUTTING · GEOFFREY O'BRIEN · MEGHAN O'GIEBLYN · FRANK O'HARA DANIEL O'MALLEY · MEGHAN O'ROURKE · MILLER OBERMAN · NICK OBOURN · SARAH PAUL OCAMPO · ED OCHESTER · GINA OCHSNER · JENNY OFFILL · CHRIS OFFUTT · ALIX OHLIN · KRISTIN OHLSON · CHINELO OKPARANTA · ARIKA OKRENT · BEN OKRI · SHARON OLDS · ALICIA OLTUSKI

MICHELLE ORANGE · PETER ORNER · LAWRENCE OSBORNE · DAN OSWALT
ABBEY MEI OTIS · MARY OTIS · WHITNEY OTTO · CYNTHIA OZICK · TIM PAGE
CAROL PAIK · GRACE PALEY · ANGELA PALM · JESS PANE · GREGORY PARDLO
DOMINIQUE PARENT-ALTIER · DIANA PARK · JEFF PARKER · MORGAN
PARKER · SCOTT F. PARKER · OLIVIA PARKES · CECILY PARKS · ROY PARVIN
ELENA PASSARELLO · ANN PATCHETT · JUDITH PATERSON · CHRISTIAN
PATTERSON · JAMES PATTERSON · VICTORIA PATTERSON · ALLYSON PATY
VERA PAVLOVA · EDMUNDO PAZ-SOLDÁN · ALEXANDRA PECHMAN · DALE
PECK · MICHAEL PECK · CATE PEEBLES · ALISON PELEGRIN · BENJAMIN
PERCY · CRAIG SANTOS PEREZ · TONY PEREZ · LUCIA PERILLO · MICAH
PERKS · CARLA PERRY · MARISSA PERRY · SARA PERRY · KIKI PETROSINO
PER PETTERSON · RICHARD PEVEAR · LIZ PHANG · CARL PHILLIPS · HELEN
PHILLIPS · JAYNE ANNE PHILLIPS · TOMMY PICO · MARGE PIERCY · BOOMER
PINCHES · WANG PING · SALVADOR PLASCENCIA · SYLVIA PLATH · DONALD
PLATT · MARK JUDE POIRIER · ROBERT POLITO · DONALD RAY POLLOCK
MAURICE PONS · JAY PONTERI · MAYA C. POPA · RICHARD POPLAK · REGINA
PORTER · D. A. POWELL · DAWN POWELL · PADGETT POWELL · RICHARD
POWERS · MARTIN PREIB · VICTORIA PRICE · MICHAEL PRINCE · FRANCINE
PROSE · MIRA PTACIN · ERIC PUCHNER · LIA PURPURA · SHPRESA QATIPI
JAMIE QUATRO · KHADIJAH QUEEN · ANNALISA QUINN · KEVIN RABALAIS
ALICIA JO RABINS · EMILY ISHEM RABOTEAU · NATASHA RADOJČIĆ-KANE
DANIEL RAEBURN · BIN RAMKE · CAMILLE RANKINE · BARBARA RAS · RON
RASH · A. J. RATHBUN · HENRY RATHVON · GRAHAM RAWLE · WENDY
RAWLINGS · JON RAYMOND · TRIPP READE · MICHAEL REDHILL · JESSICA
REED · JOHN REED · DAVID REES · ROGER REEVES · NECEE REGIS
ELIZABETH REICHERT · HOLIDAY REINHORN · HARRIET REISEN · NANCY
REISMAN · PAISLEY REKDAL · REBECCA RENNER · RACHEL RESNICK · IRINA
REYN · JILL MALLEY REYNOLDS · ADRIENNE RICH · NATHANIEL RICH · CAT
RICHARDSON · JAMES RICHARDSON · ROBIN RICHARDSON · STACEY
RICHTER · RACHEL RIEDERER · KATHERINE RIEGEL · MOLLY RINGWALD
DAVID RIVARD · SAM RIVIERE · SARA ROAHEN · MAGGIE ROBBINS · ANDREW
MICHAEL ROBERTS · MICHAEL WAYNE ROBERTS · ROBIN ROBERTSON
LEWIS ROBINSON · MARILYNNE ROBINSON · ROXANA ROBINSON · PETER
ROCK · CATHERINE ROCKWOOD · ANDREW ROE · HOYT ROGERS · PATTIANN

ROGERS · STEPHANIE ROGERS · MATTHEW ROHRER · KATIE ROIPHE · ROBIN
ROMM · PATRICK ROSAL · LIZ ROSENBERG · AMY KROUSE ROSENTHAL
MICHAEL ROSENWALD · SAM ROSS · THEODORE ROSS · THOMAS ROSS
COLETTE ROSSANT · BARNEY ROSSET · HENK ROSSOUW · JESS ROW · JOHN
ROWELL · TADEUSZ RÓŻEWICZ · HARRIET RUBIN · LEV RUBINSTEIN · MARY
RUEFLE · MICHAEL RUHLMAN · KAREN RUSSELL · KENT RUSSELL · ETHAN
RUTHERFORD · DAVID RYAN · HUGH RYAN · PATRICK RYAN · IRA SADOFF
EDWARD W. SAID · TOMAŽ ŠALAMUN · JAMES SALTER · LYNNE SAMPSON
RICHARD A. SANCHEZ · BARRY SANDERS · JOHN SANFORD · LUC SANTE
JOSÉ SARAMAGO · MARIN SARDY · HIROAKI SATO · MARJANE SATRAPI
THOM SATTERLEE · GEORGE SAUNDERS · SAM SAX · NATALIE SCENTERS-
ZAPICO · ROBIN BETH SCHAER · ELISSA SCHAPPELL · ANDREW SCHEIBER
LOGAN SCHERER · MICHAEL SCHIAVO · DAVID SCHICKLER · JAMES SCHIFF
LIESL SCHILLINGER · CHRISTOPHER SCHMIDT · KATE SCHMIER · JASON
SCHNEIDERMAN · ZACHARY SCHOMBURG · DANNIEL SCHOONEBEEK
BRANDON R. SCHRAND · AMY NEWLOVE SCHROEDER · HELEN SCHULMAN
EDWARD SCHWARZSCHILD · SARAH V. SCHWEIG · JAMES SCUDAMORE
WILLIAM TODD SEABROOK · PARUL SEHGAL · WILL SELF · HEATHER
SELLERS · NATHAN SELLYN · NAMWALI SERPELL · SUSAN SEUBERT · STEVEN
SEYMOUR · KAMILA SHAMSIE · S. SHANKAR · DANI SHAPIRO · SUSAN
SHAPIRO · JENN SHAPLAND · BRENDA SHAUGHNESSY · B.T. SHAW · WALLACE
SHAWN · ANNE SHEFFIELD · JIM SHEPARD · KAREN SHEPARD · SU SHI
DAVID SHIELDS · BRANDON SHIMODA · JASON SHINDER · LORI SHINE
MAGGIE SHIPSTEAD · MIRIAM SHLESINGER · EVIE SHOCKLEY · KATHERINE
SHONK · MOHAMMAD SIDIQ · MATTHEW SIEGEL · ROBERT ANTHONY SIEGEL
ELENI SIKELIANOS · RICHARD SIKEN · JOAN SILBER · ALAN SILLITOE
MICHAEL SILVERBLATT · SONDRA SILVERSTON · CHARLES SIMIC · NINA
BERNSTEIN SIMMONS · BENNETT SIMS · ALYSON SINCLAIR · SEAN SINGER
GEORGE SINGLETON · HAL SIROWITZ · JEFFREY SKINNER · ED SKOOG
ANN TASHI SLATER · JULIA SLAVIN · MARCUS SLEASE · TOM SLEIGH
VERTAMAE SMART-GROSVENOR · ALEXIS M. SMITH · BRUCE SMITH
CHARLIE SMITH · DREW NELLINS SMITH · JEFF SMITH · LYTTON SMITH
MAGGIE SMITH · MATTHEW B. SMITH · MIKE SMITH · PATRICIA SMITH
RICH SMITH · SARAH ELAINE SMITH · TRACY K. SMITH · ZAK SMITH

JEFF SNOWBARGER · SCOTT SNYDER · MATTHEW SOCIA · STEPHANIE SOILEAU CHRIS SOLOMINE · CHRISTOPHER SORRENTINO · CHRISTOPHER SOTO TOM SPANBAUER · STEPHEN SPARKS · CARLA SPARTOS · MATTHEW SPECKTOR · SCOTT SPENCER · ROB SPILLMAN · DANA SPIOTTA · JENNIFER SRYGLEY · JUSTIN ST. GERMAIN · DAVID ST. JOHN · JERRY STAHL · SOFI STAMBO · FRANK STANFORD · SAŠA STANIŠIĆ · MAURA STANTON · MARK STATMAN · MELISSA STEIN · DARCEY STEINKE · MARK STEINMETZ · SAM STEPHENSON · GERALD STERN · J. DAVID STEVENS · J. JEZEWSKA STEVENS DEANNE STILLMAN · ALISON STINE · BIANCA STONE · EMILY STONE NOMI STONE · ROBERT STONE · MEG STOREY · GINGER STRAND · MARK STRAND · EMMA STRAUB · PETER STRAUB · TIMMY STRAW · CHERYL STRAYED · LEE STRINGER · ELIZABETH STROUT · JOE SUMNER · TERESE SVOBODA · ANTHONY SWOFFORD · ARTHUR SZE · MARY SZYBIST · WISŁAWA SZYMBORSKA · ANTONIO TABUCCHI · ELIZABETH TALLENT · BRIDGET TALONE · DOROTHEA TANNING · MICHAEL THOMAS TAREN · DONNA TARTT JAMES TATE · JUSTIN TAYLOR · MIA TAYLOR · TESS TAYLOR · ALEXANDRA TEAGUE · THOMAS TEAL · CRAIG MORGAN TEICHER · HANNAH TENNANT-MOORE · DUMITRU ȚEPENEAG · ANDERSON TEPPER · ABIGAIL THOMAS AMBER FLORA THOMAS · CAROLINE O'CONNOR THOMAS · JOHN THOMPSON KARA THOMPSON · TED THOMPSON · MELANIE RAE THON · DANIEL TIFFANY JULIA CLARE TILLINGHAST · LYNNE TILLMAN · HANNAH TINTI FRAN TIRADO · SALLIE TISDALE · ALLISON TITUS · EZRA TITUS · HÉCTOR TOBAR · JACKSON TOBIN · OLGA TOKARCZUK · TATYANA TOLSTAYA · TOM TOMORROW · DANIEL TORDAY · JUSTIN TORRES · NICK TOSCHES · JEAN-PHILIPPE TOUSSAINT · PAULS TOUTONGHI · WELLS TOWER · SARAH TOWERS · TOMAS TRANSTRÖMER · ROBERT TRAVIESO · NATASHA TRETHEWEY · DAVID TRINIDAD · QUINCY TROUPE · DANIELLE TRUSSONI JOANNA TRZECIAK · JENNIFER TSENG · KEN TUCKER · TATIANA TULCHINSKY · FREDERICK TURNER · LORI LYNN TURNER · CHASE TWICHELL · DEB OLIN UNFERTH · GIUSEPPE UNGARETTI · RACHEL URQUHART · LUIS ALBERTO URREA · CORINNA VALLIANATOS · JEANNIE VANASCO · CAITLIN VANCE · SHAWN VANDOR · MAI DER VANG · VAUHINI VARA · DAVID VARNO · KATHERINE VAZ · INARA VERZEMNIEKS · VANESSA VESELKA · SHAWN VESTAL · ENRIQUE VILA-MATAS · PETER VILBIG